POINT OF IMPACT

Also by John Nichol, with John Peters

Tornado Down
Team Tornado

POINT OF IMPACT

John Nichol

Hodder & Stoughton

First published in Great Britain in 1996
by Hodder and Stoughton
A division of Hodder Headline PLC

10 9 8 7 6 5 4 3 2 1

British Library Cataloguing in Publication Data

Nichol, John, 1963–
Point of impact
1. English fiction – 20th century
I. Title
823.9′14 [F]

ISBN 0 340 68450 X

Typeset by Hewer Text Composition Services, Edinburgh
Printed and bound in Great Britain by
Mackays of Chatham PLC, Chatham, Kent.

Hodder and Stoughton
A division of Hodder Headline PLC
338 Euston Road
London NW1 3BH

This book is dedicated to the memory
of all those aircrew who have given their lives
in the pursuit of excellence.

Acknowledgements

As this is my first novel, I have drawn heavily on others' experience in order to produce a readable end product. To thank everyone would take far too long, but I would like to single out a few individuals without whom I would have been lost:

Mark and George, the intrepid Lucas brothers, who have spent many hours helping me put the whole thing together. Suzie and Sue, for struggling through the first draft and offering their criticism – always constructive! Finally, Neil, for his constant help and advice. Thank you all.

Even in peacetime, the Royal Air Force expects to lose £100 million worth of equipment and ten lives each year through training accidents.

In the five years between January 1991 and May 1996, eighty-three military aircraft were lost in crashes during training, resulting in the loss of over seventy lives. This excludes Gulf War losses. Eighteen of the aircraft were Tornados.

Twenty-eight of the accidents were attributed to 'aircrew error'. Another nineteen are still under investigation.

These are the facts; what follows is fiction . . .

John Nichol, June 1996

Prologue

The Tempest flashed around the shoulder of the hill, a black dart, stark against the pale winter sky. Contour-flying, hugging the ground, the jet soared over ridges and swooped down valleys, burning across the sky at five hundred miles an hour, vapour trails streaming from its wingtips.

It was ten years to the day since the navigator had made his first sortie in a Tempest. Now he was guiding a young pilot through his maiden flight, a twenty-one-year-old in charge of thirty million pounds' worth of sophisticated electronics which one momentary lapse of concentration could convert into a useless pile of scrap.

During the long months of training, the pilot had been like a learner driver with the controlling hand of an experienced instructor always resting on the dual controls. Now he was at last flying free, both nervous and elated.

The navigator had flown a thousand sorties over every conceivable terrain from the Arctic tundra to the deserts of Iraq, but, like all air crew, he had never lost the thrill of fast-jet flight. He loved it all, from the smell of kerosene fuel and the whine of the electronics as the jet sat ready on the ground, to the moment when it punched through the cloud ceiling into the zone where the sun always shone and the blue of the sky began to darken into the black of space.

The navigator knew the Yorkshire Dales landscape flashing below them almost as well as he knew the streets of his home town but he gazed down for a moment with fresh eyes, seeing it as the pilot was seeing it. A flash of silver light reflecting from the jet's fuselage momentarily lit the moon face of a sheep farmer staring upwards, as remote from them as a coin sparkling in the depths of a well. As the black shadow of the jet passed overhead, the roar of its engines shook the earth. Startled by the storm – first the lightning, then the thunder – the farmer's sheep scattered over the green fields.

He shared in the young pilot's mounting excitement, even as his voice – cool, clinical, detached – forced him to focus on the humdrum routines of the flight. 'All you've learned to do in training so far is to fly the aircraft. Now you have to learn to operate it. Let's make sure of the fuel checks – check balance, check contents . . . That's good. Your nearest diversion at the moment is going to be Finnington, which is fifty miles, heading two-seven-zero. Okay, take it down the right-hand side of that lake, Semerwater.'

The jet-wash rippled the surface of the water, glinting in the early-morning sunlight. The aircraft's hawk-shadow sent the moorhens, wings splashing, scattering for the cover of the willows and alders on the shore.

'If you come hard right now, you'll see Hawes on your nose.'

The village flashed underneath them and was gone, a blur of grey stone, casting a long shadow in the low sunlight.

The navigator saw the altimeter start to rise a little and forced his pilot to keep down at 250 feet. 'Make sure we stay low round this bend. Try not to climb as you come around the spur of the mountain. Don't balloon over the ridge line.'

The pilot nudged the stick, making minute and largely unnecessary adjustments like a learner driver. He pushed the Tempest into a hard, low-level turn.

'Okay,' the navigator said, 'we've got a little fuel to spare, so let's have some fun before we go home. Come hard left around that fell there. Increase speed to max power and keep the power on as you come round the corner.'

The jet flashed around Shunnor Fell, the pilot plugging in the after-burner to boost their speed; but, as their G-pants started to inflate under the force of the turn, there was a sudden clamour of attention-getters on the cockpit warning panels and a Christmas tree of lights began to flash.

'My God, what's that?' Panic edged the pilot's voice.

'Level the wings.' The matter-of-fact tones of the navigator belied his own unease, but the pilot responded instinctively to the command, stabilising the aircraft as he had been trained to do.

Red lights still flashed insistently while warning sirens whooped in their headsets.

Sensing the pilot's continuing indecision, the navigator's calming voice betrayed no hint of the danger. 'Pull up. Get away from the ground.'

The pilot did not react for a moment, staring frozen at the computer screen, where a caption should have identified the problem. There was nothing but the battery of lights. Over the headset, his breathing sounded faster and shallower by the second.

The navigator barked the order once more. 'Get the nose up. Get away from the ground.' His voice was now urgent, but still betrayed no emotion.

This time the pilot moved swiftly, though he continued to stare in horrified fascination at the warning lights. The navigator checked his screens again, but the Tempest's computers still offered no explanations. Like the pilot, he had practised every conceivable emergency in the simulators until he could carry out the drills in his sleep. Unlike the pilot, he had also faced and survived many real emergencies, but in each of them there had been some identifiable fault and a prescribed response.

He had seen nothing like this before.

The first priority was to keep the plane stable and gain height. Only when safely clear of the dark, looming fellside would he allow himself to dwell on the possible cause. His hand moved involuntarily towards the black-and-yellow-striped handle under his seat as the pilot wrestled the controls. The aircraft started to come up, but too swiftly.

'Don't get the nose too high.' The navigator's warning was an irrelevance. As he spoke, the jet began to barrel-roll to the right.

'I can't control it,' the pilot screamed, paralysed by the sight of the hill rushing up to meet them.

As his instruments showed 135 degrees of bank and the blue sky over the cockpit turned to green grass and black rock, the navigator yelled, 'Eject, eject.'

They both grabbed the handles at the same moment, as the aircraft hurtled towards the ground.

The ejector rockets fired and the canopy blew away with a crack as the plane spiralled, but the rockets that should have thrown them three hundred feet upwards into the safety of the sky blasted them directly into the mountainside. The aircraft smashed into the ground an instant later. An explosion more deafening than a clap of thunder echoed around the hills as an inferno burst from the wreckage. Then there was silence again.

Four seconds had elapsed between the first warning siren and the impact, four heartbeats separating life from death. There was no trace of either pilot or navigator, no movement but the belching flames and the oily smoke spiralling up into the sky, alongside the rooks startled from their treetop nests.

Chapter 1

'Mountain Rescue call-out. Mountain Rescue team report to Hangar Seven immediately.'

Drew Miller was sitting in the crew room at RAF Finnington, drinking a cup of coffee and doodling absent-mindedly in the margins of his newspaper, when he heard the alarm on the Tannoy start to sound around the station.

In a base making daily use of the most advanced electronics and engineering, it was an incongruously old-fashioned signal, a man blowing three blasts on a whistle, like a referee signalling full time in a football match.

As the alarm sounded, all over the base men scrambled from their work. The Mountain Rescue team were all volunteers. Engineers servicing aircraft on the line outside the hangars downed tools and ran, a cook washing dishes in the mess sprinted for the door, still wearing his apron, and a member of the firecrew dozing in his bunk, leapt up and hurried out, hopping from leg to leg as he tried to pull on his boots. There was a fusillade of slamming doors as they rushed outside, jumped into their vehicles and raced towards Hangar Seven.

Drew dropped his pen and ran for the door, cursing as he

brushed against his cup of coffee and sent it spilling onto the floor.

'Sorry, I've got a call-out,' he shouted over his shoulder. 'I'll clean up the next one.'

'That'll be the day,' came the reply, but Drew was already out of the door.

He jumped into his car and tore off towards the Mountain Rescue headquarters on the other side of the airfield. He screeched to a halt outside the armoury for a moment to pick up his deputy on the MR team and then bucketed on across the airfield, swerving across the bows of a lumbering Hercules transport as it taxied out towards the runway.

'Christ, go steady, Drew.' His passenger ducked instinctively as the Hercules towered above them. 'We're supposed to save lives, not lose them.'

Drew grunted, but kept his foot down as they sped through the secret core of the base, the two squadron sites, clustered around one end of the seven-thousand-foot runway. He took a shortcut through the web of taxiways connecting the runway to a warren of hardened aircraft shelters – burrows of concrete and steel, each just large enough for a single Tempest. Fuel and arms dumps were hidden nearby, submerged under even thicker carapaces of reinforced concrete.

'Shame isn't it?' Drew said, gesturing to the shelters as they sped past. 'As much concrete as the Berlin Wall and just as redundant these days.'

His deputy laughed. 'Don't let the boss hear you talking like that or you'll be on a permanent posting to the Outer Hebrides.'

The jokes stopped as they braked to a halt outside Hangar Seven. It was already buzzing and Drew looked on approvingly. Without the need for any orders from him, the individuals had melded into a team, going about their preparations coolly and methodically, without a wasted movement or superfluous word. The kit was quickly checked and packed and the vehicles – two Land-Rovers and two HGVs – lined up outside the hangar.

The teleprinter was chattering in the corner. One of the team ripped off a message and brought it to the control desk. Drew scanned it hurriedly and then called the team around him. 'A Tempest from 71 Squadron at Coningsby, callsign Raven 2-1, has been overdue for an hour. Smoke and flames have been sighted near Gunnerside in Swaledale. No reports of the crew so far. The suspected crash site is Crowgarth Farm on the edge of Ivelet Moor, grid reference 401319. The helicopter is already on its way. We will deploy by road – it should take about fifty minutes to get there. Despite the urgency, let's make sure we all get there in one piece. Drive safely. Let's go.'

His deputy smiled to himself, knowing Drew's normal driving to be anything but safety-first.

The members of the team piled into their vehicles and set off with blue lights flashing and sirens sounding. An armed guard raised the barrier as they sped through the entrance gate of the base. He turned to his fellow guard, watching through a slit in a concrete pillbox, with only his eyes and gun barrel visible in the gloom. 'There they go – another one bites the dust. I tell you what, you wouldn't catch me flying a Tempest.'

'I suppose it would be a bit of a step down from your Honda 50,' his mate said sardonically, turning his attention back to the approach road.

The convoy headed west from Finnington, climbing steadily as it negotiated the winding roads leading up into the hills. Twice Drew's Land-Rover, leading the way, was forced to a juddering halt as he rounded a bend to find a farmer's tractor blocking the road.

'Come on, Farmer Giles, out of the bloody way,' he muttered irritably, turning on the siren to emphasise his urgency, but the second farmer was not to be hurried. He whistled in his dogs and even lit a cigarette before easing himself ponderously into his seat to move the tractor.

Drew inched his way past and climbed higher, burrowing through dark tunnels of single-track road where the trees met over their heads, shutting out the weak sunlight. Damp walls of rock rose on either side, moss and ferns sprouting from every crevice. They branched off at last onto a rough track, marked with a mouldering wooden sign, lichen almost obliterating the legend directing them to Crowgarth Farm.

As Drew pulled into the farmyard, he saw a yellow Sea King helicopter in the corner of the field. The Tempest crew's locator beacons had been superfluous. The pall of smoke from the jet's funeral pyre had been visible for miles.

As he yanked on the handbrake, Drew was already halfway out of the door. He raced across to speak to the winch-operator from the Search and Rescue helicopter, by now an old friend. 'Anybody get out?'

'They got out, but that's all they did. They're over there.' He pointed up the hill.

Drew and his men walked quickly to the edge of the wood but there was little to be seen. The aircraft had tent-pegged, rolling over and going into the ground nose first. Only the jet pipes and the tailplane were visible above the ground, a fierce fire still raging around them. A small amount of wreckage was scattered around the site.

Drew looked round at the winchman. 'Where's the rest of it?'

He jerked his head towards a huge ash tree. 'Over there.'

Walking further into the wood, Drew winced as he saw the bases of two ejection seats. One was embedded in the side of the hill, the other had smashed into the ash tree, twelve feet above the ground. A yellow survival pack dangled uselessly below it.

A severed arm lay on the ground a few feet from the base of the tree. Drew looked up and had to suppress a shudder as he saw the pilot's legs and lower body still strapped into the seat. The head and torso had disappeared, pulverised on impact, with only a dark red stain on the trunk of the tree to show where a man's life had ended.

His men gathered around him, gazing in disbelief at the sight facing them. There was a gagging sound. Drew turned to see a newcomer to the Mountain Rescue team vomiting, tears pouring down his face.

Drew took a last look at the mangled seat above him and then turned away, briskly issuing orders. 'Okay guys, no survivors from this one. Get a temporary crash cordon organised immediately. Jack, take three men over there, Harry, over there with another three.'

He left them to mount the crash guard and headed back to the Land-Rover, nodding curtly to the farmer and a handful of locals standing in a circle in the farmyard, muttering to each other.

The farmer's face was still white with shock. The twin poles of his life were his two hundred acres of steep, sparsely grassed hillside and the livestock market in Hawes, barely ten miles away, where he sold his sheep. In his fifty-two years, he had travelled further than Hawes only a handful of times. He had often paused as jets flashed overhead, sour but not a little envious of the freedom of air crew who could traverse that distance in less than a minute and span a continent in a couple of hours. Now he had seen at first hand the price that some paid for that freedom.

Drew called in to base. 'I'm at the crash site. It's a Tempest RS3. No survivors. We'll need a full crash cordon organised as soon as possible. I'm sending a Sea King down to pick them up.'

His orders were immediately relayed around the base by Tannoy.

'Crash procedures in operation. Each section to organise three guards with full overnight kit, to report to Hangar Two in fifteen minutes.'

No one was spared: every sector from filing clerks and kitchen porters to engineers and air crew had to take an equal part in one of the Air Force's least popular duties.

The reluctant conscripts pulled on several layers of winter clothing and then began straggling towards the hangar, less than enthusiastic at the prospect of spending a cold night on a bleak hillside. By the time they had assembled, the Sea King was already clattering in to pick them up and ferry them to Crowgarth Farm.

Drew was standing in the farmyard ready to greet them as they clambered awkwardly out of the helicopter. 'Right, we haven't got much daylight left. Your job is to secure the site; the investigation begins in the morning. Meanwhile, I don't want any curious locals, souvenir hunters or bloody tabloid reporters within a hundred yards of here. No one gets close to the site and no one takes anything; let's keep it as it is for the investigators.'

The senior medical officer from the base had also arrived to confirm that the men were dead, prising his bulk out of the helicopter and struggling up the field, his brogues slipping and sliding in the mud.

'It doesn't take a sodding doctor to see they're dead,' muttered a chef from Finnington, a less-than-willing volunteer, dragged from his warm kitchen for the cold, all-night guard duty. 'That's about as bleeding pointless as dragging us up here to guard the site: there's nothing to nick and no one up here to nick it, even if there was. There's nothing but bleeding sheep for twenty miles.' He kicked at a pile of droppings to emphasise the point.

As the shadows lengthened, Drew's team hurried to disentangle the mangled remains of the pilot and navigator from their ejection seats and place them in two black rubber body bags, laid out side by side on the trampled grass beneath the trees.

Drew detailed his most experienced man to climb the ash tree and secure the ejector seat with some rope. The seat was stuck fast, driven into the trunk like a nail, and his men had to bring up ladders and hack at the tree with axes for twenty minutes before the seat could be prised loose and lowered gingerly to the ground.

So little of the pilot remained that not even his mother could have identified him, but the name patch was still visible on the navigator's bloodsoaked flying suit.

Drew read the name and turned away, groaning aloud. 'Shit, Jeff Faraday. I went through training with him.'

There was a long silence, as the men around him stared at the ground. Few of them had not lost friends in similar circumstances.

Finally Drew said gruffly, 'Right, let's get on,' his men stirred and went back to their task, avoiding each other's eyes.

The team medic had the job of lifting the remains of the pilot's body out of the seat and placing it in the body bag alongside the severed arm. He zipped the bag closed and helped to carry it to the helicopter as the last rays of the sun touched the moortop high above them. Carrying its grim cargo, the Sea King rose into the rapidly darkening sky and was gone.

It was a long, cold night for the men on the crash cordon.

Drew made an hourly circuit of the perimeter, to make sure that they were awake and alert, but the only intruders were owls flitting like wraiths among the trees and foxes which gave the grumbling guards a wide berth. In between his rounds of the crash cordon Drew paced the yard, brooding on the death of his friend.

He remembered Faraday encouraging him through his flight training and rescuing him when his impatience and hot temper led him into confrontations with senior officers. In true British style, Drew's thanks and his admiration had been expressed only as an unspoken subtext. Now it was too late to repair the omission.

As the sun at last showed above the ridgeline to the east, the rooks around Crowgarth Farm shook the frost from their feathers and took off, cawing indignantly at the guards down below. Drew stood motionless at the edge of the farmyard, his eyes following the flight of the rooks against the dawn sky, though his mind was far away.

He stretched and rubbed his face wearily with his hands, then began walking up the field towards the guards. They stamped their feet, scuffing black streaks into the frost, while their breath condensed in clouds of vapour, drifting up like the smoke from the still-smouldering wreckage. A couple of them were holding out their hands towards the tailplane, trying to warm themselves, as if standing by a brazier.

Drew tried to push the image of Faraday's corpse from his mind as he addressed the guards with an enthusiasm he did not feel. 'Morning, guys. The good news is that you should be relieved in an hour and we'll chopper you straight back for breakfast in the mess. Meantime, stay alert.'

'And the bad news, sir?' asked the chef warily, wise beyond his years to the cruelties of officers.

'The bad news is that you're back here at 1800 hours to guard the wreckage again tonight.'

There was a chorus of groans.

'Isn't there anybody else could do it, sir?' asked the chef.

'Two men died over there yesterday,' Drew said, his voice level. 'Be grateful the closest you come to that is cutting your thumb on your kitchen knives or giving us all food poisoning with your bloody awful cooking. Now, any other complaints?'

The chef scowled but said nothing as Drew turned on his heel and walked back down towards the farm. He called up base to confirm that the relief guard was on its way. As he finished his call, his eye was caught by the farmer standing at his front door, bleary-eyed in the dawn.

'Morning.'

The farmer nodded, eyeing him narrowly as he scratched the grey stubble on his chin.

'Morning. You look as rough as I feel,' grunted the farmer in a thick Yorkshire accent.

'Did you see the crash?'

'Aye, I saw it. It's not something I'll forget in a hurry neither.'

'What happened?'

The farmer licked his lips. He had already told his story a dozen times in the local pub the night before. Each time he told it, the speed of the jet increased by another fifty miles an hour and the crash site moved a few feet closer to where he had been standing. Despite the repetitions, he was far from bored with the tale and began again with relish.

'I was up by High Riddings there,' he said, gesturing up towards the moor. 'I was foddering my yows when the plane flew over.'

His rambling monologue included frequent diversions to cover local points of interest and bits of sheep-farming lore. 'They've shifted some hay this winter, I can tell you. It's been a thin winter. It's not come a big heap of snow as it can do, but I've never known it so cold, windy and wet – what we call clashy weather.'

He paused to pull a battered packet of cigarettes out of his pocket and lit one before continuing, eyeing Drew smugly as he did so. Drew was itching to get to the point, but forced himself to be patient.

'Anyway,' the farmer said, exhaling a cloud of blue smoke into the still air, '. . . where was I?'

'The crash.'

'No,' the farmer said, playing him like an angler with a trout, 'I hadn't got to that – I was talking about the winter.'

'Yeah, but . . .'

But the farmer was enjoying his fifteen minutes of fame and was not to be rushed. His eyes flickered craftily towards Drew. 'Anyway, what about my yows? That crash'll have scared them half to death. There'll be a few abortions and stillbirths come lambing time.'

Drew gave him a knowing smile. 'I'm sure you already know how to apply for compensation. Now, about the aircraft?' he asked, a note of desperation creeping into his voice.

'It came around yon hill, very fast and low. I'd only just gathered my yows to fodder them and the noise of it scattered them like a fox in a henhouse.'

'The crash . . .' Drew said wearily.

'I were just telling you,' the farmer replied indignantly. 'It came over the hill, just there over what we call Robin Hole – it's a cave that goes back about twenty yards into the hillside. It has a spring that has never been dry in all my life, nor my father's neither.'

'But what happened to the aircraft?' Drew felt a mounting urge to seize the man by the throat and strangle the story out of him.

'I'd be able to tell you, if you didn't keep interrupting. It came over Robin Hole, like I said, and then just sort of dropped out of the sky.'

'Did you see an explosion or any smoke or flames before the crash?'

'I didn't see anything like that, just the plane flying along and then hitting the hillside. It fair shook me up, I can tell you. Now about my compensation . . .'

Drew looked at him with distaste. 'Thank you. You've been most helpful,' he said. 'I'm sure the official accident investigator will be very interested to hear all about your sheep.'

'It's been my pleasure,' the farmer said. 'I hope he's as good a listener as you.'

Hearing the clatter of the Sea King's rotors, Drew turned away and walked back up the field. He briefed the incoming relief guard and saw his own team safely on their way back to base, the chef still grumbling as the helicopter took off.

The downwash from the helicopter whipped up a whirlwind of dead leaves, a couple sticking to the tailpipes of the crashed Tempest. Within seconds the leaves were smouldering and then bursting into flame. Drew stared at them for a long time, watching the skeletons of the leaves show through and then crumble as the leaves disintegrated into ash.

'Looks like it'll be a while longer before we can start examining the engines.'

Drew jumped in surprise and wheeled around. A blue Rover had pulled into the farmyard as the Sea King was taking off and its two occupants had walked up the field and joined Drew at the still-smouldering wreckage.

He gave a broad smile of recognition. 'Hello, Tom, good to see you.' He checked, half-embarrassed. 'In the circumstances, that is, if you know what I mean.'

Tom nodded sympathetically. 'I know what you mean.'

'You're still with the Accident Investigation Board then? I thought you'd be back flying by now.'

'No such luck,' Tom said, shooting a sidelong glance at his companion. 'I've still got another twelve months of my ground tour to do. I'm counting the days till I get back in the cockpit again.'

'Even when you keep seeing things like this?' Drew asked, gesturing to the wreckage.

He nodded. 'Even when I see things like this. You know the aircrew motto, Drew: it won't happen to me.'

There was a pause, broken as Tom's companion cleared his throat peremptorily.

'Sorry, Richard,' Tom said, giving Drew the ghost of a wink. 'You haven't met Drew, have you? Flight Lieutenant Drew Miller, this is Squadron Leader Richard Enfield, who's leading the accident investigation.'

Enfield acknowledged Drew's greeting with a barely perceptible nod then cleared his throat again. Drew decided that it was a mannerism he could very quickly grow to dislike.

'Let's get on, shall we?' Enfield said, his clipped speech, almost colourless grey eyes and very short iron-grey hair, emphasising the austerity of his manner.

Drew briefed them on what he knew of the crash and the

steps taken to protect the site. 'There's also a witness. The farmer down there saw the aircraft come down. Don't start a conversation with him if you haven't got plenty of time to spare, but if you live long enough he may finally get to the point.'

Tom smiled; Enfield merely gave a brief nod. 'Any sign of the accident data recorder?'

'Not that I could see.' He gestured towards the tailpipes. 'I imagine you'll find it under those.'

Enfield grunted in agreement, then said curtly, 'Thank you, that will be all.'

Tom intercepted the look Drew directed at Enfield's back as he turned and walked away into the wood.

'Don't mind him, it's just his way. He's actually quite a nice bloke when you get to know him.'

'I'll have to take your word for that.'

Tom glanced at him, trying to read the expression on his face. 'So it was a pretty messy one, was it?' Drew nodded slowly, his lips compressed. 'Did you know the guys?'

'I knew the nav, yeah. I went through training with him.'

'I'm sorry. It's bad enough hearing about a friend's death. It's even worse when you're the one who has to deal with the body.'

He waited for a reply, but Drew said nothing, his eyes staring at the thin plume of grey smoke drifting upwards from the wreckage of the jet.

Tom watched him thoughtfully. 'You know, Drew, we both see a lot of crashes and they're often people we know, but there's always one that really hits you hard.'

Drew looked up suspiciously but Tom's face, framed by a mop of dark-brown hair, was open and friendly.

'When I came up for officer training,' Tom said, 'I was just a raw lad from Wigan surrounded by what looked and sounded to me like a lot of entrants for the Upper Class Twit of the Year.' His Lancashire accent grew even broader as he summoned up the memory.

'Only one bloke befriended me at first, Michael Flynn. He was from Belfast and felt just as out of place among all the Ruperts as I did. We became really good mates but we lost touch when we were posted.

'The first incident I had to go to after I joined the AIB was the crash that killed him. His nose-wheel collapsed as he landed and the jet just flipped over.'

Drew started to say something in reply, then frowned and shook his head. They both stood in silence for a couple of minutes, then Drew squared his shoulders. 'I'll have to be getting back, Tom.' He paused. 'We must have a beer together sometime; it would be a real pleasure to meet somewhere that wasn't a crash site for a change.'

'I'd like that.' Tom shook Drew's hand, then turned to follow Enfield up into the wood.

The investigators went about their business, taking photographs, notes and measurements, Enfield pausing occasionally to give Drew a curious look. There was nothing more for him to do at the site, yet Drew was reluctant to leave.

Finally, Enfield walked back down through the wood to where Drew was standing, still staring unseeingly into the smoking wreckage.

Enfield cleared his throat once more. 'Was there something else you had to tell us?'

Drew's eyes came back into focus. He turned his head to glance briefly at Enfield, then looked away, shaking his head. 'Nothing you'd understand.'

He took a long final look round the crash site. Then he walked slowly down the hill and, ignoring the still-hovering farmer, drove off down the narrow, rutted track.

It was a perfect winter morning, a pale sun shining from a cold, cloudless sky, but Drew had no thoughts for the day or the gradually unfolding landscape as he followed the road winding alongside the river down the dale.

His mind was filled with blazing warning lights, wailing sirens and earth and sky spinning faster and faster until everything ended in a scream of tortured metal and a detonation that shook the earth.

He was jerked back to reality by the insistent blaring of a horn. He looked up to see the Land-Rover drifting well over the crown of the road, into the path of a cattle truck pounding up the dale. He hauled frantically on the wheel. The cattle truck filled his windscreen for a moment, then there was a crack as Drew's wing mirror shattered.

The truck hurtled by, the driver screaming abuse above his blaring horn, while the cattle thrown around in the truck added their own bellows of protest.

Drew pulled into the side, his heart pounding and his brow clammy with sweat. He got out, walked down to the edge of the river and bathed his face in the icy water. Then he went back to the Land-Rover and drove on down the dale, the music blasting from the radio drowning out the clamour of his thoughts.

Chapter 2

It took Drew another hour to drive back to Finnington. As he crested the last hill before the windswept flatlands on the edge of the Plain of York, he saw the base ahead of him, sprawling over twenty square miles. Again, he pulled into the side of the road for a moment.

From this distance Finnington could almost have been any small town – a ring of suburbs surrounding a cluster of shops, banks and churches – but for the vast expanse of grey concrete at its heart. As Drew watched, a formation of Tempests flew in from the east, the sun glinting on their wings as they banked to make their approach to the runway.

He drove on down to the base, his black mood deepening. He left the Land-Rover outside Hangar Seven and hurried away as a mechanic began tutting over the shattered wing-mirror.

Drew should have checked in with his squadron before going home to try to get some sleep, but his nerve failed him as he hesitated in the corridor outside the crew room. He could not face the laughter and noisy banter of his crew-mates and was about to turn and slip away, when a hand touched his shoulder.

He whipped round. 'Bloody hell, Nick. You scared the life out of me.'

His navigator laughed. 'Nerves of steel. Just what I like to see in the pilot I entrust my life to five times a week.' His smile faded as he studied Drew's face. 'Are you all right?'

'Yeah, I'm fine,' Drew muttered, trying to ease past him.

'Are you sure? You look rough as guts.'

'Honestly, Nick. It's nothing. I'm just tired.'

Nick put a restraining hand on his arm. 'Nothing my arse. What's up?'

Drew shook his head, but Nick maintained his hold on Drew's arm.

'Look, I'm fine. I'm off home for a kip, I'll see you in the morning.'

Nick reluctantly released Drew and stepped aside. He watched him walk down the corridor, then shrugged and pushed open the crew room door.

Drew made his way slowly out along the main road through the base. All he wanted was to get back to his flat and close the door on the last twenty-four hours, but it seemed to him that every single one of the three thousand servicemen on the base and their five thousand dependants were trying to cross the road in front of him. He held his impatience in check and eventually left the crowds behind as he passed the last of the housing estates and two-storey blocks of flats in the suburbs just inside Finnington's perimeter fence.

Clear of the barrier, he joined the high-speed procession down the A1. He concentrated hard on his driving, the memory of his earlier near miss with the cattle truck still vivid in his mind. Twenty minutes later, he eased through the gates of a converted Georgian mansion on the north side of the town square.

He killed the engine, then sat for a moment, looking around the immaculately manicured grounds and watching the branches of the ancient cedar waving hypnotically in the breeze.

At last he hauled himself wearily out of his car and walked over to the house, his footsteps crunching on the gravel. Letting himself into the dark, echoing hall, he picked up his mail, arranged on a silver salver like the visiting cards of society ladies, and walked upstairs to his flat.

Drew dumped his letters unread on the table, made some coffee and then slumped down in an armchair, listlessly turning the pages of a newspaper.

He awoke with a start. The newspaper still lay across his lap, but the room was in darkness. He looked around for a moment, then swore and leapt to his feet, groped his way to a light switch, then swore a second time as he looked at his watch and saw the time.

He rushed to the bathroom, brushed his teeth and dragged a comb across his head, then grabbed some fresh clothes from the wardrobe and hurriedly changed. He ran downstairs, still buttoning his shirt, and sprinted down the drive and out through the gates.

Finnington Hall stood just below the town square, its grounds sweeping down to the river. Drew rushed up the drive but then paused for a moment, trying to compose himself. Then he hurried up the steps and burst into the foyer of the restaurant, banging the door against the wall. He scanned the startled faces at the bar, then saw Josie at a side table.

As he walked across to join her, she glanced up and gave him a quizzical look.

'I know,' Drew said, 'I'm really, really sorry.'

Josie shrugged. 'It's all right. It gave me time to do some thinking.'

'That sounds ominous.'

She gave a brief, brittle smile and looked away.

Puzzled, Drew went on hesitantly. 'While I'm apologising, I haven't got your present either. It's ordered, but I just didn't have time to pick it up. I'm really sorry. I'll get it for you tomorrow.'

She shook her head. 'Not unless you've ordered it from Copenhagen, Drew. You're going on detachment, remember? That's why we're doing this tonight instead of on my birthday.'

Drew began to stammer out another apology, but she held a hand up. 'Don't worry. It honestly doesn't matter at all.'

'On Monday then,' he said, but Josie just gave another thin-lipped smile.

He studied her face for a moment, half hidden by her long, dark-brown hair, then shrugged and signalled to the barman.

When the champagne arrived, Drew raised his glass to Josie. 'Happy birthday. You look sensational.'

'Thanks. You bought the dress for me last year, remember, so you deserve some of the credit.'

He smiled. 'I do remember some things, Josie. Green suits you. It goes with your eyes.'

It was a joke – Josie's eyes were dark brown – but she barely registered it. Instead she returned the scrutiny, shaking her head. 'You look like hell.'

He grimaced. 'Yeah, I know, tough day at work.'

She waited for a further explanation, but there was none forthcoming. A frown flickered across her face and her expression became even more set.

They ordered their meal and then exchanged desultory small talk, neither seeming to have their heart in it. Drew remained preoccupied, Josie even more distant and brooding. She answered most of his questions in monosyllables. Drew felt himself floundering.

After they were seated at their table, he made a last effort to rescue an evening apparently slipping into terminal decline. 'So how was your day? Not good, I'd say.'

She grimaced. 'I've been working on a story for weeks. It's the biggest one I've ever been involved with. I've built it up from nothing, tracking down sources, following up every lead, sweating blood to make it absolutely watertight. Do you know what happened to it?'

Drew could have made a pretty fair guess, but he prudently shook his head.

'It's been spiked. Not because it's not true – every word of it is – but because, and I quote, "there may be legal complications". That's editor-speak for, "the fat-arsed industrialist involved is a substantial donor to Conservative Party funds and his libel lawyers are like rottweilers, so thanks for the story, Josie, but why don't you go and do a feature on the fashion industry or six interesting ways to serve potatoes?"' She gave a bleak smile. 'So I suppose you could say it wasn't the best day I've ever had.'

'Is that why you're so quiet?'

As she was about to reply, the waiter arrived with their first course. She checked and changed the subject. 'How was yours?'

'Not the best one I've ever had,' Drew said, staring blankly at his plate.

Josie waved away the hovering waiter and as Drew looked up she held his gaze for the first time that evening and asked gently, 'Want to talk about it?'

He shook his head. 'Not really.'

She bit her lip and lapsed back into silence.

'What's the matter, Josie? Is it just work?'

She smiled fleetingly to herself, drained her glass and laid her hands, palms down, on the tablecloth in front of her. 'No, Drew, I'm not like you. When I go home at the end of a day, I try to leave all that stuff behind me.'

He mechanically refilled her glass. 'I try not to bring it home either.'

'But you leave a part of yourself behind. You're not really here with me now, are you? A part of your mind is somewhere else. Isn't it?'

Her stare challenged him to deny it. He nodded.

'So where are you right now, Drew?'

He shook his head, his gaze downcast.

When he looked up again, her eyes had filled with tears.

'Josie, I'm all right, really I am,' Drew said, reaching across the table to take her hand.

She pulled it out of reach and shook her head, gulping back the tears. 'You don't understand do you? It's not that at all.' Josie took a long drink from her wine. 'It's not going to work, Drew. It's never going to work. We can't do this any more.'

'You mean split up? Move out?'

She gave a sad smile. 'You can hardly call it that, Drew. I've never really moved in. I've never been allowed to be part of your life. I'm just permitted to drop in for a visit occasionally, to take my toothbrush for walks.'

Even as Drew began to argue, he knew in his heart that she was right. 'I can't ask you to share the sort of life I lead,' he said quietly, as if trying to convince himself as much as her. 'When I go to Germany, we both know you'd never be happy to tag meekly along behind. Three years of loyalty and submissiveness, flower-arranging classes and coffee mornings isn't really your style.'

Drew read her expression and fell silent for a few moments, knowing what she was thinking.

'I can't tell you what you want to hear, Josie.'

She nodded. 'I know. I wouldn't want you to. You'd be doing it for the wrong reasons. If you passed up the posting to Germany, it would always be lying there for the rest of our lives, ready to be picked up and thrown in my face in an argument.'

'That's not fair.'

'Perhaps. Anyway, it doesn't matter now, does it?'

She blinked away another tear and met Drew's gaze with a level stare. 'You know it's the only thing to do, don't you?'

Drew looked away, remembering the night he had told Josie for the first time that he loved her. Later he had lain awake with her sleeping body cradled in his arms. Filled with a love so intense it almost hurt him, he had looked down at her face, hungrily absorbing every detail. Her lips were slightly parted in a smile as she slept, showing the faint gap in her front teeth that he still found ridiculously attractive.

Stooping to kiss her, he had made a vow to himself. If ever he was tempted to break with her, he would recall the way he had felt at that moment. He was doing so now, but the intensity of feeling had faded like a sepia photograph. The intimacy between them had once seemed as constant and natural as breathing; all he felt now was an aching hollowness. He nodded slowly.

They continued to sit in silence, Josie seeing him as if for the first time, taking in every detail and committing it to memory – the ruffled black hair, dark-brown eyes and the slightly crooked nose, broken when he was a child and clumsily reset. It contrasted oddly with his classical good looks, as if vandals had attacked a statue of a Greek god with a hammer.

Drew stared at his hands.

As if reading his thoughts, she said, 'Remember what you once told me? "Never let us part on a cross word. Too many pilots go flying and don't come back. If my number comes up, I don't want our last words to each other to have been angry ones."'

He nodded.

She reached for the bottle and refilled their glasses. 'Let's not part on cross words or long silences now, let's just enjoy what's left of the evening.'

He smiled gratefully and raised his glass in a toast. 'To Drew and Josie, the ones that got away.'

She laughed, a little too harshly, and Drew pretended not to notice.

She searched his face, then said, 'It's nobody's fault, Drew.'

He shook his head. 'You're being polite.'

'Perhaps a little,' she conceded, 'but you've got your career, I've got mine and there just aren't enough points of contact between them. Even when you were in the country, you might as well have been operating on Eastern Standard Time for all I saw of you.'

'It's called daytime, actually. You wouldn't recognise it since you don't have to crawl in to your office until eleven. By the time you get home again, I'm already yawning and counting the hours to my next dawn briefing.'

She smiled. 'Was it my imagination or was there an edge creeping back into that last remark?'

He bowed his head in mock shame. 'We could scarcely have found two more mutually antagonistic occupations, could we?'

Josie laughed, this time an unforced one. 'Nor two more hostile groups of friends. Do you remember those disastrous evenings when we tried to put your Air Force mates and my media friends in the same room?'

Drew nodded, wincing at the memory. 'It was like having six Arthur Scargills sitting down to dinner with half a dozen Margaret Thatchers. They either argued furiously or just sat and gazed at each other in total incomprehension.'

Josie smiled at the memory. 'When they'd all gone home, we used to howl with laughter.' She gave a bright, brittle smile. 'At least we'll avoid the usual problem in break-ups: our friends having to choose between us. I can't think of a single friend we've got in common.'

'Nick and Sally?'

She shook her head. 'Hardly. Sally's always been much too fond of you for my liking. Anyway, you're even worse. I bet you can't name a single one of my friends that you'd willingly meet for a drink.'

'It's worse than that,' Drew said, grinning. 'I can't name a single one of your friends. It's not just them, though. I call the people on squadron mates, but if I'm honest Nick's the only really close friend I've got there. I can't think of anyone else that I'd actually phone when I was away from the base and say, "Fancy a drink?"'

'I don't believe that.'

He shrugged. 'It's true. You're all thrown together, you work together and inevitably you socialise together, particularly when you're overseas. You even entrust your lives to each other, but . . .'

'Are you sure you're not just talking about yourself? It sounds awfully like Drew Miller syndrome to me – show no emotion, reveal no weakness.'

He shook his head. 'It's everyone. Perhaps it's just self-protection. If you don't get too close to people, you don't feel as much pain when they don't come back from a sortie one day.'

He fell silent again, his face clouding.

'Drew?'

He spoke in a low voice, staring down at his hands as they traced patterns on the tablecloth. 'You know when you asked me where I was earlier on?' She nodded. 'I was back on a hillside in the Dales. I'd been helping to scrape a mate's brains off the trunk of a tree. We put all the bits of him we could find into a black rubber body bag. When we'd finished doing that we had to start all over again with the even more mangled remains of a pilot so young that he probably didn't start shaving till last week. I was at the site all night.'

'I'm sorry.' Her voice was gentle.

He shrugged, trying again to distance himself from his memories of the crash site.

She watched as he wrestled with his thoughts, fighting the urge to wrap him in her arms. 'This one seems to have hit you really hard.'

'This one was different.' He hesitated. 'It's the first crash where I've seen a real mate, a true friend, killed. Not just killed, but mangled, mutilated, torn apart. There'll be no viewing of the body at his funeral.'

He pulled himself back to the present and gave her a sheepish smile. 'Sorry to lay that on you.'

'Don't be. I wish you'd been like this more often. You never tell me anything about what you do.'

Drew looked wistfully at her. 'It's funny, now we've decided to split up we're getting on better than we have for months.'

She laughed, though her eyes remained sad. 'It's because we're demob happy, Drew. It's like the end-of-term party: even if you didn't like school, you always enjoyed the bit just before you got the hell out of it.' She saw the hurt in his eyes and added, 'I don't mean it quite like that . . .'

'Josie . . .'

She shook her head. 'We'd better go.'

Drew signalled for the bill. 'Do you want to come back to the flat?'

'I'll come back, but only to pick up my toothbrush and a couple of bits and pieces.'

'Get them another time.'

'No, Drew, it's better if there isn't another time. Really.'

They left the restaurant and walked back to his flat in silence, their footsteps echoing across the deserted town square.

He opened the heavy front door and switched on the light. As usual, it cut out again before they had walked the length of the cavernous, oak-floored hallway and he had to grope his way to the next switch at the bottom of the stairs. It was an odd but altogether typical touch of parsimony from the owner of the house: the vast crystal chandelier, studded with a dozen light bulbs, was operated by a time switch to save money.

As soon as Drew unlocked the door of the flat, Josie disappeared into the bathroom to collect her things. She came out a few moments later and stood facing him by the door. She gave him one last searching look, her head tilted to one side. 'I hope you'll be really happy with someone one day, Drew. I'm sorry it couldn't be me.'

'Me too.'

She kissed him quickly on the cheek and then slipped out. Drew heard her heels clicking on the wooden floor. There was a dull thud as the front door swung shut, and then silence. He ran to the window and watched her walking out across the gravel in the moonlight. She turned in the gateway, as if she knew he was watching, and raised a hand in farewell. Then she was gone.

He closed the curtains, sat down and stared dully around him. He had lived there for four years, but the flat still had an air of impermanence. It was well, if austerely, furnished, but could easily have passed for a hotel suite, save for the stack of paperbacks on the floor, patiently waiting for Drew to put up some shelves. In those four years it had acquired none of the clutter or the patina of use of a family home and there were times, as now, when it felt as hollow as a drum.

He walked through to the bedroom, undressed and got into bed. He tried to read, then switched the light off, but lay awake a long time, staring into the dark.

The alarm rang at six, jolting Drew out of sleep. He showered and dressed and went into the kitchen to make some breakfast. The fridge was barren but for a pint of milk, a tub of yoghurt and some cheese. He sniffed the milk, then washed both it and the yoghurt down the sink.

He picked up his bag and was on his way out when he saw a note on the doormat. He opened it eagerly but then groaned as he saw the microscopic, anal-retentive handwriting of his next-door neighbour: 'If guests are leaving late at night, please ensure that the front door is closed quietly, avoiding disturbance and annoyance to others.' He crumpled it into a ball and stuffed it back through his neighbour's letterbox, then walked out, shutting the front door with a crash that resounded throughout the building.

As he unlocked his Audi, he glanced up at the first floor. On the nights when she had stayed there, no matter how tired she was, Josie would always be at the window to wave to him as he drove off.

Only ghosts looked down at him today. He swung the car around fast, carving crescents into the newly raked gravel, then drove off through the gates and across the square, heading east. After half a mile he turned off into a tree-lined suburban street to pick up his navigator.

Drew pulled up outside a red-brick Victorian house, once the vicarage for the church at the bottom of the road. He opened the gate and walked round to the back door, picking his way through a forest of kids' toys, bikes, buckets and spades.

He rapped on the glass and stepped inside. Nick's wife, Sally, was standing in front of the Aga, cooking toast and trying to soothe the baby bawling in her arms. Nick was chasing their elder son, Martin, around the big pine table in the centre of the kitchen, while the other boy, Simon, sat at the table yelling encouragement and spraying cornflakes in all directions.

Their little daughter, Jane, was lecturing her teddy bear loudly as she tried to feed it bread and jam. The kettle was whistling, the dog was barking furiously and, ignored by everyone, breakfast television was blaring out of a portable TV in the corner.

'Uncle Drew. Uncle Drew.' Martin ran over and hugged Drew's legs. Drew ruffled the boy's hair and then released him back to the chase.

He sat down at the table and within seconds the two-year-old was clambering up on to his lap, clutching a book, her face a mask of raspberry jam. 'Read story, Drew. Read big story.'

A flannel came flying across the room. 'Give her face a wipe, Drew, or we'll have to hose you down before you go to work.'

Nick glanced at his watch. 'Sorry, princess, no time for stories. We're going to be late.'

Nick scooped up each of his children in turn, then slipped an arm round Sally's waist and kissed her tenderly. 'I'll miss you. Look after yourself and look after the brood, especially this one.' He kissed the baby, who babbled and smiled back at him.

Drew watched them, then looked up to meet Sally's amused gaze. 'Bit of a soft face there, Drew. I'd say it won't be too long before you and Josie are having a couple of little ones yourself.'

His face clouded. 'Don't buy a new hat just yet. 'Bye everyone.'

As he turned towards the door, Sally shot a questioning look at Nick, but he just shrugged his shoulders and followed Drew out to the car.

Nick flopped into the passenger seat, banging the door as always, while Drew winced.

'Created by robots, destroyed by morons.'

'And a *vorch sprung durch technik* to you too! Great morning, Drew.'

'Is it?'

'Uh-oh, what's the problem this time – sex or money?'

'Josie. It's her birthday tomorrow, but as we're going to Denmark I took her out for dinner last night instead. I think it would be fair to say that the evening didn't go quite as I planned.'

'A big row?'

Drew shrugged. 'Not really, but we did end up agreeing to part.'

Nick raised an eyebrow. 'What was the problem – the posting to Germany?'

'That's part of it.' Drew paused as he accelerated to overtake a lorry. 'But not all of it.'

Nick studied Drew's profile for a moment, then gazed through the windscreen as he spoke, picking his words with care. 'You've got to think about what you really want for yourself, inside or outside the Air Force. If you want a career in fast jets, then you really have to go to Germany. If you don't, the Air Force isn't the be-all and end-all. There are lots of other things you can do.'

'I know,' Drew said, swinging the Audi through an S-bend, 'but there aren't many that are this much fun. I've got a friend who's a lawyer in the City. He makes a stack of money, but it takes him an hour and a half to get to work every morning and his job bores the tits off him. Then there's my mate Hamish. He's a farmer up in the north of Scotland. It's a beautiful place, but he's up to his neck in nettles and cow shit, and the most exciting thing that ever happens is when he gets rid of the double-six playing doms. It's a great place to fly over, but I wouldn't want to live there.'

He thought for a few moments, then spoke again, slowly,

as much to himself as to Nick. 'I keep thinking that I should stop messing around with the *Boy's Own* hero stuff and take a ground job, but if I wasn't happy doing it I'd only make Josie' – he gave an embarrassed smile – 'I mean whoever I'm with miserable as well.'

He glanced across at Nick. 'You've done your two tours in the front line. You've got a nice wife and kids and have every reason to settle down with your pipe and slippers. I've still got things I want to do in the Air Force.'

'Then it sounds like you've already made your decision . . . and a bit less of the "pipe and slippers" if you don't mind.'

Drew smiled and flicked on the radio for the news. There was a terse report, buried halfway through the bulletin: 'The RAF have still not released the names of the Tempest fighter crew killed in a crash in the Yorkshire Dales the day before yesterday. Investigators are at the scene working to establish the cause. An RAF spokesman said that the parents of one of the dead men are on holiday abroad and the names of the crew cannot be released until the next-of-kin have been informed.'

Drew turned off the radio. 'Imagine coming home from holiday to that.'

'Imagine being told that, period,' Nick replied. 'It must be the worst thing in the world for parents to outlive their children.'

Both men sat in silence for a while. After a few moments Nick looked up. 'Sorry. These crashes must be getting to all of us. That's the third in four weeks.'

'Did you know that Jeff Faraday was one of the guys who died?'

Nick shook his head. 'He had two kids, didn't he?'

He fell silent again, then asked, 'Do you know what happened?'

'Not really. I was with the Mountain Rescue team up there. It was a hell of a mess. I had to sit still for the whole bloody life story of the farmer who saw the crash, but the only thing he could tell me was that he wanted compensation for the shock to his sheep.'

Drew pulled out onto the outside lane of the dual carriageway and gunned the engine. Like most pilots, he was an excellent driver, but with a correspondingly high opinion of his own skills and a complete lack of patience with other motorists.

'Look at that dickhead.' He flashed his lights and sounded his horn at a Montego doing the legal maximum and stubbornly blocking the outside lane.

'What's it matter?' Nick asked. 'We're almost at the turn-off anyway.'

'I know that, but he doesn't.' Drew switched to the inside lane. He shot past the Montego but then braked and sped down the slip road, catching a glimpse of the Montego driver soundlessly mouthing obscenities at him as he disappeared.

At one time anyone could have driven right up to the guardroom at the heart of the base before being challenged. Since the IRA began its bombing campaign, every visitor, no matter how familiar, was now stopped by armed guards at the main gate. The barriers were flanked by concrete screens solid enough to stop a speeding truck.

'Morning. ID, please . . . Oh, hello, sir.' The guard was a technician on Drew's squadron.

'Morning, Mike. How are things?'

'Murder. The new baby's going for the UK All-Comers record for screaming. The only time I get any sleep is when I'm on guard duty. OK, sir, drive on.'

Chuckling at his own joke, the guard nodded to a colleague invisible in the gloom of the featureless concrete blockhouse. As the barrier swung silently upwards, the gun barrel protruding from the narrow slit in the blockhouse swung away from them and onto the next car waiting in line.

Drew accelerated away, driving in through the suburbs towards the heart of the base. He paused again at a second checkpoint, then passed another barbed-wire fence separating the commercial area from the operational sector, off limits to all except authorised personnel.

Chapter 3

Drew drove past the ranks of two-storey brick buildings, as functional and featureless as a 1950s industrial estate, before pulling up outside the 21 Squadron crew room.

Round the corner of the building two armed guards with a snarling Alsatian paced across the concrete. Drawn up on the line outside an enormous hangar were ten sleek grey killing machines, bristling with missiles slung under fuselage and wings. Drew stared out across the airfield, punctuated by the concrete and blue glass of the control tower and a revolving black steel radar dish, restlessly scanning the skies.

Nick stood waiting with mounting impatience. Finally he called, 'There's a tour bus leaving in ten minutes. Want me to book you on it?'

'Sorry,' Drew said, 'I was miles away. Shall we check the flight programme or get a cup of coffee?'

'What a question to ask a professional,' Nick said. 'Always do the important stuff first; let's get the kettle on.'

As they entered the crew room, Drew gave the squadron mascot, a stuffed tiger, an absentminded pat, dislodging a further couple of hairs from its ever-diminishing pelt.

Ancient as it was, the tiger was still slightly younger

than 21 Squadron. The 'Fighting Tigers' had an illustrious history dating back to the First World War. Their emblem was emblazoned on the sleeves of 21's flying suits and the tiger motif also extended to everything from the crew room coffee mugs to the squadron tie.

The tiger was much loved, even though its once luxuriant fur was threadbare and its ferocious snarl had been cruelly emasculated by their sister squadron, 26. The 'Screaming Eagles' had kidnapped 21's tiger on a drunken, pre-dawn raid and removed all its teeth with a pair of pliers. 21's honour had been satisfied only when 26's mascot – a stuffed eagle, naturally – had been taken down from its perch, plucked, dressed, and left on a silver serving salver, surrounded by pork chipolatas. The toothless tiger had been restored to its podium in the 21 crew room, doubling as mascot and repository for surplus flying kit.

Drew dropped into one of the battered old armchairs grouped around the fireplace. He looked around the room. Sometimes this was the only place he felt at home.

David 'DJ' Jeffries, the most junior member of squadron, glanced up from the toaster behind the coffee bar and called, 'Hello, Drew, has my watch stopped or are you actually on time for once?'

Drew yawned and stretched. 'Punctuality is only a virtue for those who aren't smart enough to think of good excuses for being late.'

Nick had been rummaging through the cupboards. 'There's no bloody coffee.'

'Tea will do,' Drew said.

Nick emerged frowning from beneath the counter. 'No, this is too serious to let go. Who's the coffee-bar officer round here?'

'I am,' DJ said, unsure whether this was a genuine complaint or yet another crew-room wind-up.

'Well, it's not that difficult to run a coffee bar, is it?' Nick asked. 'If you can't fly a kettle and a toaster, God knows what you're like in a jet.'

'Pretty crap on recent evidence,' Drew said. 'He cocked up his starting checks as he was winding his engines up the other day and dumped two hundred gallons of avgas all over the tarmac. He was still running down the line to the spare jet shouting "Wait for me" when the others took off.'

There was a burst of laughter. DJ flushed, gazing uncertainly from one to the other, but his tormentors were already off on another tangent.

'Better luck next time, DJ,' his navigator, Nigel 'Ali' Barber called, half hidden by the fug of steam and smoke. 'By the way, anyone heard anything about that crash?'

'A little,' Drew said. 'It was an RS3 from 71 Squadron at Coningsby. I went up to the site with Mountain Rescue.'

'I know,' DJ said. 'I was the one who had to clean up the coffee you spilled in all the excitement.'

'Such ingratitude,' Drew sighed. 'I go out of my way to give him the chance to make himself useful and he turns on me.'

'So anything grisly at the crash site?' DJ asked.

'Just the body of a good friend of mine.'

DJ's face fell. 'I . . . I er . . .' He twisted a strand of hair between his fingers.

'Do we know why it happened?' Ali asked, coming to the rescue.

'Not yet,' Drew said, 'but they were only flying a routine sortie and it was perfect visibility.'

There was a brief silence. Then Drew said, 'Right, are you ready, Nick? Let's go check out the programme.'

As he reached the doorway, he turned. 'DJ, a word.'

Nick walked a discreet distance further down the corridor as DJ followed Drew out of the crew room. 'Drew,' he began, 'I'm really sorry about your friend. I didn't realise—'

Drew cut him off. 'Forget it. That's not why I want to talk to you. But I did think about you while I was helping to pick up the bits of the pilot that died in that crash. I don't know who he was – the nav was my mate – but he was very young. Too young to die, certainly.'

DJ waited for Drew to continue.

'What I'm trying to say is that you've got to learn a lesson from that. Sheer bloody bad flying causes most crashes. You're good, there's no doubt about it, one of the best young pilots I've seen.'

DJ blushed slightly at the praise.

'But you're still very young and inexperienced and you're

impulsive. You take risks that a more seasoned pilot never would. People who don't know you think you're arrogant, but we both know that air of supreme confidence you try to project is just camouflage. You'd rather make a snap decision – even the wrong one – than risk being thought indecisive. I'm telling you this now because I don't want to be scraping your brains off a hillside one day.

'So starting today, when we go to Denmark, I want you to concentrate on the basics. Forget the flash moves, forget pushing it to the limit.'

He caught DJ's sullen expression. 'Yeah, I know it's boring, but it's the stuff that keeps you alive. If you try to cut the corners, somebody ends up dead. Okay?'

'Yeah, thanks, Drew,' DJ said, without enthusiasm.

Drew nodded and walked down the corridor.

'More of Mother Miller's homespun wisdom and handy hints?' Nick asked.

Drew scowled. 'Something like that.'

They walked across the car park and left the bright sunlight for the gloom of the Hard – the Pilots' Briefing Facility – built from two-foot-thick reinforced concrete and designed to withstand a direct hit from a bomb. Having seen the footage of concrete buildings disintegrating during the raids on Baghdad, Drew was less than reassured.

In times of tension, the Hard became a closed world behind thick steel security doors and pressurised airlocks. Today was just a normal day: the doors stood wide open and there was no guard behind the bulletproof glass screen. A repair man parked his van and walked into the nuclear bunker to service the photocopiers.

Drew and Nick followed him in. They passed the racks of rifles and respirators by the airlocks separating the outer layers of the Hard from the core and squeezed between the filtered chambers and the dormitory. Known as the Submarine, it was a stiflingly tiny room filled with racks of beds on three tiers. They spent many a sleepless night here on exercise, preparing for Armageddon.

They found the squadron commander, Bert Russell, in the Ops room. In his mid-forties, Russell was inevitably nicknamed 'Jack'. He sat with his feet on the desk, preening his handlebar moustache.

Drew sighed to himself. In his present mood, he would have preferred to avoid him. Russell saw himself as an open and approachable father figure to the squadron, but Drew regarded him as a humourless stuffed shirt.

Russell's clerk was pressing him for a decision on the day's programme, without obvious success. 'Are we still flying the first mission this morning, sir, or are we trying to keep the jets serviceable for the deployment to Denmark this afternoon?'

'I haven't decided yet. Just give me a moment, will you?' he snapped.

'I have to let Ops and Air Traffic know.'

She looked to Drew and Nick for help, but they only shrugged. Giving a bollocking to a senior officer was not normally regarded as a good career move.

'I see Russell's charisma bypass operation is still a success,' Drew muttered to Nick. 'Play it safe and by the book and, if that doesn't work, procrastinate. We'll be lucky to get a flying programme for Denmark before we actually arrive there.'

Russell swivelled in his chair. 'What was that, Miller?'

'I was just talking to Nick about the detachment in Denmark, sir. I don't suppose there's a flying programme yet?'

His smile was not returned. Russell looked at him with something close to distaste, then hauled himself upright.

'Okay, let's bin the morning missions. Let the engineers have the jets back, then at least we have ten serviceable for two o'clock this afternoon. Drew, you and Nick are going to lead the push-out – God knows why I let you, when all you do is give me a hard time. Make sure you've got the flight plans in and everything's sorted for a one o'clock brief. Now does anybody mind if I go to the lavatory? I might at least get a bit of peace in there.'

'I doubt it,' Drew said. 'We just saw Jumbo heading in there with the *Telegraph* crossword and a very purposeful look on his face.'

It was a daunting thought. Jumbo was seventeen stone of prime Scottish beef. Beneath a crop of tightly curled fair hair, his florid face was a tribute to his idea of a balanced diet – a pork pie in one hand and a can of beer in the other.

Russell raised his eyes to heaven. Drew winked at the clerk and followed Nick through to the map room. They spent the next couple of hours scattering maps, poring over computer screens, typing in coordinates and drawing up flight plans, punctuating their deliberations with regular refuellings of coffee.

By one o'clock they were ready to brief the sortie. The Tannoy called the squadron together: 'Nitro, briefing for detachment now.'

When all the guys had assembled in the briefing room, Drew took the platform. 'Okay. Met brief. The weather here is fine, light easterly winds. We're going to be working just off Flamborough Head, where conditions are similar, with the wind likely to strengthen slightly and back round to the south-east by mid-afternoon. The forecast for Aalborg is good all day, so we should have no problems getting in.

'Tirstrup is our diversion. Make sure you have enough fuel for that and bear in mind that we are going to a new base at Aalborg. We haven't been there before, so let's not arrive with minimum fuel. Make sure you've got an extra couple of hundred KGs to flog around if we get messed about by Air Traffic Control.

'We haven't flown with the Danes for almost a year now, so you all know why we're going over there – and it's not for the nightlife. This isn't just a jaunt. We could easily find ourselves shipped out at any time to fight alongside them in some faraway place with an unpronounceable name, so we need to catch up on any changes in their tactics and try and surprise them with a couple of ours. They've also had a new radar warner fitted apparently, which they're keen to try out on us.'

Jumbo grinned. The Air Force abbreviation for the Danish detachment was TDPU – Tactics Discussion and Principles Update – but they all knew that the wives' scathing alternative, Thinly Disguised Piss-Up, was much closer to the truth.

Drew called them back to order. 'Any questions? Right. Back to today's mission. Nick and I will be doing one v one air combat with DJ and Ali. The rest of you straight transit over there and make sure everything's set up on the ground. You're going to be responsible for starting the liaison with the Danish guys as soon as you land and that includes the compulsory pickled herrings and North Sea oil.'

Groans greeted the Air Force nickname for Gammel Dansk, a frighteningly potent brew which had the same colour, texture and, many swore, the same taste as Brent crude. The herrings were not to everyone's taste, either, raw and pickled in spiced vinegar – or battery acid, according to some jaundiced veterans.

'Tomorrow morning we'll do the serious business. We're going to be flying basic dissimilar combat, starting off with standard two v ones and building it up from there. We'll be under the control of Danish radar and they've been told it's a full-up sortie, so we'll be playing with hard rules. Any questions? Okay, the time is thirteen-seventeen . . . now. Let's do it.'

The men filed out, heading for the changing room, where they struggled into their flying gear under the watchful eye of the corporal who presided over their equipment. He sorted through the mountain of flying kit dumped in a heap by the returning air crews and produced it, cleaned and neatly folded, ready for the next day's sorties.

'No matter how many times you do this, it doesn't get any easier, does it?' Nick battled with his rubber immersion suit.

Drew grunted as he hauled the top half of his suit over his head and forced his arm down the sleeve. He had three layers of clothing under the suit. On ninety-nine per cent of sorties, they would just make him hot, sweaty and uncomfortable. On the hundredth, they might save his life; an unprotected pilot ejecting into the North Sea would die from hypothermia in minutes.

He bent down to pull on his G-pants, securing the clips and zips, then straightened up and put on the thick, heavy life-support jacket. He glanced at Nick, raising an eyebrow. 'Ready?'

Nick nodded. They picked up their helmets. Some of the ground crew were already working on the jets, the rest, wearing the headsets they plugged into the aircraft to talk to the pilot, followed the aircrew out.

Drew checked the jet over externally and signed to assume responsibility for the aircraft while Nick clambered up the ladder, climbed into his seat and began programming the inertial navigation kit and feeding the routeing of the mission into the computer.

Drew joined him in the cockpit, the familiar electronic whine growing louder as he climbed the ladder. He checked the ejector seat and then lowered himself into his tiny, rock-hard seat. It was a straight trade between comfort and safety – no cushion, no shattered vertebrae if they had to eject.

He began strapping himself in, helped by one of the ground crew who had followed him up the ladder. He fastened his leg restraints, bending double despite the bulky flying gear, then pulled his thigh and shoulder straps tight and locked them into the quick-release buckle in his lap.

Next came the connections to his life-support equipment: the rubber tube feeding him oxygen, the cables with radio communications, the air hose to inflate his G-pants and stop him from blacking out under the G-force as the jet turned, climbed and dived, and the survival pack that might keep him alive if he had to eject. Finally he attached his arm restraints. Like the ones on his legs, they would ensure that he did not leave any limbs behind during an ejection. By the time he had finished, he was streaming with sweat.

While the ground crew connected the generator, Drew and Nick began the near-endless sequence of pre-flight checks. Initial checks complete, the power unit fired up with a throaty roar and Drew flicked the switch to start the right engine. There was a high-pitched whine, a rumble like thunder as the engine caught and started, and then a deafening, teeth-rattling blast. He repeated the procedure on the left engine, watching the temperature gauges on the turbines soaring from twelve degrees to over four hundred in a matter of seconds.

'Closing canopy.' Drew lowered his visor and punched a button.

A siren wailed. The failsafe plastic explosive used to blow the canopy apart if it failed to jettison during an ejection had been known to explode as it was lowered into place, sending jagged chunks of Perspex flying like shrapnel. The ground crew disappeared under the wings or clustered behind the generator, re-emerging as the siren faded after the canopy had snapped shut.

The engine noise inside the cockpit dropped to a bearable level, but a rising tide of sound washed over the airfield. The hum of electronics was counterpointed by the bass rumble of the generators and the throaty roar of Tempest engines as more jets blasted into life. There was a low rumble as a formation from 21's sister squadron, 26, flashed down the runway and soared into the air.

The pilots checked in with him one by one. Down the line, Drew could see the heat shimmering above their engines. He led them out in formation along the taxiway.

As they moved out, there was a sharp crack on the side of the canopy. Drew and Nick ducked instinctively then glared out of the cockpit. A nine-hole golf course had been laid out on the land surrounding the runways and the ninth crossed the taxiway. The golfer on the ninth tee raised a hand in apology. Drew responded with a less conciliatory gesture.

The players on the green stopped and clapped their hands to their ears as the Tempests thundered along the taxiway ten feet away.

Drew and Nick completed their final set of pre-flight checks as they rolled to a halt on the far side of the airfield, awaiting clearance from Air Traffic Control to take up position. They had gone through the same sequence of challenges and responses two or three thousand times during their Air Force careers and could have recited them in their sleep, but nothing was left to chance. The checks were still made by reading them from a card, rather than from memory, for even one missed could mean disaster.

'Abort brief,' Drew said. 'Light easterly, dry runway. For a major loss of thrust or major emergency while the wheels are still on the runway, I will abort, engaging thrust reverse, braking and using the hook if necessary. If there are any problems from Rotate, I'll select combat power, climb straight ahead and deal with it at height. If I can't maintain the climb, I'll call "Jettison" and you shed the under-wing tanks. If that doesn't sort it, I'll call "Eject" and see you in hospital.'

'By the time you've called "Eject", I'll already be in hospital.'

Air Traffic Control radioed clearance to take off and they eased their way onto the right-hand half of the runway. DJ and Ali drew up alongside, with only six feet between their wingtips.

Drew glanced across to the cockpit of DJ's jet and signalled to wind up the engines. Holding the jet hard on the brakes, Drew pushed the throttles forward and the engine note changed to a rising howl as he wound up the power.

The usual army of plane-spotters waited in the specially built compound just outside the perimeter wire. They raised their binoculars and long lenses, shouting excitedly, their voices swept away by the storm of engine noise.

Tongues of flame flew thirty feet behind the engines as they juddered under the strain, held immobile by the brakes even though they were generating power enough to light a small town. The ground trembled and buildings shook, windows rattled and babies sleeping a mile away were jolted awake.

With a final scan of the dials and captions, Drew glanced across to DJ, gave a curt nod and released the brakes, pushing the throttles smoothly forward to maximum re-heat for a moment and then easing them back to eighty per cent. The Tempests leapt forward together like greyhounds from the traps, rocketing along the tarmac, wingtip to wingtip.

Drew and Nick kept up a constant dialogue, Nick chanting a mantra of ascending speeds, punctuated at the three key points on the brief, earthbound phase of their journey:

'100 knots. Cable' – the last chance to take the arrester cable.

'130 knots. EMBS' – the last chance to bring the plane to a brake-burning halt on the runway.

'160 knots. Rotate' – take-off speed.

'Engines good, captions clear, rotating.' Drew pulled back on the stick. There was a clunk as the wheels lifted and the Tempest was airborne, still with DJ in perfect alignment alongside.

'Gear travelling . . . and the flaps.'

'250 knots,' Nick said.

'Out of re-heat.' Drew eased the throttles back, though they kept accelerating up to 350 knots, standard climb speed for departure.

DJ stayed with him as they tore upwards through the cloud layers. Drew caught a brief glimpse of his face, framed in the cockpit. He was frowning with concentration, his eyes never wavering from Drew's wingtip. Even at four hundred miles an hour, less than a metre separated them.

Nick kept up a running commentary as the cloud grew more dense. 'DJ's working for his money today. I can't see his cockpit now, but I can still see the wing. He's still hanging in there. Whoa, he's gone now.'

His voice remained level even though an invisible twenty-ton steel projectile was now flying blind somewhere out in the cloud. The discipline of the air was deeply ingrained. Drew held rigidly to his original course, knowing that, as soon as DJ lost sight of his wingtip, he would instantly swing away out of danger, then follow a parallel track until they came out through the top of the cloud.

A smile spread across Drew's face. He had been flying Tempests for four years; over a thousand take-offs, yet each one gave him the same buzz as the first – that awesome surge of power pinning him back in his seat, the airfield blurring, then disappearing, as the wheels lifted, the steep-angled climb through the overcast that covered the airfield on 250 days out of the 365 and the glorious, exalting moment as the jet punched through the top of the cloud into the sunlight. Flying higher than eagles, higher than Everest; if that feeling did not make your blood pound in your veins, then you might as well be dead.

They levelled off at twenty thousand feet. Drew dispatched the other six crews, bound directly for Aalborg.

'Save me a blonde Dane,' DJ called.

The response was immediate. 'How about a Great Dane?'

'The nearest he'll get to a blonde will be a golden retriever.'

The departing crews signed off, their aircraft rapidly disappearing into the haze to the east.

'Right,' Drew said. 'Can we get some work done? Okay Nitro Two. We'll split fifty miles apart and then go for it. This is your last sortie before we start letting you play the games for real, so let's make it quality work. Base height is ten thousand feet – bong the base and you're dead. Don't get carried away if you think you've got a chance of a kill. Keep checking fuel and checking your height. Be safe; better to bug out and run away to fight another day than press on in and get killed.'

'Whatever you say, Grandad. If I'm too quick for you, just let me know and I'll ease up. I don't want to embarrass you in front of your friends.'

'Talk's cheap, DJ. Let's see you live up to it.'

Nick's voice came over the intercom. 'Cocky little bastard isn't he?'

Drew threw his jet around. 'Let's see if he can back it up.'

The two aircraft split fifty miles apart, the maximum range of their radars, and then turned inwards, their pilots' hearts beginning to pound, adrenalin pumping. It was a video game, played for real. They probed each other's defences, reacting to the radar warner, ducking and diving to break missile locks.

They met head to head at 1500 miles per hour, DJ and Ali flashing down the left hand side of Drew's aircraft. Nick braced himself against his computers as he cranked his head around over his left shoulder, trying to keep DJ's jet in sight.

Each crew was battling to get on the other's tail – the six o'clock – the killing zone. Once an opponent was there, a heat-seeking missile would be homing on your tailpipe before you even had a chance to say your prayers.

'Looks like they're evading south,' Drew said. 'Hard starboard.'

He jerked the stick to the right and heard Nick's 'Unnh' as his helmet banged against the side of the cockpit.

'He's in a hard left turn now,' Nick warned. 'Coming nose-on. Let's go high.'

Drew yanked the jet into a four-G climb, looping over the top. He was grunting with the effort of fighting the jet, his breath rasping. He could taste the sweat dripping steadily down his face, mingling with the rubbery tang of his oxygen mask.

DJ was pushing even harder, screwing his turns tighter and tighter and gradually getting closer to their tail.

'He's threatening us, he's threatening us,' Nick yelled, his voice distorted by the strain as Drew fought to squeeze a little extra G into his turn. Lubricated by the sweat, his helmet slid on his head. The technicolour landscape blurred as the jet came hard around, and suddenly changed to monochrome.

Instantly he tensed his muscles and grunted aloud, like a weightlifter bench-pressing the maximum. The colour of the landscape returned, flickered and then faded back to grey as the G-force steadily increased. This time Drew nudged the stick back slightly towards the centre and the colour flooded back again. Greying out, as aircrew called it, happened under high-G turns. If you kept pressing the turn, the greyout would become a blackout. The next step was death.

Try as he might, Drew could not shake DJ from his tail. He barrelled over the top, still pressing, as Drew flashed beneath him.

'He's pulling hard, he's pulling hard,' Nick shouted, straining every sinew as he fought to get his head around and keep DJ in sight. 'Come on, Drew, get us out of it. Oh God. Look out!'

As Drew glanced up, a dark shadow blotted out the sun. The sweat seemed to freeze on his forehead. DJ's jet was dropping out of the sky, twenty tons of metal in a free fall towards them. Even as Drew registered the danger, he reacted instinctively, yanking the stick savagely to the left and ramming the throttles all the way forward.

The engines bellowed in protest and he gasped at the G-force plastering him to his seat, but the Tempest responded agonisingly slowly as the black mass hurtled down towards them.

The frenzied action of combat seemed to slow to a crawl. Drew froze, flesh creeping, felt his aircraft disintegrating under the impact, the other jet's wing slicing through the cockpit like a buzz saw. He heard the shrieking of tortured metal, the bang as the canopy fractured and the scream of the slipstream ripping at him, followed only by blackness and silence.

The black shadow swelled and filled Drew's vision for an instant, then there was a blinding flash of reflected light as the other Tempest's wing slashed past him like a cut-throat razor. Drew tensed, half closing his eyes as he waited for the impact. There was nothing. The plummeting jet flashed no more than six inches past Drew's right wing and was gone.

With a curious detachment he watched DJ jerking about like a puppet in his cockpit, his mouth opening and closing soundlessly as he dropped from sight.

He pulled himself back under control immediately, as the discipline of endlessly repeated emergency drills took over. He centred the stick and pulled back the throttles, then began taking stock of the aircraft. All checks showed nothing amiss.

His vision was a little blurred. A blood vessel had burst in his right eye, but he had no time to worry about it. He swung his own aircraft into a wide, spiralling descent, keeping DJ's jet in sight as it hurtled downwards. The once-sleek flying machine was tumbling helplessly, spinning like a sycamore leaf in the wind. He could see the controls flapping as DJ tried to save his aircraft.

'What's happening?' Drew shouted into the radio. 'DJ, what's happening?'

'I don't know. I can't control it.'

Drew watched helplessly. Plumes of vapour streamed from the wings as the jet plummeted, nose down, accelerating faster and faster under the remorseless pull of gravity.

He watched the jet shrink as it hurtled away from them, then he began yelling into the radio, 'Eject. Eject. For Christ's sake, eject.'

There was no response from DJ, no puff of smoke as the ejectors fired, no orange and white flowers as two parachutes opened. Instead, far below him and seemingly beyond recall, DJ's jet stopped spinning. There was a heart-stopping pause, then the aircraft bottomed out a few hundred feet above the sea and Drew saw it begin to climb.

His relief was replaced by cold fury. 'What the hell's going on, DJ? What happened?'

'I don't know. It wasn't me, it was the aircraft.' The fear in DJ's voice was obvious, even through the crackle of the radio.

'Don't give me that. Aircraft don't just fall out of the sky. I warned you about this before we started.'

'Drew, this isn't the right time,' Nick said. 'He's probably messed his pants already. He doesn't need you messing with his head.'

'He nearly fucking killed us,' Drew said. 'I warned him this morning about trying the funny stuff before he'd got the basics sorted out. What does he do? He goes straight up in the air and pulls a stroke like that.'

'I know,' Nick said. 'But give him a chance to explain when we get on the ground. We don't know what happened.'

'I could see what happened. He tried to pull too bloody hard round the corner.'

'Perhaps. But we've both had a pretty close call. Let's get back and sort it out on the ground.'

Drew thumbed the button. 'Okay DJ. Let's knock it on the head and get to Aalborg.'

Shrugging off Nick's restraining hand, Drew strode straight across to the other jet as DJ and Ali were clambering out at Aalborg.

'I warned you about this, didn't I? You can throw away your own life if you want to, but you nearly killed us as well. What the hell were you doing? We've already briefed the loss-of-control drills. How did you manage to do that?'

'I don't know what happened,' DJ said plaintively. 'I was just pulling over the top of the circle, trying to get my nose onto you, and I just lost it completely – it fell out of the sky. I thought I was going to have to eject.'

Drew was not even listening. 'You're too cocky by half. You think because you've been on squadron for six months you know it all, but you know jack shit. You've got to keep your aggression under control and learn the basics of flying before you start trying to be a smart-arse.'

'But I didn't do anything,' DJ said. 'I was doing it how you taught me to do it last week.'

Drew ignored his protests. 'I should put you on review for a stunt like that.'

'But I really don't think I did anything wrong.'

'Then you haven't learned anything from it. You'll just go up and keep cocking it up until you kill yourself, Ali and anyone else unlucky enough to be within range.'

Drew rubbed his eyes with his hands. When he spoke

again his voice was even. 'Look, DJ, I'm not going to write you up for it. If we report it now, the aircraft could be grounded. That would screw up the detachment and maybe put your flying at risk as well.' He paused. DJ's face was sullen. 'It's your choice.'

'All right.' DJ turned away.

The greeting party from the hosting squadron trooped forward uncertainly. Drew and Nick met them with broad smiles and handshakes. RAF traditions were observed: while the engineers rushed around, clambering over the jets, refuelling, waving dipsticks and screwdrivers and wiping canopies, the air crew set about getting pissed, standing in a circle amongst the aircraft.

After a brief speech of welcome, the Danes offered them a dish of pickled herrings and glasses of Gammel Dansk.

'The things we do for international relations.' Nick chomped a herring and tossed his glass back in one. He smiled and smacked his lips appreciatively, partially masking the sound of DJ gagging.

Still pale, DJ was led to a flatbed trailer with seats bolted onto it. Drew, Nick and Ali also hopped aboard, still clutching their drinks. A tractor pulled them across the base, belching diesel fumes.

Their crewmates were already comfortably ensconced outside the crew room. Drew was relieved to see that the Gammel Dansk had been replaced by cans of Carlsberg. He helped himself to one and joined the others, but DJ sat by himself. Nick looked across at him and then motioned Drew to one side.

'Look, DJ may have been a prat, but he deserves the same benefit of the doubt that you'd expect yourself.'

Drew started to argue, but Nick put up his hands. 'I know it looked bad, but we weren't in the cockpit with him. Something could have gone wrong with his jet. Even if he did cock it up, he needs to learn the lessons and go on from it, not have his confidence shredded so totally that he jacks it all in. Did you never make a mistake when you were working up to combat-readiness?'

Nick's point struck home. Three years before, Drew had lost track of one piece in the three-dimensional chess game while flying a two v two training sortie and had almost flown into his wingman. Nick had been in the back seat.

Drew gave a grudging nod.

'In any case,' Nick said, 'you were right out of order sounding off at him in public like that. If he deserved a bollocking – and he probably did – it should have been done in private, quietly, not broadcast on Radio Aalborg.'

'You're beginning to make me feel like it was my fault.'

Nick laughed. 'Good. Now you know how DJ feels.'

Drew walked off to get himself another beer but, when he thought Nick was looking the other way, he went over to DJ.

'Look, maybe I went at you a bit hard. If so, I'm sorry. I got as big a fright as you did.'

DJ smiled. 'I'm sure a couple of pints will help me forget the whole thing.'

Chapter 4

Drew awoke with a start, streaming with sweat. The telephone was ringing and he fumbled blearily for the receiver.

'Good morning,' said a recorded Danish voice. 'This is your alarm call, the time is six-thirty.'

Dog-tired and badly hung over, Drew unleashed a useless volley of abuse down the phone and slumped down again. He still had his head glued to the pillow an hour later when a hideously cheerful Nick called him up. 'Come on, you're late. Transport's in fifteen minutes.'

Drew fell out of bed. A gorilla appeared to have broken into his room during the night, breaking a light fitting, strewing his clothes all over the room, battering his head with a baseball bat and taking a crap in his mouth. He shuddered, drank some water and brushed his teeth, but his head went on pounding and his stomach felt as if it was full of broken glass.

It was the worst hangover he had ever had. He had been falling down drunk once or twice as a teenager back home, but ever since he joined the Air Force he had prided himself on keeping a cool head, knowing when to stop while others drank themselves sick or stupid. It was not a boast he would be able to make this morning.

He stared at the vision from hell in his bathroom mirror. Nice going, he thought to himself. You can't blame anyone else for this. What are you, a professional pilot or a professional piss-artist? He turned away and stumbled into the shower.

It did little to revive him. He could not face breakfast and met Nick and the others down in reception, just in time to catch their transport to the base.

Nick took one look at him and burst out laughing. 'God, Drew, I thought I was rough.'

'You are, it's just that I'm worse. You're going to have to drive the car. There's no way I can drive in this state. I shouldn't be flying, either, but we've got to do it; we can't lose face with the young lads.'

Drew and Nick were again paired with DJ and Ali, going up on a Combat Air Patrol, two v one with a Danish F16. DJ and Ali briefed the mission, but made a mess of it, transposing a couple of digits in the coordinates. Had Nick not corrected them, they would have been exercising over the centre of Copenhagen instead of the North Sea.

While most of his colleagues laughed off the mistake, Drew said, 'For Christ's sake, DJ, get your act together.'

'Shit,' DJ breathed to Ali, 'if this is what he's like when he gets a hangover, I hope he's not going to be mentoring us all week. He's going to be a real pain in the arse.'

Nick leaned over to Drew. 'Can't you get off DJ's case for a while? In a few minutes he's going to be taking up the jet he almost died in yesterday. He's going to be shitting himself as he goes down that runway, wondering if whatever happened is going to happen again. What he needs is reassurance and confidence, not another bollocking.'

Drew knew he was right, but was too hung over and bad-tempered to acknowledge it. He did not interrupt the briefing again, but nor did he give DJ any reassurance. He took his foul mood and his foul head with him into the air.

Flying in a foreign country for the first time, DJ was having problems both with Danish Air Traffic Control and with setting up the CAP position, but Drew made no attempt to help him.

Drew sat in his aircraft with the switch set to 100 per

cent pure oxygen. Medics insisted it was an old wives' tale, but pilots swore it could cure a hangover. 'Christ, Nick, I shouldn't be up here. I'm sweating pure North Sea Oil.'

'Just make sure you don't screw up,' Nick warned. 'One near miss is enough to be going on with.'

Drew did not reply, too busy gulping and swallowing as saliva flooded his mouth. Just as DJ got everything set up, with the two Tempests and the F16 all in the right places in the sky, Drew gulped again, tore off his face mask and reached for his blue Nato-standard sick bag, guaranteed not to spill or burst even at thirty G.

Drew retched miserably, then dabbed ineffectually at his chin. He stuck down the self-seal tag, groaned and called DJ on the radio. 'Nitro Two, I've got a bit of an in-cockpit snag.'

'What's up?' DJ asked. 'Anything we can do about it?'

'No, no,' said Drew hastily. 'It's just in-cockpit, but we'll have to get back to base now.'

'Do you need to declare an emergency?'

'No, no,' Drew said testily. 'It's very minor. Don't worry, we'll be fine as soon as we get on the ground.'

DJ cursed to himself, but called up the F16 and then wheeled his jet around to follow Drew back down to Aalborg. They touched down and taxied back in, the journey back along the taxiway seeming at least twice as far to Drew as it had on the way out.

After he pulled to a halt, he fumbled again with the sealing strip of his sick bag. It was designed to stay sealed even under combat conditions and took him another minute of sweat and struggle to get it open.

Nick laughed. 'Probably the most expensive drink in history. Getting two RS3s and an F16 up into the air over Denmark must have cost the taxpayers about £100,000.'

Drew just groaned and bent over the bag again. When he'd finished, he clambered unsteadily down from the cockpit and went across to DJ and Ali as they were walking away from their jet. 'Look, I'm really sorry.'

DJ's glance took in Drew's greenish tinge and the blue sick bag half hidden behind his back.

Drew followed his gaze and added shamefacedly, 'I should

know better at my age than to fly with a hangover. Sorry to wreck your sortie.'

DJ let the silence last long enough for Drew to remember their previous conversation on the Aalborg tarmac, then said, 'That's all right. I'm sure you'll have to do the same for me before the week's out.'

Though the words were friendly, the tone was not.

They had been sitting drinking coffee for an hour while Drew nibbled on pieces of dry toast, when a stunning young Danish airwoman came sprinting in with a flash signal from Finnington. She handed it to Russell, who was alone in showing more interest in the message than the messenger. He scanned it and then leapt to his feet.

'What is it?' Nick asked.

'An immediate recall to base. It doesn't say why. You've got half an hour to get back to the hotel, pack your bags and be back here ready to fly.' He paused and looked pointedly at Drew.

'I'm fine now. No problems. I think I must have had a bad herring,' Drew said, but Russell was already halfway out of the door.

'Here we go again,' DJ said, 'the knee-jerk reaction. Something's happened, let's all rush off home immediately. This must have happened five times in the last six months and every time it's been something trivial.'

Ali laughed. 'Never mind, DJ. Perhaps Mariella will wait for you.'

Russell radioed the crews still flying their sorties. Those with enough fuel transited straight to Finnington, while the rest landed back at Aalborg, refuelled and were airborne again inside the hour. As usual, the ground crew were left to tidy up the mess, collect all the equipment and fly home later on the lumbering Hercules transports.

As soon as Drew and Nick touched down at Finnington, they rushed into the Ops room, where several other members of the squadron were already haranguing Russell.

'Come on, boss, what's going on?'

'Just wait till everybody's in and I'll tell you.' Russell puffed on his pipe, enjoying being the focus of attention.

'We'll have a briefing in half an hour. Make sure everybody knows about it.'

Drew sat in the crew room with the rest of the squadron for half an hour, drinking coffee and exchanging increasingly wild speculation. Before they filed into the briefing room, rumours ranged from an escape attempt by Russell's budgerigar to an outbreak of nuclear war in Bosnia.

Nick sat calmly through the frenzied speculation. 'Why don't we just wait and see?'

'What?' Drew said. 'And let the facts spoil a good story?'

'It's probably another squadron to be mothballed,' Jumbo said gloomily, buttering himself another piece of toast. 'Wonder if it's us this time?'

Russell was already standing by the podium. He waited until the last man was seated and then cleared his throat.

'As you may have guessed from the news bulletins over the last few days, we are very likely to be called forward to set up an air exclusion zone again over Bosnia. We'll be responsible for ensuring that nothing gets off the ground and if it does we'll be ensuring that it is in no state to land on a runway again.'

'Just like last time, boss?' Drew asked. 'Seven thousand violations in three years and only one engagement?'

There was a knowing laugh from the rest of the squadron. Russell ignored it. 'We have got to be ready to move in twelve hours, though we're just as likely to be on standby for a month or even longer. We may not even go at all. Most of you have been in this situation before, with the Gulf, Somalia, Rwanda and Bosnia the first time around, so you should be getting used to it.

'Let's not forget the lessons we learned. Let's not try and reinvent the wheel. Those of you who were out there last time, prepare briefs for the newer guys telling them as much as possible of what they can expect.

'Right, we're knocking it on the head for today. The engineers are preparing all the aircraft as fast as they can and, providing we haven't been given the order to go, we start training tomorrow. 33 Squadron are sending their Pumas up.'

He waited for the buzz to die down. 'As you know, the Puma's traditionally a troop carrier and battlefield support helicopter, armed only with nose guns and a door-mounted machine gun operated by the crewman. These are the new generation, however, carrying rocket packs in addition to the nose and door guns. They'll be simulating the tactics of the Serb helicopter gunships, so that we can start practising our helicopter affiliation.'

Even the most world-weary members of the squadron showed a flicker of interest at the news, for their day-to-day work was purely fast jet against fast jet. Learning to fight helicopters would be new to almost all of them.

'Everybody can take the rest of the day off to sort out your affairs,' Russell said, 'but be back in for met brief at seven tomorrow morning.'

They started to get to their feet, but hesitated as they realised that Russell had something more to say. 'I know we've all been having a wild time in Aalborg – even if we were only there for twenty-four hours in the end – but this is serious business now and I want strict adherence to the twelve-hour bottle-to-throttle rule.'

Drew avoided catching his eye.

Drew dropped Nick at his house and then sped home to a cold and empty flat. He turned on the heating and sat down at the table with a pen and paper, spent the next few minutes doodling aimlessly and then threw the paper in the bin.

Abruptly he got up and began to pack his bags. When he'd finished, he prowled from room to room, pausing to leaf through a magazine and then impatiently throw it away. Twice his hand hovered above the phone, but each time he resumed his pacing without making the call.

By early evening he was slumped on the couch, staring blankly at the television. He thought of DJ and Ali, already out on the town, and he imagined Nick and his wife, playing and laughing with their kids as they got them ready for bed.

He smiled ruefully to himself as he took in his surroundings. You really know how to live, Drew, he thought. This could be the last night before you go to war. What a way to spend it, sitting in an empty flat watching *Coronation Street* and eating a takeaway pizza straight out of a cardboard box.

The rest of the pizza followed the paper into the bin. He left the television blaring and walked out, heading for his local pub. He stood at the end of the bar, gazing blankly ahead of him, too dispirited even to make the attempt to start a conversation with anybody. He stayed in the pub for an hour, talking to no one but the barman who served him, then walked slowly home.

The noise from the television did nothing to disguise the emptiness of the flat. He sat at the desk and methodically sorted through his papers, throwing away every letter and postcard from Josie and every photograph of her. Then he turned off the television and threw himself down on the bed.

Faint traces of Josie's perfume filled his nostrils. He leapt up, stripped the sheets from the bed and stuffed them into the washing machine. He went back into the bedroom, remade the bed and then dragged it on its protesting castors to the other side of the room. He moved the dressing table and wardrobe as well and then lay down on the bed and picked up a book.

It was still lying on the bed, unread, when he woke the next morning. He shoved it aside and dragged himself into the shower. A search of the kitchen cupboards revealed only an empty bread wrapper and some cereal, but no milk. He contemplated rescuing the cold pizza from the bin, then thought better of it and went to scrounge breakfast at Nick and Sally's house instead.

'How did last night go?' Nick asked as they were setting off for work.

'It didn't.'

Nick raised an eyebrow. 'So it wasn't much of a farewell-to-freedom night?'

'You could say that,' Drew said. 'I went for a few drinks, just for a change.'

As they passed through the barrier into the base, they both noticed the air of anticipation. The squadron had moved onto a war footing and the customary laid-back attitude had disappeared. People moved about their business briskly, purposefully, and even the morning tea-and-toast rituals in the crew room were over in a few minutes.

Russell called the senior aircrew to a conference in his

office. He beamed around the room, like Santa Claus about to open his sack.

'Right, we're on a war footing. With luck, that means that peacetime constraints will be eased and, within reason, we can have whatever equipment we want, without worrying about budgets or the date of the next General Election. So what do you all reckon we need?'

The others were almost falling over themselves to speak, like kids let loose in Hamleys.

'We'll need new chaff dispensers . . .'

'And flare dispensers . . .'

'And let's try to get that new French jamming pod. It defends against ground missile systems and hostile aircraft.'

'Is it available?'

'Yes, I saw it in *Jane's Defence Weekly* a few weeks ago.'

Santa was already back-pedalling, stuffing toys back into his sack. 'I don't know,' Russell said nervously. 'I can't go to HQ and ask for all this in the present financial climate.'

'Look, boss,' Nick began, 'this is our one and only chance to get the kit improved to the standard we need to do our job properly. Instead of an adequate aircraft we could be flying a capable one.'

Drew followed his lead. 'And surely it's our job to tell HQ what we actually need. It's their job to tell us whether they can afford it.'

Russell frowned. 'I hope you're not lecturing me on my responsibilities.'

'Of course not, but—'

'Thank you gentlemen, that will be all,' Russell said. 'I'll get on to Strike Command immediately and do what I can on equipment. Now let's get out and get everybody crewed up. Sort out who flies with who, to get the best blend of experience.'

Christmas was over. The men filed out, their elation forgotten. 'We'll be lucky if he asks for a rubber band and a box of paper clips,' Drew said as he shut the door.

'Come on, Drew,' Nick said. 'I think you're being a bit harsh. I'm sure he'll ask for two rubber bands.'

When Russell arrived in the crew room half an hour later, Drew could tell from his manner that he had got a dusty answer from Strike Command. He nudged Nick. 'Here comes Mr Bumble. Who's going to be Oliver Twist and ask for some more?'

'Not me and not you if you've got any sense. You've already rattled his cage enough for one lifetime.'

Russell stood at the coffee bar. 'Chaff dispensers are ordered and should be with us inside twelve hours. Flares are a bit more of a problem. We can't get more than the training allowance. We can have them for combat, but we can't practise with them. I'm sorry, but I'm afraid that's the way it is. With all the cutbacks, we just can't afford this kind of stuff any more.'

He surveyed the circle of faces. Drew waited for someone else to speak, but realised no one was going to. 'This is bloody ridiculous. You're telling us we can have flares for combat but we can't train with them. So the first time we get to use them is when someone fires a missile at us?'

'I'm afraid so. I fought as hard as I could.' Russell flushed.

'And the French jamming pods?' Jumbo asked forlornly.

'Not a hope in hell, I'm afraid. This isn't like the Gulf. We haven't got the Saudis and Japanese picking up the tab. It's coming out of our own budget and there's just no more money in the coffers.'

'So it's okay for the MoD to spend seventy grand on some curtains for an Air Vice-Marshal's house, but there's not enough money in the budget for us to even fire off a seventy-quid flare,' Drew said. 'Let's just hope the Serbs don't have anything more advanced than bullets to fire at us, or you'll be looking at an even bigger hole in the budget when they have to replace all the Tempests that have been shot down.'

A look at the near-mutinous faces staring back at him told Russell that this was not the moment to lock horns. He turned and went back to his office.

While they waited for the additional equipment, the engineers worked flat out, testing and retesting the jets, checking over and over for minor defects. In routine, day-to-day operations these would go unnoticed or unreported, but with a possible conflict looming nothing was left to chance.

As the engineers sweated and cursed over the jets, other ground crew practised loading the weaponry, aiming to service a returning aircraft and prepare it for a further mission in the time it took to refuel.

With no immediate sign of the call to fly out to Bosnia, the air crew waited impatiently for the arrival of 33 Squadron's Pumas. Russell strolled into the briefing room just as they were about to begin the Met brief for the day.

'Okay guys, I've got some important news for you. Air Vice-Marshal Power will be in the crew room at nine o'clock this morning. He wants to have a bit of a chat.'

'Come on, boss, be reasonable,' Drew said. 'This is no time for distractions. We're trying to sort all the new briefs and we've got some serious training to do.'

'Let's just humour him,' Russell said. 'I want you, Nick, Mike, DJ and Ali in the crew room when he gets here. Make sure you've got your boots cleaned. And DJ, get rid of that yellow tee shirt, you look like a bloody canary.'

Two hours later, Russell ushered the honoured guest into the crew room. Power paused for a moment, apparently scrutinising one of the fading pictures of air crew on the wall, though Drew suspected he was actually checking his reflection. He looked pleased with what he saw. Power was in his early fifties. He stood ramrod straight and the cut of his uniform suggested that its origins lay closer to Savile Row than RAF Supplies, Northolt. His grey hair, cut as impeccably, was slightly longer than the military norm and his face was deeply tanned.

Power turned and favoured Russell with a regulation smile. 'So how are things going?'

Russell tried not to make it obvious that he would have preferred a conversation in the privacy of his office. 'Okay, sir, thank you. The helicopters from 33 Squadron arrive this afternoon. The chaff dispensers are on their way up from the depot, but we have a bit of a problem with the allocation of flares. We're being told that we can't even train with them . . .'

Power pulled a small leather-bound notebook from his pocket and made a note with a silver propelling pencil. 'I don't think we need to worry about that.' His voice was quiet, but commanded their attention.

The instant gratification of a need that had been only half expressed startled Russell. He decided to push his luck. 'One of the crew has also seen an article on the new French jamming pod.'

'You know how it is these days,' Power said. 'Even war has to be fought under Treasury constraints.'

He spread his hands, palms up, signalling the end of the discussion. 'Let's meet these men of yours, shall we?'

When he reached Nick, he asked, 'Now then, how do you feel about going out to Bosnia?'

'As long as we get the backing, sir, we'll do the best job we can.'

Power glanced sharply at Russell, who suddenly became very interested in the toes of his freshly polished boots.

'You'll get the backing, Flight Lieutenant,' Power said. 'Just do the job you're paid to do.'

'Any idea when we might be out in Bosnia, sir?' DJ asked.

'I'm afraid not. We must all keep working and training hard. When the call does come, I know you'll do us all proud.' He was already turning to go when Drew called after him.

'Just one more thing, sir. You're in charge of the Accident Investigation Bureau, aren't you?' Power raised an eyebrow and nodded. 'Do you know anything yet about the crash in the Dales the other day? We normally get a bit of a hint about what happened, but we've heard nothing at all. There hasn't even been a forty-eight-hour signal, as far as I'm aware.'

Power looked at him thoughtfully. 'The investigators' report is not yet complete. But it was a young pilot who had only been on the squadron a week. A young pilot, flying his first sortie—' He let his words trail off. 'Let's put it this way. All the evidence to hand indicates that the aircraft was serviceable at the point of impact.'

'If it's really that straightforward, why was there no forty-eight-hour signal?'

'I don't think you need trouble yourself about operational matters outside your own area of expertise, Flight Lieutenant.'

'With respect, sir, we fly these aircraft,' Drew said, ignoring

Nick's tug on his sleeve. 'I'm just trying to establish what made this crash so unusual.'

Power's tone remained assured. 'I hope you're as aggressive in the air as you are on the ground, Flight Lieutenant. Now, I mustn't keep you chaps from your work. Well done, carry on.'

The Air Vice-Marshal strode out, with Russell in tow. Once they were safely out of earshot, there was a burst of laughter.

'I don't know about you guys,' Drew said, 'but that's certainly boosted my morale. I really feel like going and dying in Bosnia now.'

Nick grabbed his arm and pulled him to one side. 'What was that about?'

'What was what about?'

'Come off it. The crash. Is there something you're not telling me?'

'Not really.'

'Then why were you winding up Power? Russell was practically giving birth.'

'I don't know,' Drew said. 'I just think it's very strange that there's been no official word on it. Power was very evasive, wasn't he? And those hints about pilot error don't really tie in with what the farmer said to me up there.'

'What would a farmer know about it?'

'Enough to know if something was flying or falling.' He paused. 'I've started thinking about what happened with DJ on the way to Aalborg. What if there's a connection?'

'But you told me yourself what happened; you couldn't wait to tell DJ, either.'

Drew nodded. 'Perhaps I was wrong, though. It wouldn't be the first time.'

'You won't get any disagreement from me about that, but why don't you let the AIB sort it out? That's what they're there for.'

Chapter 5

The sound of rotor blades grew louder as the sleek black shapes of three Puma helicopters appeared over the horizon. They skimmed in over the boundary and hovered menacingly for a moment above the airfield, their air intakes gaping like eye sockets in a skull.

Nick and Drew had been detailed to go and pick up the crews in the squadron taxi, a beaten-up old Austin Allegro, hand-painted in squadron colours. Drew winced at the grinding of the gears and the creaking of the springs.

Nick peered through the windscreen at the Pumas. 'Did you know that Michelle Power is flying one of these?'

'No I didn't.' Drew waited in vain for a word of explanation. 'So who's Michelle Power?'

'Oh come on. She was all over the press: one of the first woman pilots to come through the system. And the Air Vice-Marshal who gave us that inspiring speech this morning is her old man.'

Drew rolled his eyes. 'Oh yeah? No prizes for guessing how she got through the course.'

'I wouldn't bet on it. My mate Scabs was on the base she trained at. He says she's as good as any Puma pilot he's seen.'

'Well we'll soon find out when we start flying against her.'

'Give her a break, Drew. You haven't even met her yet. At least wait until you've clapped eyes on her.'

Drew smiled. 'If she's that good, why isn't she flying fast jets?'

'She wanted to stay with helicopters apparently. She was a technician on one of the chopper squadrons and wanted to know what it was like to fly them. So she's an ex-ranker . . . just like you.'

'Not quite. My father was a docker, not an Air Vice-Marshal.'

Nick laughed. 'That's what I like about you, Drew. You're perfectly balanced, a chip on both shoulders.'

Drew shrugged. 'Why would someone whose father could pull any amount of strings have wanted to be a grease monkey in the first place?'

'You'll have to ask her. You might enjoy it. Scabs says she's a looker.'

The pilot of the first Puma jumped down and walked towards them. The co-pilot and crewman followed, dragging out their bags.

'Hello, I'm Michelle Power. This is Sandy Craig and my crewman is Paul Westerman, known as Kraut. Except when we're stationed in Germany.'

Drew turned to face them. Paul Westerman was tall, square-jawed with crewcut hair so blond it was almost white. A scar ran down his left cheek from the corner of his eye to the angle of his jaw. Sandy Craig was shorter, with a plump, round face and a slightly startled expression.

Drew nodded to the two men, then turned back to Michelle Power. She met Drew's gaze with a challenging look which suggested that she didn't suffer fools gladly, but her voice had an unexpected warmth. She also had a dazzling smile and startlingly blue eyes. Drew found himself smiling foolishly as he introduced himself.

She gave them a firm handshake, then turned away to help with the bags.

'Let me give you a hand,' Drew said, starting towards the helicopter.

'Thanks, I can manage.' She threw her own bags into the back of the car and, as she brushed past him, he caught a faint trace of perfume.

'Obsession?' he asked.

She smiled faintly. 'Poison, actually.'

'It makes a change from sweat and avgas.'

She laughed. 'You certainly know how to turn on the charm, don't you?'

She gestured to her bags. 'By the way, do you make that offer to everybody?'

'Just the ugly ones,' Drew said. 'I'm that kind of guy.'

She smiled. 'If it's a battle of wits you're looking for, I hope you're well armed.'

Drew met her gaze and his own smile grew broader.

She arched an eyebrow. 'Was there something else?'

'I was waiting for you to take off your helmet and shake out your mane of blonde hair.'

'You've been watching too many shampoo ads. It's not like that in real life. Still if it makes you happy . . .'

She took off her helmet and shook out a mane of blonde hair. Her crewmen burst out laughing.

Drew turned around and caught Nick trying not to smile. 'What's your problem?'

'Wow,' breathed Nick. 'I don't care who her father is. She's okay by me.'

They drove over to the crew room and planned the next day's training. Drew noted the way the other helicopter pilots deferred to Michelle. They obviously shared Scab's opinions.

Late that afternoon, they adjourned to the bar for welcome drinks. Everyone from 21 Squadron was there; 26 was in town as well, not long returned from NATO's Red Flag exercise in the Nevada Desert, complete with suntans and Las Vegas tall stories. The banter between the rival squadrons flew to and fro across the bar.

Drew watched her from the other side of the room, admiring the way she dealt with a chorus of would-be suitors. She managed to give each of them the brush-off in a way that neither offended them nor extinguished their hopes completely.

Only a very raw flight lieutenant, full of drink and fuller

of himself after a fortnight in Nevada, took Michelle's gentle rebuff as an affront to his manhood.

'You're only here because your old man's an Air Vice-Marshal.' His jaw jutted, his red face aggressively close to hers. 'You wouldn't be flying at all if it wasn't for him. Women just aren't up to the job.'

'Nice to know Jurassic Park isn't the only place where dinosaurs still roam the earth,' Drew murmured to Nick.

He nodded. 'I think this one's close to extinction.'

All those within earshot fell silent, waiting for Michelle's response. She hesitated for a moment, while he swayed truculently in front of her, his face flushed as much with embarrassment as beer now that all eyes were upon them.

'I'm sorry,' she said in a small voice. 'I'm afraid I don't know much about flying Tempests. Are they very different from Pumas?'

He gave her a suspicious look, but then blundered ahead. 'As different as a Ferrari from a tricycle.'

'And you must have been to some really interesting places.'

Bathed in the radiance of her deep-blue eyes, he puffed out his chest. 'I've been on detachments in Alaska, Italy, Denmark and Cyprus, and I've just been on the biggest NATO exercise of them all, Red Flag in the Nevada Desert.'

'It all sounds fascinating,' Michelle said breathily, 'but I don't think you'll find it's any substitute for the real thing. I've obviously not had as much excitement as you have, but I have seen action in Northern Ireland and Iraq. I've watched one of my mates killed by ground fire, and I've seen the IRA blow up an army patrol – boys about your age – with one of their booby traps. There was hardly enough left of them to fill one body bag.

'I also did CASEVAC in the Gulf War. I brought back the crew of a Tempest once. They had to bang out over the Iraqi desert. Unlike them, I got my aircraft there and back every time. Perhaps I'll have the pleasure of meeting you under similar circumstances one day. Until then though, I'm afraid you'll have to excuse me: my friends and I are going for dinner.'

There was a burst of laughter and the normal hubbub

resumed as the pilot, his face beetroot, slunk away to the far end of the bar.

The floor show over, Nick turned to Drew. 'Are you off back to an empty flat? Why don't you come and have dinner at our place?'

Drew gazed after Michelle as she left the bar. 'I'm sorry, what did you say?'

Nick laughed. 'I said, I've never seen anyone look that good in a flying suit. Do you want to come for dinner at our place?' He paused again. 'Hello . . . Drew . . . are you receiving me? Over.'

'What? Yes, sorry, that'd be great.'

As they opened Nick's kitchen door, they were buried under a warm avalanche of kids. Drew hugged each of them in turn and then walked over to kiss Sally. 'Evening, Sally. God, you're beautiful after dark.'

He ducked as a piece of toast buzzed past his left ear. 'Very droll. If you think I'm beautiful now, you'll die when I'm not two stone overweight and knackered from breast-feeding every five minutes.'

Drew pretended to study her again. She was in her mid-thirties, but even after four children could have passed for much younger. She had a tangle of thick, shoulder-length, dark hair and her hazel eyes were full of humour.

'You're right,' he said. 'I can see it now. You need a couple of laps around the block, but for a woman of fifty you're actually in very good shape.'

'You'll pay for that,' she promised. 'Here, hold this, will you?' She thrust her two-month-old daughter at him.

'I certainly will not,' Drew said, recoiling in mock horror. 'It might be loaded.'

He sat listening to the children's excited chatter until Nick rounded them up for their bedtime stories.

'Get yourself a drink, Drew,' he called over his shoulder as he followed them up the stairs, 'and tell Sally all about your new friend at work.'

Drew could hear him laughing as he chased the children into their rooms.

Sally gave him a quizzical look as he pulled the cork on a bottle of Chardonnay and handed her a glass. 'New friend?

Don't tell me, let me guess. You've crossed swords with another senior officer.'

'That's not as much fun as it used to be. No, Nick's talking about a helicopter pilot.'

'Smart-arse was he?'

'She. No. Just smart.'

'And beautiful?' she asked, with a sly glance.

'And beautiful.'

She hooted with laughter. 'For steely-eyed pilot Hunk Masters and blonde heiress Sharon Cleavage it was hate at first sight. But as international tension rose, warfare was the last thing on their minds . . .'

Drew gave what he hoped was an enigmatic smile. 'You're wearing too much eyeliner, but otherwise you'd make a great Barbara Cartland.'

Sally choked on her drink. 'You charmer,' she said. 'That helicopter pilot will be fluttering her eyelashes like captive pigeons and beating her fists against your manly chest by the end of the week.'

'I think I might wait a bit for Josie's imprint to fade from the mattress.'

There was a brief, brittle silence. Sally took another sip from her glass. 'Nick told me about it. I'm sorry.' He nodded, staring into his drink. 'So . . . how is it going?' She gave him a gentle smile. 'As your surrogate mother, I have a right to know these things.'

He shrugged. 'All right, I suppose. I think it was probably best for us to split, but had things been a little different I'm sure we could have been very happy. Does that sound perverse?'

She shook her head and glanced towards the stairs. 'Even in the best relationship there are times when you find yourself thinking what if? But . . .'

She met Drew's eyes for an instant and then continued. 'Sometimes you have to go through the pain of a break-up, just to learn to avoid some of the mistakes in the next relationship that you made in your last. Of course, it's not much consolation to your ex to know she's helped you make your next relationship more permanent.'

'But that won't happen with you and Nick?'

'No, I don't think it will. We're very happy now, but there

were times when it wouldn't have taken too much of a push for one of us to have been heading out of the door.'

She gave an embarrassed smile. 'How is it that you always get me to talk so much about myself without ever giving anything about yourself away in return?'

'Natural talent and years of dedicated training.'

'I'm serious,' she said.

'I don't know. Perhaps I don't know the answers to the questions I get asked.'

She raised an eyebrow. 'Or perhaps you're just afraid of the answers?'

'No comment,' he said, reaching across the table for the wine bottle.

'So what's next?'

'Another glass of Chardonnay. In the longer term, I'm going to concentrate on my flying for a while, put my career first.'

'That's a refreshing change,' she said dryly. 'That should really sort things out.'

Drew stuck his tongue out at her and filled their glasses again.

'Really, Drew. You can't keep on buttoning up your emotions. I know you think flying is the biggest thing in your life at the moment, but please don't let the Air Force get in the way of your personal life. In the long run that's what's important.'

He started to protest but she cut him off. 'I remember when Nick was first posted to a Tempest squadron up at Leuchars. The senior pilot there wasn't that much different from you. He had a lovely wife but he seemed to care more about his career than he did about her. She certainly thought so, because in the end she left him. I still see him now and he's a sad spectacle. I doubt if he'd admit it openly, but I'm sure deep down he knows he's ruined his life. You know who I'm talking about, don't you?'

Drew shook his head.

'You should do, you know him better than I do.'

Drew stared blankly at her.

'Bert Russell.'

'Oh come on, Sally, you're not seriously comparing me with that stuffed shirt?'

'You didn't know him then, Drew. Ten years ago he wasn't the sad character he is now.'

She held up her hand as he started to protest again. 'You've got a lot going for you. For God's sake don't wind up like Russell in ten years' time, living for the Air Force and going home to an empty flat every night.'

Sally watched him for a moment, then said, 'Right, that's enough of a lecture from me. What about this helicopter pilot?'

Drew shrugged. 'What about her? I only met her today. There's a queue of at least five hundred people all trying desperately to get into her pants and I'm probably number 499. Not that I'm interested.'

'Of course you're not.' Nick laughed as he came down the stairs. 'You've got far more important things to do. The kids want Uncle Drew to come and read them a story.'

Drew got to his feet with a show of reluctance, but, when Sally tiptoed upstairs ten minutes later to rescue him, he led the chorus of 'Just five more minutes' himself.

She shook her head firmly. 'Don't argue – dinner's on the table.'

Over dinner Sally was distracted.

'What's the matter?' Nick finally asked.

She looked up quickly and smiled an apology. 'Sorry, I was miles away.' She hesitated, then said abruptly, 'What the hell's been going on with the jets recently?'

There was an awkward silence, then Nick put a hand on her shoulder. 'It's pretty straightforward: not enough men, not enough spares, and everyone trying to do more and more with less and less. We're knackered and so's the hardware.'

'And now we've got the delights of Bosnia to look forward to again,' Drew said, instantly regretting it as Sally shivered.

'I wish you didn't have to go.'

Nick hugged her. 'We may not even go.'

'You will, you know you will.'

'Look love, even if we do go, it'll just be another milk run. The only danger will be dying of boredom.'

She pushed his arm away angrily. 'That's bullshit and you know it, Nick. Don't patronise me. People were shot at last time and people were shot down. Don't tell me lies, not even little white lies.'

Embarrassed, Drew sat staring at the stem of his wine-glass as he twisted it in his hand.

'What's the matter, Sally? This isn't like you,' Nick said gently.

'I don't know. Maybe it's the crashes.'

He put his hand back on her shoulder. 'I've been flying jets for twelve years and I've still got all my bits.'

She nodded, still looking as if she was on the brink of tears. 'I know. Maybe it's because you've been flying so long. Maybe it's Jeff Faraday. I just can't get the thought out of my mind of his wife and kids opening the door to see some squadron leader or wing commander standing on the doorstep. Before he even spoke you'd know. Your world would be falling apart and all you'd have would be this stranger sitting in front of you, mouthing platitudes about the ultimate sacrifice.'

She looked across the table at Drew, urgently holding his gaze. 'If anything ever happens to him, Drew, I want *you* to come and tell me. I don't want to find out from some starched uniform.'

'Nothing will happen to Nick—' Drew began.

'But if it does?'

'Er, Sally,' he said, trying to lighten the mood, 'if something happens to Nick, it'll happen to me too. We're flying in the same jet.'

'Promise me anyway.'

Drew looked vainly to Nick for help, then nodded. 'All right, I promise.'

Uncomfortable, he drank the rest of his wine, then glanced at his watch. 'Time I was off home. Thanks for dinner.'

He got up and walked round the table, giving Sally a squeeze and kissing her forehead. 'And stop worrying. Neither of us are going to be dumb enough to put ourselves in danger for the sake of those barmy bastards in Bosnia.'

She smiled gratefully up at him. 'I know, but thanks anyway.'

'Stay the night if you want,' Nick said. 'You'll be back to pick me up in a few hours and you practically live here anyway.'

Drew grinned. 'Thanks, but your kids are already starting

to call me Daddy as it is. Besides, I need to go home at least once a day, just to annoy the neighbours.'

For once, Drew was out of bed in good time in the morning. He showered, shaved and was back outside Nick's house before he'd finished his breakfast.

'You're keen,' he said, slumping into the passenger seat, still clutching his last piece of toast. 'And what's that smell? Aftershave?'

'It may be.'

'Well,' Nick said, smiling to himself. 'It'll certainly help clear my head. I'm coming down with flu. You'd better take another nav up with you today. The only thing I'm going to fly is a desk.'

'Is Sally okay this morning?'

'Yeah,' Nick said shortly. 'She's worried, but it's just a bad case of Air Force Wife Syndrome.'

Drew nodded. 'There's no known cure.'

When they got to the base, Nick disappeared into the crew room, clutching a packet of Beechams powders. Drew went to the seven o'clock briefing for the training sortie, stopping to read a notice on the wall in the corridor. Michelle brushed past him, then checked and wrinkled her nose. 'Calvin Klein?'

Drew shook his head. 'Sweat and avgas.'

She laughed. 'Have it your own way.' She looked at her watch. 'Seven o'clock – mustn't be late for my own briefing.'

Drew followed her into the briefing room and dropped into a spare seat next to his navigator for the day, Mike 'Smiler' Hartley, a tall, gangling West Country man. His nickname was ironic; Drew could not remember ever seeing him smile, let alone laugh.

Michelle stepped up to the podium. 'Morning. Met brief: the weather is fine at the moment, patchy cloud, wind westerly, fifteen knots, gusting to twenty-five, but wind speeds are forecast to increase, strengthening later in the day. Rain and a cloud ceiling down to eight hundred feet are also forecast. We should have time to get the sortie in, but if the weather turns ugly we'll knock it on the head immediately and come home.

'For this sortie we're going to go one on one; we're hiding, you're hunting. We'll be simulating the resupply of front-line troops. The Warcop range in the Eden Valley is the front line, Penrith is our home base. Our mission is to get from Penrith to Warcop – your mission is to stop us.

'For those of you who haven't done any helicopter affiliation before, we can give you a couple of handy hints. We only do about one hundred knots, so catching us won't be a problem for you, but don't waste your time trying to get into our six o'clocks, because helicopters don't have them. We can turn on a sixpence – whatever that is – so, by the time you're in there, it'll be twelve o'clock instead. Doesn't time fly when you're enjoying yourselves?' There was a rumble of appreciative laughter.

'The other thing we can do that you can't is to stop dead, so, if you haven't got your wits about you, you'll have overshot us before you can blink. The difference in velocity means you'll only get one crack at us on each pass and, by the time you've completed your turn to come back in, you'll be six or seven miles away and we'll be hiding down in the weeds.'

She paused and smiled at them. 'And that's all we're going to tell you. You can work the rest out for yourselves. See you up there.'

Drew took off. Mike Hartley was not as confident as Nick, and Drew had to prompt him a couple of times to load information into the fighter's kit. 'Keep it updated, Mike, don't forget the basics. I need to know where the best diversions are going to be. And keep an eye out for the weather ahead. Help me make any weather decisions.'

They took up position, sitting on CAP, waiting for the call, high above the pock-marked landscape of the army artillery ranges in the Eden Valley. The radio crackled into life. It was Michelle's voice.

'We're at Penrith, running south now.'

'Okay,' Drew acknowledged. 'Right, Mike, we know where they're coming from and we know where they've got to go. Let's find them.'

The G-force pinned Drew into his seat as he swung the jet into a hard turn to the north-west, using the after-burners briefly to gun the speed up to 500 knots. He looked contentedly around him.

The clouds scudding across the sky beneath them were painting deep pools of shadow on the landscape. In the valley floor the river meandered through a patchwork of vivid green meadows, the water flashing silver as a stray beam of sunlight struck its surface.

Further from the river, the fields changed in colour as they climbed the fellsides, dulling slowly through every shade of green until they merged finally into the barren browns and bleached greys of the sea of moorland stretching away far to the north.

'What a great day to go flying.' Drew sent the jet soaring and swooping as he revelled in the freedom of the skies.

Mike was enjoying it rather less in the back, trying to concentrate on the radar despite his head bumping around as Drew toyed with the stick. 'Just look at this, Mike,' Drew said. 'It beats the hell out of being stuck in an office.'

'I might as well be, for all I'm seeing of it,' came the voice from the back. 'And you don't get airsick in an office.'

Looking in the rear-view mirrors, Drew could see Mike face down in the green screen, working the radar for all he was worth.

'Get your head out of the cockpit for a bit. It won't be much consolation that you plotted the perfect intercept if we collide with a stray jet that neither of us has seen coming. If you look out more it'll cure your airsickness too.'

Mike took a cursory glance around, then went back to his screen.

'Anything on the radar yet?' Drew asked.

'Nothing yet . . . nothing yet . . . got them. Contact south of Penrith heading one-four-zero, doing about one hundred knots.'

'Okay, good work.'

'The weather's not looking too clever, though,' Mike said, looking up again. 'The cloud's building and the wind speed's picking up.'

Drew looked out towards the west, seeing the first outriders of the coming storm, thick pillars of grey-black cloud boiling up over the horizon. 'I think we've got time for this before we cut and run. Don't lock them up on the radar – we don't want to alert them. We'll come in from high, spiral down into their six o'clock and see if they're looking out.'

As they closed with the target, Mike kept calling directions, his confidence growing as they began the intercept. 'Target left forty degrees, fifteen miles . . . ten miles. Come left ten degrees. Yeah, that's it . . . Six miles.'

'Okay, tally ho,' Drew called a few seconds later. 'I've got him on the nose, about three miles. I'll just take it up a little bit higher.'

He pulled back on the stick and saw the helicopter far below him, skimming over the green fields outside Appleby.

'Coming below the left wing now,' Drew said. 'Are you tally with him, Mike?'

'Yeah, I've got him.'

'Here we go.'

Drew gripped the stick harder, as if trying to merge with the machine, then began the spiral dive, pulling a hard, four-G turn. His G-suit inflated, pressing in on his stomach and compressing his thighs as the Tempest dropped towards the helicopter like a hawk diving on its prey. The height unravelled on the altimeter almost as fast as Mike could count it off, his voice growing steadily less distinct as the G-force dragged his mask to one side of his mouth.

'Thirty thousand . . . twenty-five thousand . . . twenty thousand . . . fifteen thousand . . . ten thousand . . .' Mike grunted aloud with the effort of forcing his head around to keep the helicopter in sight. Under the G-force, his two kilogram helmet now weighed four times as much.

Michelle had seen them coming. Drew saw the helicopter come around hard left as Michelle gunned it, flying fast and low, chasing for cover in a steep side valley.

'Okay,' Drew said, 'coming around, three miles, good position. Coming hard left.' He nudged the stick rapidly from side to side, trying to stay in a firing position on the helicopter as Michelle zigzagged.

Drew was sweating heavily and could hear Mike grunting and groaning, his head thrashing about as the jet bucked and swerved.

'Stick top armed. Tracking . . .' Drew cursed as the helicopter slid in and out of the cross-hairs on his Head-Up Display, his aim thrown off by the yawing of the jet and the turbulence of the humid air rising from the valley floor.

The Puma slid through the gunsight again, then was trapped in the cross-hairs as Drew anticipated Michelle's next turn. 'Tracking, tracking . . . Guns! Guns! Guns!' He squeezed the trigger as Mike whooped his triumph, and then yanked back on the stick to send the Tempest soaring skywards again.

The calm was suddenly shattered as the alarms and warning lights went crazy. The streamlined electronic jet turned into a twenty-ton deadweight and started an uncontrolled dive.

Mike was screaming in the back, 'What the hell's going on?' his previous confidence disappearing as fast as the vapour trailing from the wingtips. As the jet plummeted downwards at fifteen thousand feet per minute, the tiny green squares beneath them grew into meadows and the dark specks became houses.

Drew's voice was reassuringly cool and measured, though his heart was pounding and his mouth was dry with fear. 'There's no feel in the stick – it's barely responding to any inputs. Stand by, we're going to have to come out.'

As Drew fought ineffectually with the controls, a fellside village loomed ahead of them.

Mike shouted, 'Come on. What are we waiting for?'

'Hold on, I've got to get it away from this village.'

Drew kept wrestling with the stick. It felt like he was stirring cement with a teaspoon, but he won a grudging and agonisingly slow turn from the jet.

'Hurry up, Drew. For Christ's sake, hurry up.'

'Just a few more seconds . . .'

'No. Bang out, *now*!' Mike screamed. He could see nothing through the canopy but a wall of trees. He reached down in front of him and yanked the yellow and black handle for all he was worth.

Drew felt the restraining straps tighten, dragging his legs and arms inwards. He heard the explosions as the guns fired to set the seats rising, then the canopy blew off with a crack and, as the slipstream began to howl and tear at him, the ejector rockets fired. He felt himself seized by the scruff of the neck and hurled high into the air like a fistful of rags. He was tumbling over and over, close to blacking out as the seat blasted upwards at thirty G.

There was a massive explosion and a ball of flame flashed through the trees as the Tempest ploughed into the ground, barely two hundred yards from the edge of the village. He tumbled head over heels again and again and again, then there was a crack like a pistol shot as the stabilising parachute fired.

The tumbling slowed and stopped. The seat dropped away and, as it fell to earth, the main parachute opened with another crack. He was jerked upwards like a body on a gibbet. Then there was silence, broken only by the strengthening wind howling through his parachute rigging.

One and a half seconds had elapsed from the moment Mike had pulled the handle until the parachute opened. Drew drifted down, sick to the pit of his stomach. The sequence of events kept racing through his mind.

The ground was coming up fast. He inflated his life-jacket to protect his neck on impact and released the forty-pound survival pack.

He hit the ground with a bone-jarring thump and was dragged along by his chute, parallel to the road leading to the village, travelling faster than a passing car. It screeched to a halt, the driver staring in amazement at the sight of the stricken pilot and the fireball lighting up the sky ahead.

Drew hammered desperately at the harness release. He could feel the heat from the flames reaching out to him, but forced himself to still his mounting panic. He turned and pressed the catch and the parachute blew away in the wind. He lay winded for a moment, then hauled himself painfully to his feet, staggering back, away from the searing heat of the flames. He checked himself gingerly. He had a few bruises, but no broken bones.

Mike was lying motionless a couple of hundred yards away. Drew ran over to him. He was screaming in pain, his leg broken. A piece of bone was protruding from the side of his G-suit, stark white against the torn, bloody flesh.

'Just stand by, mate, it won't be long.' Drew affected a nonchalance he did not feel as he eyed the wound. Arterial blood was spurting out onto the grass. He felt a wave of panic rising in him, but forced himself to be calm, breathing slowly and deeply as he glanced up at the sky. The weather front was coming in fast over the hills. The outline of the peak of Cross Fell was already lost, shrouded in cloud. As Drew watched, the lower hills also disappeared from view and spots of rain began to fall.

The locator beacon in Drew's life-jacket was already going off as he knelt down beside Mike and began to examine his leg. Drew whipped a dressing out of the emergency kit in his flying suit and pressed it hard onto the wound. He improvised a tourniquet from his flying scarf, twisting it steadily tighter until the blood flow slowed to a trickle. Mike yelled with pain as the bones grated against each other.

'You bloody maniacs!'

Drew looked up. A figure was racing towards them across the field from the village school, shouting as he ran. Behind him, the children stood lining the playground wall, their eyes like saucers.

'We've been warning you about this for years,' the man gasped, panting from exertion and crimson with rage. 'Every day you cowboys come over here using our school as some sort of target. Who the hell do you think you are? It was only luck that you didn't hit the school and kill every child in it. I've been watching you playing chicken for the last five minutes. I'm going to have your hide for this.'

Concentrating on Mike's maimed leg, Drew was in no mood for a debate on low-flying. 'Do you really think we're stupid enough to play chicken with our own lives, never mind yours? You haven't got a clue what you're talking about. Can't you see that this guy needs a doctor? If you're not here to help just stay out of my way, you're only placing yourself in danger.'

'What about the danger to those kids?' the teacher began, but then blanched and fell silent as he caught sight of the bloody mess that had been Mike's leg.

Drew ignored him. Hearing the Puma approaching, he turned away and began to call it on the emergency speech channel in his locator beacon.

'Listen,' Mike gasped, teeth clenched in pain. 'If he hadn't risked his own life to steer the plane away from the school, it really would have been a disaster. I was trying to get him to eject, but he wouldn't do it until he was sure it was going to miss the village. He didn't endanger those kids: he saved their lives.'

'But they wouldn't have been in danger if you hadn't . . .' The rest of his sentence was drowned in the thunder of the Puma's rotors.

Michelle was broadcasting the emergency call as she closed on the site. 'Mayday. Mayday. Mayday. Tempest down, ten miles north-west of Appleby.' Drew threw radio procedure out of the window and instead of his callsign, he just said, 'Michelle, this is Drew. Can you hear me?'

'Thank God you're all right. We thought you were dead. What's the situation down there?'

Drew tore his eyes away from the blood still seeping from Mike's leg. 'Trouble with the natives, but we're doing all right. Mike's in a bad way. He's got a broken leg and he's bleeding badly. I'm trying to staunch it, but he needs medical help soonest.'

'We've called out Search and Rescue,' Michelle said. 'They should be with you inside half an hour.'

'I don't know if we can wait that long. He's losing a lot of blood.'

Michelle glanced around. The helicopter was being buffeted by the turbulence from the hillsides. Her co-pilot, Sandy, read her thoughts and warned, 'Go easy, Michelle. Wind speed's increasing, we don't want to get trapped in here.'

Her crewman, Paul, chimed in as well. 'We're low on fuel, Michelle – we've only fifteen minutes spare and the weather's worsening. Leave it to the Search and Rescue.'

Drew gnawed on his lip as he waited for her reply, staring at Mike's deathly white face.

'Sod it,' she said abruptly. 'We can't just leave them there. Okay, Drew, we're coming in for you ourselves.'

'The fuel, Michelle . . .' her crewman said, but she silenced his protests.

'Paul, we'll make it.'

Relief flooded through Drew for a moment, but his apprehension grew again as he looked up and saw the wall of storm clouds advancing rapidly towards them.

Blown sideways by the wind and stung by flurries of driving rain, reducing visibility to a few hundred yards,

Michelle battled to land the helicopter. The instant she touched down, Paul jumped out and sprinted over with a stretcher. They tried to move Mike gently onto it, but, as they lifted him off the ground, he screamed with pain and then lapsed into unconsciousness.

Inside two minutes, they were airborne again. Drew strapped himself into the tiny space that remained between the stretcher and the hard metal wall of the cab.

Michelle flicked over to the emergency channel. 'Hello, London Centre, departing crash site. Two survivors on board, one critical injury. Can you call Newcastle General and tell them that we're bringing them in? I know Carlisle's closer, but there's too much weather that way. We're fuel critical as it is, without having to fight a head wind.'

She contacted Air Traffic Control demanding priority over all other traffic and they roared north-east, across the spine of the Pennines and down over the sprawling western suburbs of Newcastle. Paul and Drew tended Mike's wounds as well as they could, muttering reassurances to him, though he gave no sign of hearing them. The pool of blood spread slowly wider around his shattered leg as they listened grim-faced and silent to the increasingly anxious fuel warnings.

As the hospital appeared ahead, they let out a yelp of relief. Michelle brought the Puma in to land on the helipad on the hospital roof and shut down the engines.

Even before the rotors had stopped moving, an emergency team lifted Mike out, connected a drip and wheeled him hurriedly away. The Perspex doors clattered shut behind them and Drew could hear the doctor shouting urgent instructions to his team.

'Thanks, I'll walk down.' Drew tried to turn down the offer of a horizontal ride on another hospital trolley.

'Just get on and lie down, sir, we give the orders here,' the orderly said.

Drew shot him a look, but did as he was told. As the orderly got ready to wheel him away, Drew glanced up at Michelle. 'Thanks, we owe you big time.'

'Forget it,' she said. 'Unless you've got a few gallons of fuel handy. There's no way in the world this thing is taking off again without some.'

'I'm right out of avgas,' he said, 'but I'll definitely buy you a drink. All of you,' he added lamely, suddenly remembering Sandy and Paul.

He gazed back towards her until the plastic doors banged shut, hiding her from view.

Chapter 6

Drew woke the next morning to see a nurse beaming down at him. 'Well, Mr Miller, it seems you're a hero.'

She showed him a copy of the *Sun*. Splashed across the front page was the headline: JET HERO RISKS LIFE TO SAVE SCHOOL.

She began quoting from the story, pacing up and down at the foot of his bed. 'Listen to this: "Eye-witnesses who saw the plane crash only yards from the village primary school reached the scene within seconds of the injured crew landing. Navigator Mike Hartley fought back the pain of a badly broken leg, as he told me: 'If it wasn't for the heroism of my pilot, Drew Miller, the jet would have crashed into the school.'"'

'What crap,' Drew snorted, but the nurse kept reading.

'"An inquiry is already under way and the black box has been recovered. Miller's commanding officer at RAF Finnington, Wing Commander Bert Russell, added, 'I cannot comment on any aspects of the incident except to say that we are proud of the actions of our air crew in risking their own lives to ensure that the jet crashed away from the village. I would have expected as much from any of my men.'"'

'Russell wouldn't know what to expect from his men.'

The nurse ignored him. '"But furious schoolteacher Andrew Morris, who witnessed the crash, said, 'Despite this man's alleged heroism, it does not alter my basic complaint. We have been warning of the danger of these low-flying jets for years. Will it take the deaths of our children to make the Air Force finally act?'"'

The nurse offered him the paper, 'Do you want it?'

'Thanks,' Drew said. 'It's a load of bollocks, but my granny will love it.'

When she had gone he lay back in bed, reading and rereading the story, secretly pleased that his name was in lights. He thought back to the crash once more. At least they found the black box, he thought to himself, so they'll know it wasn't my fault.

He looked up to see two men in RAF uniform approaching his bed. He recognised both of them and suppressed a smile. Flight Lieutenant John Millns was tall, long-faced and thin; Squadron Leader George Gordon was rotund, balding and even had a small black moustache. They looked like Laurel and Hardy.

'Good morning, Flight Lieutenant Miller,' Gordon said. 'Don't get too carried away with the newspaper reports.'

Drew stuffed the newspaper into the bedside table, then smiled at Millns. 'Hello, John, I haven't seen you for ages. How are you doing?'

'I'm fine, Drew, but I'm afraid this isn't a social visit.'

He looked pointedly at his companion. 'This is Squadron Leader Gordon.'

'I know. We met at Fairford three years ago,' Drew said.

Gordon smiled perfunctorily. 'So we did. So we did.' He cleared his throat. 'I have to tell you that we have been appointed as the Accident Investigators, so we are not here to discuss old times: we're here to talk about what happened yesterday.'

'It's pretty obvious what happened,' Drew said, 'though I couldn't identify a cause from the warning panel. There were just one hell of a lot of warning lights, followed immediately by a near total loss of control.'

'That may be obvious to you, but it's far from obvious to us,' Gordon said. 'We've already found the ADR – the media's beloved black box – and had it deciphered.'

'Good,' Drew said, puzzled by Gordon's attitude. 'If you've got the ADR, you'll know exactly what happened.'

'Unfortunately we don't, because all the signs are that the aircraft was completely serviceable until the point of impact. How do you explain that?'

Drew looked at him in disbelief. 'What can I say, except that it's not true? It obviously wasn't completely serviceable, because it went out of control. I did everything I could to save that aircraft. I've been flying the same way for four years. Suddenly an aircraft goes out of control and hits the hillside, but that's not my problem.'

Gordon stroked his moustache as Drew talked. 'I think you'll find that it is going to be your problem. According to the ADR, there was nothing wrong with that aircraft. We have to warn you that you are under investigation. We will need an immediate initial statement from you.'

'I don't believe this,' Drew said. 'Five minutes ago I was reading a paper telling me I'm a hero and now you're telling me that I'm a villain.'

'Not quite. I'm sure there's a perfectly logical explanation for the accident. Our job is to discover it . . . and we've always found it to be more effective to have accident investigation carried out by RAF personnel rather than the tabloid newspapers.'

He favoured Drew with a brief, thin-lipped smile. 'Now, as I was saying, we need an initial statement from you, to form the basis of the forty-eight hour signal, which, as I'm sure you know, is the mandatory first step in the investigation. It's just a straightforward factual statement: "This is what happened to the aircraft," and so on.'

Drew fought to control his anger. He hated Gordon for his smug, patronising attitude and for apparently having already made up his mind. 'All right,' he said. 'I was flying along the Eden Valley—'

'Just a minute,' interrupted Gordon, 'while John gets his tape recorder working. Right, away you go.' His eyes were cold and unblinking.

'I was flying along the Eden Valley, heading north-west towards Appleby, at thirty thousand feet and five hundred knots. I went into a spiralling descent and as I made a series of turns to engage the target the aircraft went out of control, heading towards buildings on the edge of a village. I got enough response from the controls to steer away from the buildings and, as I did so, Flight Lieutenant Hartley ejected us from the aircraft.'

'Thank you, that will do for now.' Gordon snapped his notebook shut and turned to leave.

'Look,' Drew said, 'I just can't understand what the problem is. I didn't lose control, the jet did.'

Gordon paused and looked back at him. 'Perhaps, perhaps . . . Good morning.'

Millns smiled sheepishly at Drew and followed his superior out of the room.

As soon as they had gone, the nurse came in again, holding the *Daily Mirror*. 'You're in this one as well.'

'Bloody marvellous,' Drew said. 'I'm such a sodding great hero that I'm about to lose my job.'

He slumped back down in the bed, playing the events leading up to the accident over and over in his mind.

His reverie was interrupted by the consultant sweeping through on his morning rounds. 'Good morning. Any problems?'

'None that you can help me with.'

'That's the spirit,' said the consultant, face already buried in Drew's notes. 'Well, we've had a look at the X-rays and you seem to be fine – no fractures, no cracks, no crushed vertebrae. You're an old hand at this, aren't you, so you'll know that we would normally like to keep you immobile for a few days, just in case of any problems we might have missed. Your commander wants you back in a hurry, however, so you'll be on your way home in the morning, but at the first warning sign of any discomfort or any back pain – beyond the bruising of course – get in touch with your medical officer immediately.'

'What about my mate?'

'Mr Hartley? He's making good progress, but he obviously won't be leaving with you tomorrow and he won't be going flying again for several months . . . if indeed he ever does. He's a very lucky man; he lost a lot of blood. A few more minutes and it might have been too late.'

'Can I see him?'

'Not today, I'm afraid. He's still in a lot of pain and we're keeping him sedated.'

Drew spent a miserable day and a sleepless night. He eventually fell asleep just before dawn and woke with a start a couple of hours later to see Michelle sitting beside the bed.

'This is a much better dream than the one I've just been having,' he said, rubbing his eyes. 'What are you doing here?'

'Your boss wanted Nick to come and pick you up, but he had to go to the dentist, so I volunteered.'

'Do I look as rough as I feel?'

'I've seen worse, but you might have to put a bag over your head if we see any of my friends as we're driving home.'

'Listen, Michelle, I just want to tell you that you did a hell of a job to get the helicopter down in that weather. You probably saved Mike's life.'

Michelle held up a hand. 'I don't know about his life, but we probably saved his leg. But don't go on about it, you'll only embarrass both of us. You might get the chance to return the favour one day.'

'I doubt it. Have you tried landing a Tempest in a field?'

She laughed. 'My, you are feeling better aren't you? Okay, I'm going to find a cup of coffee while you get dressed.'

'Are you sure you wouldn't rather stay and watch?'

'No, it might be a disappointment for us both. Five minutes.' She gave him another of her dazzling smiles and left the room.

Drew scrambled out of bed and started dragging a comb through his hair.

'Hmm, not too disappointing after all.' Michelle's face was framed for a moment in the mirror on the wall. He heard her laughter as she walked away down the corridor.

Driving down the A1, Drew found himself gazing out at the speeding traffic as the crash kept preying on his mind. Then he remembered the way Michelle brought in the Puma. 'So how did you learn to fly like that?'

She looked at him quizzically. 'Why, haven't you heard the crew room version?'

'Don't be touchy, I'm only asking.'

'Sorry. All right, as you've probably heard, my father is an air vice-marshal, in charge of the RAF logistics system and the Accident Investigation Bureau. I had the same kind of childhood as most servicemen's kids.'

She glimpsed Drew's private smile from the corner of her eye. 'I know, I know. The rather privileged upbringing of a senior officer's kid. But it wasn't all it's cracked up to be. We moved much more frequently than the standard three years. I hated always being the new girl in school, always the outsider. I didn't really form any lasting friendships until I joined the Air Force myself.'

'I find that hard to believe,' Drew said with a smile.

She laughed. 'Oh, there were plenty of boys, but I never seemed to stay in one place long enough to make long-term friendships. Every time we moved on it would be the same. We'd write letters every week to start with, then once a month, then we'd stop altogether, except for a scribbled note on a Christmas card. After a while it hardly seemed worth the effort making friends in the first place.'

'Stop, stop,' Drew pleaded. 'This is almost too sad to bear.'

'Keep it up, Drew – a few more smart-arse comments and you'll find yourself suddenly very alone on the hard shoulder of the motorway.'

Drew threw up his hands. 'Cast out into the frozen wastes of the unexplored territory of – erm – Northern England. I don't know how I'd survive. This may come as a shock to a refugee from the Home Counties like you, but there are actually people out there, some of them human.'

She signalled and pulled onto the hard shoulder. Drew played along, reaching for the door handle, but she accelerated away again. 'That was just a warning. Now are you going to sit there taking the piss all day or do you want to hear the rest of this riveting story?'

'Yes I do. I promise not to interrupt again.'

'When I was seventeen my father finally took up a staff job in London, so I enjoyed a stable Home Counties home life for all of six months.'

'Do you get on well with him?'

'Better than most air vice-marshals I know.' She laughed. 'Yes, we do. We're very close.'

She didn't speak for a moment. 'You haven't mentioned your mother,' Drew said gently.

'I know. I don't really remember much about her. She died when I was seven.'

'I'm sorry.'

She shrugged. 'It was a long time ago.'

'I know, but it still hurts.'

She looked curiously across at him.

'We have that much in common,' he said. 'I was twelve when my mother died. No fun is it?'

'No. Are you very close to your father?'

'Not really.' Drew changed the subject. 'So did you join the Air Force despite or because of your father?'

'I don't know – a bit of both probably. I've tried to steer as clear of the family influence as possible, but it would be naive to think that it hasn't helped.'

She glanced across at Drew, trying to read his expression. 'I'm not going to apologise for any of that, Drew. So don't give me that "when I were a lad we lived in a cardboard box" look.'

'I never said a word.'

'You didn't have to.'

'So they taught you telepathy as well as flight engineering?'

She smiled. 'Anyway, I started off as a technician, partly to prove that Daddy's girl didn't mind getting her hands dirty, I suppose, but I soon found that I bloody loved it.

'I applied to become a pilot as soon as the RAF was finally dragged kicking and screaming into the twentieth century – just in time for the twenty-first. And before you ask, I never, ever wanted to fly fast jets. Helicopters have always been it for me.'

She waited for his rejoinder, but he was gazing intently at her face.

'You are listening, aren't you, and not just admiring the view?'

Drew had been wondering what it would be like to kiss her neck, where it joined her collarbone beneath the tangle of blonde hair.

'Absolutely, every word,' he lied.

'I was posted to 17 Squadron and did two three-month detachments in Northern Ireland. I also went on Desert Storm with 17, flying casualties back from the front line. I joined 33 two years ago . . . and that's enough about me. What about you?'

'I was born in Glasgow, but I hardly remember it. My parents moved to Liverpool when I was very young and I grew up there. My dad was a docker and he thought there'd be more work in Liverpool. Ironic wasn't it?'

Michelle smiled sympathetically and turned her head. Her deep-blue eyes at such close quarters were even more distracting.

'Shouldn't you be watching the road?' he asked.

'Well?' she said after a brief pause. 'What happened next?'

Drew shrugged. 'I left school as soon as I was sixteen.'

'Back up a minute,' she said. 'What happened to childhood and adolescence?'

'Not a lot,' Drew said.

Michelle gave him a curious look, but let it go.

There was a strained silence before he continued. 'My teachers wanted me to stay on at school, take A-levels and go to university, but I hated school so much I just wanted to get out. I tried a few dead-end jobs and then joined the Air Force, on a whim as much as anything else.

'I learned my legendary driving skills ferrying air crew to their aircraft and I guess I must have got the flying bug from them. I started going to night school to get the qualifications and came through the long route. After four years of graft, you realise that all you've achieved is the same starting point as a "chap" coming straight into officer training, which, by the way, I hated.'

'So did I,' Michelle said. 'I'm no good with all the rules and regimentation. So where have you been so far?'

'The usual circuit – RAF Arsehole-of-the-Universe, Lincolnshire, and then four years at Finnington.'

'Four years?' Michelle sounded surprised.

'Yeah, it's still my first tour.' He hesitated. 'I asked for an extension. I wanted to stay in the area because of my girlfriend, so they gave me another year. I'm being posted to Germany after we get back from Bosnia.'

'And the girlfriend?'

'She's taken voluntary redundancy.'

'I'm sorry.'

Drew shrugged. 'It's all right. How about you?'

'Not at the moment thanks.'

He laughed. 'So why were you spying on me in my bedroom?'

She cocked an eyebrow. 'You're all right in a *Boy's Own* kind of way, but I could never sleep with a combat virgin.'

'I've seen my share of action,' he said. 'So who's the man in your life – a contract killer for the SAS?'

'Not right now. Relationships do tend to get in the way of a flying career, don't they? Or do I mean that the other way round?'

They pulled up at the barrier at Finnington. 'Here we are,' Michelle said.

'That's another favour I owe you,' Drew said. 'Can I buy you a lunch in part payment?'

She shook her head. 'Sorry, I'm flying this afternoon and you've got a meeting in—' she glanced at her watch – 'exactly twenty minutes. Your boss wants to see you at twelve-thirty sharp for a briefing.'

The guard waved them through and she accelerated away towards the operational area.

'He means a bollocking,' Drew said. 'The accident investigators came to see me in hospital this morning. They claimed the ADR shows nothing wrong with the aircraft. They as good as told me I'd caused the crash. I can't understand it. The jet just went out of control – no warning, no chance.'

As Drew opened the car door, she put a hand on his arm. 'Don't worry about the investigation. You'll come through okay.'

He smiled gratefully. 'Thanks. I hope you're right.'

Russell looked up from a pile of papers as Drew entered his office, and motioned him to a chair. 'With you in a moment,' he said, pipe clamped between his teeth. 'Everything from a requisition for Skyflash missiles to an order for toilet rolls seems to pass across my desk.'

Drew smiled politely as Russell scanned and initialled each document in turn. After a few moments he signed his name at the bottom of a final paper with a flourish and consigned it to one of his four metal filing trays, lined up like soldiers on parade at the right-hand end of his desk.

Russell laid down his pen. 'Everything all right, Drew? No medical problems, no aches and pains?'

'None at all. I'm raring to go.'

There was a silence as Russell puffed on his pipe.

'So when can I get airborne again, sir? I know I'd normally be flying a desk for a fortnight after an ejection but, with a potential deployment in the offing, I was hoping you could shelve that.'

'Sometimes I wonder why I bother,' Russell said.

'Sir?'

'Do you ever read my memos?'

'Absolutely, sir, every word.'

'Then you'll know that the procedure following an ejection has been changed.'

'Perhaps you could refresh my memory, sir.'

'The Tempest crash at Coningsby last year. Since then, no one who's ejected or been involved in a major incident can fly again without the express permission of the head of AIB, Air Vice-Marshal Power.'

Drew smiled. 'I'm sure your word will carry a lot of weight in the Air Vice-Marshal's deliberations.'

Russell was unmoved. 'There's also the AIB investigation to consider.'

'But it'll be months before their report's complete.'

'Quite so,' Russell said, 'but the forty-eight-hour signal carries an imputation of possible pilot error which may give the Air Vice-Marshal pause for thought.'

Drew tried not to show his exasperation. 'Surely you're not going to ground me on the basis of that?'

'As I've reminded you, it's not my responsibility. I will, however, be arguing your case quite forcibly. We're short enough of air-crew as it is without having experienced pilots sitting twiddling their thumbs.'

Drew was amused by the idea of Russell arguing forcibly with any senior officer. But his look was respectful as Russell delivered the final part of his sermon.

'I've got complete confidence in your ability, Drew, but I must warn you that my confidence is not shared by everybody on the station. You're your own worst enemy sometimes. That air of impatience, arrogance even, does not go down well.'

Drew kept his expression neutral. 'Thank you, sir, I'll take that on board. Will that be all?'

'For the moment, yes, but I hope to have Air Vice-Marshal Power's verdict later on, so don't go too far away.'

Drew found Michelle in the crew room.

'How do you manage it?' Jumbo asked him as he made his way over. 'We go out and do our job every day and nobody even notices. You go and throw thirty-million-pound aircraft away and you're suddenly a hero.'

Michelle grinned. 'I hope you're not coming to me for sympathy. I've been getting that shit for years. When are you going to get back in the air?'

'I don't know,' Drew said. 'It's up to your father.'

'My father? It's nothing to do with him yet, is it? The AIB always takes months to grind through its investigations. Even if they're going to blame you – which I'm sure they won't – they can't ground you till the accident report's complete.'

Drew shook his head. 'They've changed the system. Every time you eject now you need the head of AIB's permission to get back in the air. I'm surprised you hadn't heard.'

'Really,' Michelle said. 'Have you ever seen anyone eject from a helicopter? It's a bit like sticking your head into a food processor. I'm surprised you hadn't heard.'

'Point taken,' Drew said. 'It all changed after a crash at Coningsby last year. The guy had been involved in an incident in Wales six months before. He'd been told that a lot of blame was going to be laid at his door and warned that he might be court-martialled. Even though the results of the Board of Inquiry hadn't come out, he was sent back flying again.

'A few weeks later, he was just coming back after a normal sortie over the North Sea and forgot to put his landing gear down. He hit the runway at a hundred and fifty miles an hour, with no wheels. He slid off to the side and the aircraft flipped over. He didn't stand a chance.

'The Board of Inquiry thought that he might have been

distracted, worrying about the report on the previous crash. As a result, the Chief of the Air Staff has now given your father sole authority to make the decision about when a pilot who's lost an aircraft can go flying again.'

'Let's hope he's in a good mood at the moment then,' Michelle said, getting to her feet. 'See you later, Drew. Right now we've got a couple of your mates from the squadron to torment. We've found a lovely bit of the Lake District to go and hide in. See you in the mess for Happy Hour?'

'What? Yes. Great.'

'Loosen your bullets, Flight Lieutenant,' Michelle said. 'I'm only talking about a drink.'

There was laughter from Drew's mates, who were hanging on every word. As she picked up her maps she gave him a gentle smile and whispered, 'See you later.'

Everyone headed for the changing rooms to prepare for their sorties, leaving Drew sitting on his own in the crew room. He settled down with the papers, alarmed to see that his name figured prominently in all of them. He threw them into a heap and stared out of the window.

Russell bustled into the room, clutching a sheaf of papers.

'Ah Drew, there you are,' he said, as if it was a major surprise. 'I've got good news and bad news. Which would you like first?'

Drew said evenly, 'I just want to know whether I can go flying again, sir.'

'Well that's the good news. I managed to persuade Air Vice-Marshal Power that you played too vital a part in the squadron to sit around the crew room reading newspapers all day, so you're cleared to resume flying with immediate effect.'

'That's great news, sir. Thank you very much.'

'The Air Vice-Marshal took a great deal of persuasion, however. He was very unhappy about the implication of pilot error in the initial report, but I've assured him that he'll be given no cause to regret the decision.' Russell's voice caught at the memory of the conversation with Power. 'I really had to go out on a limb for you over this, Drew, so don't let me down.'

'Don't worry, I won't. I really appreciate what you've done for me,' Drew said, not entirely believing him.

'I'm afraid there's still the bad news,' Russell said. 'The accident investigators have arrived to give you the third degree again. They're waiting in my office.'

Squadron Leader Gordon and Flight Lieutenant Millns proved no more friendly than on their first visit. Drew repeated the details of the crash, but, the more he did so, the less convincing he knew he sounded.

Gordon listened with impatience. 'We know there was nothing wrong with the aircraft, Flight Lieutenant Miller – the ADR has already told us that. Why don't you save yourself the months of waiting as the Board of Inquiry considers its verdict and admit what we both know to be the truth now? You simply cocked it up, didn't you? You lost concentration or you pushed just a little too hard – perhaps showing off to that rather attractive helicopter pilot – and in the process you lost control of your aircraft. Isn't that what really happened?'

Drew watched Gordon as he spoke. Everything about him – the smugness, the ridiculous moustache, the pink jowls trembling with indignation – filled Drew with distaste.

'I'm sorry to spoil your theory,' he said wearily, 'but that isn't what happened at all. I don't know why the aircraft went out of control but it certainly wasn't down to any error of mine. I've replayed that sortie a thousand times in my head. Everything I did was by the book and well within normal operating limits. The fact that the jet is now a pile of scrap certainly indicates that there's a problem, but you must look for the solution in the aircraft's systems, not the conduct of the man flying it.'

Gordon's eyes drilled into Drew. 'Your comments are noted, Flight Lieutenant Miller,' he said. 'The engineers will be examining the wreckage thoroughly. If your theory's correct, we'll certainly be able to prove it. At the moment, however, all the evidence points in exactly the opposite direction. We will be interviewing you again, but for the moment I really don't think we need detain you from your duties any longer. Good afternoon.'

As Drew rose to go, John Millns buried himself in his notes, unable to meet his eye.

Chapter 7

Drew called DJ over when he arrived back in the crew room from the sortie. He had a quick look around, making sure no one was near enough to eavesdrop. 'DJ, I owe you an apology.'

'What for?'

'That near miss before we went to Aalborg. I didn't believe you at the time, but now I've seen it for myself.' Drew hesitated. 'Look, DJ, I need your help. The accident investigators don't believe me any more than I believed you. They've as good as told me that I caused the aircraft to crash.'

'So how can I help?'

'I need to be able to prove that there was a fault with the Tempest, even if it didn't show up on the ADR. I'm not sure I can convince the investigators on my own.'

DJ looked embarrassed. 'I don't know, Drew. I'm not really sure about it myself now. I was just flying along and suddenly it went bananas. I thought I was doing it by the book, but I could have overcontrolled or something. To be honest, I don't know what happened. I don't even know how I pulled it out. I was panicking so much I even let go of the stick and it suddenly righted itself.' He paused. 'Apart from anything else, we didn't file an incident report or anything at the time, so if I report it now we're both going to get into some pretty serious trouble, aren't we?'

'Yeah, you're right.' Drew stood lost in thought for a few moments, while DJ studied the toecaps of his boots. 'I could try a CONDOR report, I suppose.'

'A CONDOR?' DJ's brow furrowed.

'Those forms on the back of the toilet doors. With your cock-up record, I'd have thought you'd have known them by heart.'

DJ grinned. 'Never read them. I always take the *Daily Mirror*.'

'They're Confidential Occurrence Reports. They put them in the bogs so that you can pick one up without anyone knowing. You grab one from the back of the door, fill in your name and the details of the incident and send it to the AIB, where it goes straight onto Power's desk.'

'Just a minute,' DJ said. 'How can it be confidential if it's got your name on it?'

'It's on a tear-off strip, so only the head of AIB actually sees it and he's only allowed to use it if he needs further clarification. After that he bins the name and personal details and circulates the rest of the form around the stations so that lessons can be learned.'

'So is that what you're going to do?'

Drew shrugged. 'I've got to do something. I can't just sit on my hands until Gordon's kangaroo court's finished with me. If I'm lucky I'll be permanently grounded and if I'm not I'll be court-martialled and kicked out of the Air Force with a dishonourable discharge. If the CONDOR to Power doesn't help I'm going to have to prove it myself.'

'How the hell are you going to do that?'

Michelle's voice startled both of them. 'I hope you're not planning to set up in competition with my father. I don't want anyone ruining the family business.'

Drew smiled distractedly at her.

'Not that I think you'll pose too much of a problem,' she continued. 'You've no expertise, no evidence, no research data and no way of getting proof.'

'So you don't believe me either?'

'I didn't say that.'

'Well you're in a minority,' Drew said. 'Most of the guys think I just cocked it up.'

'Look, Drew, I have to go now. We're going back up to let another couple of top guns have a crack at us, but I'll see you later in the mess. I'll tell you something then that may help.'

'Can't you tell me now?'

'It's pretty insubstantial,' Michelle said, 'but it's worth a dinner.'

Drew was due to take a jet up himself later in the afternoon, a routine flight to get himself back in the groove. Nick gave him a quizzical look as they collected their flying kit and sat down between two rows of grey lockers.

'Are you sure you're ready for this?' Nick asked. 'From what I hear, you've a lot on your mind just now. I mean the accident investigators,' he added drily.

'Air Force gossip is unbelievable. If I farted in Fairbanks, Alaska, they'd know about it here before the smell had faded.'

He felt a sense of relief at the monotony of the pre-flight routine, but he was unusually tense as the Tempest began to roll down the runway, catapulting forward as he unleashed the brakes and pushed the throttles. Sensing his nervousness, Nick kept his own voice neutral and dispassionate as he ran through the endless cycle of checks and counterchecks.

Once airborne, Drew kept the Tempest well within its operating limits as they rose into the overcast sky, the airframe bumping and juddering in the turbulence as they passed through the cloud layers.

They levelled out at twenty thousand feet and flew east over a rapidly changing cloudscape, soaring over towering cliffs and deep valleys of swirling vapour. Chinks and gaps in the cloud began to widen, giving Drew brief glimpses of the North York Moors far below them. By the time they crossed the coastline, the cloud was well broken and the North Sea shimmered blue as the Mediterranean in the sunlight.

'Let's take it up to the top and have a good look round,' Nick said. 'It's not often we get a free sortie with nothing to do but sightsee.'

'Sounds good to me,' Drew said, hauling back on the stick and opening the throttles to send the Tempest higher.

He levelled it out again at forty-eight thousand feet, eight miles above the earth, the maximum height they could fly. He looked around him, revelling in the sight. He could see virtually the whole east coast, from the Farne Islands far to the north, down past the Wash and the pregnant bulge of East Anglia. Out to sea, tankers and freighters were ploughing up and down the congested sea lanes like trucks on a motorway.

As he swung the jet into a turn to follow the coast south, a light flashed and an alarm sounded. His jaw clenched and he held his breath, his fist tightening around the stick as he scanned the warning panel.

As he read the caption, he exhaled slowly.

'All right?' Nick asked.

Drew grunted. 'Yeah, just a glitch in the computer system. It's reset, nothing to worry about.'

As he flew along the coastline he began to relax again, glorying in the freedom of the skies.

'Not that bad is it?' Nick said, sharing his enjoyment.

'Not bad at all. I tell you what, Nick, I'm not going to let the bastards take this away from me without a fight.'

'Spoken like a man,' Nick laughed. 'Okay, it's nearly time for Happy Hour. Let's go home.'

Drew pulled the Tempest into a sweeping turn, the sun glinting on the wings as they began the long descent back into Finnington.

The bar was already packed when they got to the mess. Michelle was in the far corner. As the drinks went back to full price and the crush began to thin, he worked his way over to her side. 'Ready to go?'

Michelle nodded. She interrupted the latest in a long line of would-be suitors in mid-flow. 'Sorry, must go and powder my nose.'

Drew listened to her circle of admirers exchanging increasingly implausible stories about flying and women, as they waited with diminishing optimism for her to return, then he slipped out.

Michelle was waiting. They jumped into Drew's car and sped out of the base. 'Some of those guys have been trying to chat me up every twenty minutes since I arrived here,' Michelle said. 'They've had more knock-backs than a weak server at Wimbledon.'

'I'm flattered to have got through to the last sixteen.'

'You should be.'

At Finnington Hall, the head waiter steered them impassively to a table by the window, overlooking the river. Drew ordered champagne.

'Celebrating something?' A smile played around Michelle's lips.

He laughed. 'I'm an incurable optimist.' He toasted her silently.

'I didn't want to say anything in front of the others,' Michelle said. 'But there was a crash in the Brecon Beacons last year. A Tempest from 35 Squadron at Valley.'

Drew nodded. 'I remember it.'

'Well they reckon that aircraft was perfectly serviceable, too, before it hit the deck. They blamed pilot error, but I knew Alastair Strang. He was one of the best pilots around and one of the coolest guys under pressure I've ever met.'

'It sounds like you knew him pretty well,' Drew said gently.

She smiled, though her eyes were sad. 'Yes, I knew him very well. He's one of the reasons why I don't date air crew.'

'This isn't a date?'

'No, this is a dinner. It's only a date if you get to kiss me at the end of it.'

'And I don't?' She shook her head. 'Sorry,' Drew said. 'I'll stop interrupting.'

'The details don't really matter, but having been to one lover's funeral, I don't want to have to go to another.'

There was a silence. Drew longed to reach out and take her hand, but as if reading his thoughts Michelle sat back in her seat and folded them in her lap.

'I also had to watch my co-pilot from 17 Squadron die in front of me.'

'Who was he?'

'Dave Williams. We were doing CASEVAC around Lurgan. There was a call to say a bomb had gone off and two members of a patrol were injured. We were about half a mile short of the site when I heard a bang and the canopy suddenly turned red. I thought we'd hit a flock of birds, but then I realised the blood was on the inside.

'The IRA had been lying in wait and put a burst of heavy-calibre fire up through the floor. I was lucky – I wasn't even touched. But a round blew off David's kneecap and then ricocheted into his chest. The impacts on the cab and his knee distorted the bullet so much that it punched a hole this size' – she gestured to her dinner plate – 'in his chest.'

Drew winced at the thought.

'There was blood absolutely everywhere,' Michelle said. 'I was covered in it and I had to wipe it off the canopy before I could see anything. He died before we set down at base.'

With a visible effort, she pulled herself back to the present. 'It could be worth your while talking things over with some of the guys on Alastair Strang's squadron. They reckoned there was definitely something strange about the crash that killed him.'

Drew paused. 'Thanks. I'm really grateful. Particularly since I might be about to make waves for your old man.'

'He's head of the AIB, Drew. That means he *likes* finding out why aircraft drop out of the sky.'

He hesitated, feeling suddenly sheepish. 'What's it like having an Air Vice-Marshal for a dad? I mean, what's he like out of uniform?'

'Pink with a certain amount of grey hair.'

'Does he have gold braid on his pyjamas?'

'I don't know. I've never slept with him.'

Drew was embarrassed. 'I'm sorry. You must have stupid pricks like me asking you this stuff all the time.'

'I'm sorry too.' She reached out and touched him briefly on the arm. 'He's all right. These days we don't see each other as much as we did, but we're still close. As far as I can remember, he was a bit aloof when I was young. When my mother died it would have been easy for him to have packed me off to my grandparents and then sent me to boarding school. He never did that. He was wealthy enough to afford a nanny, but he did keep me at home and spent as much time with me as he could.

'He treated me as an equal, an adult almost, and was

always as straight as the crease in his trousers with me. He's never ever told me a lie. When I asked him if there was a Santa Claus, he just said, "Of course not, but don't tell your friends – they might be disappointed."'

She smiled at the memory. 'What about your father? You said you weren't that close, didn't you?'

He nodded. 'We're not close at all. We never have been really, not even after my mother died.'

'Tell me more.'

Drew moved a little uncomfortably in his seat. 'My mother always felt that marriage was for life no matter how bad things got.' He frowned at the memories. 'My dad had been in and out of work all the time we were in Liverpool – always casual, never a steady job – and the longer we were there, the less he went out and the more he drank. He was one of the old school though: he never lifted a hand around the house. That was woman's work, beneath a working man's dignity, even when the working man wasn't working at all.

'My mother just wore herself down in the end: getting up at four to clean offices, hurrying home to make breakfast before I went to school, doing domestic cleaning for middle-class ladies in Aintree all morning, then hurrying home again to clean our own house and leave us a dinner in the oven before she went back out from five o'clock to nine at night to clean yet more offices.

'She died of cancer, but it was everything else that really killed her. Afterwards my dad took us back to Glasgow. It was a foreign country to me and to him by then, and there was no work there either. He drank more and more and I couldn't wait to get away.'

He looked up, embarrassed.

She gave him a few moments, then said, 'Perhaps we've had enough history for one night.'

They swapped Air Force gossip and tales of bad behaviour on detachment for another hour, then Michelle glanced at her watch and looked around the restaurant, deserted save for a knot of tired and grumpy waiters. 'I think we ought to go.'

Drew nodded. 'I know. The head waiter's been preparing to bring out the hoover for the last twenty minutes. It makes a refreshing change to have a waiter trying to catch my eye.'

Drew tried to pay the bill himself, but Michelle shook her head. 'We'll share it. Don't spoil your new-man image by going antediluvian on me.'

She asked the waiter to phone for a taxi.

'Don't you want to come back for a nightcap?' Drew asked.

She shook her head. 'I told you. I don't date air crew.'

'What if you fall in love with someone?' Drew asked.

She met his gaze and shook her head. 'I won't.'

'How can you be so sure? If you meet the right person, surely you can't stop yourself from falling in love?'

She looked at him quizzically. 'Can't you? From what I hear around the crew room, you've been managing it pretty successfully.'

'I hadn't met the right woman,' Drew said.

Michelle took another sip of her wine, raising an eyebrow at his use of the past tense. 'Perhaps. Anyway, can we drop the subject of my dating habits?'

Her growing irritation was obvious, but he pressed on. 'At least if your husband was a pilot himself, he'd understand the risks.'

'Look,' snapped Michelle, now coldly angry. 'This is a restaurant, not the marriage guidance council. I don't need any advice on how to run my personal life, least of all from someone who's known me less than a week.'

Drew flushed. 'Michelle . . .'

'Forget it,' she said coolly. 'Let's just go, shall we?'

There was an awkward silence as they waited for their coats.

Drew surveyed the ruins of a once-perfect evening. 'It seems as if every time I go out for dinner these days, the evening ends in silence.'

The taxi was already waiting, Michelle paused with her hand on the door. 'I'm sorry. I did enjoy the evening. Most of it, anyway. Goodnight.'

Drew watched the taxi lights fade into the darkness and then walked home through the deserted square, kicking an empty can in front of him.

His alarm woke him from a very short night's sleep. He showered and then phoned the base. Always the first to arrive in the morning and the last to leave at night, Russell was already at his desk, even though it was only 6:15.

'Fine morning, Drew.'

'Is it, sir? I'm afraid I haven't had time to notice. I've been sequestered in the smallest room since half past three.'

'Oh dear. Montezuma's revenge, eh?'

'I'm afraid so, sir. I don't think I'll be flying anything today that isn't connected to plumbing.'

'All right, we'll hope to see you tomorrow.'

Drew hung up and five minutes later was in his car heading south. It took him three and a half hours to reach his destination. The first hour was a high-speed motorway run, the last two and a half an endless procession of traffic on the road snaking along the North Wales coast.

Finally he cleared the road bridge over the Menai Straits and drove across the island to the base. It was a typical Anglesey day: grey, cold and teeming with rain, making RAF Valley look even more dismal and unwelcoming than usual.

Drew showed his ID to the guard on the gate and asked directions to 35 Squadron. The crew room was deserted, but, looking out of the window through the driving rain, he could see a formation of Tempests coming in on the runway.

He helped himself to a coffee and settled down to wait, peering idly at the photographs of aircraft and air crew on the walls.

Twenty minutes later Alastair Strang's former crewmates began to straggle through from the changing rooms. 'Hello there,' said one of them. 'Where are you from?'

'Drew Miller, 21 Squadron. Is the weather always this bad?'

'Bad? This is just a thin overcast and a light shower. Wait till it really starts raining.'

'No thanks. If I'd wanted to drown, I'd have joined the navy.'

Drew went along with the banter until he had a chance to steer the conversation on to the ever-popular crew-room topic of equipment shortages. 'It's getting bloody ridiculous,' one of the older pilots responded. 'They're expecting more and more out of the air crew and the aircraft, but providing less and less to do it with.'

'I know,' Drew said. 'It's playing hell with safety too. I had to go to yet another crash with the the Mountain Rescue Team a couple of weeks ago up in the Dales. You probably heard about it.'

There were some answering nods.

'It looks like they're going to blame pilot error,' Drew continued as casually as he could, 'but I went to the crash site and it didn't look like pilot error to me.'

He waited, hoping someone would bring up the Strang crash, but there were just a few nods and grunts.

'Didn't you have an incident like that a while ago?' Drew asked eventually. 'Alastair Strang?'

The warm welcome was instantly replaced with suspicion. 'Why, were you a friend of Alastair's?'

Drew shook his head. 'I never knew him, but Michelle Power told me about him. She seems to think that pilot error wasn't the cause of his crash either.'

Nobody spoke, but a couple of them looked at him closely and then exchanged a glance.

Drew decided to level with them. 'Look, I almost died in a similar incident. Now the accident investigators are telling me that I was responsible. I'm just trying to get to the bottom of what happened to my aircraft.'

There was a noticeable thaw in the atmosphere. The older pilot elected himself group spokesman. 'We're sure the accident report wasn't right. Alastair had been in the Red Arrows before he retrained to fly Tempests and was the best pilot on squadron, bar none. He was such a perfectionist that, if he wanted to be flying at twenty thousand feet and was at twenty thousand and one, he'd nudge it down an inch at a time until he got it there. If he was refuelling at night, blindfold, he'd still get the probe in the basket first time every time.'

He stopped, a little embarrassed. 'Sorry, I sound like the founder member of his fan club, don't I? But the others will tell you the same thing. He was a bloody good pilot. If he crashed because of pilot error, then I'm the Minister of Defence.'

Drew held up his hands. 'I'm convinced. Have you heard about any similar incidents?'

'Not really. There are always rumours, aren't there, but

nothing definite.' He paused. 'It's not much to show for the journey from Finnington I'm afraid.'

'It's something,' Drew said. 'Thanks.'

He was just south of Manchester when he came to an abrupt decision. Instead of heading east – the direct route back towards Finnington – he took the M6 north, through the rusting cotton-belt towns of Lancashire and out into the cleaner air of the Cumbrian fells.

Night had already fallen when he turned off at a run-down, grey Victorian railway town, straddling the main line at the foot of the granite mass of Shap Fell. He stopped to study his map briefly and then drove on another dozen miles before turning off again onto a B road that climbed the shoulder of another fell. Scattered farms threw tiny pinpricks of light into the blackness of the night.

For eight miles he passed nothing but peat bog and wild moorland, the only sign of human occupation a few stretches of crumbling stone wall and a handful of ruined sheepfolds. Then the ground began to drop away and he found himself looking down into a narrow, steep-sided dale.

He halted to check his map once more, then drove on, swinging off the main road over an ancient, arched pack-horse bridge and climbing steep twisting lanes. He almost missed the turn. He braked hard as he caught a glimpse of a familiar lichen-encrusted wooden sign. Two minutes later he was pulling to a halt in the yard of Crowgarth Farm.

A faint glow of yellow light came from the farmhouse. As Drew got out of the car, two dogs chained in the yard went into paroxysms of barking. He stepped around them, carefully gauging the length of the chains, and banged on the door. There was a long silence, save for the barking of the dogs. Then he heard footsteps and a woman's voice bellow. 'Jess, Floss, be quiet! Who is it?'

The barking dropped a few decibels, but Drew still had to shout to make himself heard. 'My name's Drew Miller. I'm one of the RAF men who was here after the aircraft crashed.'

There was the sound of several bolts being drawn and then the door opened a crack. 'What do you want?'

'Is your husband in Mrs, er . . .'

'Alderson. No he's not.'

'When will he be back?'

'When he's had a bellyful of ale, I wouldn't wonder. He's playing dominoes at the Farmer's Arms.'

'Where's that?' Drew asked.

She clicked her tongue at the stupidity of offcomers. 'It's the only pub between here and Gunnerside.'

Before Drew could thank her, she had banged the door and begun slamming the bolts back into place. The dogs redoubled their barking as Drew ran for the car and drove off back down the hill.

He found the pub easily enough, a whitewashed, low stone building, set back from the edge of the road in the heart of the village. He pushed open the door and walked in. A row of flat-capped farmers in dun-coloured clothes were shoulder to shoulder at the bar. They swivelled to look at him as he came in, then swung back.

The hubbub of conversation faded and died as Drew walked towards them, feeling as welcome as a gunslinger entering the Last Chance saloon. The wall of farmers' rumps showed no sign of parting. He caught a glimpse of the barmaid over one of their shoulders and ordered, then turned to scan the bar for his quarry.

He couldn't see him at first and turned back as his drink was served. 'Has Mr Alderson been in?'

A slow ripple of laughter spread away from him, washing along the bar and out to the tables clustered around the walls.

The barmaid gave him a pitying look. 'This is Swaledale. Two-thirds of the people in here are called Alderson.'

'Sorry, Mr Alderson from Crowgarth Farm.'

She pointed to a corner table. 'He's sitting there with his back to you.'

Drew pushed through the crowd. Alderson glanced up briefly, furrowed his brow, then nodded to himself with satisfaction. 'You're that RAF feller aren't you? Never forget a face,' he added to his approving circle of friends.

'I wondered if I could have a quick word with you,' Drew said.

'Not now, lad, not now,' Alderson said, gesturing to

his dominoes. 'When we've finished. Now then, whose drop is it?'

Drew leant against the wall and waited for over an hour as Alderson and his cronies played one interminable game of dominoes after another. A few other farmers stared at Drew with curiosity from time to time, but no one engaged him in conversation, and his own attempts to speak to them were answered with monosyllables or grunts.

Finally Alderson stood up and stretched. 'Come to learn a bit more about yows?' He winked at his mates. 'That's sheep to you townies.'

'I came to ask you a bit more about the crash.'

'Not that again,' one of Alderson's cronies said, grimacing. 'He's about bored the arse off me already with that.'

'What do you want to know then?' Alderson asked, looking meaningfully in the direction of the bar.

Drew took the hint. 'Pint?' he asked.

'Whisky,' Alderson said, smiling to himself. 'Large one. Famous Grouse,' he added. 'I drink no other.'

Drew was beginning to remember why he had disliked Alderson on first acquaintance, but smiled politely and bought him his drink.

'Right,' Alderson said. 'Ask away.'

Drew looked around at the sea of expectant ruddy faces, all tuned in to his conversation. 'Did you see an explosion or any smoke or flames before the crash?'

Alderson took an appreciative sip of his whisky, then put his head back and tipped the rest down in one. 'No. I didn't see any of that, just the plane flying along and then hitting the hillside.'

'Did it seem to be under control right up to the point of impact?'

The farmer gave Drew the look of a teacher faced with a particularly backward child. 'How would I know? I'm a farmer, not a bloody flyer. All I can tell you is it looked to me like one of those other sort of low-flyers we have on the moors here.'

He waited, watching Drew from under his bushy eyebrows.

'You mean a plane?'

'No, a bird. A game bird.'

'A grouse?'

'Thanks very much. I'll have a large one,' Alderson said, presenting his glass. There was a roar of laughter from the farmers.

Drew passed Alderson's glass back across the bar.

'Have you never seen a grouse in flight?' Alderson asked, having sent the second whisky the way of the first. 'Low-flyers we call them. That plane were just like a grouse on the twelfth of August. One minute it were skimming over the moor, following the slope of the ground, the next it just fell out of the sky, like a grouse that'd been shot. Not as good to eat though.' He chuckled.

'But it did definitely fall to the ground, rather than flying too close to it?'

'That's what I just said in't it? It just dropped out of the sky . . .'

He reached over to the bar and picked up a half-eaten pork pie. Holding it out at arm's length, he let it drop. It splattered on the flagstone floor.

'Just like that,' he said, kicking the mangled pie under a table.

'Would you be willing to sign a statement to that effect?'

'I might,' Alderson said, looking once more at his empty glass.

'A Commission of Inquiry would be cheaper than this,' Drew said, but he passed the glass back over the bar.

'So you'll sign a statement?' he persisted, as Alderson smacked his lips over his third large Scotch in five minutes.

'I will if you like,' Alderson said, 'but I've already signed one for those investigators of yours. I told them the same thing as I'm telling you: it fell out of the sky like a sack of spuds. They asked me the same questions and I gave them the same answers, though I didn't even get a drink out of them.'

He winked at Drew and turned back to his mates. Drew could hear them laughing and slapping him on the back as he pushed his way out of the pub, into the cold wind keening down the valley from the moors.

He was scarcely aware of the road as he drove away down the dale, turning over and over in his mind what Alderson had just told him. If the jet really did fall out of the sky in the way the farmer had described, how could Power and the AIB be so confident that it was pilot error? If it wasn't, what was going wrong with the aircraft? Drew now knew of four loss-of-control incidents involving the Tempest, two fatal, two near-fatal. How many more were there?

Chapter 8

Drew did not get home until well after midnight, but he was at the base by seven the next morning. He went straight to the crew room and told Nick what he had learned at Valley and in the Farmer's Arms.

Nick waited until he had finished and then said quietly, 'Don't quote me on this – I'm already under suspicion of being a card-carrying communist just because I'm your mate – but there were also quite a few rumours about a Tempest from 71 Squadron that crashed in Alaska last year.'

Drew nodded. 'The word on the grapevine at the time was that the guy had simply flown into the ground while trying to evade an F16.'

'Maybe, but my mate Spud, who was on 71 Squadron at the time, said it didn't add up.'

'Did he see it himself?'

'No, but he was out there with them and spoke to the pilot of the F16. They'd already broken off and were about to climb back to height when the Tempest flipped, hit the deck and exploded.'

'So they weren't even in combat when it happened?'

'Not according to the guy driving the F16.'

'Can we talk to Spud?'

'Difficult – he went on an exchange tour to America last month.'

Drew stood in silence for a moment.

'I was just thinking,' Nick said, glancing round the deserted crew room. 'If we were to have a snag with the jet at the north end of our operating area on the sortie this afternoon, the nearest diversion would be Leuchars. By an amazing coincidence that happens to be where 71 are based.'

'Nick, I'm surprised at you,' Drew said. 'What could possibly go wrong with a Tempest?'

'But purely hypothetically, just supposing it did,' Nick said, 'what do you suppose that snag might be?'

'I suppose, purely hypothetically, it could be fumes in the cockpit. We'd have to get straight down on the tarmac. We wouldn't want to be overcome by fumes, would we?'

'We certainly wouldn't, Drew.'

'Are you sure about this? There'll be some serious shit hitting the fan if we're rumbled.'

'With your recent track record who could possibly suspect us of anything so underhand?'

Ninety minutes later, as they were flying off the coast near Berwick, Drew began sniffing loudly.

'I can smell burning oil, Nick.'

'Me too,' Nick said.

Drew turned the jet to the north and flicked the radio switch. 'Pan. Pan. Pan. Tiger 2–1. Fumes in cockpit. Request immediate diversion to Leuchars.'

Descending towards Leuchars, Drew could see the massive road and rail bridges spanning the Forth and Edinburgh Castle jutting proudly above the city skyline to the south.

A pair of golfers on the links at St Andrews shaded their eyes and craned their necks to watch as the Tempest swept in over the sea. The sandy beaches slipped away under the left wing as Drew banked the jet for the final approach.

'You should see it during the Open,' Nick said. 'You can't get into Leuchars for all the jets lined up on the side of the runway. Every air marshal, vice-marshal and group captain who can swing it is there, strictly on Air Force business of course.'

The Tempest skimmed over the waves and Drew put it down onto the start of the runway, just thirty yards from the sea. The nose-wheel bounced and steadied and the puff of blue smoke from the tyres blew away in the slipstream. The plane juddered under reverse thrust as it slowed to taxiing speed.

A retinue of fire engines and ambulances had been scrambled to meet them. As they pulled to a halt, the engineers swarmed all over the aircraft, while the medical staff concentrated on them.

After twenty minutes of having their temperature and blood pressure taken, Nick led the way to 71 Squadron, showing Drew around Leuchars like a proud old boy on speech day.

They found half a dozen bored air crew in the crew room. To Drew's delight, Nick did not recognise a single one. Drew knew a couple of them from training courses and nodded a greeting.

'Drew, what brings you here?'

'Oh just the usual, Bob, an emergency.'

'Serious?'

'No, not really, just fumes in the cockpit.'

'Had a curry last night?'

Drew grinned. 'I can see why they put you on Quick Reaction Alert.'

'Well that's more than I can,' the 71 pilot said miserably, gesturing to the bulky flying kit he was wearing. 'It's been like this for the past four weeks. The only time I take this off is to crap and sleep. I wouldn't mind if there was some point to it all, but unless I'm missing a trick, I have the feeling that the threat from the East isn't quite what it once was.'

'But don't relax your vigilance for an instant,' Drew cautioned. 'Down at Finnington we're privy to some pretty high-grade intelligence reports and I happen to know for a fact that the Faeroe Islands are assembling an invasion force even as we speak. And if your jets are in the same state as ours, that's probably about all you're equipped to repel.'

The pilot nodded. 'Glad to know we're not alone. You should know by now, the top priority for spares are the

Tempests that are really vital to the UK's air defences: the ones we've sold to assorted Middle East sheikdoms.'

'And to think Nick calls me cynical,' Drew said, laughing.

'It's true though, isn't it?'

Drew nodded. 'Yeah, it's true all right.' He hesitated, unsure of how to broach the subject. 'Look, speaking of crap equipment, a couple of us on 21 have both had a problem with a Tempest recently, a sudden and total loss of control. The other guys managed to recover theirs, but I had to bang out of mine.'

There were no cynical comments this time from the 71 Squadron air crew. 'We haven't heard anything official.'

'I know, nothing shows up on the ADR either. They're trying to blame pilot error.'

The pilot studied Drew's face carefully. 'Are you sure that's not what it was?'

'I'm sure. I wondered if there were any similarities with the Tempest crash in Alaska last year. What was the story on that?'

'BA would be the one to tell you that.' The pilot got to his feet and shouted down the corridor. A few minutes later, a tall, dark-haired man sauntered in, wearing a ripped U2 teeshirt.

'Drew, this is BA,' the pilot said. 'It stands for Bad Attitude, by the way, not British Airways. He was flying the same sortie.'

'Drew Miller, good to meet you,' Drew said extending his hand.

BA gave Drew an appraising look. 'BA Stokes, what can I tell you?'

'What happened to the guy in Alaska last year?'

'His name was Mike Hanson. He died,' BA said shortly. 'Why do you want to know? Idle curiosity or something more?'

'Something more. I had to bang out of a Tempest over the Eden Valley recently, a mysterious fault that hasn't shown up on the ADR. I admit I'm clutching at straws, but I hoped you might be able to tell me something about the Alaska incident that would shed a little light on mine.'

BA shrugged. 'We were on a sortie protecting a package

of RS1s, being tapped by two F16s from the Air National Guard. Mike was countering an attack from one of them. It had just begun to pull away from him when he suddenly inverted and flew into the ground.'

'But according to the accident report it was pilot error,' Nick said.

BA looked contemptuous. 'Pilot error my arse. That's what they called it, but that's not what it looked like to me. I told them as much, but as usual they're not interested in what a lowly flight lieutenant has to say, especially if it contradicts the words of wisdom handed down from the ivory towers.'

Drew and Nick walked back to their aircraft, pretending not to notice the suspicious glances from the chief engineer, a dour lowland Scot. 'We've spent hours running these engines and I'm buggered if I can find anything wrong with them. Are you sure you didnae dream the whole thing?'

Drew gave him a smile as he signed the Form 700 to reassume control of the Tempest. 'That's fast jets for you. The only thing to do is go back up and wait for it to happen again.'

He bounded up the ladder into the cockpit.

'The fumes-in-cockpit ploy worked pretty well,' Drew said as soon as they were safely airborne. 'We'll have to use it again sometime.'

'Drew, don't forget the voice-tape,' Nick said.

'Why worry? They're not allowed to pull it unless we crash. And if we do, we'll probably be past caring.'

'All right,' Nick said. 'Don't say I didn't warn you. So what do we do now? It seems to me we've got a lot of puzzling coincidences, a few suspicions and a bit of hearsay, but nothing that couldn't be brushed off as paranoia by Power and his boys at the AIB.'

'Yeah, you're right. But the number of suspicious Tempest incidents is now up to five; I think it's high time I found out exactly how many more there've been.'

'How are you going to do that?'

'I'm going to lean on a friend.'

'Not me, I hope.'

Drew smiled. 'No, not you. Surprising though it may seem, I do have others.'

He made a phone call as soon as they had landed back at Finnington. 'Tom? That drink we talked about in Swaledale. How about it?'

'You've left it a bit late, mate. I'm going home for the weekend and then I'm off on attachment to NATO in Brussels next week.'

'How about tonight, then?'

'Well I've still got to pack,' Tom began. 'Oh, what the hell, why not? Where and when?'

'About nine o'clock? And a pub near you would suit me.'

'All right, the Cross Keys in Buckwell village. Know it?'

'I'll find it.'

Drew hung up, thought for a moment, then went in search of Russell. He eventually found him slumped, puce-faced, in the changing room after a game of squash.

Russell greeted him guardedly, but exploded when Drew talked about Strang and Hanson. 'What on earth does this have to do with you? It's bad enough you winding up your own squadron, without going round stirring up trouble elsewhere as well. My neck's on the line as well as yours, Drew, and I'm telling you, this is getting out of hand. Stop rocking the boat.'

'You're not going to tell me that there were fi—' Drew checked himself, remembering just in time that Russell had never been told about DJ's loss-of-control incident. '. . . Four entirely unconnected incidents in the last twelve months: the Swaledale crash, a guy from Leuchars, a guy from Valley, and me?'

Russell ignored the question. 'What were you doing at Leuchars anyway? The engineers there say there was nothing wrong with your aircraft.'

Drew hesitated, astonished at Russell's knowledge of his movements. 'Who told you?'

'I have my sources,' Russell said. 'Now, I've had enough of this. I forbid you to carry on these ridiculous amateur investigations. For the last time, it's a good aircraft. Just fly it – that's your job. Accident investigation is not your department. And in case you didn't get the message, Drew, that's a direct order. Do you understand?'

He pulled off his sweat-soaked squash kit and stomped into the showers.

Drew gazed thoughtfully after him, then glanced around the deserted changing room. He listened for the sound of water, then eased open Russell's locker and riffled through his uniform. He found what he was looking for in the breast pocket.

When he walked into the crew room, he found Michelle drinking coffee with Paul and Sandy. She raised an eyebrow as he dropped into the seat next to her.

'Michelle, I need a word with you in private.'

She looked at him coolly. 'Go ahead. I've no secrets from my crew.'

'It's about Alastair Strang.'

Her lips tightened as she glanced at the others. 'All right. Back in a minute, guys.'

She followed Drew out onto the edge of the airfield. They stood looking out across the acres of grey concrete as a jet rolled towards the end of the runway.

'What about Alastair?'

'I went to Valley and talked to some of his crewmates about his crash. They're sure it wasn't pilot error.'

'For Christ's sake,' she said. 'That's why I told you about him.'

He held up a hand. 'Just a minute, there's more. Nick and I diverted to Leuchars this morning. We talked to the guys at 71 Squadron about a crash in Alaska last year. The official version was that he flew into the ground during mock combat.'

'And?' She was now intrigued.

'The American F16 pilot he was up against said they'd already disengaged and were starting to climb back to height when the Tempest spun and crashed.'

Michelle started to speak but he interrupted her. 'Hang on, there's still more. On the way back from Valley I took a detour to go and talk to the farmer who witnessed the crash in Swaledale last week. He insists that the jet didn't fly into the ground: it simply fell out of the sky. He says that was in his statement to the AIB investigators.'

'A farmer's scarcely an expert witness.'

'He may not know the technicalities, but he can tell the difference between a flying object and a *falling* object. He said it came down like a shot grouse.'

'Even so, that still doesn't rule out pilot error. The pilot was a novice. He might have stalled it or lost it for all sorts of reasons.'

'No. Tempests aren't like choppers, Michelle.' He broke off immediately.

'I have flown fast jets, Drew.'

'I'm not patronising you. Tempests are different. The fly-by-wire system in a Tempest won't allow you to lose it like that.'

He paused as some air crew came straggling in after finishing a sortie, their flying suits stained with sweat.

'The stick used to be physically attached to the control surfaces of the aircraft by rods, levers and wires,' he said, when the last one had disappeared inside. 'Now it's attached to nothing but a computer. We still use a stick, but it could just as easily be a mouse or a keypad.

'When you pull on the stick, it doesn't move the tailplane mechanically: it sends a signal into the computer, which tells the tailplane what to do. When you push the throttles in your throttle box forward to engage combat power, the computer orders the fuel system to supply more fuel.'

'Thanks,' Michelle said drily. 'I always wanted a GCSE in aircraft mechanics.'

'It also thinks for you. If you're going to do something that will send the aircraft out of control, it will stop you from doing it.'

'That must be particularly valuable for you.' He gave her a weary look. 'Sorry,' she said, 'no more smart comments.'

'That I don't believe.' Drew smiled. 'Anyway the fly-by-wire system computes every command you make through your movement of the stick and the throttles. If it feels an instruction you've issued risks the aircraft departing from controlled flight, it'll countermand the order with another, safer one.'

Michelle remained unconvinced. 'Surely you're not saying there's no such thing as pilot error.'

'Of course not. The fly-by-wire isn't omnipotent. It can't

see if you're too close to the ground or about to fly into a hillside, and it can't tell if you've pushed too hard on a turn and blacked out under the G-force, in which case it might well allow you to plummet straight into the ground. But, if a jet in normal straight and level flight just drops out of the sky, it can't be pilot error.'

A Tempest began its take-off, drowning out any possibility of conversation for a minute as it rocketed down the runway, its massive engines bellowing.

They clapped their hands to their ears and Michelle stood lost in thought as it lifted off the runway and began a turn to the south. 'So where does all this leave us?' she asked finally.

'We have a series of five Tempest incidents already and those are just the ones I know about. The AIB is trying to blame pilot error for all of them – or the four they know about anyway. I know for a fact that it wasn't the cause of mine and the evidence I've heard so far suggests it may well not be the cause of any of them.'

Michelle's face still showed traces of doubt.

'Look Michelle. They're saying that your friend Alastair Strang – one of the best pilots on his squadron – killed himself by flying like a novice. What if there is actually a fault on the Tempest which they're concealing? It's bad enough that they're blackening the names of people who can no longer speak for themselves, but they're in danger of adding to the list.'

'Are you really suggesting a conspiracy?'

He spread his hands, palms upwards. 'I don't know what else it could be.' He gave her a long, appraising look. 'You know where this could lead, don't you?'

'If there is a cover-up – and I doubt it – it has nothing to do with my father. I know him, Drew.' She continued to hold the look, challenging him to disagree with her.

Finally he dropped his gaze. 'If you tell me that, then of course I believe you,' he said.

There was an embarrassed silence before Michelle spoke again. 'So what's the next step?' she asked.

'I've arranged to go and see a guy I know tonight.'

'But you're station duty officer. You're supposed to remain on the base in case the Russians invade or the toilets get blocked.'

'Yeah I know, but I don't have a choice.' He broke off. 'I can trust you, can't I?'

'Do you have to ask?'

He shook his head, embarrassed. 'No, of course not.'

'What's so important that it can't wait till you're off duty anyway?'

'I know a guy who works in the Accident Investigation Bureau. We've met at a few crash sites when I've been there with the Mountain Rescue team. He can get access to all the incident reports on the Tempest, but I have to see him tonight, because he's going on attachment to Brussels next week.'

Michelle looked puzzled. 'So why not go to see him tomorrow?'

'Because I'm under investigation myself and Russell's already on my back.'

'What will you do if something happens while you're off base?'

'It won't, but if it does I've got my bleeper.'

Michelle shook her head and laughed. 'You're mad. What'll happen if Russell finds out?'

'I hope he'll be far too busy sitting at home, playing with his model aeroplanes and polishing the buttons on his uniform.'

'So what time do you think you'll be back?'

'About midnight, I should think. Why?'

'If I'm still awake, I might drop by for a coffee.'

That evening, Drew slipped off the base and set off to Lincolnshire. The Cross Keys was a Brewer's Tudor road-house, a mile down the road from the AIB building at RAF Buckwell.

Tom was already standing at the bar, nursing a pint. He bought Drew one and then allowed himself to be steered to a corner table, away from the handful of regulars warming themselves by the log fire.

'It's good to see you,' Drew began. 'I'm glad I caught you before you left.'

Tom smiled and sipped his pint. 'So it's not just social then?'

'Not entirely, no,' Drew admitted. 'I need some help.'

'What kind of help?'

'Information.'

Tom frowned. 'Let me guess: about your Tempest incident?'

'How did you know?'

'I saw your name on the forty-eight-hour signal about the incident in the Eden Valley.' He fixed Drew with a steady gaze. 'I'd like to help you, Drew, but you must know that I can't discuss any aspect of the investigation with you. If you've questions to ask, they can only be addressed to the two officers conducting the inquiry.'

'But I don't want information about my crash,' Drew said, 'not specifically anyway. I want to know about Tempest incidents in general.'

'Keep your voice down, Drew, for God's sake. We're not discussing recipes here – you're asking me for classified information.'

Drew glanced around the pub. The regulars remained locked in their own conversations. 'Relax, Tom. The thought police have got the night off.'

Tom shook his head slowly. 'You're not that naive, Drew. Every telephone call in or out of the AIB building is logged. It won't look good for either you or me if it's discovered that a pilot under investigation has been in unauthorised contact with a member of the AIB staff.'

'So why did you agree to meet me, then?'

'Because I didn't think you were such a bloody fool.'

'But since I'm here . . .' Drew persisted.

Tom paused. 'Since you're here, you might as well get whatever it is off your chest.'

Drew glanced round the room again. 'Can you get me a printout of every Tempest incident in the last couple of years?'

Tom burst out laughing. 'Are you really that naive? It's not just phone calls: every single sheet of paper that goes through that printer is logged against the recipient. I've no reason to access that information, let alone print it. And even if that wasn't detected, any copy of it turning up elsewhere will automatically be traced straight back to me.'

'No one but me will see it.'

'I'm not taking that chance. I've got a nice cosy posting in Brussels for a couple of months and then I'm back in the cockpit. I'm not going to risk that by ruffling any feathers in the meantime.'

'Come on, Tom, I'm not asking you for the crown jewels here.'

He shook his head emphatically. 'You don't know what it's like to be stuck in a ground job, Drew. My career's on the line if I do this.'

Drew held his gaze. 'Your life might be if you don't.'

'Isn't that a bit melodramatic?'

'I don't know,' Drew said evenly. 'I only know of three fatal crashes so far, so perhaps the odds aren't too bad. How many do you know about?'

Tom looked away.

Drew allowed the silence to deepen. 'You know more than you're saying, don't you, Tom? You know there's something wrong with it. Do you sleep well at night?'

'Get off my case, Drew,' Tom said angrily. 'You keep pushing me and I'll walk out of that door and you'll get nothing.'

Drew looked him straight in the eye. 'I'm counting on you.' Again there was a long silence. 'Look, if you can't print anything off, just tell me instead.'

Tom hesitated. 'I can't. I don't know it all. A memo came down from on high well over a year ago, saying that all material relating to Tempest incidents would in future be handled by the office of the head of AIB. Anything that's come in since then has been passed straight up the line. I've been to a couple of the crash sites, as you know, but I've had no part in the subsequent investigations.'

'Who's been handling it then?'

'Air Vice-Marshal Power and his deputy. They co-opt other personnel as they need them, not necessarily AIB.'

'Like Squadron Leader George Gordon?'

'Could be. I've seen his name on quite a few reports, so Power obviously thinks highly of him.'

Drew pushed his hands through his hair, fighting his frustration. 'There must be something on computer though.'

Tom ticked the points off on his fingers. 'There's the bare details of each incident: where, when, fatalities, probable cause listed in the forty-eight-hour signal, the final conclusion of the Board of Inquiry – in those incidents where it's reached one.' He glanced at Drew. 'And any disciplinary action taken against the pilot.'

'Can you show me what you've got?'

Tom shook his head, exasperated. 'I could, but if you drive up to the gate, the guard will record in his log that Drew Miller visited Tom Marshall. If you make any use of the information, that entry in the log will be enough to drop me right in the shit.'

'You'd be in that anyway,' Drew said. 'According to you, they've already got a record of my call this afternoon. But Drew Miller isn't coming to see you tonight.'

Tom looked at him suspiciously. 'What do you mean?'

Drew smiled. 'I'll give you five minutes' start. Just go back to your office and wait. Someone will be along to see you, but it won't be me.'

'I really shouldn't be doing this,' Tom said, half to himself, but he was already rising to his feet, leaving the rest of his drink unfinished on the table. Drew waited a few minutes, then followed him out into the night.

Chapter 9

Drew stopped a few hundred yards from the barrier at RAF Buckwell, pulled a card from his pocket and peered at it. He hesitated for a moment, then abruptly put the car into gear. He drove past a sign warning: 'This is a restricted area within the meaning of the Official Secrets Act. Use of deadly force is authorised.'

He waved the ID card as imperiously as he could at the night guard, a military policeman in combat uniform. Stamping to keep himself warm against the chill of the night air, he held an assault rifle, its muzzle pointing down towards the ground.

'Wing Commander Russell to see Flight Lieutenant Marshall. I'm expected.'

The photograph looked nothing like Drew, but at night and with the weight of his rank behind him, Drew reckoned he could bluff his way through.

The MP sprang to attention but to Drew's horror, he took the ID from his hand and then stepped back into the pool of light from the gatehouse.

He studied it carefully, raised his eyes to stare at Drew and then looked down again at the card, shaking his head. 'I know most of these cards make people look like Dracula's grandmother, sir, but this is going beyond a joke. I'm going to have to go and make some security checks on this.'

Drew sat sweating in his car as the MP disappeared inside and picked up the phone, keeping a wary eye on him through the window. Drew was not remotely reassured to see that the muzzle of the MP's rifle was now pointing directly at him.

He kept his face impassive, but panic was mounting in him. Shit, he thought. Why did I get myself into this? I've really blown it this time. Although he tried to force himself to keep calm, he could see no option but to make a break for it. In the absence of the duty officer, the guard would be put through to Russell's house and, when Russell discovered that Drew was absent from his post, it wouldn't take a genius to put two and two together.

He slipped the gear stick into reverse. He waited for a couple of seconds as he steadied his breathing and measured the distance to the guard and the assault rifle cradled in his hands.

How long would it take the guard to drop the phone, get out of the gatehouse, slip off the safety catch, raise the rifle to his shoulder, aim and fire? Drew reckoned he might have four seconds, more if the guard froze in surprise. He glanced in his rear-view mirror: it was twenty metres back to the main road.

There was a stand of pines at either side of the entry. If Drew could hit first gear before the guard had taken aim, he doubted if he would be able to get a shot away at all before the car disappeared behind the trees.

Even if he got away, Drew knew that a hue and cry would be raised long before he could get back to Finnington, but he'd have to try to bluff out the reason for his absence. Of course if the guard had already noted his licence plate . . .

Drew reached forward to switch off his lights, hoping the MP would assume that he was just conserving his battery. The man glanced up but made no move to come out of the gatehouse.

Drew decided to wait until he began speaking into the phone before making his break. He gripped the wheel tightly with his right hand, his left holding the handbrake off the catch.

As he waited, he visualised the escape run: floor the accelerator and, as soon as the back wheels were clear of the fenceline, spin the steering wheel left, hit the brakes, crash-change into first gear even while the car was still travelling backwards and roar off up the road fishtailing under the acceleration.

He could feel the hairs on the back of his neck rising as he imagined the guard drawing a bead on him with his rifle. He swallowed nervously as he watched the man fumble with the RAF directory and then start to run his fingers down a list of numbers. Finally he began dialling, mouthing each number in turn as he did so.

There was a long pause.

Drew was about to release the handbrake when he saw a glow in the darkness behind him. A car was travelling along the main road. Cursing, he forced himself to wait for it to pass, not willing to risk a collision that could leave him a sitting target.

The car took an eternity to reach the gap in the pines. As it did, it swung off the road, the lights still on main beam, dazzling Drew as he stared into the mirror. Before he could react, the car was pulling up behind him, trapping him against the barrier. The driver tooted his horn, but the MP merely glanced up and waved an acknowledgement with the telephone handset.

'It's the guard at RAF Buckwell here.' The MP's voice carried on the still night air. 'I've got an officer who says he's Wing Commander Russell at the gate, but the picture on his ID is just about unrecognisable.'

Drew started to sweat harder as the man said something into the phone that Drew did not catch, then looked up and stared intently at him. He put the phone down and came out of the guardhouse, walking to the front of the car. He wrote down the registration number.

The MP went back inside and picked up the phone again. As Drew listened to him reciting the number down the phone, he resigned himself to the worst.

He heard the guard say, 'Of course, immediately,' and watched as he came out of the gatehouse again, assault rifle still held at the ready.

'Sir?' Drew pretended to look up. 'Will you step out of the car, please sir?'

The guard moved back, keeping his distance as Drew opened the door. He looked blankly at the MP. 'What now?'

The man gestured towards the guardhouse. 'The phone, sir, an officer at Finnington wants to speak to you.'

Leaden-footed, Drew walked into the guardhouse and picked up the phone. Even though he knew any attempt at deception was now futile, he could not stop himself from making a feeble attempt to disguise his voice as he said, 'Hello.'

The answer was a peal of laughter. 'That's twice I've rescued you now.'

The guard was momentarily out of earshot, round the far side of Drew's car. 'God, Michelle, you nearly gave me a heart attack. What are you doing there?'

'I thought I'd just mind the store for you. It won't do any good if anything serious happens, but I can answer the phone . . . and save you from a court martial when a guard gets suspicious.'

Drew lowered his voice as the MP reached the front of the car. 'What did you tell him?'

Michelle laughed again. 'I said the duty officer was in the bog, but I'd vouch for the Wing Commander. I told him you were always being stopped, because the photo on your ID is an old one and the handlebar moustache makes you look like Biggles after a bad night in Borneo. I said the saddest thing of all was that you won't get a new one because you actually think the picture makes you look good.'

'Why did the MP come peering at my number plate?'

'I gave him your car registration number as a double check. Now hurry up and get back here.'

'Why, losing your nerve?' he said, recovering slightly.

'No, I want that nightcap when you get back.'

The guard glanced up at him and chuckled as Drew walked back to his car. 'Quite a sense of humour that Flight Lieutenant Power, hasn't she?'

'Oh yes,' Drew said, 'quite a sense of humour.'

He put the car in gear to drive through the gates. The guard paused with his hand on the barrier and called out,

'Sir, just one more thing.' Drew shot him a nervous look. 'I don't care what anybody else says, the picture makes you look very distinguished . . .'

Drew noticed the guard's lip tremble as he stifled a laugh.

'. . . but please get a new photograph taken. Your own mother wouldn't recognise you from this one.'

'You're probably right, Sergeant. I'll do that.'

Shoulders shaking, the guard waved Drew on towards the mock-classical frontage of the AIB building and retired to his gatehouse.

Tom stood waiting just inside the huge double doors.

'What the hell was going on with the guard? I had about five sets of kittens while I was waiting.'

'You had kittens? It was me the gun was pointing at.'

Tom led Drew through the echoing corridors of the darkened building, punching in security codes on two doors marked RESTRICTED ACCESS.

In a sprawling open-plan office, he accessed the computer and called up a file on screen. Drew's eyes flickered over the heading: 'Secret, authorised personnel only', as he began to read.

The file was a listing of dates of Tempest incidents with minimal detail. He scribbled frantically in a notebook, recording each incident as Tom scrolled steadily down the screen. When Drew had finished, he scanned back over his notes, staggered. In the last two years alone, there had been nine Tempest crashes and nine other serious incidents involving temporary loss of control.

They gazed at each other.

'Didn't you know how many there were?' Drew asked.

Tom shook his head. 'I had no idea there were this many. None of us did, as far as I know.'

'There are no names or squadrons listed on this. How am I going to find the guys who survived those crashes?'

Tom shrugged. 'There's nothing on computer, so, unless you're going to try stopping air crew at random and asking them, I don't hold out much hope for you.'

Drew thought for a minute as Tom still stared at the screen. 'Are there any other files I can see?' Tom shook his head. 'What about the individual reports?'

'I told you, the investigations have been handled directly by Power's own office.'

'But there must be something on computer?'

Tom shrugged helplessly. 'If there was, I wouldn't know where to find it.'

Drew stared at him, unblinking. 'You must know something else.'

'All I know – and it's nothing more than a rumour really – is that there's a project code-named Operation Brushfire.' Tom hesitated. 'There's supposed to be a Tempest set up on a test bed at Barnwold. It's in a secure hangar in the skunk works site, so no one can get anywhere near it. Apparently they're doing everything short of dropping bombs on it, to try and replicate the problem.'

'And what have they found?'

Tom shrugged. 'As far as I know, nothing.'

'So call up Brushfire on the computer and see what comes up.'

Tom stared at him, incredulous. 'Jesus, Drew! You don't want much do you? Why don't you just drive down there and ask to see it?'

'Please, Tom. Just do me this one last favour and I'm out of here and out of your hair.'

Shaking his head, Tom turned back to the keyboard. A few seconds later there was an electronic tone and a message flashed up on screen: 'Authorisation Code?'

Tom frowned

'Do you have the code?' Drew asked.

'I'm not sure. It depends at what level of secrecy it's been classified. I'm only cleared up to a certain level.'

'Try it,' Drew said impatiently.

'Come on, Drew, be reasonable. Haven't I stuck my neck out far enough already?'

Drew gave him a baleful look. 'Listen Tom, just to get here tonight, I've already deserted my post and impersonated an officer, using a stolen ID card. I make that three potential court martials. All I'm asking you to do is access a file.'

Tom still hesitated.

'Something is very wrong here, Tom,' Drew went on more gently. 'You can see that as well as I can. There is a fault on the Tempest – the aircraft that we both fly – that is killing people, friends of you and me.'

He paused to allow Tom to weigh his words. 'I know you, Tom. I've watched your face when you've seen the bodies at crash sites. You go to an awful lot of them but you've never become so hardened that you've forgotten your humanity. You're not going to sit by and let more people die needlessly if you can do something to help stop it.'

Tom gave Drew a long, hard stare, then punched in a code.

There was a second, louder electronic tone and another message flashed on screen: 'Access Denied.'

'Shit, shit, shit.' Tom put his face in his hands.

'What is it?' Drew asked.

'Any unauthorised attempt to access a secret file is logged by the computer and the details sent to security.'

Drew shrugged his shoulders. 'Just play the innocent. Tell them you were curious what Brushfire was and didn't realise you weren't cleared to see it. They're not going to shoot you for it, are they? You didn't get access, so you didn't find anything out.'

'And it's that simple is it?' Tom said with heavy sarcasm. 'Look, Drew, just go now, will you? I'm in enough shit as it is for one night.'

'All right,' Drew said quietly, 'and Tom? Thanks.'

Tom just grunted in reply. As he was about to lead the way back out of the office, Drew's bleeper sounded. Tom waved him to a phone.

As soon as Drew heard Michelle's voice, he knew he was in trouble. 'Drew, I'm out of my depth I'm afraid. There's been an intruder alert. I tried to pacify the guard here and told him you'd gone staggering off to the bog with a bad case of diarrhoea, but when he couldn't find you straightaway he insisted on calling out Russell. I'm going to do a runner before he gets here. Sorry, I've done what I could.'

Drew hung up and turned to Tom. 'You'll be glad to know we're both in the shit.'

Tom showed him to the door. Drew shook his hand, then ran to his car. The MP was still grinning at him from the gatehouse as he raised the barrier.

Drew flogged the car up the motorway at over a hundred,

but it still took him ninety minutes to get back to Finnington. A nervous, flustered-looking young airman stopped him at the barrier. 'Your ID, sir, please.'

Drew reached into his pocket and handed over the card. The airman fumbled with it and it slipped from his fingers and went under the car. 'Sorry sir,' he said. 'It's been a bit of a nerve-racking evening.'

'What happened?' Drew asked, getting out to help.

'We had an intruder alert. I've spent two hours thinking some IRA man was going to sneak up behind me and blow my head off, and in the middle of all the panic Wing Commander Russell arrived with no ID, demanding to be let in.'

Drew froze and then dropped to his knees alongside the airman and began searching feverishly under the car.

'Got it,' the airman said, triumphantly brandishing the card. Drew snatched it back from him.

'Sorry,' he said, his heart pounding. 'Just remembered, that's my squash club membership card.' He took his own ID out of his wallet and handed it over, slipping Russell's card back into his pocket. 'What happened about the Wing Commander?' he asked as his pulse rate returned to normal.

'I had to keep him waiting at the barrier for twenty minutes, until another officer arrived to vouch for him. The Wing Commander got very heated about it,' the airman said unhappily, 'but I'm new at Finnington and I didn't know him, so I couldn't just wave him through, could I, sir?'

'You did exactly the right thing,' Drew assured him, smiling.

He drove in to the operational area but sneaked into the deserted Ops room and used the photocopier for five minutes before heading for Russell's office. He found the Wing Commander pacing the floor, incandescent with rage.

'Where the hell have you been, Miller?'

'I'm really sorry, sir. I slipped out for ten minutes to meet someone but then I couldn't start my car and it took the AA an hour to get to me.'

Russell held his hand up for silence. 'I'm not interested in your excuses. This isn't a prep school where you can skip lessons if you feel like it and get away with an hour in detention. This base is a vital part of the defence system of this country. You were left in charge of it overnight as duty officer and you abandoned your post on a whim. It's tantamount to desertion. I put my trust in you and this is how you repay me. Any further trouble and you'll be on a one-way ticket out of the Air Force altogether.'

Drew waited until Russell simmered down. 'Thank you, sir. It won't happen again.'

'You're damn right it won't. Now, can I take it that you'll be able to manage the rest of your stint without popping out again on some errand or other?'

'Yes, sir.'

Russell turned on his heel and headed for the door, but Drew called him back. 'Sir, before you go there's something I think you ought to know.' He produced his notebook from his pocket and began reading the list of crashes and near misses.

Russell stood silently through the recital, then held out his hand for the notebook. 'Let me see that.'

Drew hesitated for a moment, then shrugged and handed it over.

Russell glanced impatiently through it but then, visibly shocked, he read the entries again more carefully.

Finally he looked up. 'This is clearly classified information. Where did you get it?'

'I'm afraid I can't tell you that, sir, but you have to agree that it rather supports my point of view.'

'I will raise this through the proper channels,' Russell said, regaining his equilibrium, 'but there's nothing concrete here. Coincidence isn't evidence.'

'But you must warn the Tempest squadrons.'

'Must?' Russell said. 'On whose say-so, pray? A flight lieutenant with an axe to grind? Tempest RS1s and RS3s have probably flown well over twenty thousand operational sorties and many hundreds of thousands of flying hours in the past four years. Yet you want me to try and get them grounded because you don't believe there's such a thing as pilot error?'

Russell turned to go.

'Sir?'

'Yes?' Russell said, exhaling heavily.

Drew held out his hand. 'If that'll be all, I'd like my notebook.'

Russell shook his head. 'I'm afraid not.'

'But it's just a list of dates and coincidences, sir.'

'No, Drew. This is classified material, however insubstantial, and I'm retaining it. And that, Flight Lieutenant, is my final word on the subject.'

Drew waited until he heard the sound of Russell's footsteps recede down the corridor, then opened the door and walked to the changing rooms. He dropped Russell's ID on the floor and kicked it under a bench for the cleaners to find in the morning.

A few hours later, Drew nosed his way into the early-morning traffic. He took a circuitous route home, past the Conservative Party offices. A large billboard stood to one side of the building. Beneath the headline NORMAN FEATHER MP – A LOCAL MAN SERVING LOCAL PEOPLE, a grey-haired, patrician figure stared out into the bright future that awaited him and his constituents.

Drew pulled in for a moment, scribbled down the telephone number printed at the bottom of the poster and then drove back to the flat. As soon as he had shut the door, he dialled the number.

He reached the MP's secretary, only to be politely but firmly brushed off. 'If it's a constituency matter, Mr Feather holds surgeries on Saturday mornings between ten and twelve.'

'It's not a constituency matter,' Drew interrupted. 'It's a matter of national security.'

'I see. And who might you be, sir?'

'I'm . . . I'm a serving officer in the Royal Air Force. It's vitally important that I contact him.'

'I'm afraid he's here in London until Friday evening.'

'Then I'm happy to see him there. Is there not a five-minute hole somewhere in his schedule?'

'I'll have to check with him,' she said doubtfully. 'Give me your number and I'll call you back.'

Drew had wandered into the kitchen to make some coffee when the phone rang. 'Norman Feather's secretary here, Mr Miller. He could see you at the House of Commons for a few minutes at six tomorrow evening.'

'Thank you. I'll be there.'

Before he collapsed into bed he also phoned Michelle. A drowsy voice answered him. 'Hi, this is your wake-up call,' Drew said. 'Vital mission briefing, my flat, eight o'clock tonight.'

'I'd better bring the crew along.'

'No, that won't be necessary,' Drew said. 'It's confidential, strictly on a need-to-know basis.'

'All right, I'll come alone. Anything I need bring with me?'

'Don't worry,' Drew said. 'I've already got all the essential equipment.' He didn't wait for an answer.

The alarm sounded at three p.m. Drew spent the next few hours shopping, cooking, dusting, hoovering and polishing. He cleaned the bedroom, changed the sheets and was just applying the finishing touches to the dinner table when the doorbell rang. Surprised, he looked at his watch.

'Fifteen minutes early. God, you're keen,' he said as he opened the door, then faltered when he saw Russell standing there. 'Oh, it's you sir.'

'Evening, Drew, may I come in?' Russell answered his own question by stepping past Drew into the flat.

'I've got someone coming round shortly, sir,' Drew said.

'This won't take a moment. I've taken up the issues you raised through the relevant channels. As I suspected, you've rather got the wrong end of the stick. I'm not at liberty to tell you what action is being taken, but you can rest assured that it is being dealt with. They're very concerned about the security aspects, however.'

'The security aspects?' Drew said blankly. 'National security?'

'The unauthorised acquisition of classified documents. The Military Police may want to talk to you about that in due course. In the meantime I don't want to hear any more from you on the subject of the Tempest. From now on keep your mind on the job and your mouth shut.'

Drew was about to reply when the bell rang.

He opened the door. Michelle was on the step holding a bottle of champagne and a pair of chocolate handcuffs. She gave him a glorious smile. 'I know you said you'd got your own equipment, but these might come in useful; if there's a raid, I can eat the evidence.'

She started to laugh at Drew's look of consternation, then caught sight of Russell.

Russell gave her an ingratiating smile as he stepped towards the door. He eyed the chocolate handcuffs. 'Flight Lieutenant Power. I'm not sure your father would approve of the company you keep.'

'I'm not sure the company I keep would be any of my father's business,' she said. 'In case you hadn't noticed, sir, I'm not only past the age of consent, I'm also off duty this evening, but I'll be sure to mention your concern for my welfare next time we speak.'

'So what was that about?' Michelle asked when Russell had gone.

'Nothing much – another bollocking for daring to suggest there might be something wrong with the Tempest.'

He kicked the door shut and took the champagne from her, raising an eyebrow at the handcuffs.

'Don't let your imagination run away with you,' Michelle said. 'The only things on the menu tonight are dinner and conversation.' She looked around the living room. 'Nice place, Drew. Does anyone live here or is it just a shrine to early-nineties Habitat?'

'No, it's definitely occupied. If you look closely you can see the imprint of a pair of mid-nineties RAF buttocks in the armchair.'

She waited for him to pop the cork on the champagne. 'How's the investigation coming along? Was it worth going AWOL last night?'

He hesitated for a fraction of a second. 'There are one hell of a lot more Tempest incidents: eighteen in all over the last two years, nine of them fatal.'

The laughter vanished from her eyes. 'Jesus! Any idea why?'

'None at all. The investigations are all being handled directly by the head of the AIB's office . . .' He paused to study her expression.

'Just because his office is investigating it doesn't mean my father's personally involved.'

'Oh come on, Michelle. That's like the Prime Minister saying he didn't know about it because it was only discussed in Cabinet.'

There was a long silence and when Drew glanced up, Michelle was giving him a baleful stare.

'All right, I'm sorry,' Drew said. 'No more barbed remarks about your father.'

'Good,' she said, relenting a little. 'So what are you going to do?'

'I'm going to give the information to my MP. I've arranged to see him at the House of Commons tomorrow evening.'

'It's not Tam Dalyell is it?' Drew shook his head. 'A pity. Don't hold your breath then. Even if he does raise it for you, the odds are that the answer will either be waffle or they'll invoke national security and that'll be the end of his interest in the subject.'

Drew shrugged. 'I don't have too many other choices.'

She sipped her drink, studying him for a moment over the rim of her glass. 'What about the press?'

'That would really be stepping outside the system.'

She almost choked on her champagne. 'Unlike deserting your post, impersonating an officer and faking a problem with your jet?' She was silent for a moment. 'Of course you could always wait for the AIB to sort it out; that's what they're there for, after all.'

His look was incredulous. 'Are you serious?'

'Why not? You're surely not suggesting that they're not even trying to find the fault?'

Drew shook his head. 'I'm sure they're trying to find it, but I'm equally sure that they're going to keep sweeping the problem under the carpet until they do.'

'And what if that's the best thing to do?'

'And meanwhile, Tempests keep crashing and air crew keep dying,' he said. 'How can it be the best thing to do? It's already cost eighteen lives. God knows how many more it might claim.'

'Including yours, perhaps. How can you keep flying an aircraft if you know – or at least strongly suspect – it's flawed? How can you keep getting back in the cockpit?'

Drew measured his words. 'The thought had occurred to me, but what's the alternative? Stop flying altogether? Leave the RAF? I couldn't do it. Flying fast jets *is* risky. There's also the feeling . . .' He broke off and gave an embarrassed smile. 'This sounds stupid . . .'

'Go on,' Michelle said.

'I also have the feeling that if I stop flying I'm ratting on the mates who keep doing it. If I don't go up, someone else has to fly my sorties.' He struggled to say more, then shrugged his shoulders. 'I can't explain.'

He drained his glass and poured himself another. 'Anyway, lightning doesn't strike twice, does it?' His tone was brittle.

'Don't count on it,' she said. 'I remember reading a story in a magazine about a man who'd been struck by lightning five times.' Michelle gazed into her drink, watching the bubbles spiralling to the surface as she swirled the glass around in her hand. After a while she put it down on the table and said, 'I'm sorry, this stuff suddenly doesn't taste right any more.'

When she stood up to leave, Drew made no attempt to dissuade her.

To his surprise, Michelle was waiting for him when he and Nick pulled up at the squadron the next morning. Nick smiled to himself as he greeted Michelle and then disappeared inside the building.

'How are you getting down to London today?' Michelle asked Drew.

'Catching the train.'

'I'll give you a lift if you like. I've got to take a Puma down to Northolt this afternoon.' She hesitated a second. 'And what are you doing after you've seen your MP?'

Drew shrugged. 'Going home again, I suppose.'

'Do you want to come and have dinner at my place?'

'Back here?'

'No, our house in St Albans. You could stay over and come back up with me first thing tomorrow.' She bit her lip. 'My father'll be there as well.'

'You didn't mention this last night.'

'It was a spur-of-the-moment thing.'

'I'm not sure how thrilled he'd be to have me on the guest list.'

'He suggested it, as a matter of fact. I told him you were going to be in London and he said he was keen to meet you.'

Drew tried to keep the disbelief from his voice. 'We didn't exactly hit it off the last time. Why would he want to do it again?'

Michelle shrugged. 'Because you're a friend of mine, I suppose. I don't think he's planning to size you up as potential son-in-law material, if that's what's worrying you.'

'No, that's not what's worrying me at all.'

Michelle gave him a look of exasperation and turned to walk away. 'If the idea doesn't appeal to you, Drew, just forget it.'

'Sorry,' he called after her. 'Yes, I'd like the lift and the dinner very much.' He pushed through the doors and walked down the corridor towards the crew room.

Chapter 10

Michelle brought the Puma skimming in to land at Northolt late in the afternoon. Looking south, Drew could see the giants of the London skyline – the Telecom tower, the Nat-West tower, Canary Wharf – lit by the afternoon sun.

She followed his gaze. 'Not bad is it? The tourists pay a thousand pounds for a sightseeing trip like this and you're getting it free.'

She shut the engine down and pulled off her flying helmet, then turned to Drew and handed him a piece of paper. 'Call me when you know which train you're getting and I'll pick you up from the station.'

Drew caught the tube into London, picking up the Circle Line round to Westminster. He joined the queue of visitors to the House of Commons, shuffling through the electronic security gates and presenting their bags for inspection by the police. The benches in the lobby were full of people talking in huddles or gazing at the ceiling as they waited for their MPs.

He gave his name to the clerk and sat down on the bench, looking curiously around him. Five minutes later, his name was called. He walked back to the clerk's desk where Feather, more florid than in his photograph, detached himself from a group of people and held out his hand. He was wearing a regimental tie and pinstriped, three-piece suit.

'Flight Lieutenant Miller, a pleasure to meet you,' the MP said with casual insincerity. 'Why don't you join me for a drink and tell me what's so vital to our national security that it won't wait until my constituency surgery on Saturday?'

He led the way to Annie's Bar and bought Drew a beer, rebuffing his offer. 'Regulations of the House, I'm afraid. Can't have outsiders getting us drunk. We're perfectly capable of doing that for ourselves.' He gave a short, barking laugh, glancing surreptitiously at his watch as he did so. 'Now, tell me how I can help.'

Drew outlined the problem with the Tempest while Feather listened attentively and made a few notes.

'You did the right thing coming to me, Flight Lieutenant,' Feather said. 'As a former military man myself, I know what courage it takes to go outside the normal channels. There is clearly a matter of concern here. Rest assured that I shall be raising it with the Minister at the earliest possible opportunity.'

'On the floor of the House?' Drew asked, not entirely won over by Feather's smooth assurances.

'Or in a written question. Sometimes these things are better handled that way, particularly where national security can so easily be invoked to avoid a direct answer to a spoken question.'

He held out his hand. 'Let me have all the documentation and I'll see what I can flush out of them.'

Drew hesitated for a second, then handed over one of the photocopies he'd made in the Ops room when he got back from Buckwell.

Feather scanned the pages. 'That should be enough to set the ball rolling. I'll drop you a line to let you know the response.'

'I'm just worried that the MoD may try to sweep it under the carpet.'

'Don't worry on that score, young man. I have a reputation for straight talking,' Feather said, allowing his gaze to settle for a moment on his reflection in the mirror behind the bar. 'When Norman Feather gets his teeth into something, it takes more than a few pen-pushers and Whitehall mandarins to stop him getting at the truth.'

He glanced at his watch again. 'Now, I'm afraid you really must excuse me. I'll show you out. This place is like a rabbit warren.'

Drew followed him back to the lobby, where the MP offered a perfunctory handshake and a fleeting smile and then disappeared back into the maze of oak-panelled corridors.

Drew stepped out into a damp, grey London evening. If Feather did not force something out of the MoD, it was beginning to look like the newspapers were his last hope. The thought did not please him at all.

He phoned Michelle from the station, then caught the train to St Albans. She was waiting for him in a dark-blue Jaguar.

'Very nice,' Drew said as he dropped into the passenger seat.

Michelle nodded. 'And before you ask, yes, it *is* courtesy of the taxpayer.'

She drove quickly across the town centre and down a steep hill past the abbey. At the bottom she slowed and turned in through a stone arch. The electronic gates swung silently open at their approach. She pulled up by the iron-studded oak door of a substantial manor house. A wisteria, its trunk as thick as Drew's waist, twisted up the honey-coloured stonework and warm light glowed from the leaded windows.

As he got out of the car he could hear the whisper of water somewhere beyond the sweeping lawns and glimpsed two ghostly white shapes unfurling their wings in the shadows by the trees.

'Geese?' he asked.

'Swans.'

'Is there a pond in the garden?'

She laughed. 'Yes, though we usually call it the lake.'

She led him inside, through an oak-panelled hall and into a huge drawing room. Drew looked around. A log fire was blazing in the inglenook fireplace, its light reflected in crystal and porcelain vases. A series of portraits of long-dead nobles gazed sternly down from the walls, defying anyone to sit in the chesterfields or armchairs in their presence. Copies of

The Field, *Horse and Hound* and *Country Life* were stacked neatly on the table, and a large, rather overblown flower arrangement stood on a plinth against the wall.

'Very nice,' Drew said, turning back to Michelle. 'Does anybody live here or is it just a shrine to 1620s Habitat?'

She smiled. 'Careful, Drew, your chips are showing.' She gestured to the sofa. 'My father'll be down in a minute. Make yourself at home, I'll get you a drink.'

Michelle sauntered out and Drew wandered around the room, pausing to peer at the photographs crowding the lid of the grand piano. Charles Power's face stared out of many of them, expressionless but for the faintest of smiles. Drew picked them up one by one: Power with Margaret Thatcher, Power with Norman Schwarzkopf, Power with Prince Charles, Power surrounded by sharp-suited civilians, shaking hands with an Arab sheik.

He looked round as Michelle came back into the room, followed by her father. Drew extended his hand. 'Hello, sir,' he said. 'A pleasure to see you again. I was just admiring the room. Nice curtains.'

Power exchanged glances with his daughter, but his urbane expression did not even flicker.

'Right,' Michelle said. 'I'm going to let you two do a bit of male bonding, while I check on dinner.' She picked up her glass and moved off towards the kitchen, ignoring the silent plea in Drew's eyes.

Power motioned Drew to one of the armchairs, then stood with his back to the fire. 'So, Drew, you're champing at the bit to get to Bosnia, no doubt?'

Drew could not decide whether Power was being ironic.

'Absolutely, sir. There's no place I'd rather be.'

'Good, good,' Power said, deadpan. He pressed the tips of his fingers together and rested his chin on them for a moment, studying Drew like a surgeon planning his first incision.

'Tell me, what do you know about Operation Brushfire?'

Drew was startled by the directness of the question, but he kept his face straight. 'Nothing at all. What is it?'

Power was watching him narrowly as he replied. 'A classified operation. I rather thought you might have got wind of it in the course of your freelance investigations into the safety record of the Tempest.' Drew shook his head. 'I don't know what documents you've been shown, nor how you came to have access to classified information outside your own sphere of activities, but a man of your intelligence must realise how dangerous it is to base conclusions on partial knowledge of the evidence.'

Drew did not respond.

Power let the silence grow for a minute before speaking again. 'If there is a problem with the Tempest, it must be dealt with. There is no dispute between us about that. Our only difference of opinion may be in how to go about doing so.'

He reached for a drink, the ice clinking in the glass. 'I know you're acting from the best of motives, Drew, and I admire you for it, but there is a better way of dealing with this situation. The Tempest is not a perfect aircraft – none of them are – but it is a damn good one. We're aware of the possibility of a problem, however slight it may be, and we're looking into it with our customary thoroughness. If there is a fault – and so far the evidence is entirely circumstantial – then we shall find it. Have no doubt about that whatsoever.'

'That's very reassuring, sir,' Drew said, his tone neutral.

When he spoke again, Power's voice had taken on a harder edge. 'Even supposing we accepted your hypothesis that there's a mysterious fault with the Tempest, what would you like us to do? Take fifty per cent of our front-line aircraft out of service? How do you think it would be looked on if we were unable to meet our commitments in Bosnia or the Falklands? Do you imagine the politicians would be happy about that?'

'We might find out the answer to that sooner than you think.'

Power's smile deepened. 'I wouldn't expect too much from Norman Feather if I were you. If you'd done your research properly, you'd have discovered that he's not only a member of the Select Committee on Defence, he's also a member of my club.

'Norman spoke to me after your tête-à-tête with him earlier this evening and I was able to confirm that we have taken energetic steps to investigate the cause of the recent Tempest losses while maintaining our nation's air defences in an efficient and – most importantly – cost-effective manner. There are plenty of politicians less responsible than Norman Feather, who would jump on any bandwagon to force through defence cuts: "If the planes are no good, then scrap the lot of them" – that sort of thing. Is that really what you'd like to see?'

'Obviously not, but I think we've strayed from the point.'

Power shook his head. 'The point is that, in the present climate, it's up to all of us to pull together. By spreading needless concern about the safety of the Tempest, you're not only making waves for yourself, you're making waves for your squadron and its commander. The Defence Review is imminent and we're likely to lose another squadron . . . and see more redundancies among air crew.'

He left the threat hanging in the air. 'We're by no means unsympathetic and, as I've said, we're all working flat out to ascertain the facts. But meanwhile, the best – the only – option is to carry on as normal. Flying has always been a risky business and there may or may not be an additional risk in flying Tempests, but that is nothing compared to the risk to the country's security and our NATO commitments, if we ground them on the basis of nothing more than rumour and coincidence.'

'Is that really all it is?'

'Until there's some hard physical evidence to the contrary, yes.'

Power's expression was challenging, but urbane. The silence that hung between them was broken by the ringing of the telephone.

It stopped as Michelle picked it up in the kitchen. A moment later, she called out, 'My boss on the phone for you – says he's returning your call.'

'I'll take it in the study,' Power answered. He turned back to Drew. 'I've also got some paperwork to do, but we can carry on the conversation after dinner if you like.'

Michelle came in a moment later. 'Had a good chat?'

'Fascinating. He seemed particularly well informed about me.'

She showed no reaction. 'Good. Dinner's in forty-five minutes. We've time for a swim if you fancy one.'

'Is there a pool near here?'

'Quite near – it's in the basement.'

'Sorry, we didn't have too many houses with swimming pools in Liverpool. Not the bit I lived in, anyway.'

'I know. And you had to carry your boots to school so as not to wear out the soles.' She smiled. 'We could skinny-dip, but the Air Vice-Marshal wouldn't approve, so perhaps it's better if I lend you a pair of his trunks.'

'Great,' Drew said, recovering. 'Can I have the ones with the gold braid and medals?'

'I'll do my best. I'll dig some out and see you down by the pool. Third door on the left as you go down the hall.'

The phone began ringing again, but Power picked it up in his study.

'Shit, that reminds me,' Drew said. 'Can I phone Nick and warn him I can't collect him tomorrow?'

'Sure, use the one in the hall. I'll see you downstairs.'

Drew heard the murmur of Power's voice from the study and then silence. He waited a moment, then walked into the hall and picked up the handset.

Power was still on the line. Drew started to put it down again, but then had second thoughts. He raised it to his ear and covered the mouthpiece with his hand.

'Yes,' he heard Power say, 'but I can't guarantee how much longer I can do so.'

'You have to, Charles. It's as simple as that.'

There was a click as the connection was broken.

'Get through?'

Drew whirled around, almost dropping the phone. Michelle touched his arm. 'I'd take something for those nerves, Drew. Did you get Nick?'

'Er . . . no, engaged,' he said. 'I'll just try again.'

She draped a pair of old-fashioned swimming trunks on his head. 'All his others have got elbows. I can't wait to see you in these.'

As she pushed open the door and ran down the stairs to the pool, Drew dialled 1471. The recorded voice recited back a number that meant nothing to him, but he scribbled it down on a scrap of paper as he dialled Nick. He left a hurried message with Sally, then followed Michelle downstairs to the pool.

She was swimming lengths underwater, the light dappling her body like a Hockney painting. She broke the surface close to where Drew was standing and swung easily up and out of the pool, her jet-black costume clinging to her body, beads of water glistening on her skin.

Their eyes locked for a moment and Drew felt the heat building in the pit of his stomach. He took a step towards her. 'Michelle . . .'

She seemed about to respond, but then smiled a secret smile, turned and dived back into the pool. As she surfaced, she called out, 'Remember Baden-Powell, Drew: total immersion in cold water cures everything.'

He smiled back. 'Who needs cold water when I've got your father's trunks?'

Drew changed quickly. He lowered himself into the pool and swam to the far end. By the time he reached it, Michelle was already out of the water and towelling herself dry.

'Is it my imagination,' Drew said, 'or are you always one step ahead of me?'

'In every way, Drew, in every way. I'm going to change. See you back upstairs.'

He swam a few more lengths then showered and put his clothes back on. When he got upstairs he found Michelle and Power waiting for him. Michelle looked stunning in a black Versace dress. Power had changed into a charcoal-grey Savile Row suit. Drew felt suddenly uncomfortable in his off-the-peg jacket and trousers.

Power made no further references to the Tempest as he led the dinner conversation. Drew could not decide if the references to Glyndebourne, Grenoble, Henley, Ascot and Bermuda were designed to emphasise the social and financial gulf separating his daughter from him. He dismissed the idea that he was simply making conversation; he did not believe Power ever did anything without a purpose.

Michelle brought the evening to a close. 'Drew, I'm off to bed. We'll need a five o'clock start to get back to Finnington. I'll show you your room.'

He nodded and rose to his feet.

'I'll drive you into Northolt in the morning,' Power said. 'I need an early start as well.' He turned to Drew. 'Goodnight. Give some thought to what I said earlier.'

'I'll certainly do that,' Drew said.

There was no warmth at all in either of their smiles.

Michelle led Drew upstairs to his room. As he paused in the doorway, she leaned into him and kissed him fleetingly, her lips just brushing his. Then she disappeared down the corridor and a moment later Drew heard her door shut. He touched his fingers to his lips and then closed his own door and went to bed.

When Power dropped them off at Northolt the next morning, Drew waited until the Jaguar had disappeared from view. 'Change of plan, Michelle. I'm going to nip into London and then catch a train up. Do you mind?'

'What's the matter?' she said. 'Can't take the pace?'

'I thought I might do some shopping.' He smiled and kissed her on the cheek. 'See you later.'

When he got into London he made his way to the Farringdon Road. It took him four calls before he got through to Danny Mulvoy.

'Drew,' he said. 'How are things? How's Josie?'

'We've split up – but don't worry, I haven't called to cry on your shoulder. I've got a story for you. I'm in London. Can you spare me a minute or two?'

'No problem, where are you?'

'In the payphone across the street.'

Danny laughed. 'Then perhaps we should meet here. It'll be less cramped.'

Drew hung up and walked across the street and into the *Guardian* offices. He looked curiously around the sprawling, neon-lit newsroom as Danny led him to his desk. 'I'm disappointed,' he said. 'Just a lot of desks and VDUs. There's not a green eyeshade in sight and no one's shouting "Hold the front page".'

'You're a bit early for that,' Danny said. 'Come back just before deadline and it might be a little more exciting.'

Drew turned down the offer of a cup of coffee and Danny picked up his notebook. 'So what's happening?'

'It's the Tempest,' Drew said. 'They suddenly go out of control for no apparent reason. There've been almost a score of incidents in the last two years. The people flying them at the time are either dead or as baffled as I am by what caused them. There's no obvious reason. One minute you're flying along, the next every alarm in the aircraft's going off and there's no response from any of the controls. If you're lucky – like me – you may get time to eject or even pull things round. If you're not . . .'

Danny nodded. 'What evidence have the RAF looked at?'

'Every scrap. There's a Crash Procedures book on the desk in every squadron, a big bright pink folder that tells you what to do. You impound absolutely everything: all of the flying order books, the aircraft and weapons manuals, everything to do with the squadron's flying – and everything to do with the aircraft, because the engineers impound all of the engineering records as well. Everything is immediately frozen and within two or three hours a three-man Board of Inquiry's been selected from other stations and they're on their way – to Finnington in my case. They take immediate informal statements within hours of the incident and then they formally interview you later, under oath.'

Danny kept scribbling. 'Who else has to give a statement?'

'Anyone who so much as glanced at the aircraft in the previous few weeks. The pilot and the navigator say that they flew the aircraft correctly; the engineers say that it was entirely serviceable when it took off.

'They also recover the wreckage and go through it minutely. They can tell things like whether a warning light went on before or after the crash. If you've told them that you had a right-hand fire warning, they'll know from the state of the filament whether that's true.

'They'll know whether the engines were serviceable before they hit the ground, even if they're in a million pieces and spread all over the crash site. There's also the Accident Data Recorder – the spy in the sky – like a tachograph in a lorry driver's cab. It's a digital recording that tells them every detail of the flight up to the moment of impact. It also has a voice tape, so they can listen to the pilot and nav talking to each other.

'The inquiry can take months to report, but they put out their best initial guess of the cause of an incident in what's called the forty-eight-hour signal. Then they take several months to reach a more considered verdict. If it's not an obvious mechanical failure, it could be a fire or a fuel leak.

'It might also be pilot incapacitation, either through contamination of the oxygen system or a heart attack, where the pilot just dies at the controls; or it could simply be a cock-up – pilot error. Once they've decided, then that's it; unlike a court of law, there's no right of appeal.'

'And all that has produced no hint of a cause?'

'Not as far as I know. They just keep blaming pilot error.' Drew shook his head before Danny could even frame the question. 'Definitely not.'

'Okay,' Danny said, closing his notebook. 'What have you got to back this up?'

'Not much,' Drew admitted, handing him the photocopied notes. Danny read them quickly and looked doubtful. 'Is that it?'

'Isn't it enough?'

'Not as it stands, no. I'll do some digging around and see what I can come up with.'

'I'm not making this up, Danny,' Drew said.

'I'm sure you're not, but there's a big difference between the truth and the truth you can prove. Our libel lawyers are really only interested in the second sort, I'm afraid.'

He looked back through his notes, frowning. 'To be honest, I think the most we'll be able to get out of this will be a piece about the strange number of Tempest crashes recently. We can't go dropping hints about mysterious faults without some facts to back them up.'

'Well leave my name out of it for the time being, will you? As soon as I get some, I'll let you know.'

Drew spent the journey north staring uninterestedly out of the train window at a landscape faintly tinged with the first green of spring.

When he got back to the flat, he dumped his bag and changed his clothes. As he transferred his change from his pocket, his fingers closed on a slip of paper. He pulled it out and found the telephone number he had scribbled the previous night. He picked up the phone, punched in 141 to conceal the source of the call and then dialled.

It rang twice and a woman's voice answered. 'Good

afternoon,' Drew said. 'British Telecom, we're following up your complaint of a fault on the line.'

'We've made no complaint.'

'Someone's reported a fault, perhaps a caller trying to dial you. Is this a business or private phone?'

'It's a private one.'

'And it's Mr and Mrs David Richards?'

'No.' The voice was becoming increasingly irritated. 'Mr and Mrs Henry Robertshaw.'

'And what line of business is Mr Robertshaw in?'

'What? You're not from British Telecom. Who is this?'

Drew hung up and stood motionless in the deserted flat. Then he dialled Danny at the *Guardian*. 'Does the name Henry Robertshaw mean anything to you?'

'Off the top of my head, not a damn thing. Who is he?'

'I don't know,' Drew said, 'but I'd like to find out.'

Nick was already waiting outside when Drew arrived to pick him up the next morning.

'So how did it go?' he asked, as soon as he was settled in the passenger seat.

Drew gave him a suspicious look. 'How did what go?'

'The meeting with the MP, of course.'

'Oh that. Absolutely perfectly. I told him the story and by the time I got to Power's house forty-five minutes later, Norman Feather had already been on the phone to him. It turns out they went to Charterhouse together.'

Nick stared at him. 'Sod Charterhouse, what about Power's house? You actually went there?'

Drew nodded. 'By invitation.'

Nick whistled. 'Hell, Michelle must be keen if she's already inviting you back to meet the folks.'

'If only. I don't think it was even Michelle's idea. Big Daddy wanted a friendly fireside chat about the Tempest.'

'And what did he say?'

'Much the same as Russell the previous day though more subtly. Power would never be this obvious but the message was: butt out or we'll break your balls.'

Nick swivelled in his seat. 'So what now?'

Drew sighed. 'I'm not going to get anywhere going through official channels. You should have seen the photos on

Power's piano. He's so well connected – the Queen probably bows when he walks into the room. I'm going to have to go outside the system.'

Nick smiled. 'Would that be revolutionary warfare or Fleet Street in the first instance?'

'You tell me.' Drew fell silent for a moment. 'I also eavesdropped on a snatch of a very strange phone conversation while I was at Power's.'

'Saying what?'

'Power was complaining about the difficulty of keeping the lid on something.'

'Who was he talking to?'

'Someone called Henry Robertshaw, I think.'

'And who's he?'

'I don't know. Who would have an interest in keeping the Tempest fault quiet?'

'The Air Force, the government and the manufacturers, for a start. But you don't even know that's what Power was talking about, do you?'

'What else would he want to keep the lid on?' Drew asked as he swung the car onto the Finnington slip road and pulled up at the barrier.

'His septic tank?'

'Morning, sir.' The guard checked their ID. 'Either the Queen's paying a visit or we're going to war. There's all hell broken loose this morning.'

'Bet you it's Bosnia,' Nick said.

As he drove towards the squadron, Drew could see the whole base buzzing with activity. Even the cooks, clerks and administrators seemed to be more purposeful.

'Looks like a major deployment,' Nick said. 'You don't get the paper-clip squadron breaking sweat for anything less.'

Outside the squadron, air crew were swarming over the jets and a fleet of Hercules were being loaded with equipment under armed guard. Drew was amazed to see the amount of weaponry being put on board.

'It seems a bit of a waste doesn't it?' Nick said, following his gaze. 'Using million-quid missiles just to knock poxy old Serb helicopters out of the sky? The missiles probably cost more than the choppers.'

'There's nothing poxy about their Hind helicopter gunships. You won't be lying back in your seat like that if we come up against one of those.' Drew yanked on the handbrake and jumped out.

He hurried into the crew room. DJ glanced up. 'Briefing in twenty minutes. Six to four on it's Bosnia, ten to one against a surprise birthday party for Russell.'

Russell was already standing at the podium when they filed into the briefing room. 'You're probably wondering what all the activity is about this morning.'

'Not really,' Nick whispered.

'Let me put you out of your misery straight away. We're off to Bosnia again.'

'Surprise, surprise,' Drew said, 'alert the media.'

'We're deploying to Gióia del Colle in Italy today and we begin patrolling the exclusion zones from dawn tomorrow. You have ninety minutes to go home, pack what you need and be back on base ready to go to work.'

When Russell finished speaking, there was a buzz around the room. Drew could see DJ and Ali sharing excited speculation about flying over Bosnia, though he suspected it was also tinged with apprehension at the thought of their first combat. As they filed out of the briefing room, they hurried to overtake Drew and Nick and began bombarding them with questions.

'What was it really like last time?' DJ asked.

Drew exchanged glances with Nick. 'Ninety-nine per cent boredom and one per cent pure, unadulterated terror.'

Nick nodded. 'You'll sit there in the skies over Bosnia with your thumb up your bum and absolutely nothing happening for day after day. Then all of a sudden, for no discernible reason, someone will start shooting at you.'

'Come on,' DJ said, looking from one to the other. 'You were just as excited as us in there. This is what we joined up for.'

Drew shook his head. 'Not really. We're not defending our country, we're not really defending anything at all, because if it's like last time both we and the Serbs know we won't be allowed to strike back. All we're doing is flying the flag for the politicians. So don't get too carried away. If you die out there, you're not dying in some great heroic cause, you're just dying, and no one will thank you for it.'

Subdued, DJ and Ali wandered back to the crew room.

'You were going in a bit hard there, weren't you?' Nick said as they walked out to the car.

'Just trying to make sure all that youthful enthusiasm doesn't wind up getting them killed.' Drew floored the accelerator.

'There's obviously been a misunderstanding,' Nick said, peering through his fingers at the swathe Drew was cutting through the traffic. 'I thought the combat missions didn't start until tomorrow.'

'Just testing your nerve. If you can't handle a threat from a Ford Cortina on the A1 near Finnington, there's no hope for you against a SAM 2 over Banja Luka.'

Drew screeched to a halt outside Nick's house and dropped him off, promising to be back inside twenty minutes.

Back at Finnington, Drew emerged from the briefing room and hurried down to the crew room. 'Anyone seen Michelle?' he asked.

'Yeah, you've missed her,' Jumbo said, as he smeared peanut butter on a pile of cold toast. 'She was looking for you a while ago, but she's airborne now. They were taking off as we came out of the briefing.'

'On a sortie?'

'No, recalled to base.'

Chapter 11

Drew and Nick were in the first formation of Tempests to touch down at the enormous base at Gióia del Colle. Like the seasoned veterans they were, they made an immediate dash for the accommodation block and claimed two of the better rooms for themselves. Then they drove out of the domestic site on to the perimeter track leading to the operations area.

They passed a number of open doors as they walked down the corridor to the crew room. The detachment commander, a group captain, was already at his desk, wrestling with the problems involved in shoe-horning the Tempest and Jaguar personnel into a space barely big enough for a single squadron.

Across the corridor was the Ops room. 'Nice to see the mud-movers hard at work,' Nick said, nodding to the Jaguar pilots already planning missions at their operations desk, surrounded by racks stuffed with Ordnance Survey maps.

The Tempest crews had a separate area, presided over by the authoriser, who was flanked by a battery of status boards and secure radios to talk to the aircraft, Combat Operations Centre and Air Traffic Control. An engineer stood ready to report on the availability of the aircraft and a met man was busy fumbling with his charts.

The crew room was at the far end of the corridor. Drew nodded to DJ, Ali and the others, then stood contemplating the bare concrete floors, second-hand equipment and decrepit furniture.

He gestured towards the geriatric kettle and chipped mugs on the table. 'The Americans bring everything from coke machines and jukeboxes to a fully fledged Dunkin Donuts franchise. What do we bring? A small jar of Nescafé and a packet of digestive biscuits.'

'We can't afford to get too comfortable,' Nick said. 'We're on dawn patrol tomorrow.'

The room fell silent, each man lost in his thoughts. Combat was what they trained for, but it was also what got them killed.

As Drew settled down in a corner with a paper, DJ came over to him. He took a look around, making sure the others were preoccupied with their own conversations. 'Drew, can I have a word?'

Drew saw the strain in DJ's face. He put down his paper.

'You'll think I'm stupid, but . . .' DJ began.

'Try me.'

DJ gave him a grateful look. 'I'm scared I've lost it. Every time I go up there I'm thinking about what happened on the way to Aalborg. I still don't know if it was me or the aircraft, but I'm scared it's going to happen again. If I lost it in training, how will I keep it together in combat?'

Drew paused, searching for the right words. 'We're all scared, DJ. We all have that, no matter how many times we go up. Anyone who tells you he isn't every time he crosses into hostile territory is a liar. But you can't allow it to take hold of you. Use the fear as the fuel to keep you alive. It can make your eyes keener and your reactions sharper, but only if you control it. If you don't, it'll take control; panic will kill you quicker than anything.'

DJ nodded, but Drew knew he was still unconvinced. 'Take a look at my face as we go out of the changing rooms tomorrow morning, DJ. I guarantee what you'll see is white, tinged with pale green. I'll be shitting myself all the way to the aircraft, but, as I start to strap the jet on, I'll push that fear to the back of my mind. Do the same.' He paused. 'What happened on the way to Aalborg has made you a better pilot: you've looked into the abyss and come back from it. I don't have any worries about going into combat with you as my wingman. I just feel sorry for the Serbs.'

DJ gave a weak smile.

'Anyway, I don't know what you're worrying about. Nothing that happens up there could be more dangerous than breathing the same air as him.' He gestured towards Ali, who was lighting his next roll-up from the stub of his last.

An alarm call woke Drew at two the next morning. He showered but was still bleary-eyed as he shuffled into the canteen. He had to force himself to eat some toast. Nick sat down next to him, immediately wolfing down an enormous cooked breakfast.

Drew shuddered.

Nick smiled and reached across him for the toast. 'You should get stuck in. If we're shot down, this could be the last meal you'll get in a week.'

As they rose to go to the Ops room, the ground crew began to file into the canteen for their own customary, artery-furring mixture of bacon, sausages, eggs and fried bread.

As lead crew, Drew and Nick had to prepare the briefing for the sortie. Four crews had come in prepared to fly the two aircraft and they lounged around the makeshift briefing room as Drew began talking them through the mission. 'Everybody here? Where's Bob? We can't start without him.'

Jumbo held up the Ops room cat, which had been nestling on his lap.

'Right. Welcome to Operation Decisive Edge.' Drew gave a grim smile. 'Only time will tell if there's an "in" missing from the title.'

There was a knowing laugh from veterans of the previous Bosnian patrols.

'Unless AWACs tells us different, we're flying a roving CAP over north-west Bosnia, from Dohovacu in the east to the Bihać pocket in the west. We're there to patrol the no-fly zones, to identify and if necessary intercept any aircraft. The rules of engagement are that calls for authorisation go back to AWACs – codename Magic – back to the COC – codename Sunray – and then back to the UN – codename Gotham – who answer whether you can engage . . . unless they're out at dinner.'

Once more there was laughter.

'The callsign of the tanker is Texaco, we're refuelling three times off him today. Aviano and Bari are the diversions we're using. Make sure you've got the authentication codes for the day. You'll almost certainly be challenged when you check in with the AWACs controllers and, if you're in doubt about any identifications and orders, be cautious and challenge the other person. Even if you recognise my voice, there's nothing to stop someone recording it and playing it back to spoof you.

'There are fixed points for entering and leaving the hostile air space. No deviation is permitted from this except in emergency and only then after receiving permission from AWACs. Our height is twenty thousand feet, our specified entry gate is Gate 5 and we will be travelling along the fixed corridor to our drop point – Drop 4. After that, we're free to fly our particular CAP as we – or the AWACs controller – think fit.

'We're flying with live weapons, live flares and live chaff. Make sure that you make the weapons safe every time you come out of the area to go to the tanker.' He smiled. 'And if you cock things up and accidentally let off some chaff, a flare or, God forbid, a weapon, there are codes to let AWACs know we didn't really mean it. The Serbs will have to work it out for themselves.

'If we're switched to a static CAP, boredom will be the main problem . . . apart from Triple-A and SAM missiles.' He raised his watch. 'Right, take-off is 0500 hours, the time is 0310 . . . now!'

Nick took over. 'Okay, combat survival brief. Rule One: the whole of Bosnia is hostile territory. There are no friendly forces. Stay in the air if you possibly can; if you must hit the ground, the only people likely to help you rather than shoot you are the American troops in the rescue helicopters.

'Today's word is Bullfrog, the letter of the day is B for

bravo, the number of the day is twenty-two. Please commit these codes to memory. If you get shot down or have to bang out, they could save your life, but they could also get you blown up if you forget them or get them wrong. I know you all know this, but I have to stress it again, particularly for those of you flying over hostile territory for the first time.'

He gave DJ and Ali a wink. 'When Combat Rescue come in, they may ask just the number or letter of the day, or if they're feeling particularly fiendish they may ask the number of the day minus seventeen, or the third letter of the word of the day.

'Please also review your ISOPREPS. Make sure that all the information is correct and that your fingerprints, photograph and dental record are on the form; they are sometimes needed. All they found of one bloke in the Gulf was a hand and he had to be identified from his fingerprints.

'You must also check your four personal questions. You've chosen them, so you ought to remember the answers, but you'd be amazed how many people forget the name of Auntie Nelly's budgerigar or Great Aunt Maud's secret lover from Bridlington when they've been shot down and are under major stress. If you don't remember the answers when the rescue team come looking, don't be surprised if you're suspected of being a Serb and blown away.

'Finally, dress to egress, and that means arctic survival gear. It'll make you uncomfortable in the cockpit, but it could save your life if you have to bang out over the mountains. Your other lifesaver – in theory at least – is your UN blue beret. We haven't got many – there's a UN shortage apparently – so you'll have to sign them in and out. We could only get seven in sensible sizes, so the last to pick one up will find it sits on his head like a cocktail cherry on an ice cream.'

Drew added, 'Whether you wear it if you have to bang out is entirely up to you. The theory is that no one will shoot at you if you are, but the UN casualty rates so far suggest that isn't entirely correct. It'll also make you stand out like a teetotaller at a squadron party; there's not much point in wearing camouflage if you're going to put a pale blue Belisha beacon on top of your head. Official

Air Force policy is to wear them, but the final decision is yours.'

Drew paused to let it sink in, then nodded to the intelligence officer.

'Intelligence brief,' she said crisply. 'These missile sites are active. There are SAM 2s around Banja Luka and mobile SAM 6s at the places marked with smaller red circles on your maps. There was heavy gunfire around Donji Vakuv last night and helicopter activity over Banja Luka yesterday afternoon.

'There's also an unmanned aerial vehicle in the area marked blue, spotting Serb gun positions. It's flying round in cloud between five and twenty thousand feet. It can't see you, so be aware if you're between those heights in that area – you may suddenly find something the size of a sofa coming straight at you.'

She paused and gave a thin smile. 'And finally, we have already reached a total of nine hundred and ninety-two violations of the no-fly zone. I'm counting on you to get us past the magic one thousand mark today.'

The met man, a round-shouldered Welshman with a diffident manner and a soft, almost inaudible voice, stood up next. 'Met brief.'

'Louder,' came the immediate call from the back of the room.

He cleared his throat and began again. 'Met brief. The weather here is fine, cloud ceiling at five thousand feet. Expected to break up after dawn, no visibility problems anticipated. Cloud's on the deck over the target at the moment.'

Those crew who preferred boredom to danger smiled, those who didn't frowned. With low cloud, there was no threat of hand-held missiles or Triple-A being fired at them, but it would mean flying around all day without seeing anything at all.

'However, we expect it to lift within the next few hours,' he continued, 'giving reasonable visibility, say six miles.'

After the briefings, Drew and Nick had one final official duty to perform. All air crew were deeply superstitious and failing to feed Bob, the Ops room cat, was tempting fate. The lead crew on the dawn patrol always did so and even the most sceptical crewman would give the cat a furtive stroke as he filed past on his way to fly a sortie.

Ninety minutes before take-off, the crews started to get ready. Drew began putting on his combat gear. Every item of clothing had been sanitised – stripped of identifying marks and potentially embarrassing labels – even a Marks and Spencer tag could be enough to get them shot in a volatile area.

He pulled on a vest, long johns and two pairs of clean socks, then a big woollen arctic coverall and an arctic flying suit. Nick preferred an extra layer and opted for two woollen coveralls, followed by a normal flying suit. Their combat smocks were in camouflage pattern instead of the usual olive green and unmarked apart from rank tabs on the shoulders.

After hauling on their G-pants, they stuffed them with kit, mostly maps and spare water sachets. The combat jacket came next, supplied by the USAF and jammed with every conceivable survival aid from a fishing line and a sleeping bag to a combat map on canvas, doubling as an emergency blanket, which was stitched into the back of it. There was also a survival pouch with emergency rations and more sachets of water, distress flares, a first-aid kit and a second secure radio, an American one, for most rescue missions were flown by them.

Finally Drew hauled a life-jacket over the top of all his other gear. He looked around. 'If we get shot down, they'll think they're being invaded by Michelin men.'

'If they give us any more kit I'm going to have to find a new job,' Jumbo grumbled. 'I can't get into the cockpit with my combat jacket fastened. I've got to squeeze myself in first and then jam the jacket down around me afterwards.'

'You could always try a diet, Jumbo,' Nick said helpfully, 'or is that just too silly for words?'

They waddled slowly past the ops desk where the intelligence officer issued them with a pistol and two magazines – eighteen rounds of ammunition – and the code book with the remainder of the secret codes for the day. Each minute of the mission had a separate code, so that any order could be challenged and authenticated by its time code.

She also had a pile of UN berets. Drew looked doubtfully at his, but stuffed it into one of his pockets

He picked up his pile of three thousand Deutschmarks in assorted bills, for use as bribes if shot down, and his goolie chit, promising a substantial reward to a captor for returning Drew unharmed – with goolies intact.

Nick collected a stills camera, a video camera and a stabbyscope – an incredibly powerful pair of stabilised binoculars. 'It's like Christmas shopping in Dixon's. How the hell am I supposed to fit all this crap in? It's crowded enough with just you and me in the cockpit.'

Jumbo shuffled along the line, looking thoughtfully from the mountain of kit on the table to his equally mountainous form. He picked it all up, but, after a furtive look over his shoulder at the intelligence officer, he stuffed a few items into his locker. As he closed the door, he caught Drew's eye and grinned.

Drew and Nick followed him through to the Ops room for the final out-brief. The authoriser stepped up to the platform, cutting through their chat with a brisk, 'Right, pay attention. Have you briefed weather, callsigns and the tanker? Do you know who you're joining up with in the area?'

There were nods of assent.

'You're taking over from the French Mirages and the Turkish F16s will then replace you.'

'If they turn up,' Nick whispered.

'There are also American F15s and F18 HARM-shooters tasked in your area, so things might get a bit crowded.'

The crews were beginning to fidget.

'Last thing,' he said, raising his voice. 'Have you sanitised? You should all have got rid of your wallets and be carrying absolutely nothing personal other than your ID card and your UN passport.'

Several faces stared blankly back at him. 'Those of you who have them, that is . . . it's another UN shortage, I'm afraid. That's all, thank you.'

The air crew were on their feet and heading for the door before he'd finished speaking. A grey bus was waiting outside, belching diesel fumes into the dark. All four crews clambered aboard and were driven out to the shelters, where ten steel-grey Tempests stood on the line.

Drew tapped DJ on the shoulder as they got off the bus. 'All right?'

DJ nodded, though his voice cracked a little. 'I'll be fine once we're up there.'

Swathed in their layers of kit, the crews waddled across to the first four of the jets. As Drew signed for his aircraft, Nick started looking it over.

'Did I ever tell you about a guy on my previous squadron during the Gulf?' Nick said as he checked the weapon safety pins. 'He forgot to check the pins in his Sidewinders and accidentally fired one while he was winding the jet up on the ground. It killed six ground crew as it careered across the base.'

'Thanks, Nick,' Drew said. 'I'm sure we all find that very reassuring.'

The power was put into the aircraft and Nick began loading the data into their computers. An hour before take-off, Drew gave the signal to start up the engines. The jets were cold and wet and in no mood to go flying. Engines sputtered and died, inertial navigation systems wouldn't align, hydraulics systems leaked fluid.

Twice they had to jump out of their aircraft and start all over again in another one, while the engineers began working on the faults. 'At this rate we'll have to use all ten just to get two airborne.' Drew lowered himself into yet another cockpit.

'So what's new?' Nick replied as he loaded the mission data into his third computer of the day.

Twenty minutes before take-off time, Drew punched the radio button. 'Right, who's ready?'

By a miracle all the crews now had functioning aircraft. Both the nominated crews for the mission – Drew and Nick, and DJ and Ali – began to taxi out, leaving the others sitting there, engines running.

'Sorry, Tiger Three and Four,' Drew said. 'We'll do our best to break something during weapons check.'

'Like hell you will,' Jumbo said, already sweating profusely, wedged in his cockpit with nowhere to go and facing the prospect of having to stay there for another hour.

Drew and Nick, and DJ and Ali lined up on the runway and took off, tongues of flame from the Tempests' afterburners searing red streaks into the slowly lightening sky. As they swung round in a wide curve to the east, Drew glanced back at the two other aircraft in Slingshot mode – on the ground with their engines running – ready to take off instantly if anything went wrong with the jets already airborne.

Approaching the first gate off the Adriatic coast, Drew called, 'Weapons check,' and began testing every part of their weapons systems. He checked the flow of nitrogen coolant to the Sidewinder's heat-seeking head, while Nick tuned the radar missile systems.

Both crews then tried out their chaff, DJ dropping behind Drew's jet while Ali checked on the radar that the aluminium foil actually came out when Nick punched the button, and then flying ahead while Nick returned the compliment.

'Flare check?' Nick said.

'At seventy quid a time? You're joking of course. We fired one five years ago. That'll have to do until the next Gulf War.'

'You sound more and more like Russell every day.'

'Oh all right, sod the Air Marshal's new curtains. Flare check.' He pressed the button and sent a flare out behind the jet.

'Flare sighted,' confirmed DJ, as a flare like a miniature sun, burning hotter than the aircraft's engines, drifted away below them.

Fifteen miles out from the shoreline, Drew checked in with the guard ship *Red Dwarf*, an American missile cruiser steaming constantly to and fro, parallel to the coast. 'Tigers One and Two, serviceable.'

'Okay, Tiger,' came a mid-Western drawl, 'this is *Red Dwarf*, relaying message to Gióia and handing you over to Magic two-one. Have a good trip.'

Drew thought of the reserve crews huddled in their cockpits back at Gióia, hearing the welcome call on their radios to stand down.

He could imagine Jumbo's sigh of relief as he shut down the engines and began to prise himself out of the seat. 'How many layers do you think Jumbo'll dare to take off?'

Nick laughed. 'He'll be sweating like a pig in the crew room, but he won't strip off more than the outer layer. If he gets a call to scramble it'll take him fifteen minutes to finish his sandwiches, never mind get back into his flying gear.'

The banter was brittle as they approached hostile territory. Almost as soon as *Red Dwarf* cleared the radio, Drew heard the AWACs controller checking in. 'Morning, Tiger, this is Magic two-one.'

'Morning, Magic, two aircraft for Gate 5, Drop 4.'

'Roger, Tiger, Gate 5, Drop 4. Roving CAP. No change to mission.'

As they entered their gate, they crossed the invisible line separating the safe, friendly forces' areas behind them from the hostile territory ahead. Drew reached down to touch the ejection handle beneath his seat like a talisman. He knew that Nick would be doing exactly the same thing.

Drew scanned the warning panel for the thousandth time since they had taken off, alert for any flicker that might signal another uncontrolled dive, but it stayed reassuringly blank.

There were now other, more immediate dangers to worry about. As the friendly symbols faded from the radar warner, hostile ones identifying the known Triple-A and missile sites began to spring up on the screen instead. Each was greeted by a brief warning tone from the radar warner, cranking up the tension in the cockpit another notch.

Nick began chanting a mantra from the back seat: 'Triple-A, one o'clock, outside lethal range. Sam 2, three o'clock, outside lethal range. Triple-A, eleven o'clock, just outside lethal range.'

As they flashed through their drop point, Drew called up DJ and Ali. He heard DJ's voice still catching and made himself speak more slowly and calmly. 'Okay, guys, we'll take a look at all the sites where you'd normally find helicopters flying. First up Mostar, fifteen miles, twenty degrees left of your nose.'

'Looks like the met man got it wrong again,' Nick said, taking in the already well-broken cloud. 'If that's cloud on the deck, I'm Genghis Khan.'

The jets swung round to the north, following the Neretva river up to Mostar. Even from fifteen thousand feet, they could see the city clearly as the first rays of the sun tinged the rooftops with red.

'That's it,' Drew said. 'It's not much but it's home to the boys down there. The helicopters normally sit at the football stadium, which is coming under our left wing now. Nine times out of ten they're heading due north along the river valley up towards Gornji Vakuf, but we'll get to that later. Next stop Sarajevo.'

Drew put his jet into a long turn towards the north-east, pushing the throttles to climb steadily towards the snow-capped mountains. They flashed over a ridge between two towering summits and plunged down towards Sarajevo. As they circled the city, they could see the battered towerblocks pock-marked with shell craters and the black scars of burnt-out buildings. The Serbs' dawn shelling was already in progress and Drew could see the orange flash of shell bursts and puffs of grey smoke drifting west on the wind.

'Let's go down to two hundred and fifty feet and have a closer look.' He pushed the stick forward to drop the nose. They skimmed over the city, spotting a few startled white faces in the drab grey streets. Fires were raging in one cluster of buildings that had taken a barrage of Serb shells and a stream of figures hurried from it, clutching a few pathetic belongings.

'Just another day in paradise,' Nick said gloomily. Drew swung the Tempest away from the city, following a narrow twisting valley up towards Gornji Vakuf. They flew on, the deserted, thickly forested mountains punctuated by a succession of grey, war-ravaged towns, their buildings holed and crumbling like rotten teeth.

They skimmed down over the foothills to the edge of the Danube plain and swept over Banja Luka and through the Bihać pocket. Drew knew that Nick and Ali would be using both the jet's electronic eyes and their own Mark 1 human eyeballs as they searched for any sign of hostile actions. They still scanned the skies around them for hostile contacts, but much more of their attention was now focused on their green screens. They stared intently, alert and dry-mouthed, dreading the warning that would tell them that a missile was about to be launched at them or the telltale puff of smoke and dust on the ground that would show it had already been fired.

They made it safely through the danger zones and kept flying out towards the coast. Drew checked his watch and his fuel and then called, 'Magic this is Tiger, for Drop Three, Gate Eight, meeting up with Texaco Two.'

'Roger, Tiger, Claret One and Two replacing you.'

As they came out of the exit gate, Drew and Nick shut down their weapons systems. 'This always makes me think of when I was in Germany,' Nick said. 'A Phantom had just come off quick-reaction alert and he went straight into a big NATO exercise still fully armed up. He started hunting down a Jaguar, called, "Fox Two, Fox Two", and two missiles came off the aircraft. They hit the Jaguar and blew it apart. Luckily the pilot ejected just in time.'

'Is there nothing we do that doesn't remind you of someone cocking it up?' Drew said. 'In case you hadn't noticed, I'm having a hard enough time persuading myself that this thing isn't going to crack us into the hillside on its own without you finding new ways to scare the shit out of me.'

Nick chuckled. 'The funniest thing was that there was an Italian in a 104 chasing the Jaguar. When he saw it disintegrate, he radioed in, "Okay, I'm going home. The Brits are playing for real today".'

They found their tanker circling out over the Adriatic and both Tempests dropped in behind and began inching their way towards its trailing drogues.

Slipping the refuelling probe in the nose of the Tempest into the basket trailing from the tanker was as easy as threading a needle in the driver's seat of a Ferrari during a Grand Prix. Drew eased the jet forward, making minute adjustments to the stick and the throttles as Nick talked him onto the basket. He relaxed as the probe slipped home and fuel began to pump into their tanks.

Refuelling complete, he let the Tempest drop away from the tanker and, with DJ keeping station alongside, they pulled into a turn to the east, ramming the throttles forward to boost their speed as they flew back in towards their entry gate. Two other fighters were already dropping in behind the tanker for their refuelling slot.

'Traffic's heavy this morning,' Nick said.

They were four miles out from the entry gate and busy rearming the weapons systems ready for their second CAP of the day, when an F16 appeared from nowhere and hurtled a few feet over the top of the cockpit. Drew and Nick both ducked, their hearts pounding.

'Christ, that was close,' Nick said, his hands trembling. 'I could have reached out and touched him.'

'Magic two-one, this is Tiger, two aircraft for Gate 5, Drop 4 . . . and if that F16 had been ten feet closer, there'd have only been one aircraft for Gate 5.'

A laconic American drawl answered. 'Roger that, Tiger. By the way, haven't you heard? AWACs don't do air traffic control. We direct missions; it's your job to keep yourself out of trouble.'

'Sorry, Magic,' Drew said. 'I'll keep that in mind.'

As they swept back in towards Mostar, AWACs welcomed them with an update. 'Helicopter at Jellystone two-five-zero, twenty miles. Friendlies, Claret One and Two, at two-nine-zero, leaving the area for Tanker.'

The French Mirages left to take their turn on the tanker as the Tempests took up station. As they flew over the football pitch, Nick had the stabbyscope pressed to his eyes. 'Helicopters on the ground, rotors not turning. Wait for it, correction, rotors now turning.'

Drew reported immediately to AWACs.

'Roger, Tiger, monitor and report.'

They had been on station for only ten minutes when one of the helicopters took off, its dark shadow skimming over the city as it aimed for the valley snaking away to the north.

Drew immediately challenged it on Guard, the international distress frequency. 'Helicopter two miles north of Mostar, heading three-four-zero, you are in violation of United Nations Resolution number 773. Exit the area or you will be engaged.'

He could hear the AWACs controller repeating the warning and, even though he knew that nothing would happen, felt himself tensing.

He waited a moment. 'They're not responding, Magic. Authority to follow them?'

'Roger, Tiger, authorisation granted.'

They followed the helicopter for fifty miles, routinely issuing challenges and being just as routinely ignored. The helicopter finally landed in a field on the outskirts of Gornji Vacuv and began unloading troops.

'Log it,' Drew said wearily, 'violation number 993, another ethnic cleansing squad escorted safely to their destination.'

Chapter 12

As Drew and Nick returned from another refuelling slot for their final CAP, AWACs had fresh instructions. 'Go to Oscar. CAP orientation three-four-zero. Static CAP.'

Drew groaned.

'Static CAPs are bad enough to start with,' Nick said, 'but a static CAP in range of a SAM 2 site is like playing Russian Roulette with a bullet in every chamber.'

They began circling just to the south of Banja Luka, picking up the signal from the Serbian surveillance radar as it tracked them across the sky. 'As long as that's all they point at us, we'll be fine,' Drew said easily, settling into the dull but dangerous routine. He glanced out of the canopy and saw DJ's jet still in formation, to the side and slightly behind.

As they patrolled their increasingly monotonous beat, he could see a constant series of shellbursts, smoke suddenly erupting, then drifting slowly away on the wind.

'I'm glad we're not down there,' Nick said as another barrage went off.

Drew snapped upright as he saw grey smoke bursting in the sky ahead of them. 'They're shooting at us,' he yelled. 'Break right, DJ, break right and widen.'

Drew threw his jet into a hard left turn, slamming the throttle forward to max power, but as he did so he saw DJ's lurch drunkenly from side to side.

'We've been hit. We've been hit.' DJ's voice had risen an octave in six words.

Drew had to fight to control his own shock. It was the first time any of them had been hit. He waited until he could trust his own voice. 'Don't panic, DJ. How serious is it?'

'Just a minute.'

As he waited, Drew could feel his skin crawling. He scanned the sky around them constantly, tensing at every burst of grey smoke in the air. He could imagine DJ frantically scanning his warning panel and flicking switches as Ali went through the Bold Face emergency drills.

'The fly-by-wire has dropped out and we're stuck in mechanical mode. It's supposed to be triple-redundant.'

'Then something's blown a hole in all three sets of wires.' Drew's unemotional voice belied his own unease.

'We're also losing our hydraulics. We've no flaps or nose-wheel steering.' DJ's voice was cracking again.

'You're holding straight and level flight, DJ – you're going to get out of this okay. Let's get out of here first and then I'll check you for leaks.'

He called up AWACs immediately. 'Magic, Tiger 2–1 Bravo's been hit. Triple-A, from south-west corner of Jellystone. We're exiting the area now. We can't make Drop Three or Four so we're going to set a course straight for Gióia on bearing two-three-zero.'

'Okay, Tiger, we'll coordinate with the guard ships and the other aircraft.'

They could hear AWACs rattling out commands, calling in air support. Two F16s armed with cluster bombs responded to the call and went racing in towards Banja Luka.

As soon as the Tempests were out of Triple-A and missile range, Drew began a battle-damage inspection on DJ's jet, flying within a few feet of him as he checked underneath it and then rising over the top to look down on it. As he went up the side, he saw a series of gaping holes in the fuselage and a plume of escaping fuel making its own thin grey vapour trail. Suddenly the aircraft lurched dangerously close to them.

'Christ, DJ, keep it steady.'

Drew could hear the tension in DJ's voice as he responded. 'This is as steady as it gets. Every time I touch the stick it bucks like a bronco.'

Drew tried to keep his tone light. 'Okay, DJ, the good news is no fires. Most of the damage is in the area by the avionics bay, so that's why your fly-by-wire has dropped out. Fuel's leaking quite badly. Let's put out a Mayday call and head straight for home.'

As they flew on, they could hear the cross-chat between the AWACs and one of the F16s.

'Stinger 2–1, I can see more firing. Shit, that was close. Magic, Stinger 2–1 is being fired on. Request authority to engage.'

'Sorry, Stinger, no authority yet. Sunray has referred it to Gotham. Trying to get authority at this time. Stand by.'

Drew snorted into his intercom. 'What's the point of having a two-star general sitting in COC for just this kind of situation, if all he ever does is refer it back to the UN?'

For the next five minutes, they listened to the increasingly anguished requests for authorisation from the F16, and the AWACs controller's mounting anger as he tried unsuccessfully to obtain it from the Combat Operations Centre. 'I've got guys up there like sitting ducks. What the hell's going on?'

'Gotham commander can't be contacted. You have no, repeat no, authorisation to engage.'

'All right, that's it,' the AWACs controller said abruptly. 'I'll take the flak for this if there's any flying later on, but let's clear the area now. All aircraft within fifty-mile radius of Jellystone, clear the area immediately.'

'The Serbs will have helicopters up within ten minutes,' Drew said, 'shifting more troops and strafing a few Bosnian villages.'

'I know,' Nick said, 'but at least AWACs did the right thing.'

'Unlike those gutless bastards at COC.'

'Come on, Drew. There's nothing we can do about it. Let's get off this frequency and concentrate on getting DJ home in one piece.'

Switching channels, Drew heard DJ talking to Italian Air

Traffic Control and cut in. 'DJ, concentrate on your flying. I'll handle ATC.'

The Italian Air Traffic Control handed them over to ATC at Gióia. 'Mayday 2–1. Understand 2–1 Alpha is the emergency.'

'No, it's Bravo,' Drew said patiently.

'What's the nature of the emergency?'

'He's lost the fly-by-wire and he's leaking fuel. We're going to have to make an emergency cable engagement.'

'Roger. It'll take us twenty minutes to get it rigged.' The controller hit the button to set the sirens blaring across the airfield.

'It's going to have to be a hell of a lot faster than that. He's leaking fuel badly. Ready or not, we're going to have to put it on the ground inside five minutes.'

The jets dropped through the cloud ceiling to begin their approach, engines rumbling like distant thunder.

Drew thumbed the radio button. 'What's your fuel state, DJ?'

'Fuel critical. The red warning's on.'

'Don't worry, you'll make it.' Drew released the button, then added, 'I hope.' Gusts of wind shook the aircraft and he shot an anxious look at DJ. He could see his head rocking from side to side as he fought to hold the Tempest on line.

'Wind's over ten knots,' Nick said, studying the emergency drills cards. 'They're over the limits for this.'

'They've no fuel to go anywhere else,' Drew replied. 'They have to put it down here even if it's blowing storm force ten.'

'Cable rigged,' came the call from ATC. 'We're ready for you.'

Drew pushed the radio button to talk to DJ. 'Okay, you've only got one chance at an approach, so take it calm and steady. Without flaps and nose-wheel steering, this is going to be pretty hairy. Put it on the ground, slam the anchors on and hope for the best. You're technically too fast for the cable and you may just rip it out of the ground. If that happens or you miss the cable, bang out immediately. Don't hesitate for a second – you'll be off the runway.'

'Right,' DJ replied. 'We're going in.'

Drew eased back on the throttles and watched as DJ's Tempest swayed and lurched ahead of them towards the cluster of blue flashing lights by the runway.

Another gust of wind pushed DJ's jet sideways. Beads of sweat broke out on Drew's forehead as he saw it yaw away from the runway. DJ dragged it back, fighting the controls, but overcorrected and Drew saw the runway slip off to the other side. Even when DJ managed to get the nose back on the centre line, the lightest touch on the controls made it rear or drop away.

'If you're in doubt, bang out now, DJ,' Drew said.

'No, we're going in. Hook down.'

'I see your hook,' Drew confirmed.

'Okay. Here we go.'

The jet dipped and touched down just short of the runway. The landing gear bit into the soft earth and the jet wallowed and slewed, one wingtip brushing the ground. There was a dull thud as they lurched onto the tarmac, the impact on the right wheel pushing the jet back on line. It bounced a few feet back into the air and careered on.

'Shit, they're going to miss it,' Nick yelled.

As the Tempest dropped back onto the runway, the trailing hook snagged the thick steel cable. Drew saw the jet lurch as the cable brakes bit. The nose-wheel compressed. Instead of bouncing back as the shock absorbers soaked up the impact, it simply collapsed and hit the runway, vanishing in a torrent of sparks and grey smoke.

The cable hauled the jet savagely from over two hundred miles an hour to a dead stop in less than a hundred feet.

As Drew swung his jet into a wide circle, Nick gave him a running commentary from the back seat, twisting his neck around to keep DJ's aircraft in sight. 'Escape platform going in now.'

Drew caught the movement out of the corner of his eye as the mobile steel platform, perched on top of a Land-Rover, rammed into the side of the aircraft.

'Canopy opening,' Nick said. 'DJ's out. Ali's still in there. No, they're helping him out now. He doesn't look too good.'

Drew levelled the wings as they completed the turn and saw DJ and Ali hanging onto the rail as the platform reversed away at top speed. The fire crews in their yellow space suits instantly doused the jet and its trail of spilled aviation fuel with foam.

As they came in over the runway Drew saw that the massive concrete blocks anchoring the steel cable had been torn half out of the ground by the force of the impact.

DJ looked up and waved as Drew waggled his wings in salute.

'Nothing will be landing there for the next few hours,' Drew said. 'We'll use the west runway.'

Two hours later, DJ and Ali emerged from the medical centre.

'You beauties,' Drew shouted. 'Millions of pounds' worth of damage and not a scratch on you.'

'Only one,' Ali said, pointing shyly to the two stitches on the bridge of his nose. 'I forgot to lock my harness and slammed into my instrument panel.' He held up his helmet, which was split down the middle like an Easter egg.

When they walked into the briefing room, they found the intelligence officer flanked by Russell, the authoriser of the flight and an American intelligence expert, who had driven over from Combat Operations Centre to sit in on the debrief.

They gave the basic information on the incident – location, height, speed – and were immediately interrupted by the American. 'Were you breaking any of the rules? Did you overfly the Serb HQ or any of the politically sensitive zones?'

Drew answered for them. 'No. We'd been down to low level on our initial circuit but not below the minimum, and we'd been on Static CAP at fifteen thousand feet for over twenty minutes when we were fired at.'

The debrief continued for some time. Finally the American exchanged a questioning glance with the British officers and then said, 'Thank you. That's all, unless you've anything further to add.'

'I certainly have,' Drew said, ignoring Nick's warning nudge. 'Why wasn't that Serb firing position engaged?'

'We couldn't get any authority from the UN,' the American said evenly.

'What's the point of a Combat Operation Centre that has

no authority to carry out combat operations, even when its forces are being fired on?'

The American held up his hand. 'I've got every sympathy with you, really I have, but until the UN either gets off its ass or delegates authority to us, our hands are tied.'

Russell called Drew over as the others headed for the mess. He waited until they were out of sight. 'I know exactly how you feel, Drew, but there's no point in taking it out on them. They just do what they're told like the rest of us. As usual the politicians are the problem and we can't do much about them.'

'DJ and Ali could have died out there today,' Drew said. 'We're putting our lives on the line just so that the politicians back home can wrap themselves in the flag and pretend they're doing something, but it's a farce. We're not doing anything at all. We're not stopping them from flying and, even when they fire at us, we're not allowed to fire back. We might as well go the whole hog and paint targets on the jets.'

Russell nodded his agreement. 'I know. The only response after the last incident was that General Higgins wrote a strong letter to the Serb leader.'

Drew stared at him and then burst out laughing. 'A letter from General Higgins? That must really have frightened them.' He rubbed his face with his hand. 'They're not just firing at us, they're firing at undefended villages, raping the women, murdering their men. What are they going to have to do before we can act?'

'Believe me, Drew, there's nothing I'd like better than to see the squadron let off the leash, but we don't make the decisions. Do the job you're ordered to; that's all any of us can do. In the meantime,' he said, 'I'm afraid you've got another task lined up for tomorrow. The members of the Board of Inquiry are flying in to take your formal statement about the crash in the Eden Valley.'

Drew was incredulous. 'In the middle of combat operations? Well thanks for letting me know. I'm glad I've got plenty of time to prepare.'

'If you're telling the truth,' Russell said, 'you shouldn't need any time to prepare.'

Drew found Nick, DJ and Ali in the mess, just draining

the first bottle of champagne. Drew bought another one and sank his glass at one gulp.

Nick raised an eyebrow. 'Trouble?'

Drew nodded. DJ and Ali slipped discreetly away, not forgetting to take the bottle with them.

'What's on your mind, Drew?'

'The Board of Inquiry's going to interrogate me tomorrow.'

'That should be fun. Do you want me to mark your card?'

'You haven't been before one, have you?'

'Not on my own account, no, but I had to give evidence on behalf of another gung-ho pilot when I was on 13 Squadron.'

Drew gave him a withering look. 'So what's the story?'

'It's a bit like a court of law: you give your evidence under oath. Because no one's been killed, your judges will just be two air crew – a squadron leader and a flight lieutenant – almost certainly the two you've already had the pleasure of meeting. There'll also be an engineer there to advise them on technical details, and a stenographer.

'You sit facing them. They'll listen to your statement and cross-examine you. It can be quite daunting, especially if there's any hint that you may be found negligent – which there is in this case.'

Drew bristled. 'Thanks a lot.'

'I'm not saying *I* think that. I'm just repeating what they've already told you. As I said, if there's a chance you could be found negligent, they'll warn you as soon as you sit down that you could be court-martialled.'

'Any other cheerful stuff you think I should know?'

'Only that when they get round to announcing their verdict it's absolutely final. This isn't good old British justice. You can't get it declared a mistrial. You won't get a campaign going to Free the Finnington One. There's no right of appeal at all.'

He topped up the glasses and signalled to the barman for a refill. 'There, that cheered you up didn't it? Let's have another bottle and forget about it.'

Drew was called in to see the Board at ten the next morning. A room on the base had been hastily cleared and Squadron Leader Gordon and Flight Lieutenant Millns sat facing him across their makeshift desk – two canteen tables pushed together. Their backs were to the window, casting their faces into shadow. The engineer sat behind and slightly to one side of them, while the grey-haired stenographer occupied neutral ground, sitting at the end of the table at right angles to the others. She kept her eyes downcast, her only movement her fingers tapping at the keys.

As Nick had predicted, the opening salvo from Squadron Leader Gordon was direct and to the point. He raised his eyes from the documents in front of him. 'Are you 4213432, Flight Lieutenant Andrew Miller?'

'Yes.'

'Under Queen's Regulations, I must warn you that this investigation may result in you facing a court martial and that anything you say may be used in evidence against you at that subsequent court martial.'

Drew took a deep breath. 'Thank you, sir.'

Gordon glared at him. 'I know that combat air crew traditionally feel resentment and impatience with any insistence on adhering to procedures, but even in combat the correct procedures are still important. It isn't just paperwork – there's a reason for it.'

He waited for a response, but Drew remained silent. 'Right, let's get on. You are entitled to have a lawyer present during these proceedings.'

Drew raised an eyebrow. 'Gióia isn't exactly Lincoln's Inn, I'm afraid, sir. I think I'll have to manage without.'

After Drew had sworn an oath to tell the truth, the whole truth and nothing but the truth, Gordon began his most searching examination to date.

He did most of the questioning himself, with Millns only chipping in occasionally. The engineer sat behind them, leaning forward from time to time to whisper into Millns's ear. He in turn would scribble a note to Gordon, who took in the contents and then raised the point as if it had just occurred to him.

Drew's dislike for Gordon went beyond his growing hostility to the establishment. He contested every claim that Drew made and constantly disputed his version of events. But Drew kept his tone neutral as he laid out the events leading to the crash for what seemed like the thousandth time.

After two and a half hours, Gordon glanced at his two colleagues and then said briskly, 'Thank you, Flight Lieutenant. We have no further questions. If you have anything to add to your own previous statements, however, this is the moment to do so. There will be no further opportunities.'

'All I can add is that I carried out every aspect of that sortie in a routine, professional manner. A fault developed in the Tempest, forcing myself and my navigator to eject from the aircraft. My own informal enquiries lead me to believe that this is far from an isolated occurrence with the Tempest, as the incident reports held by the AIB make clear. Instead of reaching for the traditional stand-by of pilot error, I strongly suggest that the Board of Inquiry searches for a more plausible reason for the eighteen loss-of-control incidents involving Tempests RS1s and RS3s recorded in the last two years. Investigation of all incidents is apparently being handled directly by the head of the AIB.'

Gordon remained unmoved. 'That concludes the proceedings for this morning.' He looked significantly at the stenographer, who folded her hands in her lap. 'However, off the record, I have to say that I find your attempts to shift the blame for this accident absolutely reprehensible. These veiled hints at some high-level conspiracy of silence, based on little more than rumour and innuendo, do you no credit whatsoever, Flight Lieutenant. My job is to view the evidence dispassionately and objectively, and that is what I shall do. Good morning.'

Drew saluted mechanically and strode out. If there had been little doubt about the verdict of the Board of Inquiry before, there was none at all now. As he marched towards the crew room, his footfalls echoing from down the bare breeze-block corridor, Drew knew that his only hope was to discover the truth for himself. If it was left to Gordon, he would be facing a court martial before the year end.

Nick was waiting outside for him. He took one look at Drew's face and shook his head. 'I'm not even going to ask how it went. Let's get down to work. We've a mission to fly tomorrow and some serious preparation to do first.'

Drew went back to his quarters and sat on his bed. Furnished only with an iron bedstead, a wooden table, a chair and a metal wastepaper bin, it was as sterile and impersonal as a prison cell.

The only personal item was a picture in a small gunmetal frame. He picked it up. The black-and-white photograph was fading with age and cracked at the edges from the years he had carried it in his wallet.

Two faces stared out at him: a woman and a boy barely recognisable as the man he had become. Though he knew it as well as his own, Drew looked long and hard at the woman's face. Her skin was tight-drawn and almost translucent, and the eyes had a bright, fevered look, as if burnished by the disease that was eating away at her. It was the only remembrance of his mother that he possessed.

In a few weeks it would be ten years since Drew's graduation parade. Unlike his peers, he had had no family or friends to see him marching past. His father was still in Glasgow, too drunk or indifferent to make the journey, and his mother was already seven years dead. As he thought how proud she would have been if she could have been there, tears stung Drew's eyes.

The career he had built had been a validation of her struggle. Now he was about to place it all in jeopardy. He desperately hoped that she would have approved.

Chapter 13

Drew had an air of grim determination the next morning. He resisted Nick's efforts to draw him out, answered his questions distractedly or not at all and ignored the customary banter as the crews jostled in the changing room before the flight.

'What the hell is it, Drew?' Nick finally asked in exasperation. 'Pre-Mission Tension or what?'

'Something like that.'

Their mission was to CAP over a refugee centre on the outskirts of a village a few miles from Gornji Vakuf which had been coming under increasing Serb attacks. As Drew flew low over the operating area, he could see the narrow roads choked with refugees streaming away from the burning village to the north, the front line marked by a pall of smoke.

He grew even more withdrawn as he watched the devastation, but changed in an instant as their radar picked up a contact. He called AWACs as they flew to intercept.

'Request authority to engage.'

'No authority yet. Sunray has referred it to Gotham. Monitor and report.'

Drew swore. 'Not this bullshit again. You know where

this aircraft is heading – all the intelligence reports tell us that.'

AWACs did not reply.

'Four miles ahead, ten left of nose,' Nick called, talking Drew into visual contact with the target.

A few seconds later he saw the Serb aircraft. 'Tally.' The Super Galeb bomber was coming in on a course that could only lead to one destination.

Still there was silence from AWACs and Drew watched helplessly as the Serb aircraft neared its target. As it reached the perimeter of the refugee camp, it began firing its guns and rockets.

Drew grabbed the radio. 'Target now attacking the camp. Repeat, request authority to engage.'

He could see sticklike figures scattering in panic as explosions burst around them. One huddled figure, clutching a small, dark shape to her shoulder, was blasted apart by a direct hit from a rocket. All around her, others sprawled in the mud and lay still.

Staring in horror at the scene unfolding in front of him, Drew scarcely heard the laconic tones of the AWACs controller, 'Trying to get authority at this time. Stand by.'

'People are being slaughtered down there. We are tasked to protect that camp. Do you want to wait until there's no one left to protect?'

'There is no authority to fire as yet.'

'Bollocks. Engaging the target.'

'Drew, this isn't a good career move,' Nick said from the back seat.

'Just sit back, Nick,' Drew said grimly. 'Unless the Serbs send a SAM up to see us, that's all you've got to do.'

Ignoring the increasingly urgent calls from AWACs, he sent the Tempest spiralling down into the six o'clock of the lumbering Super Galeb as it turned for another strafing run. There was a high-pitched beeping as the Sidewinder's sensors locked onto a heat source – the Serb aircraft's engines. It was just half a mile short of the refugee camp when Drew pulled the trigger and yelled, 'Fox Two! Fox Two!'

The missile came off the side of the aircraft with a roar like an express train leaving a tunnel. The flare faded as it streaked away from them, weaving like the head of a cobra as it sped towards its target. Then there was a blinding flash as it detonated, followed immediately by a second, even bigger fireball, as the Super Galeb blew apart.

There was nothing left of the Serb aircraft but a corona of debris, spattered across the sky.

Drew thumbed the radio button. 'Sorry, Magic. What was that you were saying? Target engaged and destroyed.'

'For a Brit, you've got big balls,' the AWACs controller said. 'You'll certainly need them, because the shit is going to hit the fan in a very big way when you touch down.'

He ordered them straight back to base. Drew pulled into a steep turn, climbed to height and headed for the coast.

Nick sat in silence for a few minutes. 'Drew, you are a stubborn, self-willed, pig-headed, arrogant son of a bitch . . . but if you get out of this alive, I'll buy the drinks all night.'

'I've got a funny feeling that Russell is going to say exactly the same thing, apart from the bit about the drinks.'

They landed back at Gióia and taxied in. 'Don't open the canopy just yet,' Nick said as Drew nosed the Tempest onto the line outside the hangar and shut down the engines. 'Let's enjoy the last few moments of peace and quiet we are ever going to experience.'

Drew smiled. 'You think I might be in trouble then?'

'Never mind you, we're both in the deepest shit we've ever seen. This isn't just RAF rules and regulations, this is an international fucking incident. It'll come as quite a surprise to the folks back home. There they all were assuming that a declaration of war was a matter for the Chiefs of Staff and the Government and now it turns out that any old flight lieutenant can do it for them.'

'Have you finished?' Drew asked, though his confidence was ebbing fast. 'I've no problems with my conscience.' He gestured towards the hangar. 'Look, here's Russell himself coming to congratulate us.'

He took a deep breath and then flicked the switch to raise the canopy. 'Well, here goes.'

'I'll keep this short,' Russell said, his moustache quivering with indignation. 'The procedures for engagement were clearly laid down. You have deliberately chosen to ignore those procedures.'

'Because by the time we'd gone through them,' Drew interrupted, 'even supposing we'd got authorisation, the Serb bomber would have been on its way home again, leaving a lot of innocent people in bits.'

'That is irrelevant. Quite apart from the betrayal of the trust that I had personally placed in you, you have also disgraced yourself and your squadron.'

Russell waited for a response, but Drew just watched him impassively.

'I can't protect you this time, Miller. It's out of my hands.' Russell spun on his heel and strode away.

The rest of the squadron crowded around. Drew smiled wearily at their gestures of support, but knew it counted for nothing.

He stripped off his flying gear, showered and was on his way to the crew room when three military policemen confronted him. The most senior blocked his path. 'Flight Lieutenant Andrew Miller?'

'Absolutely.'

'I am instructed to issue formal notice of court martial proceedings to be undertaken against you. You are charged with gross misconduct, dereliction of duty and disobeying orders from a duly authorised senior officer. You are not obliged to say anything, but silence may count against you in court. Do you understand the charges against you?'

'Yes,' Drew said evenly.

'Do you have anything to say?'

'Yes I do: my conscience is clear.'

The MP's face registered a flicker of disapproval. 'You are grounded and confined to base until further notice. Any attempt to leave the base by any means will be treated as desertion.'

The MPs marched away, in step, down the corridor. Drew stared after them, a sick feeling in his stomach.

Nick handed Drew a coffee and sat down with him at a table. 'So they're throwing the book at you?'

'The whole library. What about you?'

Nick shrugged. 'I'll get a bollocking but I should be all right. That's the beauty of being a nav. Short of ejecting the pair of us, there was nothing much I could do to stop you, was there?'

He studied Drew's face for a moment. 'It's bad news for you, though. I can't see any way they won't kick you out for this.'

Drew tried to stop his hand shaking as he picked up his cup.

'It's a cold world, Drew. We've both been in the Air Force so long we've almost forgotten what it's like out there. People have to buy their own clothes. When their teeth need fixing they have to find a dentist. When they're ill they have to look for a doctor and join the hospital queue.'

Drew nodded. 'None of that stuff bothers me as much as the thought of what I'd do and where I'd go. That empty flat in Finnington doesn't hold much appeal these days, but I've no idea where I'd go instead.' He stirred his coffee abstractedly. 'No home, no wife, no lover, no family, no mates; perhaps Sally's right: maybe I *am* Bert Russell's spiritual son.

'The other thing that bugs me is that, if they kick me out, I'm never going to find out what's wrong with the Tempest. You're going to have to take that over.'

Nick shook his head. 'If I get out of this one alive, I'm not going to do anything to rock the boat again. I've got a wife and four children. You can tilt at windmills, if you like. I'm more interested in trying to keep the sails turning.'

Drew smiled, drained his coffee and stood up. 'One thing's for certain: we're not going to be flying any dawn patrols tomorrow, so what about that promise to buy the drinks all night?'

Nick got to his feet. 'That's the only intelligent suggestion you've made all day.'

They both slept late the following morning and were settling down to breakfast in the canteen as some of the crews were beginning to file in for lunch.

Drew looked up and smiled as he watched DJ sidle across to their table, holding a sheaf of papers.

'What are they?'

'Today's British front pages, faxed through from Finnington. I intercepted the clerk and managed to persuade him to photocopy them before he delivered them to Russell.' He tossed them on to the table.

Nick picked one up, scanned it and groaned. 'Oh no. Not Guy bloody Gibson again. Listen to this: "While not condoning the action of Flight Lieutenant Miller, it shows more clearly than a hundred empty speeches at the United Nations the extent of the mounting frustration felt by servicemen hamstrung by petty restrictions while asked to confront an increasingly desperate and ruthless enemy."

'That was the *Times* editorial. Can you imagine what the *Sun*'s going to be like?' He riffled through the pile and held up the lurid front page: GOTCHA! OUR BOY BLASTS SERB PSYCHOS.

As Nick read through the rest of the photocopies, a smile spread slowly over his face. He tossed the last one aside and grinned across the table. 'Perhaps I've been a bit hasty in consigning your career to the dustbin, Drew. You know that old chestnut about having to shoot someone or give them a medal? My guess is they're going to have to stand the firing squad down.'

Half an hour later, they checked the duty roster for the next day and found they were back on dawn patrol. 'Perhaps Russell hasn't got round to crossing us off yet,' Nick said.

'No such luck.' The authoriser looked up from his desk. 'He only put you on there ten minutes ago.'

As Drew walked back along the corridor, he came face to face with Russell, who stopped, nonplussed.

'I see I'm rostered for duty again tomorrow, sir.'

Russell flushed. 'I've been persuaded to give you another chance, Drew, against my better judgement, I might add. You can consider yourself fortunate.'

Drew kept his face deadpan. 'Who persuaded you, sir?'

Russell's mouth worked soundlessly for a moment, then he said, 'That's none of your damn business,' and hurried away down the corridor.

'He's cracking up,' Nick said, as he came up behind Drew.

'I know,' Drew said. 'That's what happens if you sit on the fence for twenty years. The railings eventually penetrate your brain.'

* * *

The intelligence brief the following morning warned of increased activity around Banja Luka and it came as no great surprise to Drew and Nick that they were assigned to that area as they checked in with the AWACs controller.

'Tiger 2–1, confirming two aircraft for Gate 5, Drop 4,' the mid-western voice said. 'Go and CAP at Oscar.'

'Great,' Drew said. 'Just what we need: another static CAP. Why is it always our turn to play at being live targets?'

'Drew,' Nick said, choosing his words carefully. 'You're not going to do anything rash this time, are you?'

Drew knew his answer was less than reassuring. 'If anything happens, let's just hope either the general back at COC has some balls for a change, or the UN commander hasn't gone for a round of golf.'

The first CAP passed without incident, but Nick grew increasingly restive in the back seat. Finally he could stand it no longer. 'I don't know about you, Drew, but I'm dying for a pee.'

'Tension getting to you Nick? Help yourself to a Nato pee bag and don't mind me.'

'For some strange reason the thought of undoing my safety harness within range of several Triple-A and SAM missile sites doesn't really appeal. If it's all the same to you, if we have to eject, I'd like to be attached to a parachute at the time.'

'Oh all right, then. I suppose we'll have to find a rest area. Honestly, if I've told you once, I've told you a thousand times, always take a pee before a long journey.' He checked his watch. 'Our refuelling bracket isn't for another fifteen minutes, but if you're really desperate I'll call AWACs and see if we can go early.'

'I'd be pathetically grateful if you could.'

'Magic, Tiger 2–1 requesting permission to exit the area fifteen minutes early for our refuelling bracket.'

'Any reason for that?'

'An in-cockpit snag, a bit of crew discomfort.'

There was a chuckle from the AWACs controller. 'You Limeys and your endless cups of tea. Go ahead. Do one for me while you're at it.'

As they came out of their gate, Drew and Nick made their weapons safe. Nick pushed the pin into his seat, then began unstrapping himself and struggling out of several layers of flying kit.

'Bag relief, NATO-issue,' Nick said, reading the label on the plastic container. 'These guys can't even write English, never mind speak it.'

There was the sound of a struggle as he fought to unite himself with the equipment. 'Mid-air refuelling is a doddle compared to this. It's like trying to get a python into a pillow-case underwater.' There was a contented sigh from the back seat, a few seconds' silence and then a groan. 'And why are they only half a pint? It's bad enough having to use them at all without having to stop halfway and change bottles.'

'You always say that,' Drew said wearily. 'It must be prostate trouble.' He began bunting the aircraft, decelerating sharply to create zero G for a few seconds. Unrestrained by his harness, Nick felt himself floating out of his seat, with his NATO-issue equipment still attached.

'Very witty, Drew. However, if you glance over your right shoulder you'll see that the first pee-bag I filled is floating straight towards the back of your head.'

Drew laughed and pushed the throttles forward, piling on a bit of G and sending Nick crashing back down on to his seat. The first pee bag squelched down on to his lap a moment later.

'Now if playtime's over,' Nick said, 'I'll just pop the equipment away and we can get back to work.'

They flew on to their rendezvous with the tanker.

'Morning, Texaco,' Drew said. 'Fill her up and check the oil and water will you?'

'Great,' the tanker pilot said, 'another humorist. That's all we need.'

Drew nosed the Tempest's probe into the basket. Fuel began pumping into the jet at the rate of hundreds of gallons a minute. Inside five minutes they were streaking back towards their entry gate, ready to take up position again just to the south of Banja Luka.

AWACs welcomed them back. 'There's a lot of activity around Jellystone. Claret 2–1's just reported heavy concentrations of troops around helicopters at 448174. He's also had SAM 2 indications a couple of times.'

As they flew in to take up station south of Banja Luka, the hostile symbols began reappearing on the radar warner, each one announced by an electronic tone, ringing out in the cramped cockpit like the tolling of a bell.

At each tone, Nick rattled out a warning: 'Triple-A, two o'clock, outside lethal range. SAM 6, eleven o'clock, just outside lethal range.'

Almost as soon as they were on station, there was a different, more strident tone. 'Surveillance radar tracking us from site Orange,' Nick said.

'We know about that one. No problem.'

'There may be,' Nick said. 'It's come up as missile surveillance now – a SAM 2, inside lethal range. Someone's having a closer look.'

Ali came through on the radio immediately with the same message. Drew called up AWACs again. 'Magic, SAM 2 indications from Jellystone area.'

'Okay, I've lost SAM 2 indications,' Ali said, but as Nick began to reply, 'So have—' he interrupted himself. 'No, it's back on us.'

As he spoke, the alarms started screaming. A bar of green light stabbed across Nick's screen, pinpointing the radar locked on to them.

'Spike! Spike!' he yelled.

The screen message, 'SAM 2 acquisition', was superfluous. Drew was already throwing the jet into a pattern of evasion and ramming the throttles all the way forward, the engine note rising to a scream as the afterburners kicked in.

As he hurled the aircraft into a hard left turn, the screen message changed to 'SAM 2 MG' – missile guidance – the missile was already in the air and homing in on them, surfing the radar beam.

'SAM launch. Get away from us, DJ,' Drew yelled. DJ and Ali peeled away instantly, afterburners blazing. 'Chaff.'

Nick responded before Drew had finished the order, pushing the chaff button as fast and often as he could, sending clouds of aluminium foil billowing out behind the aircraft.

'Clear my turn,' Drew demanded.

'Break right.'

Grunting with the effort, Drew forced the stick hard right, the G-force clamping down on him like a vice as the jet slewed. He held the turn for two seconds, then levelled the wings and yelled, 'Chaff', before sending the jet into another breakneck turn.

He heard a thud as Nick's helmet banged against the side of the cockpit under the force of the turn. 'Where's the missile?' Drew shouted, each word an effort as the G-force pressed in on him. He kept the jet diving, twisting and turning, trying to break the radar lock as Nick scanned the sky for the missile hurtling towards them.

Both saw it together, a black streak far below them, trailing a tail of grey smoke as it shrank the gap. Drew forced the stick right and watched the missle change course to follow. There was not even the slightest room for doubt about its target.

Neither Drew nor Nick wasted a word, concentrating on their jobs with cold professionalism. Accelerating to two thousand miles an hour, the missile would take a handful of seconds to reach its target. Drew had to keep dragging his eyes away from the panel on the screen, but he could not stop himself counting down the seconds to impact.

Despite Drew's manoeuvres, the alarm still sounded and the warning light still flashed. The missile kept accelerating towards them, locked to the radar beam. He hurled the jet into an even more desperate turn, fighting the stick to force it down and away to the right as he screamed for more chaff.

Numb with fear, he waited, skin crawling, hunching his shoulders as if to make himself a smaller target. There was a vivid red flash in the sky above and behind them, as the missile detonated on the last burst of chaff.

He flinched involuntarily, expecting shrapnel from the blast – white-hot metal exploding outwards, obliterating everything in its path – to come crashing through the fuselage. As he realised that they had escaped, he closed his eyes for a second in silent thanks and let his pent-up breath escape through his teeth.

He eased back on the throttles and the howling engine note began to fade. 'Shit, that was too close. Are you okay, Nick?'

Nick's voice was so shaky that his reply was almost inaudible.

Drew thumbed the radio button. 'Magic, Tiger 2–1 was engaged by SAM 2. No dam—'

He never had the chance to finish the sentence. The aircraft would not respond to the stick, lurching drunkenly from side to side, then spiralling downwards. Already at low altitude after the manoeuvres to evade the missile, Drew had no time to try to right the aircraft. He hauled back on the stick and called, 'It's no good, Nick. Prepare to bang out.'

Nick scanned his screen one last time, then thumbed the radio and began broadcasting the information that would let a rescue helicopter pinpoint the site. 'Bull's-eye point seventeen miles, zero-two-nine, present posit—'

'No time,' Drew yelled. 'Eject! Eject!'

They pulled on the yellow-and-black handles simultaneously. Straps tightened around them, pinioning their arms and legs to their seats. There was an explosion as the canopy blew off and was ripped away by the slipstream, then a roar as the ejector rockets fired.

Drew blacked out for a couple of seconds under the force of the ejection. He came to as the main parachute opened with the crack of a whip and he felt himself jerked upwards as it took his weight.

After the noise, there was silence.

He opened his eyes and glanced around. The Tempest's pyre was blazing a mile away in the same thick forest that covered the steep slopes below him. There were mountain crags rising at his back, but in front of him the forest ended abruptly in a narrow patchwork of fields surrounding a small village. A canvas-topped lorry was beginning to move out of the village in his direction, drab-uniformed figures buzzing around it.

At first Drew could see no sign of Nick. Panic seized him. Had he been trapped in the Tempest? Then he caught a movement in the corner of his eye and saw Nick's orange-and-white chute a few hundred yards nearer to the village and drifting ever closer to it on the wind. Drew hauled down hard on his own harness trying to steer away from the village and the road, but his efforts had little effect.

He saw the lorry grinding up the road towards them. As

it stopped, soldiers spilled from it and ran towards the edge of the forest.

He tore frantically at his combat jacket and pulled out his pistol. He felt slightly less defenceless now, though he knew that if the Serbs got within range of him it would be of little use against their assault rifles.

Nick's parachute drifted towards one of the last clumps of trees, then snagged, his harness entangled in the branches. He hung there helplessly, twisting slowly in the wind.

Drew dropped towards the forest canopy and could see no more for a moment. Branches whipped at him, tearing at his clothing. The parachute caught and then ripped free. He crashed on down through the treetops, cannoning off a thicker branch, then was jerked viciously to a halt as the chute caught again.

The silk drooped like a dying flower and, as it tore free again, Drew plummeted towards the ground. He screamed in pain as another jagged branch stopped him dead, ripping through his layers of clothing and gouging his side. Then it snapped and he was falling again, the last twenty feet to the forest floor.

He crashed to the ground, the branch impaling itself alongside his head. He lay there winded for a few moments, then struggled to his feet, tearing at his harness. As he looked up, he could see Nick through a gap in the trees, still dangling thirty feet up as he struggled with something in his combat jacket. There was a flash of pale blue as he waved the UN beret at the Serb soldiers hidden from Drew's sight by the trees.

His gesture was answered by a burst of gunfire. A high-velocity round hit him just below the knee, blowing off the lower part of his leg in an explosion of blood and bone. Drew stood frozen as he saw Nick's mouth fall open and heard a chilling, high-pitched scream, the sound of a tortured child torn from the throat of a man.

As the scream at last died away, there was a burst of laughter from the men on the ground. Then the firing began again – single shots – and Drew realised what they were doing. The Serbs were not shooting to kill: they were working their way in from the extremities of Nick's body, prolonging his agony for their amusement.

Another round blew away part of his other foot. There was another scream, a pause, two shots that missed and a third punched a hole clean through Nick's left hand.

Drew pulled his own pistol out of his combat jacket and ran towards them, firing twice. The effect on the Serbs was instantaneous. Nick's body jerked like a puppet as bursts of automatic fire tore tufts of fibres from his clothing. Dark stains spread across his combat jacket. His head suddenly tilted and his screaming stopped.

Drew froze again, his knuckles whitening on the butt of his pistol until the steel bit into his fingers. He saw every detail with a terrible clarity: the face of his friend in its death agony, the contorted body, the blood dripping from the mangled limbs as Nick's body twisted slowly in the wind.

As he stared, the promise he had made to Sally just a few days before came back to him. Tears misted his eyes as he thought of those suddenly fatherless children.

Fresh bursts of gunfire jerked Drew back to awareness of his own predicament. The Serbs were firing blind into the forest; bullets raked the ground and lashed the foliage around him. As the gunfire stopped he heard a fresh sound: twigs snapped and heavy, booted feet trampled through the undergrowth towards him.

He tore his eyes away from Nick and looked despairingly towards the survival box a few yards down the slope. Then he turned and ran up the hillside, dodging between the tree trunks, his feet floundering in the dense carpet of soft pine needles.

In the panic of his parachute descent, he had forgotten his combat drills and pulled the handle to inflate his life-jacket, protecting his neck on impact. The dayglo-orange jacket stood out like a target amongst the trees. He yanked it off as he ran and threw it away. His flying helmet followed. The life-jacket contained his locator beacon, but, if he stopped to retrieve it, the Search and Rescue team would only be using it to locate a corpse.

The bruise on his side throbbed agonisingly, but he forced himself on. He blundered deeper and deeper into the forest, gasping for breath, a roaring sound in his ears, sweat cascading from him.

He had no idea of how long he ran, but he kept on running until he tripped over a tree root and crashed to the ground. He slid down a steep bank into a hollow, brambles tearing at his face and body.

At the bottom, buried amongst the brambles and ferns, was a pool of rheumy water and black, stinking mud. Uncaring, he lay there, his chest heaving as he fought for breath. Gradually the pounding of his heart eased and his rasping breath quietened.

He listened. At first there was no sound other than the buzzing of the flies, but gradually he became aware of a rustling noise, which grew louder by the second. There was a sudden crack, not far off – the snap of a twig.

He looked around frantically for better cover. There was none. He wriggled deeper into the foul-smelling mud, coating the back of his body, arms and legs, and rolled his head from side to side, covering his hair and neck. Then he turned onto his front and snaked into the undergrowth.

He looked behind him, but the wet mud and brackish water had already swallowed his trail. His face lay inches from the edge of the undergrowth. It was sparse cover, but it was all there was. Peering out, he could see only a few feet of the forest floor.

He lay there motionless, his heart pounding like a hammer. Another twig snapped and then he heard a rhythmic beating as the searchers marched slowly up the hillside, line abreast, thrashing the bushes with sticks and calling to each other.

Every instinct screamed at Drew to be off and running before it was too late, but he held himself rigid, pressing himself down even further into the mire as the sounds grew louder, his fingers scrabbling into the mud as he tried to hide himself.

He found he was holding his breath and exhaled with a noise that he was sure could be heard fifty yards away. He forced himself to breathe slowly and evenly but his heart still pounded, the pulse beating in his temple like a drum. Flies buzzed around him, settling on his eyelids and lips. He heard rough, guttural shouts as the searchers came nearer. He had never felt more isolated, nor more scared.

The noise of the search reached a crescendo. A stick

whistled through the air and beat at the brambles above him. His skin tautened as he waited for the blow or the gunshot that he knew must come.

Then he heard the stick thwacking at the next patch of brambles and the footsteps moved on, scuffling amongst the pine needles. The flies, which had lifted from him as the sticks beat the bushes, returned. He was about to raise his head to peer after the retreating searchers when a scuffed and mud-smeared toecap came to rest six inches from his face. He froze again.

Instead of an explosion, there was a muffled sound he could not identify, and then silence. Suddenly a jet of steaming urine splashed down through the brambles. Drew could feel its warmth on his arm. Tiny droplets spattered onto his face. He watched in horror as the mud was washed from the arm of his flying suit.

He was sure now that he would die. Instead there was an impatient shout from further up the hill and a guttural response. The stream of urine slowed and stopped. The toecap turned away, but the soldier's other foot came down on Drew's forearm. The hobnails scoured a path across his arm as the boot slipped off and he stifled a yelp of pain. The soldier gave a muffled curse as he pulled his boot out of the mud, which released its hold with a squelch.

There was another shout and Drew watched through half-closed eyes, as the soldier came into view for a moment, hurrying up the slope, fumbling with his buttons, his assault rifle dangling from his shoulder.

The sounds of the search faded as the patrol disappeared higher up the hillside. For the moment Drew was safe, but still he stayed where he was.

He fingered the radio jammed in his combat jacket, but decided against using it. Calling up on the Guard frequency would undoubtedly have alerted the American Search and Rescue teams that he was alive, but the call could also be overheard by anyone else monitoring the frequency.

He considered his position as objectively as he could. If his luck held, he could lie up until after nightfall and then head south-west over the mountains towards Muslim-held territory. All his combat survival briefs had stressed that there was no such thing as a safe haven in Bosnia and all sides embroiled in the conflict were to be treated as hostile, but he knew that there was a UN monitoring station on the outskirts of Srebanj. It was seventy miles away, but he needed an objective and there was nothing to be gained from staying where he was.

He was haunted by the image of Nick's shattered body. As if in confirmation, he heard a shot from further up the hillside, then another and another. The searchers were returning, firing into the undergrowth to try to flush out their quarry. Drew heard them calling to each other as they moved through the forest. He tried to burrow deeper into the mud, then froze as two soldiers approached, kicking at the bushes. There was another shot and Drew heard the bullet rip through the brambles just above his head. It hit a stone and ricocheted away.

Again and again the soldiers combed the area, shouting, beating the bushes and firing into the undergrowth. Again and again they passed Drew's hiding place without discovering him.

The stagnant water seeped through every layer of Drew's clothing and chilled him to the bone, but he dared not move. Even when his leg locked in the agony of cramp, he forced himself to lie still, flexing only his toes to ease the pain. He was desperately thirsty, but could not risk moving to get at one of the water sachets in his G-suit.

He lay still, constantly alert, as he watched the shadows lengthen through the afternoon. For an instant, he found himself thinking of home and of Michelle. Only five days before, he had been sitting in a restaurant by an English river, drinking champagne, eating fine food and falling in love.

In the early evening the soldiers made one final sweep, but by then they seemed half convinced that their quarry had already escaped. They hurried down the hillside, searching halfheartedly in the undergrowth. Then they were gone.

Chapter 14

Drew heard engines revving in the distance and gears grinding as the Serb lorries lumbered away down the road. He remained where he was, fearing a trap, soldiers waiting to pounce as he emerged from his hide. When night had fallen and the first stars were pricking the sky, he crawled stiffly out of his lair.

He sorted through his pockets, lining up his survival equipment in front of him, then discarded every inessential. He was left with his water and emergency rations, a foil space blanket, a map doubling as a blanket, a sheet of camouflage netting, spare socks, hat and mittens, his pistol and a hunting knife. He also had a medical kit, a radio and a Global Positioning System receiver.

He turned his GPS on. The tiny screen lit up and within half a minute it had given him his position. The nearest rescue point lay beyond the heaviest concentrations of Serb troops, but the GPS could also be used like a compass, showing him the direction to travel and the distance he had already covered. Drew was oddly comforted by the messages on the tiny green screen.

He tossed the useless items like sunblock and sunglasses into the mud and ground them down with his boot. A thick manual on air-crew survival, its weight exceeding its usefulness, also went in, followed by his G-pants.

He thought wistfully of the survival pack from the Tempest, full of water, food, warm clothing and survival aids. It might still be lying where it had fallen. The thought of water made him rip open a sachet. He drained it and reached for another, but then stopped himself. Without the survival pack, he had only two pints, which might have to last him days; better to wait and drink from a stream as he climbed towards the mountains. He was also ravenously hungry but determined to save his rations for a real emergency.

He hesitated for a moment, unsure what to do. Then he stood up, still stiff and shivering with cold, wincing at the pain from the bruise on his side. Instead of heading up the hillside, he inched his way slowly back down the slope, retracing his route.

The moon was rising behind the clouds, but only a faint light filtered down between the trees. Every few seconds he paused, straining his eyes and ears into the darkness ahead. He struggled on, slipping from tree to tree, his breath coming in ragged bursts as each fresh sound of the forest set his heart racing.

More by luck than good navigation, he eventually reached the clearing. The newly broken end of the branch that had almost impaled him showed white in the moonlight. He saw the survival box a little way down the slope.

He hung back at the edge of the clearing, scanning every tree and every shadow. He was about to move into the open when he caught a faint scent on the breeze. He shrank back as he smelled black tobacco smoke.

He peered out again, straining his eyes to look through, not at, the cover, as his survival instructor had once told him. Directly opposite he could just make out a darker shape in the shadows by the trunk of a thick pine. As he looked there was the faint glint of moonlight on steel and the glow of a freshly inhaled cigarette.

Drew sank silently to the ground and then wormed his way forward. As the soldier took another drag on his cigarette, Drew caught a brief glimpse of his features, demonic in the red light. Then the dot turned cartwheels in the night as the soldier flicked the cigarette away.

Drew remained motionless, adrenalin pumping. Suddenly there was a rasping sound and the white flare of a match no more than five metres to his right. As he flattened himself against the ground, he heard a second soldier draw on his cigarette, cough, hawk and spit. There was a metallic click and the man called to his companion.

Both stepped out from the shadows and stood in the centre of the clearing, muttering to each other as they smoked their cigarettes. Then they slung their weapons over their shoulders and, carrying the survival box between them, headed down the hillside.

Drew crawled out of his hiding place and watched them pick their way through the trees. They paused for a moment at the edge of the forest. Drew saw them gazing up and heard them laugh. Then they walked on down the sloping field to the road. Drew stayed hidden in the shadows until the murmur of their voices faded away.

He heard a dull thump and the bang of a door, then an engine roared into life and two headlights stabbed into the darkness as a lorry disappeared into the night.

Drew moved swiftly to the point where the men had paused. Long before he saw the dark shape twisting slowly above him, he knew what they had been looking at. He stepped away from the base of the tree and listened for a moment, but the only sounds were the breeze through the treetops and the faint creaking of the parachute harness.

Every instinct told him that he must use the remaining hours of darkness to get far away from this place, but he could not leave his friend hanging there.

He peered upwards, measuring the distance to the first branch, then sprang. His outstretched fingers caught and held and he hauled himself up. Panting with effort, he swung a leg over the branch and then pulled himself upright against the trunk. He paused and then began to scale the tree.

Finally he stood on a broken branch, just above Nick's body. He inched out along it, his hands thrashing the air as he struggled to hold his balance. The branch creaked ominously and he felt himself starting to fall. He threw himself forward into space. His fingers clutched at the parachute webbing and he gasped as his bruised side banged into Nick's corpse.

The chute swung crazily to and fro. As the motion slowed, he slid down. Avoiding looking at Nick's face, he reached around for the quick-release harness, recoiling as his fingers found the catch, sticky with blood. He forced himself to press and turn it but a Serb round had jammed it shut.

He dragged himself painfully back up the harness and then, anchored by one hand, he reached into his jacket for his knife and began to saw through the strands. It took him twenty minutes, the muscles in his left arm screaming in protest as they took his weight.

The last strands of the harness parted and Nick's lifeless body dropped to the ground. Drew grabbed for the harness with his other hand. Then he lowered himself until his arms were fully extended and let himself drop.

He landed alongside Nick's body and, as he pulled himself to his feet, a gap in the clouds allowed him to see Nick's face illuminated in the moonlight.

Averting his gaze, Drew leaned down and tugged at the thin leather thong around Nick's neck. It was slippery with blood. He let it slip through his fingers until he felt cold metal in the palm of his hand. Then he jerked it free and slipped it into his pocket.

He dragged the body a few yards into the forest, tears streaming down his face, then began ripping with his knife at the soft earth between the trees. Throwing the knife aside in frustration, he scrabbled at the soil with his bare hands, scraping pine needles and forest debris aside, his fingers tearing at the network of fine tree roots just below the surface.

Without a spade, he could dig no more than a few inches down, but he made the hole as large as he could, then dragged Nick's corpse towards it, the stumps of his legs scraping twin furrows in the earth.

He scraped the soil, leaves and forest litter back over the body, covering it as well as he could. Then he snapped a branch under his boot and plunged it into the earth at the head of the shallow grave. Nick's UN beret had caught in a patch of brambles. Drew retrieved it and hung it from the branch. He knelt motionless by the grave, not knowing how to pray or what to say. Then he turned and began to move away up the slope.

He was torn between the need for caution and speed. At first he advanced stealthily, pausing every few paces to look and listen for danger, but he quickly realised that hypothermia could be as great a threat to him as the Serbs and increased his pace. He had to get warm, using his body heat to dry his clothes, before he came out through the treeline onto the barren, rocky ridges high above him. If not, he could be dead of exposure before morning.

Pausing from time to time to check his GPS, he pushed on up the progressively steeper mountainside, stumbling over tree roots hidden in the shadows as he climbed.

His luck held. He neither saw nor heard any trace of patrols and, though every hoot of an owl sent his pulse soaring, he pressed on, growing in confidence.

The tree cover grew thinner as he climbed higher, the moonlight throwing the rocky slopes above into sharp relief. At the treeline he paused and crouched down to drink greedily from a stream. Then he straightened up and scanned the ridge above him.

There was no sign of movement but it was small consolation. There was little cover to be had on the kilometre of rocky, open ground separating him from the ridge, but he had to cross it and be down amongst the trees on the other side before morning. If he was still out in the open in daylight, he would be a simple target.

Taking a deep breath, he forced his protesting body onwards, climbing up over the loose rock and scree towards the ridgeline. The wind was bitter and, despite his exertions, he could feel a numbing cold seeping through him, but he forced himself on.

He reached the ridge, starkly outlined in the moonlight, at two in the morning. With scarcely a glance towards the snowy peaks rising still higher to either side, he began to descend. The moon set behind banks of cloud piling up from the west. Flurries of snow blew around him, chilling him even more and making the ground slippery and treacherous.

In the darkness he lost his footing repeatedly and slipped and tumbled amongst the screes, once sliding out of control for thirty metres before he could bring himself to a stop. He remembered no precipices from his flying over these mountains but each hesitant footfall remained a step into the unknown.

At last he saw blacker shapes looming up at him through the darkness. He stumbled past the first stunted trees and struggled on into another dark forest, groping his way downwards. The snow had been replaced by a damp, insistent drizzle, soaking and chilling him once more to the bone. His teeth chattering with cold, he hurried on down the mountain, casting an anxious eye at the reddening sky to the east.

In the cold, grey light before dawn he came to the edge of a small clearing. He circled it cautiously, peering into the shadows, then crawled into a hole in the undergrowth a few yards into the forest, dragging branches across to hide himself.

He checked his position on the GPS, his heart sinking as he read the distance covered: a mere twelve miles in the night's travelling. At this rate of progress, it would take him almost a week to reach his destination. Even if the Serbs did not find him, he was unsure if he could keep going for that long.

Again he forced himself to be positive. Cut the crap, he thought. Nick's dead. Whatever it takes, you've got to get home and tell them what happened.

He drank another of his precious sachets of water, then wrapped himself in his space blanket and his map, and pulled the camouflage net awkwardly over the top. He sat for a few minutes, eyes blank, fingering the piece of metal on its blood-encrusted thong, then slipped it back into his pocket.

Finally he settled down to rest, but every time he closed his eyes all he could see was the body of his friend, riddled with bullets, twisting slowly in the wind.

He opened his eyes to find himself looking down the barrel of a gun. Two unshaven men, farmers, probably father and son, stood peering down at him through the foliage. The older, white-haired and grizzled, held the ancient double-barrelled shotgun. The yellowing teeth of the other man were exposed by a long scar that pulled up the corner of his mouth in a sneer. He prodded Drew repeatedly in the chest with a thick walking stick, shouting at him and signalling him to get to his feet.

Warily Drew complied, crawling out of his hide, then standing up and raising his hands above his head. As he did so, the old man stepped back, keeping a few feet between them. Drew looked back towards his hide and saw a silver flash, an upturned corner of the space blanket that had betrayed him.

His only glimmer of hope lay in making an immediate escape, before the men alerted Serb soldiers. The easiest time to escape was as soon as you were captured; he remembered that much from his combat survival lectures. But, though he felt the reassuring weight of his pistol inside his combat jacket, he knew that, if he tried to draw it, the old man would kill him in an instant.

Scarface jerked his head towards the clearing and Drew walked on ahead of them into the open, his hands still above his head. In his haste to find cover before daybreak, he had missed the wooden roof of a farmhouse nestled among the trees not two hundred metres away.

There was another shout. Drew halted and turned to face his captors. Whitehair said something, obviously asking him a question. Drew shrugged his shoulders in incomprehension. Immediately there was a flash of white light in his head and a blinding pain as Scarface smashed the stick into his face, sending him crashing to the ground.

He dragged Drew to his feet again and Whitehair repeated the question. As Drew shook his head in a show of dumb incomprehension, Scarface lashed him again. The stick shattered with the impact. Furious, Scarface began kicking him as he lay on the ground. Drew's mouth had filled with the sweet, sickly taste of blood. His left eye was closing rapidly and the Serbs' voices seemd to be coming from a long way away.

Panting with the effort, Scarface stepped back and motioned Drew to his feet. Drew dragged himself upright, shaking his head to clear it as he raised his hands above him. The old man uttered the question a third time, raising the shotgun menacingly to his shoulder.

Looking into those expressionless eyes, Drew knew he was going to be killed. Still with his hands up, he bent his right hand downwards and pointed his fingers towards his belt. Whitehair eyed him suspiciously and then nodded. Very slowly, Drew put his hand down and pulled out his wad of Deutschmarks. The old man licked his lips but kept the gun where it was.

Scarface said something and both men laughed. As he stepped forward to take the cash, he moved between Drew and the barrel of the gun. Drew let the notes slip through his fingers and the breeze caught them and sent them fluttering away.

Scarface half turned after the money and Drew shoved him into the old man and took off, diving back into the forest as a shot rang out and buckshot peppered the trees just behind him. He sprinted along a track for a hundred yards, then threw himself down behind a bush and pulled out his pistol.

Leaving the old man chasing banknotes, Scarface came running along the track, clutching the shotgun. Drew screwed up his still-closing eye and took aim with his pistol, not even sure if he could shoot the man in cold blood.

Scarface kept coming, stopping barely twenty metres away as he raised the shotgun to his shoulder. Before he could pull the trigger, Drew fired twice. The first shot hit the man squarely in the chest. The impact sent him backwards, crashing to the ground. The second shot went high, but Scarface was already dying. Pink froth bubbled from the hole in his chest

Drew stood up, rooted to the spot, staring in horrid fascination at the dying man. A shout from the old man snapped him out of it. He dragged his gaze away from the body and was off and running, deeper and deeper into the forest.

He sprinted for a few hundred yards but then forced himself to stop, reload his pistol and check his GPS. Then he ran on through the silent forest in a slow, sustainable jog, keeping to a south-west course the best he could.

As he ran, he cursed himself for his carelessness in siting his hide. Now he had lost his blankets, his radio, his map and most of his water. All he had were his pistol, some emergency rations and the clothes he stood up in. Even worse, he was now forced to move in daylight, dog-tired and an easy target for the Serbs.

He pushed the thoughts out of his mind and hurried on, ears pricked for the sounds of pursuit. He had been running for about half an hour when he heard a familiar sound, a helicopter flying low, skimming over the treetops. Hope rose in him, even though logic told him it could not be a rescue package. He had made no radio contact since ejecting from his aircraft and was now over a dozen miles from where it had crashed.

As the noise of its rotors grew louder and the downwash whipped the tops of the trees, he hid under the foliage of a fallen beech, peering upwards through the leaves at the black shape hovering like a hawk above its prey.

It was a Serbian Gazelle. Drew dropped his head in case the white of his face betrayed him and stayed motionless until the sound of the rotors had faded, then crept out of his hiding place and moved on. Several times he had to dive for cover again as the chopper returned, quartering and requartering the area, but each time it passed him by.

The trees thinned steadily, leaving him with more and more open ground to cross. Each time he lay motionless in the shadows at the edge of the wood, scanning the area for movement and listening for the telltale beat of the helicopter's rotors. Then he was off, scurrying across the open spaces, half crouching as he ran, diving into the next patch of cover, sobbing with effort and relief.

With the sun high in the sky, he found himself on the edge of open country. Ahead lay a web of rough pasture and meadow, studded with a few dilapidated barns. A single, unmetalled road wound through the fields towards a tiny hamlet.

He was working his way cautiously around the hamlet, using the walls and hedges linking the barns as cover, when he heard the rumble of engines. He stiffened and shrank back behind a low wall as he saw a convoy of military lorries come rattling along the road, trailing dust behind them. They screeched to a halt at the edge of the hamlet and soldiers piled out.

Drew's heart sank. The helicopter must have spotted him. He looked around but there was no cover between him and the edge of the woods and no prospect of reaching them without being spotted.

He flattened himself against the wall, but he knew it was only a matter of time before he was discovered. He no longer had the strength or the speed left to outrun the troops and his cover was minimal. As the Serbs fanned out to search, they could not fail to find him.

He pulled out his pistol and cocked it, prepared at least to try to kill a couple of soldiers before they shot him. He peered cautiously around the end of the wall, using a clump of thistles as cover. To his astonishment, he saw the soldiers moving away from him into the hamlet itself.

He withdrew his head, exhaling slowly with relief, but then his heart jumped as shooting broke out. He took a cautious look back around the wall. The Serbs were sprinting from house to house, firing as they ran. Punctuating the shots, there were crashes as doors were kicked in and cries as old men, women and children were dragged out into the open. They were forced to sit in a circle on the ground, their hands on their heads.

For over two hours Drew remained in his hiding place, hearing sounds plucked from the inferno. There were terrible, unearthly screams interspersed with bursts of gunfire, smashing glass, splintering wood and other nameless, horrible noises whose meaning Drew could only guess.

He heard a roar like a fire-breathing dragon, and peered around the wall. A Serb soldier with a flame-thrower sent a jet of fire into one of the houses. As flame and black smoke began pouring from the building, a figure ran from the door, hair and clothes smouldering. The soldier swivelled to track her with his weapon and pumped another burst of fire at the fleeing figure, turning her into a human torch. She tottered a few more yards, then crumpled to the ground, the flames still licking greedily at her blackened body.

The pillar of thick, black smoke rose higher into the sky as more and more buildings were torched. A young girl leapt from an upstairs window as her home dissolved in flames and ran frantically towards the edge of the village, but the Serbs were onto her like a pack of hounds. She was dragged back, her pitiful cries echoing in Drew's ears.

One soldier seized her by the hair and punched her

repeatedly in the face, then hurled her against a wooden gate. Others eagerly seized her and spreadeagled her, face down, across the gate, lashing her wrists with rope. A succession of soldiers then raped her, urged on by the men waiting their turn as they guarded the circle of terrified captives. The girl's screams kept rising and falling, her voice cracking with agony and terror.

Finally, he saw one of them fix a bayonet to his rifle. Drew buried his face in his hands as he heard the girl give a scream more terrible than any she had uttered before. Then there was silence.

When Drew looked around the wall again, the girl's body had sagged against the gate, still held by the ropes at her wrists, as a dull red stain spilled slowly down over her thighs and dripped onto the ground.

The group of soldiers were beating, kicking and punching the handful of remaining captives as they herded them into the backs of the lorries. Suddenly a man broke away and ran frantically down the road away from the village, but a barrage of shots rang out and he pitched forward into the dust. He twitched and lay still. One of the soldiers sauntered down the road, rolled the body over with the toe of his boot and, satisfied, strolled back again.

The last of the captives were forced into the lorries. The soldiers clambered in after them, carrying bottles and other loot from the houses, one even swinging four live chickens in his hands. The engines started up and the convoy rumbled off down the road, firing volleys into the air in celebration of their morning's work.

Drew watched and waited, his shoulders shaking. In the space of twenty-four hours, he had seen more dead bodies than he could count, each killed savagely, some defiled and mutilated. He felt sick with the shame of his powerlessness to intervene.

The hamlet remained silent and deserted. Nothing moved, no birds sang. Finally he got to his feet and inched his way forward, using the barns and hedges as cover. When he reached the first body, he gingerly closed the man's eyes. What he had to do was already hard enough without the accusing eyes of the dead man upon him.

He dragged the body off the road and into a ditch and

began to strip off the coat, shuddering as his fingers slipped on the blood-coated buttons.

He pulled off one sleeve then turned the corpse over to free the other arm. Air trapped in the man's lungs escaped with a gasping wheeze, as if the body was coming back to life.

His heart beating wildly, Drew managed to get the coat free and then began struggling with the trousers. The bootlaces were knotted and soaked in mud and blood. He searched his own pockets for his knife, then remembered he had left it lying on the forest floor near Nick's grave when he had blundered off into the forest.

Without it, Drew could neither undo the laces nor drag the trousers over the boots. He grew increasingly frantic, tearing at them with his fingers, which just made the knots tighter. He rifled the man's pockets, but found nothing sharp, only a piece of string and a battered leather pouch containing a few coins and a photograph of a woman and three small children.

Drew stared at the shy, smiling faces and his eyes filled with tears, but he couldn't stop now – he had to have the clothes. He searched through the undergrowth at the bottom of the ditch, for an old tin can or anything that might provide a cutting edge. Finally he saw the glint of broken glass.

As soon as he had the boots off, he began pulling at the trousers. He jerked them free, twisting the body awkwardly across the ditch, the legs obscenely white against the bloodstained mud.

In a feeble attempt to leave the man some dignity, Drew straightened him out and crossed his hands on his chest. He put the photograph of the woman and children between the stiffening fingers, then stripped off his combat jacket and flying suit and covered the body.

He hesitated over the UN beret. If he was stopped in civilian clothes he could be shot as a spy. While scarcely a uniform, the beret at least was a badge of military involvement. Abruptly he made his decision and crammed it into the pocket of the dead man's coat.

He moved to the edge of the hamlet, scanning every shadow for signs of life. The silence was now broken by a low drone as swarms of flies feasted on the bodies. Drew gagged and turned away.

A few houses had been spared the burning, though their windows were smashed and broken furniture littered the ground. The door of one swung drunkenly off its hinges. Hating himself for this further violation but driven by hunger, Drew pushed his way inside and began rummaging through the kitchen. The only food he could find was a scrap of leathery goat's cheese and a piece of stale black bread as hard as timber.

He had already swallowed the cheese and begun gnawing at the bread, when he heard a sound behind him. He whirled around. In the darkest recess of the room an old woman was hunched, her arms hugging her knees. Her white hair was matted with blood, her face was bruised and her lips cut and swollen. Her skirt lay in tatters around her, ripped open to her crotch.

She scarcely seemed to see Drew as she rocked herself endlessly to and fro, her eyes staring sightlessly at the floor. But, when he took a step towards her, she shrank back and a thin keening issued from her toothless mouth. It was the most desolate sound Drew had ever heard. Ashamed and helpless, he took out his emergency rations and placed them on the table alongside the remains of the bread. Then he turned away and stumbled out of the house.

As he ran blindly through the hamlet towards the fields, his mind reeling, he heard the clatter of a helicopter's rotors. He ran into the open, waving his hands, praying for his rescue.

The sound of the rotors grew louder, shaking the ground as the helicopter swept up the valley, hidden for the moment by a copse of trees. Suddenly the black shape loomed up over the treeline. Drew froze for a moment as his brain struggled to make sense of what he saw, then the sound of gunfire broke the spell.

He turned and ran as shells exploded around him, then threw himself over a stone wall. His foot caught and twisted, and he fell heavily. There was another rattle of machine-gun fire and he pressed himself flat, trying to bury himself in the soft earth. He lay there, his eyes shut in fright, a sickly sweet smell in his nostrils. It was strange and yet oddly familiar.

The helicopter clattered away and he raised his head a fraction and opened his eyes. Directly below him was the body of a woman, blood still congealing around a slash across her throat. He reeled away from it only to see that the woman had been pregnant. Her murderers had thrust a bayonet deep into her womb, half tearing the baby out of her.

Beyond lay another body, and another and another. Young boys had been castrated and left to bleed to death, little girls had been defiled, mutilated and then slaughtered.

Drew began to scream, the unearthly sound echoing around the hamlet as the helicopter turned for another pass. As it closed in there was another, deeper sound, from beyond the mountain ridge Drew had crossed in the night.

There was another burst of machine-gun fire. Only half aware of what he was doing, Drew squirmed deeper into the mound of bodies, pressing himself flat as the lines of bullets marched across the ground towards him. They passed close enough for a chip of stone to draw blood from his forehead and one of the bodies jerked obscenely.

The helicopter wheeled away, back in the direction it had come. There was a roar as an American F16 barrelled across the sky in pursuit.

Teeth chattering, shuddering with horror, Drew fought to free himself from the mound of bodies, but every movement seemed only to entangle him further as limbs clutched at him. He clawed his way free of the suffocating embrace and lay gasping, his face to the wall. He could taste blood in his mouth and knew it was not his. He rolled over and vomited again and again, his whole body racked with the convulsions.

As he hauled himself to his knees, keeping his face averted from the bodies, he heard a rustle behind him. He turned around, scarcely daring to look. One of the bodies was moving, the wounded chest and stomach of a man struggling for breath.

Drew tore the other bodies away but, when he looked into the man's face, two dead, staring eyes gazed back at him. As he stared down at the still-moving stomach, there was a slithering sound and something began to emerge from the wound.

Drew started to scream again as a rat crawled out, smothered in blood and entrails. As it disappeared again amongst the mound of bodies, Drew crawled backwards on his hands and knees, then stumbled to his feet and began to run towards the trees.

He blundered into the copse and threw himself into a patch of brambles, almost welcoming the pain as the thorns tore at his skin. He huddled at their centre, curled into the foetal position, and lay sobbing, the horrors he had seen crowding in upon him.

Chapter 15

When Drew opened his eyes it was dark, with only the faintest of glows in the sky to the east. For a moment he was unsure where he was. He lay still, straining his ears, but could hear no noise other than the natural sounds of the night: an owl hooting, the wind gently stirring dead leaves. Then the memories gradually returned.

As he stretched out, the brambles caught at his clothes and skin. The pain jolted him into action. He disentangled himself from the thorns and stood up. He had been asleep for almost twelve hours. His head was pounding and his tongue felt like fur. He had to find water.

The sky was brightening steadily as he watched. Just to the east, he could see the hamlet from which he had fled. A few wisps of smoke were still drifting up from the ruined buildings. He shuddered. He would rather die of thirst than go back into that terrible place.

To the west a thin line of trees curving across the fields suggested a stream. He walked to the edge of the wood and looked carefully around. There were isolated barns but no farms as far as he could see. As the sun appeared over the horizon, he emerged cautiously from the shelter of the copse and hurried across the fields.

The stream was muddy and barely a couple of inches deep. He began to follow it uphill, hoping to find clearer water. As he walked, he kept within the shadow of the trees and looked around constantly for signs of danger.

After a few hundred metres, the stream curved in close to a field barn. Drew broke cover and ran across to it. He pushed open the creaking door and looked inside. A row of eight cattle stalls gave him hope. There was no tap, but he found a trough in the corner of the yard surrounding the barn.

The water in the bottom of the trough looked rank and smelled worse. He tried to free the ballcock, which was tied up with rough string. As he picked at the knot, he caught sight of his hands, completely covered in filth.

He leaned over the side of the trough and looked at his reflection. A face he barely recognised stared back at him: gaunt, wild-eyed, its hair matted and skin caked with dried blood.

The knot finally gave way and the ballcock dropped with a hollow clang, but after a moment there was a faint rattle and a hiss, followed by a thin rusty dribble. As Drew watched, it strengthened and gradually cleared. He ducked his head under the outlet and let the water flow over his face for a few moments, then began to drink. It tasted cold and clean. He swallowed as much as he could hold.

He travelled on all day, heading south-west, skirting around farms, houses and villages. Twice dogs barked at his approach and he was forced to retrace his steps and circle even wider. He stopped only once, to drink from a stream. Late in the afternoon, weary and ravenous, he almost stumbled straight into a group of men striding along a track towards him. Only their loud, guttural talk alerted him in time.

He dived into a bed of bracken and drew his pistol, but they had not seen him and strode by without a glance in his direction. Each held a weapon, but was dressed in rough country clothes. They could have been Muslims, Croats or Serbs. It made no difference to Drew; they were all the enemy.

Uncertain if the four men were alone or the advance guard of a larger party, Drew left the track for a smaller pathway through some scrubland. With the sun sinking low in the sky, he was anxious not to be surprised just as the relative safety of darkness was approaching.

Close to exhaustion, he stumbled onwards, still clutching his pistol. As he stepped into the shadow of a clump of birch trees, two heavily camouflaged soldiers sprang out in front of him, sub-machine guns at the ready. He heard the metallic click of weapons being cocked at either side of him and knew that he was trapped.

Too weary even to think about resistance, Drew hung his head. I've lost, he thought. I've let Nick down.

'Don't move.' The command was softly spoken but menacing. 'Now drop the gun.'

Surprised by a challenge in English, Drew stood immobile, the pistol still gripped in his hand. As he saw the men's eyes narrow and their gun barrels swing up towards his chest, he let it tumble from his fingers. 'Don't shoot,' he said. 'British officer.'

There was no noticeable relaxation of tension. The soldiers still kept their guns trained on him. 'Give me the code word for the day,' their leader said. American – Jesus, they were American.

'It's . . . I don't know what the fuck it is.' Drew was almost hysterical with relief. 'I was shot down the day before yesterday so that's the last one I know. I've got this though.' Using his left thumb and forefinger, he eased the UN beret from his pocket.

'That's a hat, Jack, it's not a passport,' the leader said. 'Now why don't you tell us something useful. I guess the day before yesterday's code word would do for a start.'

Drew's mind was a blank. 'Hang on a minute,' he said in desperation. He moved too quickly and the guns came up again. 'Sorry,' he said, moving more slowly as he scraped at the dried mud still covering the back of his hand. He peered at the blurred and faded biro marks.

'The code word was Top . . . er . . . no, Tobacco.' Drew was triumphant.

The American gave a world-weary smile. 'If I hadn't seen it for myself, I wouldn't have believed it. Only a Limey could have a top secret code written on the back of his hand.'

Drew nodded idiotically, glancing from one face to another

and smiling as if his face would crack. 'I'm hellish pleased to see you guys. I had to eject near Banja Luka and you're the best thing I've seen since then. So . . .' He looked at each of them. 'How did you know I was coming? What are you doing here?'

'You blundered past a listening device and were spotted by one of our observation patrols. We'd have let you walk on by, but we thought you were a Serb. As for our mission, it's better you don't know.'

The American paused. 'We can get you out of here pretty quickly though. We're due a heli resupply at 0400 hours tomorrow, though your boys might want you out even quicker than that. Now what do you say we stop standing around and get ourselves back under cover?'

He led Drew up to a small rise in the scrubland. There seemed nothing different about the piece of ground until it suddenly opened up at Drew's feet and he found himself looking into a hide. Two more soldiers gave him a cursory glance and then went back to their work, one scanning the area through binoculars, the other sitting with earphones clamped to his head.

The leader of the patrol followed Drew into the hide and pulled a chicken-wire roof, threaded with bracken fronds, over their heads.

'Gene, dig out a drink and some food for our guest. He looks like he could use some. And get on the net and tell them we've got the Limey pilot they lost a couple of days ago. By the way,' he added, swivelling to face Drew, 'what happened to your navigator?'

Drew felt his face crumple. His knuckles whitened as he clenched his fists. 'He died.'

'Too bad.'

One of the soldiers turned on the radio and sent the signal, the information compressed into a burst lasting less than a tenth of a second.

He handed Drew food and water. 'Reconstituted beef stew, cold I'm afraid.'

Drew shook his head, not caring. He wolfed down part of it, but his stomach rebelled and he vomited it back. The Americans exchanged glances as Drew did his best to clean up the mess, but the soldier handed him a bar of compressed dried fruit. 'Try this instead. Eat it real slow this time.'

Drew nodded gratefully, nibbling at it as he pestered them with questions. 'What's been happening? I saw one of your F16s hunting down a Serb helicopter yesterday. Has the UN given the go-ahead?'

The leader nodded. 'You can probably claim the credit for that. It was your jet getting shot down that finally persuaded them to get off their butts.' Drew laughed. 'Did I say something funny?'

'I'm sorry, no. It's just that we weren't shot down.'

'That's not what your wingman said. I saw him interviewed on CNN before we were choppered in here. He said you'd been locked up by a SAM. He saw it explode and then you went out of control and ejected. Whatever, the UN passed another of their resolutions yesterday morning, handing over authority to NATO. The first raids went in late yesterday; they blew the ass out of those SAM sites.'

The radio operator leaned over his equipment as the return signal came in. The leader scanned the message. 'They're so pleased to see you, they're bringing our resupply forward and sending a welcoming party. 1930 hours at the LZ. Dress casual.'

The landing zone was a mile away at the foot of a range of hills, masked from the surrounding plain by a wood. Ten minutes before the rendezvous time, the Americans led Drew through the trees. The wood was dense and thick with undergrowth and he stumbled like a blind man, helped along by the soldiers, who all wore night-vision goggles.

Four of them took up positions at the edge of the wood, constantly alert. Two others marked out the site, using Fireflies – infra-red beacons the size of cigarette packets. The light was invisible to Drew, but he knew that anyone wearing infra-red goggles would see it from miles away.

He waited in the shadows at the edge of the wood with his two companions. High in the sky, visible for a second outlined against the waning moon, was the first wave of the rescue package, two F18 radar suppressors, their HARM missiles ready to destroy any SAM missile threat. He guessed an EA-6B Prowler would also be up there somewhere, bristling with electronic jamming equipment.

Four minutes before the RV, two American F16s blasted in low over the area. As the sound wave ebbed away, Drew heard the empty rattle of helicopter rotors. Then he became aware of a different sound, a low rumble coming from beyond the wood at their rear. Straining his ears, he could make out engines and the grinding, metallic clank of tank tracks. Thin beams of light slashed the sky as vehicles pitched over the rough terrain, closing fast. Radios crackled and the Americans moved into action.

Four Cobra gunships appeared out of the darkness and hovered over the area as two huge Super Stallion helicopters landed in line astern. The crew of the second began hurling out supplies for the American patrol and a squad of marines leapt down and fanned out to secure the perimeter as Drew heard the roar of two Harrier jets quartering the sky above the Cobras, like eagles protecting hawks.

'Hurry it up,' the troop leader barked at Drew.

'I just want to thank you guys. You saved my life,' Drew said, but the American pushed him impatiently towards the helicopters.

'Just get out of here. We're blown. Understand? Just go.'

He turned his back and began barking fresh orders into the radio. Drew sprinted across the moonlit grass and stooped beneath the idly turning rotors of the lead Super Stallion. He heard gunfire and saw two explosions as shells fell short of their target.

The Cobras had already wheeled to face the threat. There was a blast as a missile came off one and streaked away into the night, followed almost immediately by a huge detonation. Urgent voices shouted to Drew and strong hands hauled him up into the helicopter.

The gunships laid down a barrage of covering fire as the marines rapidly withdrew to the Super Stallions. Inside three minutes, both helicopters were airborne. As Drew looked down, he could see the muzzle flashes from Serb troops puncturing the darkness. His rescuers had already disappeared.

As the Super Stallion roared away out of danger, one of the crew winked at Drew. 'What's it to be? We've got coffee, Coke and there's even a can of Limey beer we brought specially for you.'

The voice seemed to be coming to Drew down a long, dark tunnel. He shook his head, unable to speak. The man fell silent and left Drew to his thoughts.

As they rattled through the night, he stared blankly down into the darkness of the Bosnian countryside. Even the towns showed barely a light, their generators destroyed by Serb shellfire.

A thin phosphorescent line was the only clue that they had crossed the coast. A few moments later the helicopter pilot called back on the intercom, 'We're out of Gate 4 and clear of hostile airspace.'

Tears flooded into Drew's eyes.

Out over the Adriatic, the Harriers waggled their wings in salute and then peeled away back to their mother ship, followed by the Cobras and the other Super Stallion. They crossed the Italian coast a few minutes later and began the approach to Gióia.

As they touched down, Drew thanked the crew and stepped uncertainly out into the glare of the halogen lights around the landing area. There was a cheer as he appeared and he realised that the whole squadron was there to greet him. Russell stepped forward and shook his hand. 'Good to have you back, Drew.'

'What about Nick?' DJ yelled as they crowded around him. Drew shook his head and walked away, leaving a sudden silence behind him.

The intelligence debrief took an hour and a half. Four senior officers from Combat Operations Centre, including Russell and a two-star American general, sat in with the British intelligence officer and her American counterpart.

Drew was constantly interrupted with a stream of questions. As he told them about Nick, the general and his aide looked at one another. Drew fought to keep his emotions in check, but the cold, clinical interrogation and the constant demands for repetition of the details of Nick's last moments were impossible to bear.

Finally he snapped. 'I told you what happened. They shot him. What more do you need?'

There was a silence before they returned to the moments just prior to ejection. Drew was emphatic that the missile had not caused the jet to crash. 'It exploded on the chaff,' he said for the fifth time.

'No one disputes that,' the British intelligence officer said patiently, 'but the shrapnel from the explosion would seem the obvious cause for your loss of control.'

'I don't believe so,' Drew said. 'The time gap between the explosion and the control loss was too long.'

The general cleared his throat and looked pointedly at his watch. 'Why don't we leave that one for the moment? The only way we'll know for sure is if we get the ADR back and the chances of that look pretty slim. The main issue as far as I'm concerned is that a defenceless serviceman, showing the UN beret, was murdered by those Serb sons of bitches. Excuse me, I'm just a regular soldier, but what brought the jet down in the first place doesn't amount to a hill of beans compared to that.' He looked around the room, defying anyone to disagree with him. 'So let's get this wrapped up and let this young man have a couple of well-earned beers. We're proud of you, son.'

Drew gave a weak smile in response and turned to Russell. 'I want to be the one to break the news to Nick's wife. I made a promise to her before we came out to Bosnia.'

Russell shifted uncomfortably in his seat. 'I'm sorry, Drew. She's already been notified that he's missing in action and I sent a signal to Finnington before the debrief, detailing a senior officer to break the news. I'm afraid she'll already know by now.'

'I promised her,' Drew said, on the brink of tears.

'I understand that,' Russell said gently, 'but we have to move fast before some tabloid reporter gets wind of the news and turns up on her doorstep. Nick wouldn't have wanted that, would he?'

Drew shook his head and turned away. He was shuffling out of the room after the Americans when the medical crew pounced on him, ready for their interminable checks.

'General,' Drew said. 'Could you help me out here?'

The general turned. 'Any back pains, Miller?'

'No, sir.'

'Any other problems?'

'No, sir.'

'There you are then,' he said to the medics. 'Why don't

you guys let him get a good night's sleep and do all your tests in the morning?'

'But—' one began.

'That wasn't a question, it was an order,' the general barked.

Drew eased himself past and went to the mess. The drink was already flowing freely.

Drew went through the motions, answering some questions mechanically and shrugging off others. His thoughts were only of a forest several hundred miles away, where Nick had met his death.

Finally he could stand it no longer. He pushed his way through the crowd and out into the night. His mates watched him go but no one followed him.

Drew stood alone on the edge of the airfield gazing out unseeingly across the deserted tarmac, his shoulders heaving, his body racked by sobs.

Still crying, he walked back to his quarters, stripped off his clothes, leaving them in a pile in the middle of the floor and got into the shower. He set the temperature as hot as he could bear and scrubbed himself over and over again, trying not to look at the water, stained with blood, as it spiralled down the drain.

Finally he towelled himself down, brushed his teeth until his gums bled and then fell into bed.

His sleep was broken by a recurring nightmare in which Russell and Power were trying to bury Nick under a pile of corpses. Drew woke, covered in sweat and shouting, 'But he's alive, he's alive.' As the realisation dawned, he turned and lay staring at the blank wall.

He got up late the next morning. A letter had arrived which did nothing to lift his mood. It was short and to the point: 'No go. Need more – much more. Danny.'

Drew turned the envelope over in his hands. It could have been his imagination, but he thought it had been tampered with. He threw it angrily into the bin and lay down again, staring at the ceiling. Hard though he cudgelled his brains, he could think of nothing to link the loss of control of his Tempest over Bosnia with the crash in the Eden Valley.

He showered again and shaved three days' stubble from his chin, then headed for the canteen. Starving though he was, he managed only a few mouthfuls before he felt full. He pushed his plate away and went to report to the medical centre.

The medics carried out even more tests than usual, then sedated him and confined him to a hospital bed for twenty-four hours. In his drugged state, he kept replaying the loss of the Tempest in his head. Something kept nagging at him, just below the surface of his thoughts; but, try as he might, he could not drag it to the front of his mind.

He woke the next morning feeling rested, cold and calm. As he shaved, he stared hard-eyed at his reflection. The face looking back at him was icily determined. After another battery of tests, the medics were forced to pass him as fit. Even the injury to his side, sustained as he parachuted down into the Bosnian forest, proved to be only severe bruising.

It was almost lunchtime when he finally escaped. He checked his watch, then went to the Sergeants' Mess in search of Neville Springer, the most experienced member of the ground crew.

Springer was holding court at the bar, but he broke off to greet Drew with genuine warmth. 'We heard you made it back, sir. Glad you did. The first one's on me.'

He signalled to the barman. 'I'm sorry about Nick Jackson, though. It's always the best blokes who go, isn't it?'

Drew nodded, his face a mask.

Springer shook his head. 'It's silly, I know, but even though they'd already put it out on the Tannoy that you'd been forced to eject, the ground crew waited on the line all day, until nightfall, just in case you got the aircraft back somehow.'

'I'd be even more touched if I didn't know that you were more worried about your aircraft than you were about us.' Drew's voice cracked.

'Quite right, sir,' Springer said. 'But we are honoured. We don't often get air crew slumming it in here. Come to see how the other half lives?'

'As a matter of fact, I've come to see if I can buy you a beer.'

Springer's response was to drain his glass instantly, but, as he wiped the foam from his lips, he paused. 'But there's no such thing as a free beer, is there?'

Drew smiled ruefully. 'Well, I did want to pick your brains about something.'

'Pick away,' Springer said evenly. 'I'm like a parking meter; I'm all yours as long as you keep putting another beer in the slot.'

Drew bought them both another drink, sat down at a quiet table, then came straight to the point. 'I'm trying to work out why we're losing so many Tempests.'

'Not really your department, sir, is it?' Springer said, swallowing half his beer at one gulp.

'Don't you start. I've been getting that from Russell non-stop for the past few weeks.'

'So what can I tell you that the combined intellectual might of 21 Squadron hasn't been able to work out for itself?'

Drew shrugged. 'There weren't the same problems with the original Tempests, were there?'

'No. We lost a few in training accidents as we always do, but nothing like the rate we've been losing the RS series.'

'When they carried out the modifications to the Tempest, what exactly was altered?'

'What wasn't? They changed the engines and replaced the weapons systems. Just about the only thing that wasn't altered was the computer. As usual, they kept upgrading the specification and squeezing the budget – more bangs, less bucks. To cut costs, they fitted one central processing unit rather than dedicated computers, so the original computer is driving some much more sophisticated weapons systems.'

'Could that be part of the problem?'

Springer shrugged. 'It's been tested to the limit on more simulators than you can shake a stick at and nothing's ever shown up, as far as I know. You really need to talk to one of the computer organ-grinders who designed it, not the grease monkeys who mend it, but I can't see any of them breaking the Official Secrets Act to talk turkey with a mere pilot, even supposing you can find one who uses English as a first language instead of MS-DOS.'

'Something's going wrong somewhere, though, isn't it?'

Springer nodded, smiling as he raised a fresh beer to his lips. 'But your guess is as good as mine. Perhaps there are just a lot of shitty pilots about. They should get ground crew to fly the jets. The blokes that have to repair them would treat them with a bit more respect.'

Drew grinned. As he got up to leave, he spotted some unfamiliar faces among the ground crew lounging against the bar. 'Who are those guys?'

Springer swivelled to follow his gaze. 'They're with a Puma squadron that flew in while you were on your holidays.'

'Pumas?' Drew said. 'Which squadron?'

'33,' Springer said, but found himself talking to thin air.

'Good to see you back, Mr Miller,' Springer said to Drew's swiftly retreating back.

Chapter 16

Drew found Michelle sitting in the spring sunshine outside the Officers' Club – a ramshackle breeze-block building, roofed with a piece of rusting corrugated iron and surrounded by a few battered iron tables and chairs. In the eyes of visiting air crew, its only saving grace was three massive fridges, each stocked with cold beer and wine. Michelle was with Sandy Craig and Paul Westerman.

As soon as she saw him, she jumped up and ran to him. She kissed him and held him fiercely, then led him back to the table, still holding his hand. Catching the embarrassed looks of her crewmen, she smiled and released Drew's hand, then sank back into her chair.

Drew nodded to the other two, pulled up a chair and added his feet to the circle on the table top.

'So,' Michelle said. 'You decided to walk round Bosnia instead of flying over it?'

'And Nick?' Paul asked.

'Didn't even get the chance to walk. The Serbs used him for target practice as he was dangling from his chute.'

'I know, I heard,' Michelle said leaning over to squeeze his hand again. 'I'm sorry.'

Paul stretched, yawned, got to his feet and said, 'Sandy and I have to go and do something. See you two later.'

'What?' Sandy said, startled.

'You know, that thing we were talking about earlier.'

'What thing?'

'Oh for Christ's sake, get out of that chair. I'll explain on the way.'

He winked at Drew and Michelle and dragged the still-protesting Sandy away.

'I wish the guys on squadron were even a tenth as tactful,' Drew said.

'I've done the same for him once or twice,' Michelle said. 'Though it doesn't always work out for the best. I discreetly left him to chat up a woman on a USAF base in Carolina once and found him two hours later with a black eye and a missing tooth. His new friend's husband had come home unexpectedly early.' She paused. 'Why don't you get me another beer. In fact, make it two more,' she said, as he stood up. 'We could take them down to the beach.'

'Only the Brits would go to the beach in March. The locals are still wearing overcoats and turning up the heating.'

Michelle flashed him a smile that set his heart pounding. 'More fool them. They don't know what they're missing.'

They walked away from the base, picking their way among the tangle of boulders, as basking lizards darted away from beneath their feet. They wandered along the shoreline until they found a quiet cove.

Michelle put down her beers and turned to face him, slipping a bare brown arm around his neck. 'It's great to see you,' she said. 'I've missed you.'

Her mouth searched for his, her tongue darting between his lips. He crushed her to him, then heard the sound of footfalls and gasping breath. They pulled apart as two puce-faced joggers came lumbering into view, staring at them as they passed, their feet floundering in the soft sand.

Michelle laughed. She held him at arm's length, still with a wry smile playing around her lips.

Drew was about to pull her to him again when his eye was caught by a flash of reflected light from the control tower on the runway. He shook his head, then smiled. 'There's a pair of binoculars pointing straight at us from the control tower. It wouldn't surprise me if they aren't broadcasting a blow-by-blow description over the Tannoy.'

'Then let's just sit here and talk.' She gave him a slow smile. 'I might just persuade you to give something away about yourself.' He hesitated. 'Don't you trust me?'

'I don't know if I trust myself.'

Michelle looked deep into his eyes. 'Was it very bad out there?'

He nodded, turning slightly away from her to stop her seeing that he was close to tears. He watched the waves roll up the beach for a while before speaking again. He told her about Nick and his escape, and about hiding on the outskirts of the village, hearing the screams. And, haltingly, he told her about the man whose clothes he had to take.

'It sounds crazy, but the worst thing was the photograph of his wife and kids. She had her arms round them and her look said, "It's tough where we are, but we love each other, so everything's going to be all right . . ."' He wiped his eyes. 'She was wrong, wasn't she?'

Michelle reached out and touched his hand. 'She made you think of your mother, didn't she?'

'Christ Almighty,' Drew said. 'For a moment I thought she *was* my mother.' He hesitated, but could no longer stop the memories from crowding in. 'My father was a real caricature Glaswegian. Though he never hit my mother, even when he was drunk, he took out a lot of his frustrations on her in other ways.'

'Like what?'

'He used to belittle her and criticise her constantly. Nothing that you could really put your finger on and say that's going too far, just a steady drip, drip, drip of negativity that stripped her of her confidence and self-respect.

'Like a lot of of women then, she put up with it and transferred all her own dreams and ambitions onto her child. She dedicated herself to me, worked her fingers to the bone for me and I took it all without even a show of gratitude, and even complained there wasn't more.'

'You can't blame yourself,' Michelle said gently. 'Every kid's the same. It's only when you've grown up yourself that you begin to realise how much they sacrificed for you.'

He nodded mechanically, his gaze still far away.

'The only thing I ever did for her was help her die.'

'What do you mean?'

'She had cancer of the brain. She'd been in hospital for quite a while. They sent her home to die, though of course that was never actually mentioned. A district nurse came in twice a day, but otherwise there was only my dad and me to look after her.

'I found it strange and very frightening. She had patches of lucidity, but there were long periods when she didn't really seem to know us at all. I opened the curtains one morning and she gasped in surprise at a view she'd seen every day for years.

'Anyway, my father began to crack up. He couldn't stand sitting around the house, just waiting for her not to be there. On the third day she was home, I'd bunked off school. My father went out to the pub about eleven in the morning and was gone all afternoon.

'I went upstairs to see if she was all right. She was deathly pale apart from two bright red spots in the middle of her cheeks, but she was sitting up in bed. She took my hand, made me sit on the bed and tell her everything I'd been doing. I was so happy because I thought she was getting better.'

He broke off, smiling at his own naivety. 'Doctors call it the brightening, apparently; it nearly always happens before someone dies. I sat with her through the afternoon, chatting to her, but she gradually fell silent again and the colour faded from her cheeks. She stopped responding when I spoke to her, though I felt she could still hear me, and her breathing grew more and more laboured and irregular.

'I wanted to call the doctor but we didn't have a phone and I didn't dare leave her to go to the one at the end of the street. I just stayed there hoping my dad would come home.

'When I took her hand again, it was icy cold. Her eyes flickered open at my touch, then closed. I didn't know what else to do, so I talked to her quietly, just saying anything that came into my head, trying to soothe and calm her.

'I talked about drifting downstream on a river: "It's warm and the sunlight is dappling the water. The air is heavy, you can hear the water lapping, the birds singing and a bee buzzing by. It's so peaceful you could just lie there all day, drifting along, drifting along." That sort of thing.'

He glanced at Michelle, but she nodded encouragingly.

'After a few minutes, the cold in her fingers had spread to her wrists. She was lying still. There was only the rasp of her breath to show that she was still alive. I heard the door open downstairs, as the nurse came in on her evening visit, but I still let my voice run on. "Just let yourself go with it, feel the river drifting away. All your friends are there on the bank. They're all waiting for you, just let yourself go, and drift away on the stream; drift down the river, under the trees, into the shade . . ."

'Her breathing stopped abruptly. I broke off and sat motionless, watching her face. There was a long, long silence. Five, ten, fifteen seconds – I don't know how long it was – as I held her hand tightly. There were tears trickling down my cheeks. I heard the nurse come upstairs and called out to her, "I think she's gone," but suddenly there was a gasp and she started breathing again.

'The nurse looked at her, then went out again, quietly closing the door. I began to talk again about the river. Her breathing stopped again, restarted with another convulsive gasp, stopped and started again. She was frail, paper-thin, but she was still fighting. I never knew how hard the dying cling on to life till then.

'There was another breath and then silence. I held my own breath and waited, waited and waited. At last I exhaled and this time there was nothing. I sat there crying, holding her cold hand until the nurse came back into the room and told me to go downstairs. My father came home an hour later. He didn't even go up and look at her. He just sat in his chair staring into the fire.'

Drew brushed the tears away again. 'I'm sorry.'

'Don't be.' She leaned over and kissed him, then looked at him in silence for a moment. 'You've changed, Drew. Just in a few days.'

'How?'

'You seem . . .' She hesitated, trying to find the right words. 'You're different. I can't explain it.'

They stayed on the beach for hours, watching the sun sink behind the hills and the sky reddening into dusk. A cool breeze had begun to blow and finally Michelle sat up and shivered. 'Come on, let's get back. I'm freezing.'

She leaned over to kiss the corners of Drew's mouth as he lay there, staring up at the sky and listening to the waves.

'Not bad, is it?'

Drew's smile faded. 'I'd better make the most of this. It could be my last overseas trip at Air Force expense.'

As they walked back along the beach, she slipped an arm through his and laid her head on his shoulder. 'I wish I could do something to help. I had to give them a statement about what I saw, but to be honest I didn't see that much. I just said that I saw the aircraft coming in high from the left, in a descending turn. The next thing I knew there was a pall of smoke.'

'I was thinking things through while I was in sickbay yesterday, and you could do something to help.'

'What?'

'I need to get back to England. I promised Sally – Nick's wife – that if anything ever happened to him I'd be the one to tell her. It's already too late for that, but I must go and see her.'

He hesitated. 'I'm also going to go and see someone at Barnwold Industries. They made the Tempest. It's in their interests to help find out what's going wrong with it.'

'Will they see it like that? They're still trying to sell them abroad. Their sales pitch won't exactly be helped if they have to admit that the aircraft keep falling out of the sky of their own accord. And, even if they were willing to help, you can't just march up to the front door and ask to see the managing director.'

Drew nodded. 'I know, but I might get to talk to one of the computer engineers.'

'Why do you have to keep putting your head on the line?'

'Because I owe it to Nick. He'd still be alive if I'd found the answer. The AIB didn't shoot him, but they let him go up in an aircraft they knew was unsafe.'

'So what can I do to help?'

'It's a big favour.'

'What's one more among so many?' Michelle said, smiling.

Drew squeezed her arm gratefully. 'I need someone to phone Russell's office and pretend to be a neighbour of my father.'

'And that someone might just be me?'

'Can you do a Scots accent?'

'Och aye, laddie. When do you want me to do it?'

'Now would be fine. That way I can get on some transport in the morning.'

'You just can't wait to get away, can you?'

Drew spun her around to look into her eyes. 'I don't ever want to get away from you.'

She allowed herself to be drawn in to his chest and kissed him. 'If you're going back to England tomorrow, we'd better make the most of tonight. Come on, let's go and phone Russell and then I'll buy you dinner downtown.'

She dialled the main switchboard from the pay phone in the foyer of the mess. After a couple of minutes she was put through to Russell's extension. 'Squadron Leader Russell?' she asked, putting on a gratingly nasal accent.

'Wing Commander,' Russell said. 'Who is this?'

'Jane Docherty. You don't know me but I'm a neighbour of Drew Miller's father.'

'Yes?' Russell said, a touch of frost in his voice.

'I'm afraid Drew's father is seriously ill. He's been rushed to hospital this afternoon.'

'What's wrong with him?'

'It's his heart,' Michelle said.

'I was rather under the impression that Flight Lieutenant Miller was estranged from his father.'

'I know,' Michelle said, improvising desperately. 'They haven't spoken for some time, but it really looks serious and he's asking for him. You wouldn't want to stand in the way at a time like this, would you, Squadron Leader?'

'Wing Commander,' Russell said mechanically. 'This really isn't the way we go about things in the Royal Air Force, Mrs erm . . . There are procedures laid down to cover precisely this kind of eventuality. However . . .'

He sighed. 'Very well. I'll see that Flight Lieutenant Russell is on the first available aircraft. What hospital is his father in?'

'What hospital? Er . . . the infirmary.'

'Which infirmary?' Russell said with exaggerated patience.

'There's only one round here. Thank you, you've made an old man very happy. Oh, and Squadron Leader?' Michelle added, ignoring a dig in the ribs from Drew. 'Isn't it a clear line? You could almost be in the next room.'

Drew silently pleaded for Michelle to stop pushing her luck, but it was Russell who cut the conversation short. 'Er, well thank you, Mrs er . . .'

Michelle couldn't remember what name she'd used and so left him hanging on in silence.

Russell finally added, 'Er . . . thank you for your call. I must be getting on, but please convey my good wishes for a speedy recovery to Mr Miller and reassure him that his son will be home to see him within twenty-four hours. Goodbye.'

Michelle hung up. She was still chuckling and dabbing her eyes when Russell came hurrying into the mess.

He stopped as he saw Drew and Michelle together. 'I've had a call from England. I have some news for you.'

'Sir?'

'It's of a personal nature,' Russell said, looking meaningfully at Michelle.

'It's all right, sir, I have no secrets from Flight Lieutenant Power.'

Russell hesitated. 'Very well. Your father is ill and has been taken to hospital, the infirmary apparently. I hope that means something to you?'

Drew nodded, putting on an expression of concern. 'What's the matter with him?'

'His heart. A neighbour phoned to say that it's serious and that he's asking for you. In these exceptional circumstances, I can allow you compassionate leave. There's a Herc returning to Brize Norton to pick up supplies in the morning. Briefing 0530 hours.'

He glanced at Michelle, who was doing her best not to smile. 'Good night.'

Drew kept his face expressionless until Russell was out of sight, then raised an eyebrow at Michelle. 'Christ, you certainly like to sail close to the wind.'

'You'd better believe it.' She smiled. 'Let's forget about

dinner downtown. I've a frozen coq au vin and a few other gourmet delights in my fridge.'

'I've got some champagne in mine. See you at your place in five minutes.'

When Drew knocked on her door, Michelle opened it wearing a blue silk kimono. The only light came from three candles flickering on the mantelpiece. She gave him a lingering kiss as she pushed the door shut and he felt the heat of her body through the thin silk.

'Dinner?' he asked, as he slid his arms around her waist.

Michelle shook her head. 'Later. Maybe.'

She ripped the foil from the champagne and popped the cork. Foam bubbled over her hand and she licked it away, never taking her eyes from Drew's face. She took a swig from the bottle and kissed him again. His tongue tingled as she let the champagne dribble slowly into his mouth.

She stepped away from him for a moment. 'This one's for me,' she said, as she took another swig. A trickle of champagne ran down her neck and over the soft curve of her breast. She gave him a slow, burning smile.

There was a rustle of silk as she let her kimono fall to the floor and stepped out of it. Then she moved towards him, wrapping her arms around him and moulding her body to his. She kissed him hungrily, unbuttoning his shirt and running her hands down his chest. From the moment she touched him, he gave himself up to her.

They sank down to the floor together and he moved over her, tracing every curve of her body with his hands, his lips, his tongue. As he moved into the soft, dark heat of her, she moaned and writhed against him.

She pulled away from him for a second, eyes unfocused, breathing hard, then stripped him naked as she covered his body with kisses. He gave a low groan as she lowered her head and he felt the warmth of her mouth on him.

Her whole body caressed his as she moved upwards, then straddled him, pushing him down again onto his back. 'Uh-uh,' she said, a slow smile spreading across her face, 'I'm flying this one, not you.'

Her nails dug into his wrists as he sank deep into her. They made love with urgency, not speaking, each taken to the brink over and over again. As she at last gave in to the waves coursing through her, Drew cried out and was swept away with her.

They lay back, their legs still entwined, bodies glistening in the candlelight. He held her gently, kissing her and whispering in her ear. Then they made love again, slowly and tenderly, gazing into each other's eyes as they moved together. When it was over, she lay with her head on his chest and he could feel her tears wet on him.

When Drew woke in the morning, Michelle was already showered, dressed and sitting at the dressing table sipping a cup of coffee.

'I thought it was the bloke who was supposed to sneak out of bed and bugger off in the middle of the night,' he said sleepily.

'It's a new idea they're testing – equality of the sexes.'

He sat up, yawning. 'It'll never catch on in the Air Force. Come back in here a minute,' he said, reaching out to grab her as she put a cup of coffee down by the bed.

'Sorry,' she said, dancing out of range. 'I've got a briefing in forty minutes.'

After the flight to Brize Norton, Drew scrounged a lift into London with one of the crewmen on the Hercules. On his way to King's Cross he stopped at a security shop. He smiled patiently through the impenetrable jargon of a nerdish sales assistant and emerged two hundred pounds poorer, carrying a tiny, voice-activated tape recorder.

He bought a sandwich and a stewed coffee in a polystyrene cup at King's Cross, then joined the line of passengers shuffling down the echoing platform to his train. He chose a half-empty carriage and stared morosely out of the window as the train began to move, rumbling through the dark tunnels and out into the sunlight.

Drew caught a taxi to Finnington from the station, picked up his car and hurried back to the flat. It was cold and musty-smelling and he felt an intruder in his own home, picking up his books and possessions with the curiosity of a stranger. He sat down at the table and picked up the phone.

He was still there three hours later, tired, frustrated and unsure where to turn next. Every attempt to make contact with one of the computer engineers at Barnwold Industries had been frustrated.

Secretaries and personal assistants gave him the brush-off, messages to return his calls were left unanswered and the only programmer he got through to heard him out in silence, then said, 'As a pilot yourself – if that's really what you are – you must surely realise that I won't discuss any aspect of classified work, either on the telephone or in person. I am bound by the Official Secrets Act. If you have any queries about the aircraft, you should direct them through the official channels.'

'But—'

'And I must warn you that I shall be reporting this conversation to my superiors. Goodbye.'

Drew hung up and gazed out of the window, trying to think where else he could turn. Abruptly he picked up the phone again and dialled international enquiries. 'Brussels. NATO headquarters.'

When he got through, he asked for Tom Marshall.

There was a long pause. 'I'm sorry,' the telephonist said. 'We have no one of that name working here.'

'You must do,' Drew said. 'He was posted a couple of weeks ago.'

'I'm sorry, sir,' she said. 'The computer lists everyone here from the cleaner to the Secretary General. If they're not listed, they don't exist.'

Drew hung up and immediately phoned the AIB at Buckwell. 'I'm looking for Flight Lieutenant Tom Marshall.'

'I'm sorry,' the operator said, 'he no longer works here. Can I put you through to someone in that department?'

'No, it's a personal matter. Can you tell me where I could find Tom?'

'We don't give out personal information over the phone.'

'I'm a serving officer myself. Tom told me he was being posted to Brussels, but NATO say they've no record of him. I really do need to get in touch with him.' Drew lowered his voice. 'To be honest with you, I borrowed some money from him a while ago and I want to pay him back. I just need to know where to send it.'

'Well that'll be the first bit of good news he's had in a while,' she said. 'He's been posted to the Falklands. BFPO 655 would reach him.'

'Poor Tom,' Drew said, pushing his luck. 'Could you give me the number as well, so I can ring him up and commiserate.'

After he had hung up, he thought for a moment, then dialled the number. He waited as an interminable chain of relays clicked and rattled, then there was a faint ringing tone. The line was terrible, but he heard a voice answer through the haze of static. 'RAF Mount Pleasant.'

'Tom Marshall, please.'

'Just a minute.'

'Ops room.'

He recognised Tom's voice. 'Tom. It's Drew Miller.'

There was a long silence. 'What do you want?'

Drew took a deep breath. 'To apologise first of all. The fact that you're in the Falklands rather than Brussels suggests they traced something back to you. I'm really sorry, Tom. The only people I gave any information to were my boss and my MP. I don't know how—'

Tom interrupted. 'I don't give a shit how it happened, Drew. All that matters is the end result. You've wrecked my career. I'm not in Brussels counting down the months till I can get back in the cockpit. I'm stuck in the arsehole of the universe instead, looking forward to another seven years of being shunted around the shittiest jobs in the RAF. I'm never going to fly Tempests again now, and to rub salt in the wounds, they've made me ops officer here. As I sit here deskbound, I have to deal constantly with the guys who, unlike me, are going flying. Excuse me if I sound bitter about it.'

'I still need your help, Tom.'

There was an explosion of rage from the other end of the phone. 'You what? You screw up my life and then phone up to ask if I'll help you out again?'

'Look, your career may have been derailed but at least you're still breathing. My best mate and I had to eject over Bosnia because of that fault on the Tempest. I went through three days of hell there before I was rescued. I saw people raped, tortured and murdered and I was nearly killed myself. But I was lucky, Tom – I survived. Nick didn't. He's another one you can add to the Tempest death toll.

'I'm going to see Nick's wife tonight and I'm going to have to explain to her how her husband died and why her four children – one less than three months old – don't have a daddy any more. Now I'm sorry for you, but I'm a damn sight sorrier for them. So I'm going to do my utmost to make sure no one else has to die because of that fault and I need you to help me this once more.'

There was a long pause. 'I've told you everything I know already.'

'Not quite. I need to know more about Brushfire. Who told you about it?'

'This is an open line . . .' Drew had to strain now to hear Tom above the static.

'And it's an open secret. Who can I go to?'

'The only lead I can give you is a man called Robin Parr.'

'Who's he?'

'An ageing computer whizz-kid at Barnwold Industries. Most of the other people there are the usual collection of suits, sharp accountants and retired generals, but Parr's a bit different. He was their youngest executive at one time, head-hunted from a rival company to become head of development. There was a big stink about it, with the rivals screaming about foul play, but Parr was smiling all the way to the bank. The glittering career hit a brick wall a couple of years ago, however. Since then he's been moved sideways, off development work, and he was passed over for the headship of the skunk works they're building.

'I was his liaison at the AIB before everything to do with the Tempest was collated by head office. I got a definite sense that he knew a fair bit more than he was telling me.'

Tom paused. 'It was pretty intangible, but I felt like he was two steps ahead of me in the conversation and would have liked to say more than he did. If you can get him away from the office, you might get more out of him.'

'Thanks, Tom. If there's anything I can do to help you . . .'

'Get promoted to Air Vice-Marshal and you might be able to. Goodbye Drew. Don't call me again.'

There was a click as Tom put the phone down. Drew listened to the hiss of static as he thought for a moment, then he dialled Barnwold Industries again.

He was put straight through to Parr's office. 'Mr Parr? I'm a friend and colleague of Tom Marshall. I wondered if you could spare me a few minutes.'

'I've a fairly heavy schedule Mr . . .?'

'Russell,' Drew supplied at random. 'Mike Russell.'

'Well, Mike, what did you have in mind?'

'I wondered if you might be free for a bite of lunch tomorrow. Somewhere quiet, away from Barnwold.'

'I see,' Parr said. 'What exactly was it you wished to discuss?'

'Something you mentioned to Tom a little while ago. I don't know if it's wise to go into too much detail on an open line.'

'Very well,' Parr said. 'What about the Pheasant at Robintree? It's about fifteen miles from here, off the Cambridge road. Shall we say one o'clock?'

Drew wandered around the flat for another hour, postponing the visit he had to make. He weighed Nick's silver locket in his hand, debating whether to throw away its blood-stained leather thong. Then he turned and hurried out, determined to make the familiar journey before his nerve failed him again.

His heart was heavy as he turned off into the tree-lined road leading to the house. The usual tangle of bikes and toys lay in the garden. He walked round to the back of the house, knocked and opened the door.

The house that had once been a bedlam of noise and laughter was now silent. Sally stood in the middle of the kitchen, holding the baby in her arms. She was death-white, with deep shadows etched under her eyes. The other children huddled around her, sullen and bewildered.

Drew hugged her to him and they stood in silence holding each other. After a few seconds, she pulled away and called, 'Rachel, can you take the children upstairs and get them ready for bed? I need to talk to Drew alone.'

As her sister shepherded the children upstairs, Sally turned to Drew and said, 'Well?'

'I'm sorry, Sally.'

Her expression did not change. 'Where is his body?'

'I buried him in a forest near Banja Luka.'

'How did he die?'

'Serb soldiers shot him.'

She held his gaze. 'I need to know everything, Drew.'

He began a halting recitation of the events that led up to Nick's death, telling her about the missile, the ejection and Nick's parachute catching in the trees.

As he hesitated, she pressed him. 'What happened then?'

'He, er . . . The Serb soldiers shot him as he was hanging there. I'm sure he didn't know much about it. He must have died pretty well immediately.' His voice tailed off.

Suddenly he felt a stinging slap across his cheek. He looked up to see her standing in front of him, eyes blazing. 'You're lying to me. I need to know what happened to Nick. I can't lay him to rest in my mind until I know everything. I don't need you to protect me – I want to know the truth.'

'You don't know what you're asking.'

'How dare you presume to tell me what I can and cannot know about my own husband's death? You gave your word to me as we sat around this table barely a week ago. Keep it.'

He stared into her eyes for a long time, then nodded slowly. 'All right. The murdering bastards shot him as he hung there, defenceless. They didn't even kill him cleanly, they took their time. They shot him in the legs first and they laughed as they did it.'

Tears poured down his face as he spoke, seeing the scene before his eyes as if he was back in the Bosnian forest. Sally was expressionless, her eyes never leaving his face.

'I escaped, hid in a swamp while they searched for me and then I went back after dark. They'd left him hanging in the tree. There were a couple of guards on the body, but they gave up and left around midnight. I watched them go, then cut Nick's body down and buried him.'

He felt in his pocket. 'I brought you this.'

She opened the silver locket and stared at the picture of herself with Nick and the children. 'When my children grow up, I'll show them this and tell them exactly how their father died, so they'll never be tempted to go and do what he did.'

She walked to the door and held it open. 'It's probably best if you don't come again, Drew. I don't want to start hating you for being alive.'

Drew stood for a moment searching her face. Then he bowed his head. 'All right. If that's what you want.'

She nodded, expressionless.

He paused on the doorstep, but she looked right through him. He closed the door and walked slowly away.

Chapter 17

Drew bought a bottle of Scotch and went straight back to his flat, but his attempts to obliterate his memories with drink did not succeed. He stayed stubbornly sober and sleep was a long time coming after he lay down on the bed.

He overslept and had to hurry through the mid-morning traffic towards the motorway. Driving south fast, he tried to drown his thoughts with the radio. He found Robintree easily enough and pulled into the car park of the Pheasant just before one o'clock.

The other customers, all couples, gave him no more than a glance. He bought himself a drink and settled down to wait. He had been there for about twenty minutes when a tall, stoop-shouldered man in his mid-forties walked in. He looked around nervously, the bar lights glinting on the frames of his gold-rimmed glasses. Drew thought he recognised him from somewhere, but could not think where.

'Mr Parr? I'm Drew Miller. I'm a pilot, flying Tempests. I didn't want to give my real name over the phone for obvious reasons.'

Parr pushed a strand of his thinning, sandy hair back from his forehead. He chose a chair that gave him a view of the rest of the bar. As he talked, his eyes constantly flickered towards the entrance, checking each new arrival.

'I recognise you, Mr Miller,' he said. 'I think I can guess what you want to talk to me about.'

Drew nodded. 'You know how many people have been killed flying Tempests in the last few months?'

Parr stared wretchedly at the floor before replying. 'I do, only too well. The aircraft that crashed in Swaledale recently was piloted by my nephew. It was his first flight in a Tempest.'

'I'm sorry,' Drew said. 'My best friend was killed after another crash and the navigator on your nephew's flight was also a friend of mine. I had to lead a search-and-rescue team to the site.'

Parr reached absently for a beer mat. He twisted and tore it into tiny scraps. 'Were they killed instantly?'

Drew nodded. 'They wouldn't even have had time to blink.' He watched Parr carefully. 'I'm trying to find a way to stop more people dying. I think you can help.'

Parr glanced around the room again, then dropped his voice. 'I can't tell you it all.'

'Then tell me what you can.'

'There were lengthy delays in completing the upgrade on the Tempest, not all of which were Barnwold's responsibility. The MoD kept changing the specification, as usual. Then the budget for the aircraft was trimmed back. Money's always a problem with these contracts, despite what the public might think. Sorry, I'm digressing, aren't I?'

'Take your time.' Drew said.

'While taking away the money with one hand, they were also pressing us with the other one to get the job done without any further delays. To maintain the profitability of the contract, we pared down the specification.' His voice trailed away into silence.

'Could you be a little bit more specific?'

'Well, the original spec had called for a completely new computer system to drive the fly-by-wire.'

'I know that already. Even the guys who put the petrol in know it should have had a bigger computer.' Drew instantly regretted his impatience. 'I'm sorry, I'm interrupting.'

Parr gave a fleeting smile. 'I fought the idea very hard.' He swallowed hard before continuing. 'Because my own belief was that in certain circumstances the computer capacity available might be insufficient.'

'Insufficient for what? What circumstances?'

'That's just what we don't know. We were under so much pressure to finish the modifications that we were never able to fully test the system; that's still being carried out now.'

Parr folded his hands in his lap, as if he had said enough. Drew was also silent, thinking through what Parr had told him.

'I need more. I now know roughly where to look, but I still don't know exactly what I'm looking for.'

Parr shook his head. 'I can't tell you any more.'

Drew looked at him for a moment, then reached into his pocket and pulled out the miniature tape recorder. He watched Parr's face as his eyes followed the microphone lead up to Drew's lapel.

Parr spoke in a monotone. 'If you use that you'll ruin me.'

'You'll be in good company. Now tell me what you know.'

'I don't know any more. What I've told you already is only supposition. We've been running a Tempest on a test bed for some time and have yet to reproduce the fault.'

'But if you know that there may be a problem, why haven't you done anything about it – apart from setting up the test bed?'

Parr gazed at the floor for a moment. 'I tried to, but I was overruled by the rest of the board. When I protested, I was warned off and when I persisted I was effectively demoted, kicked sideways into another job.'

'Why were you overruled – just to save money?'

Parr hesitated and his eyes flickered back to Drew's lapel. 'If I tell you what you want, you'll give me the tape?' Drew nodded. 'We're negotiating with two Arab governments interested in buying Tempests. If the contracts go through, the hardware alone is worth well over a billion pounds. With spares, training and other back-up, we're looking at two billion pounds' worth of business.'

Drew shook his head. 'So it's all right for British air crew to die and Arab governments to get fleeced, just as long as Barnwold can keep its shareholders happy?'

Parr swallowed again, but said nothing.

Drew stared at him, torn between sympathy and disdain.

'I have to go,' Parr said abruptly, rising to his feet.

As he held out his hand for the tape, Drew suddenly realised where he had seen him before. 'Just a minute,' he said, catching at his arm. 'I've seen you in a photograph. You, some other guys in suits, a couple of Arabs and Air Vice-Marshal Power.'

Parr nodded. 'That would be in Qatar probably. Charles accompanied us there on one of the sales trips.' As he caught Drew's expression, he added, 'There's nothing untoward about it. Senior officers are often involved in presentations to foreign governments.'

'But he knows about the billion-pound deals?'

Parr nodded.

Drew held on to his arm a moment longer, and decided to test the name he had discovered while posing as the British Telecom engineer. 'And Henry Robertshaw?'

Parr shrugged. 'As the chairman of Barnwold, he would certainly have been there. Now I really have to go. The tape please.'

Drew shook his head. 'I'm sorry. That stays with me – life insurance if you like.'

Parr's eyes clouded. 'You gave me your word.'

Drew nodded. 'I know. I'm learning to play dirty, just like everybody else. But don't worry – it won't be used except as a last resort and it won't be sent to the company. Your precious job is safe as long as you can stomach it.'

As he drove across country towards Brize Norton, Drew kept mulling over what Parr had said. He was left with the same feeling as before: the solution was so close that he could almost reach out and touch it, but there was still a gap he could not bridge.

He arrived at the base with an hour to spare. He left his Audi in the main car park, then sat in the grim departure and arrivals shed, sipping bad instant coffee from a polystyrene cup as he thought furiously about his next step.

* * *

The first person Drew saw as he stepped out of the Herc at Gióia, was Russell.

'How's your father, Drew?'

There was a pause before Drew remembered his cover-story.

'Fine, thank you sir. It was a false alarm. An attack of angina. I hope he'll heed the warning.' He smiled and hurried away.

DJ looked up as Drew entered the mess. 'Did you hear? Decisive Edge is finally gaining some teeth. Your tame American general has done the business. He reported back to NATO commanders about Nick's murder, forcing the UN to hold another emergency debate earlier today. They passed a further resolution handing operational control permanently to NATO and authorising "all necessary force" to bring the Serbs to heel.'

There was a mixture of excitement and anxiety in his voice.

'We're briefing at five,' DJ said, checking his watch. 'I'm off to write a couple of letters and then get some sleep.'

Drew nodded. 'I guess we'll all be writing those "just-in-case" letters tonight, trying to say all those things we should have said but somehow never did.'

The briefing was long and detailed. The intelligence officer, her face drawn and tired, referred frequently to her notes. 'As soon as news of the UN resolution reached the Bosnian Serb commanders yesterday, they began a push towards Srebanj. They are advancing their armour and artillery, clearly seeking to overrun the UN garrison there. Artillery and mortars are already raining fire down around the town.'

Drew's formation listened attentively as they were briefed on their part in the mission. They were to provide escort cover for Tempest RS1s and American F16s bombing the artillery and mortar sites, part of a massive package of NATO aircraft.

Drew glanced at DJ and Ali. They were being asked to fly one of the most difficult of missions, right through a firestorm of Triple-A and ground fire.

DJ met his look with a wink, but his face was pale. Ali stared straight ahead, a muscle twitching beneath his eye.

'Under cover of the bombing, a rescue mission will be mounted to extract the garrison.' The intelligence officer shuffled her notes. 'You should also be aware of a new development. There may be additional threats beyond the Triple-A defences and the SAM 2 and SAM 6 sites we've identified. There's also a strong possibility that the Serb Federation forces may come to the support of the Bosnian Serbs.

'Serbian forces have been mobilised and their aircraft are already patrolling close to the Bosnian border. Their Mig 21s shouldn't be a serious worry, but they also have four squadrons of Mig 29s.'

In the ensuing silence, Drew looked around the room. The faces of the aircrew were set. The Mig 29 had been the pick of the Soviet Union's aircraft and, even without some of the advanced technology fitted to Western fighters, it was a remarkably capable aircraft, fast and manoeuvrable enough to be a match for any of them and more than a match for the Tempest.

Drew raised his hand. 'What priority are you putting on the threat? Is it sabre-ratting or the real thing? How good is the intelligence?'

The intelligence officer laid down her notes and looked up to meet Drew's gaze. 'The short answer is we don't know, but the threat is real, don't be in any doubt whatsoever about that.'

She glanced around the room as she spoke again. 'One last thing. They have been warned that any penetration of Bosnian airspace will be treated as a violation of UN Resolution 937. As you know, it is no longer necessary to get a UN official out of the shower or off the golf course in order to obtain authority to engage a target. Have a nice day.'

'Nirvana!' DJ said. 'No more politics, no more "Land immediately or we will be forced to escort you to your final destination". Why didn't we have this from the start?'

Drew smiled, forcing to the back of his mind his worries about how the Tempest would perform against the Mig. 'Right. We all know that the Mig 29 is a very capable aircraft, but whatever advantage that might confer is nullified by the fact that we're better trained, better equipped and just plain bloody better than the Serbs who'll be flying them. There are also two of us in each aircraft, so let's make full use of the advantage that gives us. There's not a pilot born who can keep track of eight jets in close combat, so navs, help your pilots hold the big picture in their heads. Last thing: these bastards killed Nick. Remember that. Let's go.'

As Drew headed towards the changing room, he met Michelle in the corridor. He stood for a moment, lost for words. 'I wanted to see you, talk to you . . .'

'Later,' she said. 'As long as you fly back this time.'

'So where are you guys going?'

'We're the ones going in underneath you guys to evacuate the garrison from the base at Srebanj.' She squeezed his hand and then was gone, hurrying down the corridor.

Drew was left staring after her, hoping that his concern for her safety had not shown in his face.

Before walking out to their aircraft, the outgoing crews all crammed into the briefing room, weighed down with their war kit, and sang the squadron battle song at the tops of their voices. Drew found himself uncharacteristically moved, singing lustily until a lump in his throat forced him to stop.

He strode out to his aircraft quiet and determined. His new navigator, Stig Jonsson, was waiting for him. He shook his hand and grinned. 'I'm afraid I'm not great at keeping these things in the air at the moment.'

There was laughter in Stig's pale-blue eyes. 'Don't worry about a thing. You steer and I'll read the map. If that doesn't work, we can always swap over.'

Stig proved to be a methodical and unflappable back-seater, taking the customary changes of aircraft and constant reloading of computers in his stride, but Drew could feel his own tension rising. He gripped the stick a little harder and double-checked his armament switches.

He glanced up to see the vapour trails of the first waves, the Stealth bombers and F18 HARM-shooters, already returning to base. 'Lucky bastards. They'll have hit their targets before the defenders even knew they were under attack. I don't think we'll have the same luxury.'

The silver trails seemed to be pointing the way to war. He called up the other members of the formation, then taxied out to the runway on schedule and lined up alongside DJ and Ali. The other pair tucked in behind and to one side of them. The four Tempests wound up together like an erupting volcano. The ground shook as a cloud of black smoke billowed across the runway, pierced by four white-hot tongues of flame. There was an instant of stillness, then the jets howled down the runway and blasted off into the dawn.

As the package of forty aircraft formed up over the Adriatic, Drew and the other RS3s took up station at the head. They flew fifteen thousand feet above them, their radars probing fifty miles ahead.

He looked down. The formation stretched back for thirty miles. Four radar-jamming aircraft led the way. Eight HARM shooters came next, at height above two teams of six bombers. The three minutes of travelling time between the bomber formations represented twenty-one miles. There were two layers of fighter protection as well, one down in the package with the bombers, the other flying on top. He could not see it, but Drew knew that Michelle's Puma was in a formation of helicopters somewhere behind the bombers. He tried not to think about her.

Though Drew led the whole formation, he was not the ringmaster; no one was. The aircraft – German, Dutch, Danish, French, British and American – arrived from half a dozen different bases, each one precisely on its scheduled time, height and track. A few seconds too late or too early, or a few hundred metres off line or height, and an aircraft would be piling into the back of the one in front or being rammed by the one behind.

He checked his watch. 'Push-point in twenty seconds . . . ten . . . now!' There was no visible sign or signal that the countdown had begun, but the clock was now running. In exactly twenty-two minutes the first bombs would be falling, the precise computations of time and space culminating in a firestorm of explosions and flames, breaking every body and building in its path.

Drew checked in with AWACs as they approached the coast. For an instant he envied the controller, lying far off shore, miles above the earth, a chess grandmaster moving his pieces into position. But this was where he wanted to be, where he had to be. He made his weapons live and, as they moved into hostile territory, gave his ritual touch to the ejection handle.

'You expect it to feel different when it's for real, don't you?' Stig said. 'But it's not . . . not yet anyway.' He lowered his head to scrutinise the patterns emerging from the green glow of his screens.

As they crossed the coast, there were flickers on the warner as it identified Triple-A and SAM sites, but most of the known SAM 2 and SAM 6 sites had already been silenced by the F18s. Those remaining knew better than to switch on their acquisition radars for more than a few seconds. To do so was to issue an open invitation to another HARM missile. They probed the jet's defences for an instant, then hid behind a wall of silence. The only live traces on the radar screen were the RS1s and F16s streaking in towards their targets.

'They're going in,' Stig said. 'Jesus, look at that.'

The Triple-A, at first curling lazily upwards, opening mushrooms of smoke in the paths of the bombers, grew thicker and faster until towers of flame and smoke seemed to reach up into the skies. Suddenly Stig yelled, 'One's hit. One's hit.'

Drew glanced down. Frighteningly close, a bomber began trailing smoke and flame. As it dropped behind, spiralling away into a dive, two parachutes opened like tiny orange-and-white flowers scattered in its wake.

There was a burst of radio chatter from DJ and Ali. Drew felt, as much as heard, the fear in their voices.

'Keep cool, keep your minds on the job,' he reminded them. Another bomber blew apart in a flash of flame, but distance lent it a remoteness that made Nick's death suddenly seem part of a different world. The other bombers flew on and there were larger, vivid orange flashes as the first bombs began to hit their targets.

There was a warning call from Stig. 'Two contacts, Bull's-eye two-four-zero, at fifty miles, high level, high speed.'

Instantly the clinical detachment was replaced by a surge of adrenalin. Drew felt the blood pounding through his veins.

Ali called confirmation, then Stig corrected himself as two other dots appeared on the screen. His voice was urgent. 'Four contacts, now thirty-five miles. Turning in towards us.'

Drew was beginning to sweat. 'Looks like the Migs are coming to join the party.' He could hear his own voice cracking a little as he stabbed his radio button to talk to the AWACs.

The cross-talk was terse. 'Magic, four contacts, Bull's-eye two-four-zero, thirty miles. Instructions?'

'Roger, Tiger,' replied the AWACs controller. 'Stand by.' Precious seconds dragged by. 'Targets Bull's-eye two-four-zero, declared hostile. Cleared engage.'

'Authenticate,' Drew challenged.

'Time authenticate. Minute two-seven, X-Ray-Foxtrot.'

Stig scanned his authentication tables. 'That checks out.'

Drew shivered. The fight was now in their hands alone. He called the other members of the fourship. 'Okay, we're cleared, this is it. Tiger Three and Four, turn hot. Let's tap them.'

The four Tempests formed a wall as they streaked across the sky to meet the threat, their speed increasing to Mach 1 – the speed of sound. Stig was hunched over his screen like a Stock Exchange dealer, exchanging rapid-fire cross-chat with the other navigators.

Drew began the sort, flying his own jet instinctively as he concentrated on targeting each fighter onto a different enemy contact. 'Three and Four, take the two high men, we'll take the two low.'

'Twenty-five miles.' Stig counted down the distance in a voice as dry and matter-of-fact as a solicitor reading a will.

'DJ, I've got left hand low.'

The response was immediate. 'Roger, got right hand low.'

'Twenty miles.'

As they completed the sort, the calls came over the headset from each aircraft: 'Sorted.' 'Locked.'

'Fox One, Fox One,' Drew called as the radar-guided Skyflash missile came off the side of his jet with a bowel-loosening roar. Less than a minute had elapsed since the first contact. He did not pause to watch it go streaking across the sky at three times the speed of sound, for he was already hurling the Tempest into a savage turn, away from the hostile missile that might have been launched against him. As he did so, the radar warner began to clamour.

'Come hard left. Descend,' yelled Stig. 'Come out heading two-zero-zero.'

'It's okay, Stig, I've got it, I've got it. Just keep an eye on the radar.' The bombers were still weaving their own patterns of evasion against the Triple-A, but Drew had no time to spare them more than a fleeting glance. His jaw clenched and he tightened his grip on the stick still further, his muscles and sinews taut as he tried to merge himself with the machine. Flying the jet became instinctive. He struggled to hold the constantly changing three-dimensional picture in his head as his jet bucked and swerved across the sky. A micro-second's hesitation could mean the difference between life and death.

High above the bombers, Drew and his fighters began the strange ritual dance of air defenders, advancing and retreating in a murderous gavotte. He repeatedly fired a radar missile and then turned away, before swinging back in for another chicken run.

On the second run, one of the dots on the computer screen abruptly went out as a Skyflash blew the Mig out of the sky. Stig had just exultantly recorded the kill, when Tiger Three erupted in a ball of flame. A missile from another Mig had struck home, breaking the jet in two. The Tempest pilot had held his course a fraction of a second too long, condemning his own aircraft. He had gambled and lost. Somehow the crew ejected safely from the middle of the inferno. Drew gave them an anguished glance as their parachutes opened.

The Migs' prime targets were the bombers. The Tempests barring the way were an obstacle to be avoided if possible, fought if not. The fighters were now closing. The two formations spread wider as they flashed towards each other.

Stig talked Drew onto each hostile aircraft in turn, shouting to make himself heard above the cross-talk in the split seconds before the jets hurtled past each other.

'Ten miles, twenty left, two down, first man.'

'Tally.'

'Another pair ten left of him.'

'Got them.'

At a closing speed of three miles a second they were upon them before the words had been exchanged.

Even though they fought at one thousand miles an hour, Drew and his target squared up to each other like thugs in a street brawl. Stig yelled instructions and warnings, twisting his head, trying to keep track of all three enemies and watch the backs of all three Tempests.

Drew fought the jet to the limit, struggling to extract every last inch of turn, his engines screaming in protest on full combat power. They twisted and rolled. Chaff and flares flew out in bursts as first Drew and then the Mig turned and corkscrewed, trying to break a missile lock.

Drew's cockpit was a cacophony of noise. He and Stig kept up a constant cross-talk, punctuated by involuntary grunts as he threw the jet around and the scream of radar warnings as the Migs tried to lock them up for a missile shot. Frenzied radio calls from Tiger Two and Four cut across the constant rottweiler growl of their own Sidewinder aiming system: 'Chaff! Flares! Break Left! Descend! Chaff! Flares! On you! On you! Go right! Go right!'

Drew gasped for breath, his arms aching with the effort of forcing the stick. Dragging his jet into a turn, he greyed out, grunting with exertion as he inched closer to his Mig's six o'clock.

Stig shouted a warning: 'Watch out, Drew. Bogie seven o'clock high. On us! On us!'

'Shit.' Drew let his target escape as he twisted the jet into a screaming turn, throwing out more chaff and flares.

Both sides took few risks, knowing that the loss of one jet would tip the balance, but finally Drew saw his chance. Closing hard for a kill on DJ and Ali, a Serbian pilot lost track of one element of the three-dimensional puzzle and paid with his life.

As the Mig slid across under Drew's jet, he yanked on the stick with both hands, using every ounce of his strength to make the spiralling turn, throttles rammed forward all the way.

The growling of the Sidewinder changed to a high-pitched screech as the guidance locked onto the heat source, the Mig's afterburners. Drew pulled the trigger and yelled, 'Fox

Two, Fox Two,' as the missile snaked off the side of the jet, homing with deadly accuracy on the enemy aircraft.

The Serb tried to unload phosphorous flares into its track, but it was too late. The Sidewinder detonated. Thousands of titanium cubes spread outwards in a halo of destruction, obliterating anything in their path. Zirconium discs, burning at a thousand degrees Celsius, followed in their wake, igniting anything that had survived the first onslaught. When the white flash of the explosion faded, the Mig had disintegrated.

Drew watched, transfixed, but Stig yelled, 'Break right, break right, break right.'

He threw his waning strength into another plunging turn, flares and chaff flying out as the Tempest corkscrewed away. There was a flash of light as a missile streaked past their left wing. Drew did not even have time to contemplate how close it had come before he was harrying another Mig.

The odds in the battle were now stacked in their favour. As Drew hounded the Mig, he saw DJ pull to height and lie in wait. He judged his moment perfectly. As the Mig turned to evade Drew, DJ dropped in behind him.

Drew watched the Serb twist and turn desperately, then eject as the missile struck home, the slipstream hurling him back, away from his doomed aircraft. The last Mig turned and ran, streaking away too fast for Jumbo in Tiger Four.

Drew eased the throttles back out of combat power. He was drenched in sweat, his breath rasping in his throat, the muscles throbbing in his arm.

The package of bombers had turned and was already heading for home, still ducking and weaving to avoid the Triple-A.

There was a burst of chatter from DJ and Ali. Drew brought them up short. 'Good work, but it's not over yet.'

He asked each of them to check fuel and weapons status, then called AWACs. 'Magic, Tiger 2–1, fuel state amber, weapon state low, request Gate 4 for Texaco.'

As Drew made the request, Stig called, 'Four contacts, heading zero-nine-five, twenty-five miles, low level, slow speed. Looks like helis.'

There was a pause as the AWACs controller digested the new information: 'Negative, Tiger. Request you stay on task to cover Panther 2–1 at Bull's-eye one-eight-zero.'

'That's 33 on the evacuation run,' Drew told Stig, frowning as he checked fuel again. They were already too low for a supersonic intercept and had enough for only ten more minutes over the area, even at subsonic speed. All he had to protect the two Pumas were two Sidewinders and the rounds in his guns. DJ and Jumbo were in the same position.

He knew he should discuss it with Stig, but the thought of Michelle's helicopter unprotected on the ground was too much for him. 'Roger, Magic. We have fuel for only ten minutes, tops.'

'Thanks for your help. Your replacement Buckeye 2–1, will be with you in eight.'

Jumbo's voice cut in immediately. 'Negative on that. We're fuel critical, Gate 4, returning to base.'

As Jumbo's aircraft pulled away to the west, Drew had a momentary pang of guilt. Jumbo was a seasoned enough pilot to make his own decisions, but DJ was always likely to trust his leader's judgement.

Stig echoed his concern. 'Drew, there are two of us in this aircraft. Don't take my consent for granted. If any Migs return to the attack, we're not only virtually defenceless, we haven't even got enough fuel to run away.'

'Someone's got to cover those Pumas.'

Stig did not reply but Drew could guess exactly what was going through his mind. He hoped he would have made the same decision irrespective of who was flying the helicopters.

Quelling his unease, he swung his jet round in the direction of Srebanj. The Pumas would be almost invisible against the ground.

Stig was face down in his radar, searching for contacts, as Drew pushed the radio button. 'Panther this is Tiger 2–1, inbound to your location. Give your position.'

Michelle's voice crackled over the radio. 'We're south of the base now, coming under heavy fire.'

Behind the rhythmic beat of the rotors Drew could hear explosions.

Suddenly AWACs broke in again. 'Tiger, heads up, four contacts fifteen miles, on your nose, showing as Hinds.'

Drew froze.

'Christ,' Stig said. 'We wouldn't want to tangle with those bastards even with full tanks and a full weapon-load.'

Drew caught sight of them a few moments later. The Hinds looked squat and ugly as toads and bristled with menace. As well as their guns, missile pods hung off either side of their pylons.

Drew called up AWACs. 'We're visual, four Hinds. Clear to engage?'

'Confirm bandits, cleared to engage.'

Drew flicked over to speak to Michelle. 'Panther, four Hinds inbound. We should engage them short of your position.'

'Roger. We're setting down now. Will need three minutes on the ground.'

Drew swung away to the east, then swooped down on the helicopter gunships. The Hinds scattered at their approach, speeding for the steep-sided valleys that might hide them from the fighters' radar.

'I'll take the left pair, you take the right,' Drew called to DJ. 'Make sure you're set for it – you'll only get one chance at the attack.'

He closed on his first target. The Hind dodged and swerved to break the missile lock but as the growl of the Sidewinder aiming system changed tone, Drew pulled the trigger. His missile streaked towards its target. 'Fox Two, Fox Two.'

He heard DJ make the same call a fraction of a second later. Both helicopters turned into balls of flame. Drew pulled his Tempest up to height again, searching frantically for the other two gunships.

The Pumas were desperately vulnerable as they loaded the base personnel under a constant barrage of artillery and mortar fire. The few buildings still standing were ablaze from end to end. Incoming shells exploded every few seconds, hurling debris into the air.

DJ had disappeared into a side valley hot on the heels of one Hind as Drew spotted the other, flashing in low across the river towards the UN base. The Serb gunner opened up, sending a stream of fire towards the Pumas.

Drew was off to the side of the Hind and not at the best attacking angle for the missile, but fired his last Sidewinder. It thrashed through the air, seeming to home on the helicopter's engines, but suddenly nose-dived into the ground and exploded well short of its target.

Drew swore as he flashed past the Hind, forcing the stick across to make a turn back onto his target. As he looked down, he saw the line of explosions from the Hind's guns cut straight through one of the grounded Pumas. Figures were blown high into the air as it erupted and one blundered helplessly away, aflame from head to toe.

Drew stared at the wrecked Puma, praying that it was not Michelle's. Hard-eyed and determined for revenge, he screwed the turn even tighter, bringing the Tempest round as the Hind swung in for another pass. The second Puma struggled into the air, wallowing under its heavy load.

Drew fought to hold the black silhouette within the cross-hairs in his Head-Up Display. The Hind weaved to and fro, slipping across the sight without a firing solution, but a moment later the cross-hairs intersected on the helicopter and Drew pulled the trigger. The airframe juddered like a pneumatic drill and the smell of cordite filled the cockpit as the guns spat out two thousand rounds a minute.

Two lines of tracer marched the length of the Hind, like stitching. Its rotors disintegrated in a fine black spray and the helicopter plunged to the ground.

The Puma rose agonisingly slowly into the air, then swung away to the west, now pursued only by bursts of small-arms fire from the Serbs pouring into the abandoned base.

Drew made one last pass to keep their heads down, ignoring Stig's fuel warning. He emptied his guns into the troops and then pulled up and away from the town. He delayed the call for a few seconds, too scared to hear the answer. Finally he jabbed at the radio button. 'Panther, this is Tiger. What's your condition?'

'Shrapnel and small-arms damage. We've taken casualties, but we're okay. Thanks for your help.' Michelle's voice was flat and drained, but relief flooded through Drew as he heard it.

He scanned the sky for DJ as he called him on the radio, then spotted him, still in pursuit of the other Hind. His flight had taken him over the main Serb artillery positions and Triple-A was rocketing up at him. 'DJ, leave it. They're out.'

'Two more seconds, two more seconds. Fox Two, Fox Two.' DJ was exultant.

Drew saw the missile come off his aircraft and, as DJ began pulling up to height, the last Hind disappeared in a blinding flash.

'Two kills, Drew,' DJ crowed, as he flew back to reformate. 'I think we've earned a little celebration.'

'I know the adrenalin's still pumping, DJ, but take it easy. Let's head for home.'

'Stand by for victory roll.'

As he levelled out alongside him, DJ waggled his wings and then put his aircraft into a victory roll around Drew's jet. As his jet plummeted out of control, his exuberant shout died in his throat.

Drew could hear his alarms screaming. 'I can't save it,' DJ said. 'Eject, eject, eject.'

The radio crackled and went dead as the Tempest spun away and smashed into the ground, sending out a wave of fire. Seconds passed as Drew and Stig frantically scanned the sky behind them, but they could see no sign of parachutes.

'We've got to go back and search,' Drew said, hauling on the stick.

'There's no fuel,' Stig warned.

'But I've got to. It's my fault.'

'Don't be stupid, Drew. If you turn back, we'll be banging out as well. We don't have the fuel. Leave it to Search and Rescue.'

Numb, Drew nodded and turned back towards the coast. He looked behind him once more, then stared fixedly ahead.

He mechanically checked out with AWACs as Buckeye – a formation of F16s – streaked in, then he flew on in silence, piloting the jet like an automaton.

'There's still hope,' Stig said gently. 'Not seeing any chutes isn't conclusive. They were well off to the west of us and there was so much shit in the air from Triple-A and burning helicopters . . .'

'I know,' Drew said quietly. 'Let's get home shall we?'

Chapter 18

Drew landed back at Gióia drained by fatigue and in the blackest of moods. As he braked the jet to a halt on the line outside the hangar, he saw a party of visiting brass, watching the conquering heroes return.

Michelle was already out of her Puma and talking to her father as Russell hovered in the background. Drew pulled the lever to raise the canopy, then slumped in his seat.

'Are you all right, Drew?' Stig asked. 'Do you want me to stay with you?'

Drew shook his head. 'I'll be fine. You go on in and join the party.'

There had been cheers from the squadron for the returning crew as they spilled from their aircraft, but the smiles began to fade as they realised that two jets were missing. There was an anxious scanning of faces and guilty expressions of relief as people spotted their particular mates among the air crew pulling off their helmets.

Drew was still in his seat when one of the engineers scaled the ladder to the cockpit.

'All right if we get to work on her, sir?'

Drew nodded. Bone-weary, he hauled himself out of the

cockpit and walked away from the aircraft, his sweat-drenched flying suit cold against his body.

Russell hurried across to meet him. 'Drew, by God, you've done the squadron proud today.'

Drew stopped and fixed him with a level gaze. 'What happened to me and all those other guys brought down DJ and Ali's aircraft.'

'Now, Drew,' Russell began, 'you have no way of knowing that—'

Drew ignored him. 'You keep sending us up, rather than admit that the aircraft is unsafe. How many more of us are going to have to die?'

Russell's expression was frozen. He addressed a point on the horizon. 'I'm not wasting any more words on this. I make full allowance for the stresses of combat and your feelings at losing your wingman. Nonetheless, your conduct is indefensible. You're grounded and confined to base until further notice.'

Drew ripped off his helmet and stalked away.

Michelle hurried to intercept him. 'What's the matter?'

'DJ and Ali went down.'

She put her hand on his arm. 'Did they get out okay?'

'I don't think so,' he said. 'I mean, I'm not sure.'

'If they're safe on the ground, we'll find them and bring them out.'

'They weren't shot down.'

'Can you be sure?'

'I watched it happen. They weren't hit – the jet just went out of control. It can't have been anything else. Russell still won't act so I'm going to force his – or your father's – hand.'

'What are you going to do?'

'What I should have done before.'

'Come on, Drew,' Michelle said. 'Things have already moved on. Rightly or wrongly, your crash has precipitated what we all wanted anyway. The UN have finally got off their arses and authorised us to go in and sort this out. Do you really want to go back there now and say, "Sorry, my plane crashed by itself, it was all a misunderstanding"?'

She paused, searching his expression. 'You're dead on

your feet. At least sleep on it, and we'll talk about it tomorrow.'

She stared at him for a moment, then turned and walked towards the milling crowd of UN soldiers and air crew.

Drew went to see Michelle early the next morning. She answered the door yawning.

'Michelle, about yesterday . . .'

He was interrupted as her co-pilot, Sandy, ran down the corridor. 'Michelle, one of our aircraft has just picked up a signal on an emergency beacon. We're briefing as soon as possible, so we'll need to get on it right now.'

Michelle nodded. 'I'll be with you in one minute.'

Sandy glanced over at Drew. 'It's in the area where your wingman went down.'

He hurried off again and Michelle began grabbing her gear. 'We'll leave this until later.'

Drew was thinking furiously. 'Michelle.' She paused in the doorway and turned to face him. 'I want to go with you – as crew.'

'Don't be ridiculous. You're a pilot on fast jets, not a crewman on choppers.'

He held her gaze. 'Please, Michelle. I know what it's like to be on the ground in Bosnia and it's my fault that DJ's there. When AWACs asked us to cover you we didn't really have enough fuel or weapon-load for the job. Jumbo knew that and just bugged out straight away. DJ is still inexperienced, so he looked to me for a lead. I knew it was you we were being asked to cover so I agreed and DJ just fell in with that.'

Michelle hesitated. 'Have you any idea what would happen to me if I was caught giving joyrides on a combat mission?'

'The only ones who'll know are Paul and Sandy, but if anyone else does find out, you can say I said I'd been ordered to fly with you. Please . . .'

She shook her head. 'I must be mad.'

He followed her down to the map room, where Paul and Sandy were already planning a safe route in and out of the zone where the beacon had been detected.

'Boys, we've got an extra crewman today,' Michelle said.

'Get off the grass, Michelle,' Paul said. 'We're flying a combat mission, not taking a trip round the harbour.'

'Nothing personal, Drew,' Sandy added. 'We're hoping to pick up two passengers when we get to the site. We don't need an extra one before we even set off.'

'I'll take full responsibility if there are any problems,' Michelle said. 'Look, you both owe me big time. Just do this for me.'

Drew followed them self-consciously into the briefing room a few minutes later and stood behind the other crews already there.

Michelle stepped up to the podium. 'Right. We have three Pumas, with four Tempests flying top cover. I'm leading and will make the attempt to pick up the air crew once we've located them. The two other Pumas will give covering fire. If anything goes wrong with me, Panther Two and if necessary, Panther Three will attempt the rescue.

'Now because of the urgency, some of this is going to have to be seat-of-the-pants stuff. Intelligence says the Serbs have moved Triple-A into the woods south-east of Srebanj, so we'll be approaching the target from the north, following the Traj river. No other reports of significant enemy activity in the target area.

'The air crew we're looking for are broadcasting in set sequence, thirty seconds on the hour, fifteen seconds on the half-hour. Apart from the Tempests giving us top cover, there are other friendlies on CAP at Jellystone and Bedrock. Weather over the target is forecast to be the same as here: visibility fair to good, light westerly winds, air temperature around zero, some local mist patches, clearing rapidly as the sun gets up.

'Dawn is in twenty minutes. We're therefore going to be arriving and departing in daylight, so expect some ground fire. Right. Time is 0608 . . . Now. Let's get to it.'

Drew slipped out of the briefing room and hurried down the corridor to the changing room. He grabbed his flying kit from his locker, bundled it under his arm and ran out to Michelle's Puma. The ground crew were absorbed by the race to finish their own last-minute preparations for the mission.

Dawn was reddening the sky as Michelle, Paul and Sandy ran out. Drew watched as they rattled off their pre-flight checks in staccato bursts. Michelle got clearance from the tower and the three Pumas rose into the dawn sky and wheeled away to the east, over the Adriatic.

They flew in radio silence, dropping down to wave-top height as they approached the Dalmatian coast. They flashed over the flat coastal plain, startling the farmers already in their fields and then began the climb over the Kopuc mountains. As they skimmed down the thickly forested eastern slopes, they picked up the track of the infant Traj river, one of a thousand Danube tributaries springing from the chain of mountains sweeping from the Alps to the Black Sea.

Michelle was following a decoy course suggesting their target was well to the north of Srebanj, but, five minutes' flying time from the target, the three Pumas swung abruptly away to the south and sped in towards the town as the Tempests quartered the sky above them, their radar warners scanning for any hostile threat.

Michelle checked her watch. 'If they're down there we should be hearing from them in the next couple of minutes.'

As they neared the area where the signal had been detected, all of them were silent, ears pricked for the first contact. Paul hunched over his direction finder, searching for any trace of the beacon that would lead them to the target.

If DJ and Ali were still alive, they would switch on the beacon on the half-hour. When they heard the helicopters, they would reinforce the radio signal with flares. But the Serbs could pick up the radio signal as easily as the NATO aircraft and their ground forces would have been alerted by the same transmission that had sent the Pumas scrambling to the rescue.

Three times Michelle swept over the search area. Nothing but static came over the speakers in the Puma and Paul's screen stayed obstinately blank.

As they began the fourth pass, there was a fifteen-second burst of noise, followed by a shout from Paul. 'Got it! Range one and a quarter miles, bearing zero-nine-zero.'

Michelle swooped in towards the site as ragged gunfire from Serb ground troops arced upwards.

DJ's voice came up on the radio, talking them in. 'We see you now, come left a little. Red flare now.'

'Anything yet?' Paul asked anxiously over the intercom.

'Not yet . . . not yet . . . tally now,' Sandy called. 'Got it, Michelle? Just left of the nose, three hundred yards.'

'Tally,' Michelle said, as she spotted the flash of a flare and red smoke began to drift upwards. 'We see you, boys, we're coming in.'

She slewed the Puma into a turn and put it down in a clearing as close as possible to the site. Paul threw the side door open and manned the Puma's gun as Drew peered out into the forest, straining his eyes for any sign of DJ and Ali.

The seconds ticked by as they waited, rotors idling, occasional bursts of gunfire echoing through the trees. The other Pumas made strafing runs to keep the Serb heads down, but the gunfire was getting steadily closer.

Then DJ and Ali suddenly appeared, sprinting out of the trees. Paul began firing the machine gun over their heads into the forest. A hail of small-arms fire was now ricocheting through the clearing as the Serbs closed on their quarry. Drew could see the muzzle flashes from their guns.

Michelle was winding up the engines ready to lift off as DJ and Ali wove from side to side across the clearing. They had almost reached the Puma when Drew saw Ali clutch at his arm, his mouth open in a soundless scream. DJ turned and ran back, dragging him to his feet and pushing him towards the helicopter. Propelled by DJ, Ali half fell and half dived through the door. He rolled across the floor, gasping for breath, as a thin trickle of blood appeared between his fingers.

As DJ took hold of the handle by the doorway, Paul yelled, 'Go, go, go!' into the intercom, still firing bursts from the door gun into the trees. Above the deafening rattle of the gun Drew heard the rotors thunder and the Puma began to lift, the downwash flattening the grass and lashing the trees, sending broken twigs and branches cartwheeling through the air.

As he tried to pull DJ inside, blood suddenly splashed across Drew's face. DJ's head jerked back and his arms were thrown wide. He stood framed in the doorway for a moment, then toppled over backwards and fell to the ground.

As he wiped the blood from his eyes, Drew screamed to Michelle to put the Puma down again. As she did, she swung the helicopter around, bringing the nose guns to bear on the main concentration of Serb troops. The guns blasted, the sound reverberating inside the steel cab as the smell of cordite filled Drew's nostrils.

He peered down at DJ's crumpled body and saw a dull red stain spread outwards from the base of his spine. Ignoring Paul's warning shout, Drew leapt from the door when the Puma was still a few feet above the ground and sprinted across the clearing, throwing himself flat alongside DJ as bullets ripped at the ground around them.

He rolled DJ over on to his back. There was a flicker of recognition in his eyes. Drew tried not to look at the hole in DJ's stomach. He glanced back towards the Puma. He heard a '*whooomfff*!' above his head followed by a series of massive explosions in front of him as one of the circling helicopters fired a salvo of rockets into the edge of the forest.

Mud and debris rained down on him as he pushed himself upright and scooped DJ into his arms. He screamed in agony as Drew began to run with him, ignoring the bullets whining around his ears.

Drew staggered the last few feet, then fell against the Puma and heaved DJ in through the doorway. He dived after him and lay gasping on the cold metal floor as the engines howled and the helicopter lifted into the air. It shot away from the clearing, skimming the treetops, pursued by sporadic shots from the Serb troops.

Paul fired a last burst from the gun, slammed the door and ran to examine DJ. He cut the flying suit away and Drew saw him wince at the sight of the gaping hole in DJ's stomach. Paul felt for a pulse in the neck, then frantically cut the jacket away. He pinched DJ's nose and blew into his mouth twice, then began heart massage, banging his chest with a dull, double-thud that Drew could hear above the noise of the rotors.

Paul kept alternating between bursts of mouth-to-mouth and heart massage, grunting with the effort. Sweat dripped from his forehead on to DJ's face as the pool of dark blood spread wider around his body.

Despite the feeling of hopelessness that overwhelmed him, Drew's eyes never left DJ, staring intently at him, searching for some sign of returning life.

Finally Paul stooped again to feel the pulse in DJ's neck and search for the faintest breath. He straightened, shook his head slowly in response to the question in Drew's eyes and hurried to begin treating Ali's wound.

Drew cried silently, cradling DJ's head in his lap, as the blood ebbed slowly from his body.

As soon as they landed back at Gióia, the medics swarmed into the Puma, helping Ali to an ambulance and carrying DJ's body away. Ali's eyes met Drew's for a moment, but neither could find any words.

Michelle watched Drew staring from the shadows inside the helicopter as the ambulances drove off across the airfield, their red lights flashing. Her face was drawn and tired as she hugged him, ignoring the blood that covered his face.

When Drew got back to his quarters, he found Russell waiting for him, flanked by two military policemen. He led Drew to a brightly lit, windowless room, then took up station by the door. After a long wait the door opened and Air Vice-Marshal Power walked in.

He sat down facing Drew and they studied each other across the table for a moment, neither speaking. Then Power pulled a sheaf of notes from his briefcase, glanced briefly at them and cleared his throat. 'I came here specially to see you today, Flight Lieutenant.'

'I'm flattered,' Drew said.

Power ignored the sarcasm, continuing in the same cool, even tone. 'I owe you a debt of gratitude.'

'I don't understand.'

'I believe you saved my daughter from an enemy helicopter.' Drew inclined his head but said nothing. 'Please accept my thanks for that and my congratulations for your bravery in action. It was in the very highest traditions of the Royal Air Force.'

He paused for a few seconds, his pale, almost colourless, blue eyes staring straight at Drew. When he continued, his voice was emotionless. 'However, what is not in accord with any reputable traditions of the Air Force is your continued insubordination and your obsessive, amateur investigations in open defiance of orders.'

He waited for Drew's response.

'I believe there is sometimes a duty higher than that due to a superior officer, sir.'

'And what might that be – a duty to God?'

'If you like to call it that, but I'd rather think of it as a duty to human life.'

Power's tone was neutral but the anger was visible in his face. 'I don't need any lectures from you on the sanctity of human life. I did my frontline service while you were still in nappies and I saw good friends take off in the morning and never come back. There were twelve men in my training group; only four of them are still alive. My best man was killed in a training accident three weeks after my wedding. So don't you ever presume to lecture me about the value of human life.'

He stared across the table until Drew dropped his gaze. 'Unlike you, however, I need to have something a little broader than tunnel vision. The Air Force is fighting for its own life. We've been downsized by fifty per cent since the end of the Cold War, yet we're still expected to meet an expanding range of commitments, including Bosnia, without harming our prime duty, the defence of the airspace of the United Kingdom.'

'And how does having a dozen Tempests falling out of the sky for no apparent reason help that particular objective?'

'Why don't you grow up a little, Flight Lieutenant? We lost more than that in twenty seconds on the first day of the Somme. You've been around the Air Force long enough now to realise that there are more important things than individual lives.'

'When they're lost in combat, yes,' Drew said, 'but not when they're tossed away like chaff.'

Power ignored the interruption. 'When the fault first became apparent we faced two choices.'

'So you now admit that there is a fault?'

'We could have grounded every Tempest until it was discovered and rectified – a process which might have taken years, during which time our country would have been rendered virtually defenceless against air attack. The second option – the one we chose to follow – was to press ahead with an investigation with all possible speed, but to keep the Tempests airborne, accepting the losses of equipment and air crew as a necessary price to pay for our continued national security.'

'Let's not forget the back-handers from Barnwold to keep the lid on the problem while they flog a few more defective Tempests to gullible Middle Eastern governments.'

'I'm sure you're not as naive as you appear,' Power said. 'I act in the interests of the Royal Air Force and Her Majesty's Government. Where those interests coincide with those of Barnwold Industries, we work together. Where they conflict, my loyalty is solely to HMG.

'In the case of the Tempest sales to the Middle East, the government is just as keen that contracts are signed. The benefits from two billion pounds of Tempest orders will spread right through the British economy.'

Drew listened silently, his face set.

'I'm sure you'd like to find some grand conspiracy to expose, Flight Lieutenant, reaching to the very heart of government, but life just isn't like that. There are no knights in shining armour, though the popular press are doing their best to turn you into one. And there are no wicked wizards. The real world is composed of shades of grey. That's the world I have to deal with and the world that you ought to start living in.'

'Don't patronise me,' Drew said. 'The fault on the Tempest has caused the deaths of three of my friends. They didn't just fail to come back. Two of them died in front of me.' He paused. 'I'm not going to let it kill another one.'

Power rose to his feet. 'I think this discussion has gone on long enough. Let me outline the choices available to you, Flight Lieutenant. Drop all this nonsense now. You'll be given some home leave in recognition of the very real hardships you've endured and the very great courage that you've shown. On your return to duty, you'll be decorated for gallantry and promoted. You'll be a real hero, not just a tabloid newspaper tiger.'

Drew curled his lip. 'And the alternative?'

'The alternative is quite simple. You'll go home to face charges arising from the loss of your aircraft over Cumbria last month. You'll be court-martialled and dishonourably discharged from the Air Force. You'll have no career and no future.'

Drew looked from Power to Russell in disbelief. 'And if I tell my story to the papers?'

'You've no more solid information than you had the last time you tried. We could have court-martialled you for that alone, but I'm not interested in giving the left-wing press a martyr to eulogise.' Power's look was contemptuous. 'Try it again. We won't even have to put a D-notice on it. Who'll believe the uncorroborated ramblings of a disgraced pilot trying to blame his aircraft instead of his own incompetence?'

'DJ corroborated my story.'

'But regrettably I understand that he is now dead.'

Drew clenched his fists. 'You're bluffing. If you were really that confident of your position we wouldn't be here.'

He watched as Power controlled his anger. 'It's a great shame, Flight Lieutenant. A country needs its heroes and you've got the right credentials. You could have been a great morale booster for your country and a fine ambassador for the Royal Air Force, but . . .' He paused with his hand on the door handle. 'I can give you until tomorrow morning to think it over.'

Drew shook his head. 'There's no point.'

'Then you must accept the consequences, Flight Lieutenant Miller. Goodbye.'

The door banged shut behind them, leaving Drew alone in the room. Drew stared at it for a few moments, then got up. As he opened the door, he was confronted by two MPs.

'Flight Lieutenant Miller, would you come with us please?'

'Why?'

'We have orders to escort your to your quarters, sir. You're to be confined there until further notice.'

'And if I refuse?'

'I hope that you won't, sir, but we will use force if necessary.'

Drew said nothing for a moment as he looked from one to the other. Then he shrugged and walked out.

Chapter 19

Drew was sprawled on the bed with his hands behind his head, staring up at the ceiling, when he heard a tap on the door. Michelle came in, gave him a kiss on the cheek and then sat on the chair.

'How did you get past the Gestapo?' he asked.

'I spoke to my father and persuaded him to lift the siege a little. It only works one way though: I can come in but you can't come out.'

'What's he going to do with me?'

'He says he doesn't know yet. I tried to convince him that he couldn't court-martial a war hero but he just kept on about discipline overriding everything.' She rested her chin on her hand. 'What happened?'

'Did your father mention we'd been having a little chat?'

'I took that for granted. Was it the usual subject?'

He nodded. 'The vital strategic interests of the UK and my role in helping to preserve them.'

She gave him a quizzical look. 'And?'

'And we agreed to differ.' He paused. 'He's covering something up, Michelle.'

'I don't believe that.'

He swung his legs over the side of the bed and sat upright. 'Then why has he got me in solitary?'

'He says he's only doing it to stop you getting yourself into even deeper shit.'

'Oh come on, get real. He wants me out of the way so he can do a stitch-up.' He got up and moved to the window. 'You didn't see what he was like earlier on. He's no intention of allowing it to come out. I'd stake my life on it.'

Michelle walked over and held him as he stared out into the darkness. 'I know him, Drew. He asked me to trust him. He's never broken his word to me in my life.'

Drew did not turn to look at her. 'The first chance I get, I'm going to blow the story.'

'You haven't even got a story,' she snapped, exasperated. 'You still don't know what makes the Tempests crash.'

'I know *something* does.' He paused. 'I've got two stories actually. Not only does an RAF Air Vice-Marshal insist on sending air crew to their deaths in an aircraft he knows is unsafe, but he's also hand-in-glove with the company that manufactures them. They stand to lose two billion pounds' worth of Middle Eastern business if this gets out.'

He felt Michelle stiffen. 'You go to the papers with that story and you and I are finished.'

He turned as she stepped away from him. 'Michelle . . . I know this is tough, but he's compromised—'

'He's not up to anything. Of course he has links with Barnwold. He's been with them on sales trips to the Middle East a few times. But it's the government who sends him there, for God's sake. It's not something he particularly enjoys, but it's his duty. If Barnwold can sell Tempests abroad, the cost to the RAF is less.'

'And what's his price?'

Michelle's eyes blazed. 'How dare you?'

'I overheard him on the phone to the Barnwold chairman,' Drew said. 'He was discussing how to keep the lid on all this. Is that his duty to his country? A CONDOR report I sent him on the Tempest has disappeared into a black hole. He's buried every hint that there might be something wrong—'

'Let me tell you about my father,' Michelle said. 'He could have had his pick of top jobs in the defence industry at three or four times the salary, but he's stayed with the Air Force. He's one hundred per cent committed.'

Drew looked at her, overwhelmed by a sudden wave of sadness. 'Jesus – he's got you making his speeches for him, hasn't he? Go on, now tell me how the deaths of a few Tempest crew are nothing compared to the security of the United Kingdom. Tell me how it's his unenviable duty to suppress information on a fault that kills people – people like Nick Jackson, DJ Jeffries and Alastair Strang, his daughter's own boyfriend?'

'Go to hell.' Michelle pushed past him. The door slammed shut and Drew was alone.

Drew had eaten his breakfast and was gazing out of the window when there was a knock at the door. A thin, prematurely grey army officer walked in. He moved the table into the middle of the room and sat down on the only chair, gesturing Drew to the bed. He opened his briefcase and pulled out a file.

'I'm Captain James Noble. I've been assigned to your case.'

'I'm Drew Miller and I'd prefer to choose my own lawyer.'

Noble gave a nervous smile. 'That is your right, Drew – may I call you Drew? – but I'm afraid English-speaking lawyers familiar with the intricacies of a British court martial are in rather short supply in this part of Italy.

'I've flown in from Milan this morning in answer to a summons from your commanding officer and, as I'm returning to England shortly, I would be in a position to represent you at your court martial. If you still want a different lawyer when you get back, I'll of course stand down. In the meantime, maybe I can help you.'

Drew's expression did not soften.

'I assure you,' Noble added, 'I shall defend you to the best of my abilities.' He paused. 'And, with all due modesty, I'm not a bad lawyer.'

'And what are you defending me against?'

He consulted his file. 'Serious charges, I'm afraid. Insubordination, dereliction of duty, conduct unbecoming an officer and incompetent handling of your aircraft. In short, they're throwing the book at you.'

He glanced at Drew, then cleared his throat. 'Perhaps the best thing would be for you to tell me how you intend to answer those charges.'

'With a not guilty plea, of course,' Drew said. 'The truth is that there is a potentially fatal flaw in the Tempest aircraft. Rather than allow the true facts to be known, the Air Force establishment – and Air Vice-Marshal Power in particular – prefer to silence me by pressing these charges.'

Noble pursed his lips and carefully pressed the tips of his fingers together before speaking. 'I'm afraid that attitude is likely to be most unhelpful before the court martial. Even if what you say is true, an audience of senior officers sitting in judgement is hardly the ideal forum to make serious allegations about one of their number.

'It's your decision, of course, but I'm bound to say that in my experience such an attitude usually leads to a heavier sentence. Unless you're intent on denying the charges – and you can only do that by contradicting the sworn statements of several senior officers – I would suggest that a guilty plea and a statement in mitigation will be far less painful all round.'

Drew set his jaw. 'I don't intend to take this lying down and they can't impose a heavier sentence than a dishonourable discharge from the Air Force, which they're likely to do anyway, whatever I say.'

'I'm afraid they can impose a far heavier sentence than that,' Noble said. 'They can – and almost certainly will – give you a dishonourable discharge, but, before that takes effect, they have the power to imprison you for up to ten years.'

Drew felt the blood drain from his face but said nothing.

'I'll leave you to think things over for a while,' Noble said, getting to his feet. 'I'll be back to see you in the next couple of days. Think things over very carefully, but in my opinion you really do have only one course of action.'

For the next three days Drew stayed confined to his room, his repeated requests to use a phone refused by the impassive MPs. His only visitor was Noble, who called in early on the Thursday evening. He had no fresh information to give and his advice was no more welcome to Drew for a second hearing.

After the lawyer had left, Drew lay on the bed, staring at the ceiling and replaying every second of the two crashes in his mind. He was still lying there two hours later, when there was another knock on the door.

After a moment Michelle appeared. She was pale and hollow-eyed.

He scrambled to his feet as she closed the door, but then both stood in an awkward silence. 'I'm glad you came,' Drew began. 'I thought . . .'

'I thought so too.'

There was another long pause.

'What's the matter? You look like you've been crying.'

'. . . I came to apologise.'

'No,' Drew said. 'I'm the one—'

She held up a hand. 'My father took me out to dinner tonight. He had some important news he wanted to tell me.' A brief, bitter smile flashed across her face. 'Do you know what the news was?' Drew guessed, but shook his head. 'He's leaving the Air Force to take up a post in industry as an air defence consultant. Guess where.'

Drew nodded slowly. 'Barnwold.' He reached out to wipe a tear from her cheek.

She gazed at the floor. 'He actually claimed to be surprised that I was shocked. I walked out and left him there.' Her eyes began to fill with tears.

Drew put his arms round her and held her to him as she continued to sob, her tears wet on his chest. He wrapped his arms even tighter around her, murmuring gently to her and kissing her face, tasting the salt tears on his lips.

After a few minutes, she straightened up, kissed him once, cupping his face in her hands, then went to the basin and rinsed her face in cold water.

She turned to face him, embarrassed. 'I must look like the helicopter pilot from hell.'

Drew shook his head.

'I'm sorry,' she said, still holding his gaze. 'I've been so wrapped up in all this, I haven't even asked. What's happening, what are they going to do to you?'

'They're going to court-martial me for at least fifteen different kinds of high treason.'

'I'll do anything I can to help you, Drew, but I don't know what that means. I told my father I'd help you blow the whistle on him and he practically laughed in my face. As he was at pains to remind me, there's no physical evidence linking any of the crashes to a fault.'

'Not yet,' Drew said.

She looked puzzled.

Drew walked to the window and stood looking out into the gathering dusk as a jet streaked down the runway and lifted off. 'I'm not giving up. There's a transport due in from Finnington in the morning and I suspect I'll be sent back on it.' He turned back to her. 'So there isn't much time.'

'Time for what?'

'I've been over and over those two flights a thousand times in my mind,' he said. 'Every time I go to sleep, I'm flying them.'

'So?'

He took a deep breath. 'So I'm going to go back up and do exactly the same commands, in exactly the same sequence as I did over Appleby and Bosnia.'

'And what if you succeed?' Michelle asked. 'You'll have proved your point, but you'll be in a wooden box. It's Russian roulette.'

'If I don't do it, this thing's never going to end. The only way I can prove there's a fault in the aircraft, rather than the pilot, is to go back up and make it happen again.'

She nodded, but he could see her eyes brimming with tears. He reached out to take her hand.

He kissed her again, then walked into the bathroom. He lifted the cistern lid and took out a sealed plastic bag. He ripped it open and handed her an envelope and the miniature tape recorder. 'First of all, I want you to post the envelope to my lawyer in London.'

'What's in it?'

He hesitated. 'It's the tape I made of the guy at Barnwold.' She nodded. 'Then I want you to get into the control tower and tape everything I say while I'm flying the Tempest. I'll keep the link to the tower open and talk through every single move I make. Whatever happens to me, that tape will pinpoint the fault with the Tempest.'

'But there's already a voice tape in the flight recorder. Why do you need another one?'

'Because the ADR and the official voice tape will go to the Accident Investigation Board. If something happens, you've got to get the tape out.'

He saw her eyes cloud. 'Nothing will happen. We'll start manoeuvring at thirty thousand feet, so I'll have a ten-thousand-foot cushion to give me time to regain control.'

'And if you don't?'

'I can just bang out. The Air Force will lose another thirty-million-pound jet, but, as your father himself told me, accepting the losses of equipment and air crew is a necessary price to pay for our continued national security.'

She laughed despite herself. 'What if nothing happens?'

'Then I'll go back up to thirty thousand feet and do it again until either something does or I run out of fuel.'

'If you're going to duplicate the flights exactly, you need a back-seater carrying out the same actions. Who's going to be stupid enough to fly with you?'

'Can you go and find Ali and get him up here?'

She stared at him. 'Even if he agrees, you're confined to your room. How are you going to get out?'

'Simple,' Drew said. 'I'll climb out of the window.'

'On a knotted bed-sheet?'

'There's a drainpipe.'

'You'll fall.'

'Michelle, I'm about to do a thirty-thousand-foot dive. The thought of dropping another eighteen doesn't exactly terrify me.'

She was back with Ali ten minutes later. Drew wasted no time. 'I want you to be my back-seater on a sortie.'

'Not Stig?' Ali shrugged, puzzled. 'All right. No problem.'

'Not quite. Officially I'm grounded, but, since you've been on holiday in Bosnia and then in the sick-bay, there's no way you could know that. That's the good news. The bad news is I need you to help me try to re-create the fault . . . It's the only way I can prove what's wrong with the aircraft.'

Ali glanced from Drew to Michelle. 'So what if it works?'

Drew tried to sound confident. 'We'll be starting from height this time, so we'll have time to try and regain control or eject,' he said. 'I know it's asking a lot, Ali.'

'You're not wrong there.'

'You're the only person I can ask. That fault killed DJ. It almost killed you. If he hadn't gone back, he'd be alive and you'd be dead. If we fly this sortie, we can make that worth something.'

'Jesus, Drew, you know how to twist the knife.' He paused. 'All right. When do we go?'

'Now.'

Ali started to say something else, but then thought better of it. 'I'd better be the one to get clearance from the authoriser. I'll tell him I'm going up with Jumbo. He's off duty today and he's gone into town for dinner.'

Drew grinned. 'I'll meet you in the changing rooms in twenty minutes.'

Michelle turned as Ali closed the door. 'Emotional blackmail – it gets them every time,' she said. 'It's bad enough that you want to risk your own life, without making him risk his as well.'

'I didn't make him do it – he volunteered.' Drew avoided her gaze.

'Promise me one thing,' Michelle said. 'Whatever happens, even if it's nothing at all, promise me you'll call it a day after this. If this doesn't work – and I hope to God it doesn't – draw a line under it.'

He turned her face to his. 'I promise. You do understand why I have to do it, don't you?'

For an answer she pulled him to her and kissed him.

'This is my last shot, anyway,' Drew said. 'By this time tomorrow, I'll be banged up in a cell back in England.'

'Then we'd better not waste tonight, if you manage to get down again in one piece.' Forcing a smile, she kissed him again, then walked out of the door without looking back.

Drew waited a couple of moments, then stuck his head out of the door and called to one of the MPs. 'I feel a bit rough. I'm going to get my head down for a while. If anyone else wants to see me, can you ask them to come back later?'

He shut his door and turned his light out, then stood for a few moments, letting his eyes get accustomed to the darkness. He pushed the window open. Its hinges gave a faint protesting squeak. He waited, then swung his leg over the sill.

The drainpipe was four feet to the side. Drew crouched on the sill, facing inwards and grasped the steel frame of the open window with his right hand. Then he pushed himself off, swinging round with the window towards the wall and reaching out for the pipe with his left. As his fingers grasped it, the window slammed against the wall, jarring his other hand loose. He grabbed desperately for the pipe, skinning his knuckles as he slid down the wall, until his flailing feet caught on one of the brackets.

He hung on, motionless, as he waited to see if there was any response to the noise. Then he slid quickly down the pipe to the ground. He looked around, then slipped away past the corner of the building.

Ali was waiting just inside the changing room. Drew checked that the room was empty of other air crew before he spoke. 'Any problems?'

Ali shook his head. 'I just told the authoriser I needed a trip round the houses to get my confidence back after the ejection.'

Drew motioned Ali towards the counter where the corporal was scribbling in his ledger. 'Keep him distracted,' he mouthed, ducking behind a bank of lockers. He heard Ali asking for two pairs of night-vision goggles.

The corporal turned away to pull the goggles from the locked store behind him. While he had his back turned, Drew whipped his own helmet from his locker and then grabbed a handful of used flying suits from the pile on the floor. He went to the far end of the changing room, out of sight of the counter, and found one close to his size. He threw the rest in a corner.

Ali walked down to join him and they began to change in silence, keeping a wary eye on the corporal, who had returned to his ledger.

Drew had just pulled on his G-pants when he heard the door swing open. He hastily put on his helmet and threw a spare suit over his shoulders to hide the name-patch. Ali peered round the end of the row of lockers and then disappeared from Drew's sight, hurrying to waylay the newcomer.

'Hello, sir,' Drew heard him say. 'Not flying are you?'

'Sadly not, Barber, sadly not,' came Russell's reply. 'Too much bloody paperwork, I'm afraid.' There was an awkward silence. 'You getting back in the swing?'

'That's it, sir. Jumbo and I are going up for a quick spin.'

'I thought he was off duty,' Russell said.

'He was.' Ali's voice tightened. 'But I managed to bribe him into going up with me. It's costing me the best meal in Gióia.'

'No great sacrifice then,' Russell said, chuckling.

Drew could hear the voices getting closer despite Ali's efforts. He gathered the rest of his gear together and sped through the door leading to the airfield. He hurried out to their aircraft, waiting on the line outside the hangar and gave it a cursory look-over before scrawling an illegible signature on the form Springer presented to him.

'Fastest check I've ever seen in my life,' Springer said, eyeing Drew with curiosity. 'Not exactly regulation was it, sir? But then, come to that, nor's your outfit.'

Drew glanced over his shoulder and saw Ali and Russell emerging from the changing rooms, still locked in conversation.

'Look, Springer – Neville . . .'

Springer waited, cocking an eyebrow at the use of his christian name.

'That meter of yours I had running the other day.'

'Sir?' Springer said, still impassive.

'If you can fit a case of beer in it tonight, then it's Jumbo Collins in the front seat of this aircraft . . . should anyone ask.'

A smile spread across Springer's face as he took in the approaching Russell. 'Sounds fine to me, Jumbo, and by the way, I'll be drinking Becks . . . should anyone ask.'

Drew hurried up the steps and strapped himself into the cockpit as Russell arrived with Ali.

'It's just like falling off a horse, Ali: get straight back into the saddle and there's nothing to it.'

Springer gestured to his headset. 'Flight Lieutenant

Collins says would you hurry along, sir? He's got a fault showing on his pre-flight checks.'

Ali hurried up the ladder while Springer saluted Russell with the blend of deference and insolence that had taken him twenty years to perfect. As the ladders were removed, he sauntered over to the side of the aircraft, ready to start the engines, leaving Russell standing alone by the Tempest's wing.

'What's the snag?' Ali asked as he strapped himself in.

'There isn't one. That was just Springer earning his corn.'

As they fired up the two massive engines, Russell stepped back a couple of paces and glanced up at the cockpit, illuminated by the glaring halogen lights. He looked away, then snapped his head back, the smile fading from his face.

From the corner of his eye Drew could see Russell's features contorting with rage. His mouth opened and shut, his words lost in the engine noise.

'Oh, oh,' Drew said. 'I think Russell's just noticed that Jumbo bears an uncanny resemblance to Drew Miller.'

Ali glanced out. 'Come on, Drew, it's all gone to ratshit. We can't go ahead with this now.'

'Sorry, Ali. It's now or never.'

Russell sprinted across to Springer, who had his head-set plugged in to the jet. Pushing him angrily aside, Russell pressed the mike to his throat and began shouting. 'Shut down those engines now. That is an order.'

The only reply was the wail of the siren as the canopy began to close.

Russell ducked under the nose of the Tempest and, as soon as the siren died, he stepped back, standing directly in front of the aircraft, looking up into Drew's face. 'I order you to shut down those engines,' he shouted again.

Again Drew did not reply. Instead the engine note rose as he applied the power. The airframe juddered, the engines howling their frustration at the brakes holding them back. Then the Tempest began to roll forward off the line.

'Stop this aircraft,' Russell yelled. 'I am not moving. You will have to run me over.'

Once more there was no reply. The Tempest towered over Russell and at the last minute he jumped out of the way, the headset tearing free from the fuselage. He clapped his hands to his ears as they thundered past.

Glancing back, Drew could see Russell sprinting towards the Engineering Control hut.

'What now?' Ali asked.

'I imagine he'll be on the phone to Air Traffic. He'll try to get the runway blocked and stop us taking off.'

He wound up the engines further, the note rising as the jet jumped forward, rumbling along the taxiway at twice the normal speed.

'We're not going to have time for all the usual checks, Ali. We'll just have to hope everything's up and running.'

He glanced over to the wind-sock and groaned. 'Sod's Law, it's a tail wind, but we'll have to live with that as well.'

As Drew spoke, he saw the shutters on the emergency sheds further down the airfield slam upwards and the first vehicles pull out, blue lights flashing.

The radio crackled. 'Tempest, you have no clearance. Bring the aircraft to a halt.'

Drew made no attempt to reply.

'Tempest, a Hercules is on final approach, inbound to this airfield. Stop the jet now and await further instructions.'

'Drew!' Ali yelled.

'They're bluffing.'

'What if they're not?'

'Then one of us is going to have to get out of the way.'

They were almost at the end of the runway. Looking back over his shoulder, Drew could see a wavering line of blue flashing lights advancing across the airfield towards the edge of the runway.

He flicked the radio back on. 'Tiger 2–1, self-cleared for take-off. Hang on, Ali – we're going for a rolling start.'

He swung the jet around the apron, pushing the throttles forward. As they began to accelerate he saw the blue lights also begin to move again, rolling forward on to the runway itself.

'Shit,' he said, heaving back on the throttles and braking savagely. The jet lurched and shuddered as Drew swung it around. It slid sideways, the wheels drifting perilously close to the edge of the runway as he forced a turn into the maze of taxiways around the hardened aircraft shelters.

Ali groaned. 'What the hell are you doing?' he said.

'Just following our war training. If the main runway's bombed out, use the taxiways as emergency runways.'

The jet lurched again as he swung it onto a long taxiway, running parallel to, and fifty metres east of, the main strip. Instantly he rammed the throttles forward again and the engines began to howl as jets of blue flame blasted out behind them.

'Drew, there's not enough room left on this for a take-off.'

'There'll have to be.'

Drew saw the blue lights advancing again and imagined the emergency crews cursing as their vehicles bounced and bucketed over the rough ground. He sighted along the concrete strip to its abrupt end in the Adriatic, trying to work out if the jet would run the gauntlet of emergency vehicles in time. Then he shrugged his shoulders. Let them worry about it.

'100 knots,' Ali said as the jet accelerated.

They ripped past a lorry and a fire engine, which were still some way short of the taxiway, but there were more blue lights up ahead, rapidly closing on the edge of the concrete.

Drew saw an ambulance hit the brakes and grind to a halt at the side as the Tempest zipped past, but his smile faded when he saw a fire engine coming straight towards him from the far end of the taxiway.

'Speed, Ali?'

'140.'

'Can't wait any longer. Rotating.'

'Drew!'

Ali was too late. Drew was already pulling back on the stick. Still accelerating, the jet stayed on the ground for a moment, but as it reached flying speed there was a bump and the wheels lifted. The gap between the Tempest and the fire truck was closing fast as the jet dragged itself into the air, generating no lift from the following wind.

He held the stick rigid, unwilling and now unable to take evasive action. It was far too late to stop and any attempt to fly round the fire engine would simply send the Tempest's wing slicing into the ground.

As they rocketed towards the fire truck, he knew with a sickening clarity that the jet would not clear it in time. 'Look out Ali, we're going to hi—'

Drew had a momentary glimpse of two white faces framed in the windscreen, as the fire engine swerved violently off the taxiway.

It took Drew a few moments before he could trust himself to speak. He flicked a couple of switches. 'Gear travelling . . . and the flaps.' Then he eased back on the throttles as the Tempest climbed higher. 'Out of reheat.'

Chapter 20

Drew held the climb right up to thirty thousand feet and levelled off well out over the Adriatic. It was a clear, starry evening, but neither man had eyes for the beauty of the night sky. The sea far below looked black and leaden as Drew began to give the most unusual briefing he had ever delivered.

'Okay, Ali, we're starting from thirty thousand feet, so we should have plenty of room to spare, but, if we do go out of control, six thousand feet is absolute baseline.

'If we're still nose down when we come out of the spin, we'll need every inch of that to recover. Less and we won't have enough room before we hit the sea. So, if we're still going down when we get to six thousand, we're coming out without waiting to see what happens next.'

'And if we're still spinning?'

'We'll be going down too fast to eject, because the upward thrust of the seat won't be enough to counter the downward fall of the aircraft. If we're still conscious, I'll probably just have time to say sorry before we hit.'

'Then perhaps we'd better get it over with, before I begin to realise what a bloody stupid idea this is.'

They both lingered over their final checks, trying to

postpone the moment when they had to begin the dive. Drew thought of Michelle listening in the tower and longed to speak to her over the radio.

'Come on, Ali, let's get this over with. This one's for DJ.'

He rolled the jet inverted and pushed the stick forward. As the Tempest's nose dropped sharply, the panorama of stars was replaced by the black emptiness of the sea.

'Beginning a spiral dive.'

Their airspeed rose rapidly as the Tempest flashed downwards, spiralling towards the earth, the moonlight glinting from its silver wings.

'Coming around hard left . . . Increasing speed to max power . . . Pulling a hard, four-G turn . . .'

Drew's G-suit inflated, pressing in on his stomach and compressing his thighs as the Tempest hurtled down faster and faster towards the sea.

'Dropping chaff . . . Selecting air-to-air missile . . . Stick top armed . . . Max power now . . .'

There was a long silence and then Drew's voice, sounding almost disappointed. 'So that's what Russian roulette feels like. One chamber empty, climbing back to height to pull the trigger again.'

'Just our luck,' Ali said. 'Today of all days, we finally get an aircraft that works.'

Three more times they swooped down in the dive but each time the aircraft responded perfectly to its controls. As they pulled back up to height, Ali warned him, 'Fuel for just two more.'

'Okay. Let me think a minute. Where have I been going wrong? Maybe it's the speed of commands. Perhaps I've been selecting them too slowly, giving it time to part-process one set of instructions before the next comes in behind.'

Ali interrupted him. 'Drew, we've got company.'

Two dots on the radar screen were moving rapidly towards them. As Drew saw the shapes of two more Tempests outlined against the rising moon, the radio crackled. 'Hello, Jumbo, this is Jumbo.'

'I do hope we haven't interrupted your dinner,' Drew said.

'This is madness, Drew. What the hell are you doing?'

'I'm starting to ask myself the same question.'

'We're ordered to escort you down.'

'Sorry. I can't oblige you there.'

There was a long silence. 'Very well.' Jumbo took on a portentous tone. 'Tempest aircraft, you are being intercepted. We will escort you to Gióia del Colle. Should you fail—'

Drew broke in. 'Don't give me that bullshit, Jumbo.'

Jumbo ignored the interruption. 'Should you fail to comply, we will be ordered to engage.'

'Do what he says, Drew, please,' Ali said.

'If you refuse to comply, Drew,' Jumbo said, 'we will shoot you down.'

'I don't think so,' Drew said. 'I really don't think so. It took three weeks of hand-wringing and UN debates before we could have a crack at an enemy who was carrying out wholesale torture, rape and murder. I hardly think you're going to shoot down one of your own side because Russell's a bit cross.

'Now I suggest you keep well back out of range because, with any luck, we're going to be putting this jet into an uncontrolled dive. Ready, Ali? This time we're doing it flat-tack.'

The two other Tempests kept their distance as Drew began another white-knuckle ride down towards the waves, rattling out the sequence of commands as fast as the most hectic combat. 'Beginning dive. Coming around hard left. Increasing speed to max power. Pulling four-G. Dropping chaff. Selecting air-to-air missile. Stick top armed. Max power now.'

There was another long silence, followed by Drew's dispirited voice. 'Nothing again.'

'Fuel for just one more,' Ali said. 'Let's try something different. DJ had just put our jet into a victory roll when he lost it.' He paused. 'I don't know how that could have affected the computer, though.'

'Neither do I, but we might as well try it. Nothing else seems to be working.'

Once more they climbed back to height and began the long dive. As Drew rattled through the sequence of commands, he flipped the Tempest into a high-G barrel-roll. Sky and sea reversed and then righted themselves over and over again, but still the warning panel stayed stubbornly blank.

'Come on, Drew,' Ali said. 'We've no fuel for anything else. Let's go home.'

As the other Tempests trailed them, he mechanically pulled back to height and set course towards Gióia, warning the tower they were coming in. He stared dejectedly ahead, rocking the stick in his hand as he thought gloomily about the fate that awaited him on the ground. 'I'm really sorry, Ali.'

'Don't worry about it, but do me one favour, will you? I know you're depressed right now but try and concentrate on your flying until we get down. You're making the jet rock worse than a novice on a maiden flight. Even DJ at his most tense was never as bad as this.'

As if in confirmation, the jet jerked and dipped.

Drew pulled himself together. 'Yeah, you're right, I should . . .'

His mind racing, he broke off as the jet twitched again. 'What did you say?'

'I said . . .'

But Drew had already stopped listening and was staring at his hand wrapped around the stick. 'I think you've got it, Ali. Christ, you've got it. You said I was flying like a nervous novice or like DJ under stress.' He paused as he thought it through again.

'So?'

'So it's not the computer at all – or not the whole system anyway – and it's not a sequence of commands.'

'So what the hell is it then?'

'It's the way that you fly it. You can overload the fly-by-wire.'

'And how do you do that?'

'By moving the stick.' Drew had already begun making tiny movements to the stick, rocking it from side to side.

Ali waited patiently for the rest of the explanation and then exploded. 'Oh come on, Drew, don't talk bollocks. Moving the stick is how you fly the bloody plane.'

'No, Ali, you don't understand. This is the cause of it all.' He rattled the stick faster, willing his theory to be right.

'What the hell are you doing?' Ali said as the jet began to lurch violently. 'Drew!'

As Ali spoke, the jet suddenly plummeted from the sky,

the alarms shrieking and the warning lights flashing red as the altimeter unwound like a ball of string.

Drew fought against the slack controls, trying desperately to will some response into them, but the flaps continued to wave ineffectually as the jet plunged out of control, a thirty-ton deadweight.

The airframe vibrated like a pneumatic drill, setting Drew's teeth rattling in his head. He was close to blacking out but he fought with the controls again as Ali's increasingly terrified voice came over the intercom. 'Twenty-five thousand feet . . . Twenty thousand . . . Fifteen thousand . . . Prepare to eject . . . Drew!'

The lights of ships that had been pinpricks in the vastness of the sea seconds before seemed to swell as the Tempest barrelled down towards them.

Drew heard the controller in the tower add his voice to Ali's entreaties, yelling into the radio, 'Eject, Drew. For Christ's sake eject.'

The response was neither a voice nor the explosion of the ejector rockets blasting Drew and Ali up into the air, but a terrible groaning and juddering from the airframe as Drew at last felt a slight response from the controls.

He hauled at the stick, struggling to pull the aircraft out of its breakneck dive, but, though he tried desperately to level the wings, the jet kept yawing savagely from side to side. As he pushed the stick left, the jet dropped away to the right. Each pressure on it seemed to produce the reverse of what he intended and, the more he tried to correct it, the wilder the oscillations became.

'Ten thousand.'

The jet continued to drop. The sea below zoomed into frighteningly sharp focus, the white hull of a speedboat starkly outlined against the dark, midnight-blue of the water.

'Eight thousand.'

For a microsecond Drew was paralysed by indecision. Then he heard Ali yelling into the intercom, 'Let go of the stick. It's what DJ did. Let go of the stick.'

For another fraction of a second he hesitated. Releasing the stick went against every instinct and every second of pilot training he had ever had.

'Six thousand. Drew!' Ali's cry jolted him out of his indecision. He let go of the stick. Almost instantly the wild yawing stopped and the jet came back under control. Drew grabbed it again, levelled the wings and began hauling on it with both hands. The G-force still plastering him to his seat, he dragged it slowly, painfully back, until it was jammed hard into his stomach.

'Four thousand.'

They were already past the point of no return. If Drew could drag enough response from the jet, it might yet bottom out of its dive; if not . . .

They were dropping too fast to eject. 'We should make it,' Drew said. 'We're staying in.

'*Should*?' Ali shrieked.

The needle of the altimeter continued to wind down, but more steadily now as the jet slowed its breakneck plunge, easing the vibrations of the airframe.

Ali broke in again, his voice cracking. 'Two thousand feet.'

Drew could see thin white streaks in the blackness below them.

'One thousand.'

The streaks became the white crests of waves.

'Five hundred.'

There was a sudden burst of static, and then nothing. In the tower, Michelle froze as she heard the radio go dead. She was surrounded by people in the packed control room. As news of Drew's suicide mission had spread around the base, more and more of the squadron made their way to the tower to listen in.

There was a stunned silence and then a flurry of action.

'Radio check. Tiger Three, this is Gióia Controller. Are you receiving? Over . . . Tiger Three, do you read me? Come in, for God's sake.'

There was nothing.

Then the flight controller grabbed the red crash phone. As soon as he lifted it, the alarm sounded and the doors of the emergency vehicle sheds rolled upwards. 'Scramble Search and Rescue.' For the second time that night, the emergency crews went sprinting for their vehicles.

Through the window, Michelle could see the rotors of the yellow Sea King begin to turn and then accelerate to a blur. The helicopter rose from the concrete and swung away into the night.

'Rescue two-one, departing the airfield, request position update.'

As Michelle heard the call from the Sea King, there was another burst of static, followed by Drew's shaky voice.

'Sorry about that, tower, must have knocked the radio off in all the excitement. We're okay. We've bottomed out and are climbing to height. I'm not sure if we've broken this aircraft, but we've definitely bent it a bit . . . And Michelle and anyone else who's listening, hang on for two more minutes while we get these checks done. Then we'll talk you through what's been going wrong with these buggers.'

Drew took the jet back to height, forcing himself to keep his euphoria under control. He called out the checks on the jet's systems. Ali's voice was almost back in neutral as he responded.

'Damage report?' Drew said.

'Hydraulics leak. We're losing pressure.'

'How serious?'

'It's falling steadily, but it's not at danger level yet.' Ali paused. 'We may have a fuel leak as well.'

'Anything else?' Drew asked as he put the Tempest into the long descent towards Gióia.

'Well, I can't see it on the panel, but I'd say there's a severely overstressed airframe as well.'

Ali tried to laugh, but his voice caught at the memory of what they had just been through. 'You've got strong arms as well as big balls, Drew,' he said. 'This thing's tested to nine G, but it must have pulled close to fifteen as you hauled it out of that dive.

'In the few minutes left before you try and kill us again, can you talk me through that bit back there once more? I know I told you to let go of the stick, but it wasn't logic – it was sheer blind panic.'

'I was right about too many inputs in rapid succession being the problem,' Drew said, 'but I was looking in the wrong place. The fault isn't in the computer itself: it's in the fly-by-wire. If I'd used my brain a bit more and really looked hard at what all the incidents had in common, I might have seen it a lot sooner.'

Drew was lost in thought.

'So what is the link?' Ali asked, as patiently as he could.

'The one thing that links all those incidents isn't a particular sequence of commands: it's the fact that every one of us was moving the stick very rapidly just before the system crashed.

'The first time I lost it I was trying to stay on the tail of Michelle's Puma, which was zig-zagging like a hyperactive crab. DJ had been hunting down that Serb Hind and then waggled his wings like a lunatic before he went into his victory roll. The guy who crashed in Swaledale was a novice on his first flight in a Tempest. I'll bet you all the paperclips on Russell's desk that the pilot was as nervous as a learner driver taking his test and making constant adjustments.'

'What about Alastair Strang?' Ali said. 'He was one of the best pilots on his squadron.'

'He was such a perfectionist that, if he was meant to be at twenty thousand feet, twenty thousand and one wasn't good enough. He'd nudge it down until he got it bang on the mark.

'He'd also been a pilot in the Red Arrows before he transferred to Tempests. Those guys are used to flying in ultra-close formation, making minute adjustments of the stick every second. If you do that on one of these, you give the fly-by-wire more inputs than it can cope with. It's still trying to process the previous command when you input another. Eventually it becomes saturated and the system crashes.

'Even if you manage to regain partial control, the computer is still lagging behind the inputs to the fly-by-wire. You move the stick to the left but the jet goes right, because it's still responding to the previous command. You then start to panic and force the stick even further to the left, but when the jet *does* begin to come left it now has two or three commands taking it that way. As a result, it drops left like a stone.

'DJ told me the answer at Aalborg and I was too dumb to realise it. He said he was panicking so much when you went out of control over the North Sea that he let go of the stick and it righted itself, but I was too busy giving him a bollocking to listen. If I'd shouted less and listened more, both he and Nick might be alive today.

'The only way to correct it is to let go of the stick altogether, which doesn't exactly come naturally. If you hadn't told me to, we'd be on our way to the bottom of the Adriatic.'

He addressed his audience in the tower at Gióia directly. 'Here endeth the lesson, everyone. Right, Ali, let's get this aircraft down before we ruin a perfect day by running out of fuel.'

'Fuel's not the most immediate problem. We've got an amber warning now on the hydraulic fluid.'

'Then the sooner we get this on the deck, the better.'

The lights of Gióia emerged out of the darkness. 'Gear coming down,' Drew said.

He paused, then swore. There were two green lights showing that the front and left landing-gear was safely down and locked, but there was also a red warning light on the right-hand gear.

'Recycling the landing-gear.'

Drew raised and then lowered the gear again. The red light continued to glow.

He thought for a moment, then thumbed the radio button. 'Tower, we have a problem. We're not sure if the right landing-gear is down and locked. I'm going to fly past you. Can you give us a visual check?'

As the Tempest flashed over the inspection lights by the control tower, Drew glimpsed a row of white faces at the blue-glass windows.

'The gear is down,' the controller said, 'but we can't tell if it's locked.'

'All right, Ali,' Drew said. 'I'm going for the emergency system.'

He pulled a black-and-yellow lever. A blast of nitrogen flooded the system, locking the gear down permanently. The red light remained.

He flew past the tower once more, but the controller could only offer the same inconclusive message.

'Fuel's low,' Ali said. 'We can't delay any longer.' Then

there was new urgency in his voice. 'Red warning on the hydraulics.'

As he spoke, the attention-getters began sounding and the same message flashed on Drew's warning panel.

He was silent for a moment, running through the emergency drills in his mind and weighing up the chances of a safe landing.

'We've pushed our luck enough, Drew,' Ali said. 'Let's take it back out over the sea and bang out.'

Drew did not reply. He scanned his instruments once more. 'No. We've lost enough Tempests. We're going to get this one home.'

He heard Ali's dry swallow over the intercom. 'It's all right, Ali. I haven't come through all this just to fall at the last hurdle.'

'Are we going to take the cable?'

'I can't risk it. If the gear collapses, we could go underneath the cable. It'd cut through us like a cheese wire. We'll do a flat approach and land beyond it. Be ready to bang out if anything goes wrong.'

As he began the turn back towards the airfield, he saw the runway lights converging to a single point and the tower glowing an eerie blue, like a floodlit block of ice. He knew that somewhere in there Michelle was watching and waiting.

There was an unnatural stillness in the tower. Michelle looked up, seeking reassurance in the faces around her. A pilot tried to answer the question in her eyes with a confident smile, but then looked quickly away. The controller avoided her gaze altogether. Already drained, she braced herself again, but there was a cold, dull feeling in her chest.

The black shape of the Tempest was faintly outlined against the night sky as it banked to make its final approach. She heard the clamour of revving engines as the emergency vehicles prepared to track the Tempest along the runway. Their revolving blue lights picked out stray details in the darkness of the airfield perimeter: a patch of barbed wire, a speed-limit sign and a pile of twisted scrap metal – all that was left of the arrester cable that DJ and Ali had destroyed – bulldozed clear of the runway and then left to rust.

She stared out into the night, watching the Tempest

drop steadily towards the grey concrete runway, and heard Drew's and Ali's voices, taut with tension, as they counted down their height and air-speed.

The Tempest scarcely seemed to be moving, hovering like a hawk out beyond the perimeter. Then she heard the growl of the engines, faint at first, but growing steadily in volume as it swept in over the sea. It crossed the faint white surfline and skimmed the stanchions of the perimeter lights, the jet-wash stirring dust devils of sand from the dunes.

The jet yawed, then steadied again as a gust of crosswind shook it. Straining her eyes into the darkness, she watched the shrinking gap between the black shape of the landing-gear, hanging like talons beneath the sweep of the wing, and the grey, faintly luminous surface of the runway.

The flashing blue lights sent reflections dancing along the sleek flanks of the Tempest as it swept over the apron. Out of the corner of her eye, Michelle saw the fire tenders and ambulances begin to move, but her gaze remained locked onto the right landing-gear, silently willing it to be safe.

As the wheels touched the concrete, there were twin smudges of blue smoke from the tyres. The smoke hung suspended for an instant and then was blasted away in the jet-wash. Michelle had no eyes for that. She had spotted another puff of smoke from the landing-gear itself as the jet touched down.

She held her breath, her body rigid, as she stared unblinkingly at the gear. For a moment the jet roared on, straight and level down the runway. Then she sensed as much as saw it begin to develop a slight list to the right. It grew more pronounced as she watched.

She saw the outline of a dark figure in the cockpit, wrestling the stick to the left as he fought to compensate. The thrust-buckets deployed and she heard the engine note rise to a scream as reverse thrust was applied. The airframe began to judder and shake under the savage braking.

She switched her gaze back to the landing-gear. Suddenly the wing dropped a few inches, then halted. A fresh gout of black smoke spilled from the gear. Then it belched out in a constant, thickening stream.

'Eject, Drew. Eject.' Her voice sounded in her ears like a stranger's.

The landing-gear held for another split second, then shattered. She saw a glistening shard of metal burst out of the middle of the smoke like an arrow. The wing toppled and smashed into the concrete, sending out an avalanche of sparks.

There was an awful grinding, rending noise, audible even above the howl of the engines and the bedlam breaking out in the control tower. The controller shouted to make himself heard.

The air crew clustered by the windows fell silent as he rattled out orders to the emergency crews.

Like a claw, the wing gouged a scar across the surface of the runway, slicing into the concrete as if it were flesh. The torrent of sparks disappeared for a moment inside a dense cloud of smoke and dust. Then Michelle saw flames licking around the edge of the wing.

She sat like stone, her fingernails carving white crescents in her palms, as the flames flashed across the wing and writhed like serpents around the tailplane. The trail of spilled fuel laid along the runway suddenly ignited into a curtain of fire, as if a sugar-cane farmer had torched his crop.

A fire tender speeding down the runway in the track of the jet was instantly surrounded by flame. It swerved violently, teetered on two burning wheels, then crashed onto its side. Fire crew leapt from the wreck and scattered as the flames began to devour it.

The wall of fire stretching along the runway made the night glow red, making the shadows an even deeper black. The tears trickling down Michelle's cheeks were the colour of blood.

'Eject, Drew. Eject.' She repeated it like a mantra, unable to tear her eyes from the aircraft. As the wing bit deeper into the concrete, the jet slewed to one side. Then there was a huge explosion as it was torn from the fuselage. Part of it disintegrated. The rest was catapulted into the air, still blazing. It slammed down again, burying itself like an axe in the earth alongside the runway.

Freed of the spike nailing it to the ground, the Tempest spun on its axis, then careered off the runway, bulldozing its way towards the tower, engines still bellowing.

'Eject. Please. Please. Please,' Michelle mouthed the words, her voice a dead monotone.

Fire travelled the length of the fuselage, engulfing the cockpit and hiding the two stick figures from view.

There was a pause, then a whipcrack as the canopy blew away. A white flash like a lightning bolt lit the night sky as ejector rockets erupted out of the heart of the red and orange flames.

Tears blinded Michelle. 'How many?' she screamed.

'One,' 'Two,' 'I don't know,' came the replies.

Frantic, she scanned the sky for parachutes but the tornado of flame consuming the aircraft hid everything from view.

Fire tenders and rescue vehicles sped towards the doomed jet. A gust of wind cleared the pall of smoke for a second and Michelle at last saw a solitary figure drifting down under his orange-and-white parachute. Let it be Drew, she thought to herself. Please God, let it be Drew.

The figure landed and tore at his harness. As the parachute came free, the wind blew it across the burning jet. The canopy ignited and it traced a yellow line across the night sky as it whirled away downwind. Still wearing his helmet, the figure began sprinting towards the blazing jet. Rescue workers ran to intercept him and dragged him back.

Above the din in the control tower, the roar of the raging fire and the screeching of tortured metal, Michelle now heard an even more unearthly sound. One of the Tempest's engines was still running – and running out of control.

The revs steadily mounted, higher and higher, the engine note rising to a scream and then a banshee wail. She saw the rescue workers diving for cover, dragging the helmeted figure to the ground with them. Then there was a blast as the engine blew itself apart.

After the flash Michelle felt a dull concussion in the pit of her stomach. There was a long moment of silence, then bedlam resumed.

The moon-suited fire crews doused the blazing carcase of the jet with foam, working in towards the wreckage of the cockpit. Michelle was on her feet, motionless, oblivious of anything except the yellow-clad figures.

Her eyes strained into the dark, trying to pierce the dust,

steam and smoke swirling around the Tempest. Her gaze switched incessantly between the anonymous, helmeted figure, still struggling against the rescue workers holding him, and the charred, stiff body that was now being pulled from the burnt-out cockpit.

Chapter 21

Michelle gazed upwards as four dark shadows pierced the mist, the bass rumble of their engines swelling to a roar. As they came overhead, the lead Tempest suddenly pulled up and began climbing vertically away from the others, its afterburners blazing red.

It disappeared into the grey overcast, still climbing towards infinity, as the remaining members of the Missing Man formation flew on without their departed comrade. The thunder of their engines faded, leaving an echoing silence behind.

She still stared upwards, watching the mist swirling around the grey stone steeple of the church. Then she lowered her gaze as a solitary crow settled back into its perch in the bare, dead branches of an elm.

Michelle shivered. 'I thought I'd seen my last funeral for a while.'

'I thought so too.'

Neither of them spoke for a minute, gazing at the long queue of air crew in dress uniforms filing silently into the church. Russell glanced towards them and hesitated, then disappeared inside.

'What a bloody waste.'

Michelle turned to face him. 'You had to do it.'

'I threw his life away,' he said, his face haggard. 'I'll never forgive myself. We didn't do the safety checks because we were racing to take off before they blocked the runway. But I should still have checked the command ejection lever. I didn't do it.'

He rubbed his face with his hand. 'When the landing-gear collapsed, he was slammed into his instruments and lost consciousness. I pulled the handle, thinking I was ejecting both of us. I came out; he didn't.'

Her eyes had filled with tears, but she laid a hand on his arm and said gently, 'It was his job to check it as much as yours.' She paused, holding his gaze. 'It's not your fault.'

He shook his head and looked away.

She hesitated again, then reached into her handbag. 'Have you seen this?' She handed him a page torn from that morning's newspaper.

There was a large picture of Power alongside a banner headline:

FATAL FLAW IN TEMPEST

All the RAF's principal fighter aircraft, the Tempest RS3s, are being recalled, following the discovery of 'a minor fault.' Air Vice-Marshal Charles Power praised the 'diligence of the RAF's Accident Investigations Bureau' and said that two air crew serving in Bosnia, Flight Lieutenants Drew Miller and Nigel Barber had also provided useful information. A new generation of Tempests is to be introduced from next year and a rolling programme of modifications will be carried out on the existing aircraft.

The Air Force has lost a number of Tempests in crashes recently, but he denied any link. 'There's not a shred of physical evidence. The loss of aircraft in training is inevitable if it is to simulate adequately the exigencies of war.'

All the time he was reading, he was aware of Power's confidently smiling face looking up at him from the page. It was the smile of a man who knew he had won.

'Nice of him to give me a name check, wasn't it?' He

crumpled the paper and tossed it into a litter bin. As he looked up, his face clouded. 'Great. The photograph was bad enough; now here he is in the flesh.'

She followed his gaze and saw her father walking towards them. Power approached slowly.

'Michelle. Flight Lieutenant. A very sad day.'

There was a long silence.

'You're not wearing your medal, Flight Lieutenant?'

'No. I'd feel like I was taking a bribe.' He paused, his eyes locked on to Power's. 'Looking forward to life at Barnwold Industries, Air Vice-Marshal?'

'Very much, thank you,' Power replied, his face a mask. 'Of course it'll be very different from the Royal Air Force.'

'I wouldn't have thought there'd be too much difference.'

Power's lips tightened. He glanced at his watch. 'Perhaps we should be getting inside.'

He offered his arm to Michelle, but she shook her head and turned away.

Power hesitated, his arm still outstretched, then walked off alone towards the church.

As the priest appeared at the head of the church steps, looking out along the road, a black-clad figure detached herself from the queue of mourners and walked towards them.

He was shocked at the change in her. Sally had lost a lot of weight and aged years in a few weeks. She stood looking at him for a long time, not speaking, her face as white as the priest's vestments.

He put his arms around her and hugged her to him, feeling her shoulders shaking as she sobbed against his chest. He held her until she had stopped crying, then gently released her.

She straightened up, wiping her eyes. 'I'm sorry.'

'You shouldn't have come.'

'I had to . . . for Nick.'

She rubbed ineffectually at the mark her tears had made on his uniform, then turned to face Michelle. She rested her hand on her arm as she looked into her eyes. She seemed about to say something, but then shook her head and hurried away. Her children, looking small, lost and frightened, clustered around her as she led them into church.

A hearse swung in off the road and pulled up at the big oak door. Both of them stared for a moment, then looked away as the undertakers began to slide out the coffin.

'So,' Michelle said, her voice brittle. 'You're determined to stay in the Air Force, despite everything?'

He took a few moments to reply. 'It's the only job I can do. I've given up on Germany, though. I'm going for an exchange posting with the French. It's on a base in the Dordogne, three years initially, but if I like it there I could apply to stay permanently.'

'I didn't even know you spoke French.'

'I don't. I'm learning.'

He paused, watching as the pallbearers began to form up around the coffin. It was draped with a Union Jack and a peaked RAF service cap lay on top of it. 'What about you? You haven't changed your mind about leaving?'

She shook her head, her lip between her teeth. 'Every RAF uniform, every Tempest flying overhead, every Happy Hour in the mess – even the smell of Avgas in the hangar – would remind me of what I've lost.' She gave him a long, last look, reading the pain and sadness in his eyes, then kissed him on the cheek. 'Goodbye, Ali.'

She turned away, the first tears pricking her eyes as she followed the pallbearers carrying Drew's coffin into the church.

Afterword

Responding to calls from Her Majesty's Opposition to hold a full public inquiry into the recent spate of crashes involving military aircraft, the Minister of State for the Armed Forces, Mr Nicholas Soames, made the following statement in the House of Commons on Thursday 6th June 1996

It is arrant nonsense to suggest that we would do anything to jeopardise the safety of aircrew by allowing an unservicable aircraft to fly. No aircraft is permitted to leave the ground unless it is judged entirely safe to do so. The ground crews that service RAF are dedicated professionals, and are amongst the best in the world.

At the same time, the RAF continues to maintain the most rigorous training standards, which every other country in the world wishes to come and learn from. Average fast jet flying hours are well above minimum NATO levels. Operating levels and skills remain at an exceptionally high standard.

There is no reason to believe that there is any fundamental problem in the way in which operations are conducted or supported, or that this is anything other than a truly, deeply and very unfortunate coincidence. It would be premature to infer that the overall accident rate for 1996 will reveal and new or disturbing trend. There have been similar clusters of accidents in the past, but they did not reveal any new trend. Overall the general accident rate has continued to decline since the early 1980s.

I assure the House, nevertheless, that there really is no complacency. As the House will know, boards of enquiry are set up to examine the circumstances of each crash. Those investigations are extremely thorough and exhaustive, and although the work is still in progress, I can tell the House that there is no definite pattern to link any of these accidents.